Also by Allison Pang

A Brush of Darkness

D0021103

A SLIVER OF
SHADOW

ALLISON PANG

POCKET BOOKS
New York London Toronto Sydney New Delhi

Pocket Books
A Division of Simon & Schuster, Inc.
1230 Avenue of the Americas
New York, NY 10020

This book is a work of fiction. Names, characters, places, and incidents either are products of the author's imagination or are used fictitiously. Any resemblance to actual events or locales or persons, living or dead, is entirely coincidental.

First Pocket Books paperback edition March 2012

POCKET and colophon are registered trademarks of Simon & Schuster, Inc.

For information about special discounts for bulk purchases, please contact Simon & Schuster Special Sales at 1-866-506-1949 or business@simonandschuster.com.

The Simon & Schuster Speakers Bureau can bring authors to your live event. For more information or to book an event, contact the Simon & Schuster Speakers Bureau at 1-866-248-3049 or visit our website at www.simonspeakers.com.

Manufactured in the United States of America

10 9 8 7 6 5 4 3 2 1

ISBN 978-1-4391-9834-6
ISBN 978-1-4391-9842-1 (ebook)

This one's for you, Dad.

Acknowledgments

It always amazes me how many people leave their influence on a book. Sometimes it can be such a small thing, but sometimes it's the small things that make all the difference. So, with that in mind, here we go:

To my agent, Suzie Townsend—thanks for taking a chance when you didn't have to. Your support has been above and beyond anything I could hope for. (Plus you sent me Hello Kitty socks.)

To the fine folks at Pocket for doing all that they do to make these things happen. Without you, there would be no book.

To Danielle Poiesz—I can't speak highly enough of you, chica. Thanks for everything you've done and for coming through for me in some very dark moments. And for taking me to get my first tattoo.

To Jess Haines—your words of wisdom and helpful comments during this process were invaluable in the extreme. (As were your many e-mails involving things I am still not sure I have the words for.)

To my fellow Word Whores—Jeffe Kennedy, Linda Robertson, Laura Bickle, Kerry Schafer, Kristine Krantz, and Marcella Burnard—here's to Cones of Silence and ruling the world. (Hey, it *could* happen.) Seriously, you all put up with way more of me than you should, and I'm utterly grateful for it.

To Staci Myers—thanks for letting me borrow a certain French vampire. My apologies. Dahlia will make it up to him one day.

To the League of Reluctant Adults—thanks for welcoming me into the ranks of snark.

To Darchala Chaoswind—as always, your pictures are a delight (and inspiration; Talivar thanks you for his hipster scruff).

And of course, thanks to Dan, Connor, and Lucy for indulging me in my bouts of writing insanity and not complaining too much about the state of the house during deadlines. *ahem* Love you guys.

A sliver of shadow
And a destiny torn
By Three Paths woven
In an endless thorn.

One

"Run, Abby."

Sonja's warning slid around me with a wash of power. Startled, I shot up from where I huddled beneath a cluster of fallen logs, decayed bark scattering as a set of claws shredded my hiding place. I ducked, the sharpened talons slicing the air with a deadly whistle.

Grinding my teeth, I narrowed my eyes and concentrated, letting my own form shift. Small, furry, fast . . .

Hare.

The Dreaming rippled. I bounded away, sleek and long, haunches bunching and then springing forward to propel me into the darkness. Sonja's low growl of frustration echoed behind me. I didn't know exactly what form she'd taken, but my rapidly twitching nose instantly recognized the acrid scent of something feline.

The urge to go to ground vibrated through my little body, but I pushed forward, leaves sliding beneath my paws. All around me were shadows as my nails dug into the moist earth. The scenery blurred past in a haze of ragweed and pine trees, needles brushing my fur. I couldn't hear Sonja anymore and I paused, my ears rotating to cup the darkness.

The faintest breeze caught my attention, and I instinctively flattened against the grass as Sonja swooped past, this time in the shape of a barred owl.

She wheeled, but I bolted, aiming for the tinkling stream nearby. Shedding the last vestige of the hare, I leapt toward the surface, my skin sluicing into scales as I slithered into the depths. My gills opened to shunt out the water, gravel scraping my pink salmon belly.

"Good! Very good." Sonja applauded from the banks. The succubus had shifted into her more human form, the bloodred feathers of her wings shining in the moonlight of the Dreaming. Her skin had an alabaster purity that could never be matched by anything mortal. Between the hidden depths of her dark eyes and the scarlet wings, she seemed more fallen angel waif than daemon seductress. "You can come out now, Abby. I think that's enough for tonight."

My tail flicked me through the current as I changed again, pulling together the part of what made me, *me*. Emerging from the water, I squeezed the drops from my hair and pushed it from my face. "I'm getting better." I wrapped the Dreaming around me until I was dressed in a pair of jeans and a shirt.

Sonja nodded cautiously, smoothing out the wrinkles of her own tank dress. "You are, but you're still barely tapping your potential." She gestured around us with a hint of irritation. "These are *your* Dreams. You limit yourself to your own sense of physics. Becoming a rabbit was fine and you've certainly improved your shifting ability—but why not change the ground, or the trees?" She yanked on a damp ringlet of my hair. "Why waste time with this when you could instantly dry it? If you're ever going to really, truly defeat your nightmares, you're going to need more than just a few parlor tricks."

"I don't think that way. You know that. We've been

through this how many times now?" I concentrated on the water flowing over my toes before giving her a wan smile. "Have patience with me. I'm new to this." One dark brow rose at me sourly, but she let the lie pass without comment. In truth it had been over six months—six very *long* months. She was frustrated, I was frustrated. I'd been banging my head against the metaphysical equivalent of a brick wall in my attempts to break free from the confines of everything I'd ever known in an effort to make sense of the dark shadows of my inner psyche—which often took the form of vicious, man-eating sharks.

My nightmares certainly hadn't paid the slightest bit of attention either way.

If it hadn't been for a certain incubus awakening me to the existence of the Dreaming nearly eight months ago, I would have continued to experience my familiar nightly cycle of waking up from the intimate practice of having the flesh shredded from my bones. That should have meant something.

On the other hand, sometimes ignorance really was bliss. Discovering that I could visit the place where my dreams occurred was one thing. Being told I could potentially bring my nightmares to life was something else entirely.

I understood Bryston's motivation of having his sister teach me the finer points of Dreaming—we weren't exactly dating anymore, and my chances of focusing long enough past the hurt of his leaving was a bit of a toss-up. I couldn't argue against the need to control myself better, though I wasn't sure Sonja saw me as anything more than a chore. Still. The faint scent of the sea rolled past us as though to emphasize the point and I shuddered. Dreams or not, I had no wish to see the sharks again anytime soon.

The succubus sighed at my woeful expression. "You'll get there. You just need to concentrate."

I waggled my nose, annoyed. I might not quite grasp everything she tried to teach me, but I wasn't completely ignorant. "Is *that* all there is to it, Endora?" My eyes narrowed as I stared at her, the power rushing through me, a thin rivulet of the Dreaming taking form in my mind.

A small change, perhaps.

The succubus glanced over her shoulder with a surprised laugh. Her scarlet wings now gleamed a brilliant purple. "Not bad," she admitted, ruffling them with a shiver, a flush of crimson staining them back to their normal shade.

Her face sobered. "But seriously, Abby. You have enough potential to make a first-class DreamWalker. With the right training, you'd be able to slip in and out of the Dreaming at will—and not just into your dreams, but into others as well."

"Planning on having me go all Dom Cobb on someone? Let me dig up a top." Despite my words, I couldn't even begin to grasp the sort of power that might take. Hell, I could barely manage to keep from being devoured by my own nightmares—and I *knew* what caused them. What would my chances be against someone else's private despair? It wasn't any of my business, anyway.

She picked up a stick, sketching out a series of circles on the ground. "Nearly everything that sleeps visits the Dreaming in one form or another. Whether they remember it or not is another story, but I'm sure you've heard of people who have prophetic dreams or astral body projections or some such?"

"Well, sure. But the one time I actually attempted to leave the Dreaming without waking up, I ended up getting lost on the CrossRoads. And attacked by daemons." I frowned at her. The silver roads granted passage between the mortal realm and Faerie and I'd never really figured them out. "Brystion was pissed."

She waved me off. "And rightfully so, but you wouldn't be on the CrossRoads for this. Here . . . each circle represents a single person's Dreaming Heart. Let's say this one is yours." She tapped the one closest to me. "Now, the Heart of your Dreaming is sacred space, particularly for mortals. No one can enter it without permission." Her mouth pursed. "Or in my brother's case, invitation?"

I scowled at her. "It seemed like a good idea at the time."

"Indeed. Anyway, that's a bit more than the average sleeping person would normally allow, but people who are close to each other tend to form bonds . . ." She drew a few squiggles from my circle to the ones closest around it. "Friends and family, perhaps. Lovers." Her eyes met mine with a hint of amusement. "TouchStones. As a Dreamer, you could follow these pathways into their dreams."

I shuddered in distaste as visions of accidentally stumbling into Phin's personal unicorn-porn theater crossed my mind. "And what about enemies? Could they traverse those bonds to me?"

"It *is* possible," she admitted. "But that's one of the reasons why you need more training." She gestured at the thick iron gate surrounding my Heart. "The unwary have their own defenses built in—but Dreamers have defenses of a different sort at their disposal. The Dreaming itself can become a weapon if you know how to use it."

"Ah. Yeah. You know, I'm not really trying for that sort of thing." I had no desire to become any sort of neoshaman and messing with people's dreams was tricky stuff. "I'll stick with the blue pill, thanks."

"Suit yourself, but you might change your mind someday. It wouldn't hurt to at least understand the basics." She held out a hand to help me out of the stream, and we slowly ambled in the direction of my Heart. The inner sanctum of my dreams lay behind the gate in the form of the old Victorian I'd grown up in. Brystion had told me it couldn't be breached—as long as I stayed within its confines, I would be safe. Even from him.

I scanned the dark forest behind the house. My former lover had made good on his promise to be scarce and I'd barely seen any sign of him, short of the occasional sound of bells echoing like some distant memory through the trees. The few times we'd run across each other at the Hallows nightclub had been polite, if a bit strained. I didn't usually hang around to listen to him sing, and he avoided flaunting whoever his latest TouchStone was to my face, a fact for which I was utterly grateful.

The whole point of TouchStones was to give OtherFolk the ability to stay in the mortal world without limitations . . . and to travel the CrossRoads at will, usually in return for some sort of gift. The sacred bonds between mortals and OtherFolk didn't always involve sex, but in his case it had to. Knowing that didn't make it hurt any less. Knowing that after six months he probably wasn't going to come back to me hurt a lot more.

Sonja arched a brow at me and I flushed. "Have a good night. We'll try again tomorrow."

I waved at her, watching as she passed through the gate to fade away in a slurry of silver. I often wondered how she could manage the CrossRoads directly like that, but Brystion had the same talent.

I reached out and stroked the gate with a curious finger, the rusted metal flaking into my hand. Physics or not, it still seemed so real here. And as far as confronting my nightmares . . .

I glanced over at the rocky path that led to the sea. So far I'd managed to keep the worst of the memories at bay. It was chickenshit of me, but the worse the memory, the larger the shark. I wasn't any sort of hero to go facing them down. The sharks paid no mind to my efforts. They would continue to lurk in all their sharp-toothed glory, regardless.

"Always the coward." I rubbed my face before shutting the gate and locking it tight. I didn't mind keeping it open when I was here, but now that I knew there were other beings actually wandering around in the Dreaming, I disliked leaving it gaping in my absence.

The fact that I might have been locking the incubus inside didn't bother me so much. He certainly could make his own way through if he wanted to. My gaze drifted over the thick cluster of hemlock behind the garden and the heady taste of jasmine suddenly grew heavy on my tongue. I took a step toward the trees, the scent growing stronger.

Brystion.

Tempted, I gave the darkness a wry smile. "No games tonight." And I meant it.

The one time I'd actually given in, I'd wandered for hours, emerging to find myself richer only by the number of brambles stuck in my hair. I debated mooning the woods, but in the end I merely entered the house, gently closing the door behind me. And if I thought I caught my name whispered on the breeze, I chose not to acknowledge it.

Poke.

Something sharp prodded my back. Bleary, I shifted away from it.

Poke.

"Phin, if that's you, you'd better have a damn good reason for pulling me out of my training." I yawned the words and attempted to roll over.

"I thought you might want to know he's awake again." The cat-size unicorn clambered over my hip to dig his cloven hooves into my thigh.

"And he won't go to sleep for you?"

"Abby, in case you haven't noticed, I don't have hands. But I *do* have teeth, so unless you want that delicious ass of yours blemished, I suggest you get your butt out of bed. Little angel wants his mamma."

I groaned. Normally Talivar took the night shift but he'd gone to Faerie before I'd crashed. Apparently he hadn't returned yet. Some bodyguard. "What time is it?" I cracked an eye at the clock—4 A.M.

Shit.

"Fine. But I'm *not* his mamma." I sat up and snarled when my toes hit the chilly floor.

"You're the only thing here with tits. Close enough." Phineas grinned, wriggling under the warmth of the sheets I left behind. "Mmm . . . cozy," he said with a sigh.

"Don't push your luck." I glared at him, gathering my robe around my shoulders. Sure enough, now that I'd managed to pull myself out of the hazy state between awake and Dreaming, I could hear Benjamin's wailing cry down the hallway. "I'm not sure I get paid enough for this," I muttered. But who was I kidding? Moira said jump, and I jumped. Why should the job stop at a little thing like child care? Especially when it came to the Faery princess's son.

I padded down the hall with a yawn. "I'm coming, sweetie." I winced as his voice jumped two notches from slightly pissy to full-on megahowl. Upon entering the room and switching on the nightlight, the reason was quickly evident. Wedged up in one corner of the crib, Benjamin had managed to get one of his limbs wrapped around the bars. The fact that the limb in question was a neatly feathered *wing* made very little difference to the furious little eyes peering at me from a squinched-up face.

Angel, indeed. Spitting image of his father.

Startled by how much he looked like Robert when he thrust out that chin, I tsked at him soothingly, gently extricating the wing without knocking any feathers loose. His volume lowered about two decibels and I picked him up to rest his head on my shoulder. He snuffled, dark hair damp against my neck, his mouth rooting to take hold of my collarbone. "That time again, is it?" I patted his back and covered him with a blanket, starting up what had become a twice-nightly ritual of pacing.

This time Benjamin wasn't having any of it, though. I quickly changed his diaper for good measure and then the two of us headed into the kitchen so that I could warm up a bottle. I continued rocking side to side as the pot on the stove heated up. My enchanted fridge always had his milk in good supply, though what it was, I wasn't entirely sure. Moira wouldn't hear of giving him mortal formula, but I'd never actually seen her carrying a breast pump either. In the end, I supposed it didn't matter. Whatever it was seemed to keep him healthy and it's not as if I'd even know where to begin to find food for a half-angel/half-Fae child anyway. Based on the amount the little booger was going through, I could only imagine his metabolism was higher than a mortal child's, although his somewhat limited development was troubling. At eight months, a human baby would have been at least starting to wean, and certainly wouldn't require two feedings a night. On the other hand, human babies couldn't fly, so maybe the comparison was unfair.

Two weeks ago, Moira had been called away to the Faery Court to give her testimony about Maurice's betrayal. Consumed by jealousy, Maurice had concocted an elaborate scheme to remove his former lover from power in a last-ditch bid to land himself a place in Faerie—a plan I had somehow managed to thwart, although that was mostly just dumb luck on my part. Of course, the offshoot of that had nearly been my death, so it wasn't like I'd gotten away unscathed.

Undoubtedly I was on his ultimate shitlist, but I'd been spared the testimony requirement and acquired a body-guard in the form of Moira's brother, so some things had worked out. On the other hand, staying behind meant I had to run things on my own—including the task of being Benjamin's nanny.

Talivar had been happy enough to take the night shift, but when the infant had sprouted wings a few days ago, the prince had decided it was worth the risk of leaving us behind to tell his sister directly.

Regardless of what Moira had told me, the knowledge of who was Benjamin's father wasn't for public consumption, but feathers would be hard to hide for too long.

Benjamin began to whimper. The bottle was nearly warm now, so I shushed him until it was the right temperature. I retreated into the living room, and curled up on the sofa. He smacked his lips at the sight of the bottle and suckled greedily. "Better be careful," I warned him. "Keep eating like this and you'll be too heavy to fly."

If he heard my words, he ignored them, eyes closing in contentment. "Silly boy," I murmured, shifting him so that he was crooked in my elbow. Now that his needs were fully taken care of, I blinked sleepily myself, my gritty eyes burning. "Not yet. Gotta get you all tucked in first, eh?" I glanced down at the pile of loose papers on the coffee table and turned the lamp to its dimmest setting, grabbing the top few sheets.

Might as well try to get some work in.

Dear Abby . . .

I rolled my eyes. Just my luck to be stuck with the same name as the columnist. I couldn't recall exactly when the first letters started showing up, but shortly after the whole Maurice debacle, I began to find them. At first, they'd be randomly slipped under the door of the Midnight Marketplace, or even sometimes at the Pit, the used bookstore where I worked. I wasn't foolish enough to think the letters were meant for me. Not really.

Moira was the Protectorate of Portsmyth. Part of her job was to oversee disputes and issues of the OtherFolk living here. As her mortal TouchStone, I was simply a conduit to possibly getting her attention faster.

But as I tentatively began to read the letters, Moira decided I could use the practice and allowed me to try to answer. Like a floodgate opening, they started showing up on my pillow, in my bathroom, taped to the fridge. I drew the line when I found the one in my underwear drawer.

Or really, Phineas blew a gasket.

"I don't mind you having your hobbies," he'd exploded at me that morning, "but goddamn if you could keep them out of your lingerie?"

Even aside from the fact that he wasn't actually supposed to be *in* my underwear drawer either, this was one time I agreed with him.

I formally set up a separate address at the Marketplace, with occasional diversions to the Hallows, and made it clear that any letters showing up in my sheets were going to be burned.

Still, the flow kept on here and there; how useful my answers were was up for debate.

> *I was hoping you could settle a little issue between me and this ghost I'm living with.*

"Not bloody likely."

> *I'm a brownie, and I used to work for Mr. Jefferson. Now, technically, brownies work until their*

*chosen masters pass on and then we are set free. But
in this case, Mr. Jefferson did not fully move into the
light and his ghost haunts the place and refuses to let
me go . . .*

I groaned, placing the letter on the cushion beside me. I
hated these kinds of questions. Not as much as the Touch-
Stone or the star-crossed lover ones, but without knowing
both sides of the story, how was I supposed to answer this?

Even if I meant well, there was no telling what the reper-
cussions would be if I gave them the wrong advice. "Have to
find a ghost whisperer, Benjamin." Benjamin's jaw was slack
now, the nipple hanging off his lower lip, milk in the corners
of his mouth. "All right, little man. Back to bed with you.
And Auntie," I amended as the front door creaked open.

"Here, I'll take him." Talivar emerged from the darkness
with a quiet grace. The elven prince-cum-bodyguard had
finally relaxed his rather minimal dress code of tunics and
torcs a few months ago, even as he had relaxed his vigilance.

With a little shopping help from me, he had taken casual
chic to an entirely new level. Dressed in jeans and a black T-
shirt, he cut a nice figure in the dim light, his long hair tied
in a loose queue and a bit of hipster scruff on his chin setting off the strong jaw. Frankly, I found that the oddest thing
about him, given that I'd always thought elves couldn't actually grow facial hair, but I was hardly an expert.

Besides, I liked it.

The delicate points of his ears poked between the sable
strands of his hair, silver hoops gleaming near the tips like
tiny stars. He still retained the leather eye patch, though.
My threats to glitter it up had been met with a slightly chilly
smile, and in the end I'd decided to leave well enough alone.

"Ah. I didn't hear you come in." I peered up at him.
"Good trip?"

"There is much to discuss, but I think it can wait until to-morrow." He watched the baby, a strange expression ghost-ing over his face. "My sister wasn't overly happy to hear about the wings, as you can imagine, but she'll manage."

I grunted, not really sure I cared about anything other than getting back to my bed. Not at this hour, anyway. "When do you think the trial will wrap up?"

He gently took Benjamin from me, cradling his nephew's head with a careful hand. "Maurice is not being cooperative, as we suspected. His refusal to explain how he removed all that succubus blood is becoming most . . . vexing." Talivar's mouth compressed in a way that left little doubt that *vexing* probably wasn't the word he was looking for, but it curved into a crooked smile a moment later as he shrugged at me.

"I don't think it's the removal so much as what he did with it." Although probably insane on some level, Maurice had somehow discovered a way to use the blood of succubi in the form of paint. Which sounds harmless enough—until he used it on Moira and myself, among others, to trap us in portraits made of our own nightmares.

"No doubt. And Moira has given her testimony, but . . ." He hesitated. "Well, the truth is our mother is not doing as well as she might. Moira is keeping an eye on her."

"Translation: Things are fucked," I quipped with a sigh. "I already know where this is going." Visions of raising Ben-jamin to his college years filled me with a weary sort of res-ignation. "What are the chances I'll be seeing Moira again before my Contract is up?"

"Well enough, I'm thinking. The Queen won't keep her there forever."

Easy for him to say. Maybe six years didn't seem like much to a nearly ageless elf, but it might as well have been forever as far as I was concerned.

"I still think we need to tell Robert. Benjamin *is* his son, and however uncomfortable that makes people, he should know. After all," I said dryly, "who's going to teach him to fly?"

Talivar shifted Benjamin to his shoulder and shook his head. "We do not recognize paternal claims in Faerie, Abby. All lineages are drawn through the mother. By that logic, I'm actually more closely related to my nephew than Robert is."

"Yeah, I can tell, what with those *wings* and all. Still makes no damn sense."

"Yes, well, we're a rather promiscuous bunch. We cannot trust our wives to be faithful, any more than our wives could trust us. At least this way I know my sister's children are related to me. But my wife?" He shrugged at my raised brow, a wan smile on his lips. "My hypothetical wife, anyway. She could take a hundred lovers over the course of our marriage and I would have no right to gainsay her that."

"And that doesn't bother you? Knowing that you have no real acknowledgement of your own children?"

"Children are rare and precious to our kind. We tend not to look too closely at where they come from. Usually." He looked down at the baby, his gaze distant. "And that, I think, is enough for one evening. Or morning, as the case may be," he noted, glancing at the false dawn through the blinds. "I'll tend to him now. Hopefully your rest wasn't disturbed much."

"Mmm . . . you're assuming I *like* to be awakened by a horn half up my ass."

"Probably depends on the horn." A smirk crossed his face before he slipped through the kitchen and down the hallway to the baby's room. I watched him go, rubbing my eyes again. He didn't have Brystion's blatant sexuality, but there was an ethereal beauty to him that sometimes stunned me.

A pang of sadness twisted in my chest and I told it to shut the hell up, ambling to my bedroom to try to catch a few more hours of shut-eye. Today was Katy's eighteenth birthday, after all, and I had things to do—party plans to set in motion and her werewolf boyfriend to keep under control. My duties didn't get put on hold simply because I had a messy personal life.

Phineas was unabashedly drooling on my pillow, his equine mouth half open. "Lovely." I grimaced, snatching up a spare from the closet. I hunched beneath the blankets, wrapping them partway about my head as though I might shut out the memories.

The unicorn snuggled closer, making kissy sounds.

I shoved him beneath the blanket. "You're an ass. See if I make you any breakfast."

"Be still my wounded heart," he retorted. "However shall I manage without a plate of burned bacon?" There was a snuffling sound and a sigh, and then a miniature chainsaw revving next to my ear.

Out of a perverse sense of revenge I nudged him with my shoulder. "I've got to try to find a ghost whisperer today, if I can. Remind me when you wake me up again."

There was a sudden silence. On instinct, I jerked my backside away from him, peering out of my nest to catch his teeth clicking shut on the space where my ass had just been. The unicorn gave me a sour look. "Almost got you," he mumbled, flopping onto his back with his legs spread obscenely. "Ask Charlie. She's always talking to dead people."

I frowned. I hadn't spoken to Charlie in quite a while. At least not about anything that didn't end up being awkwardly . . . awkward. "Charlie as in 'the girlfriend of the angel who cheated on her with my boss and whose baby I'm taking care of'?"

"Yeah." His mouth pursed. "Hmm . . . I guess I could

see where that might be a problem. Good thing I don't have to talk to her."

"Nice." I slouched down and rearranged the blankets, rolling to the other side to keep my posterior out of range. "Whose side are you on anyway?"

"Thought you'd have figured that out by now." He yawned, one eye cocking open to wink at me. "Mine."

Two

Well she's never in the way. Always something nice to say . . ."

Benjamin promptly scrunched up his face and wailed, his hot infant breath hitting me full on in a wash of sour milk and something vaguely reminiscent of wet feathers. "Well, *you* certainly don't have anything nice to say," I said as I shifted him in my arms. "My mamma used to play this one for me all the time when I was a kid. Shut me right up."

His dark eyes blinked at me, appearing to give weight to my words. For about two seconds. As if to make his point, this time the wail was encored by a dribble of spit-up.

My teeth ground together, but I left the smile plastered on my face. "Hardly worth the effort," I scolded, rummaging through the mountain of clothes in the corner mentally labeled as clean. Baring my teeth at my iPod, I hit the shuffle button, trusting to its inner enchantment to come up with something that wouldn't resemble the Backyardigans. Rob Zombie, maybe.

"When the moon is in the second house . . . and Jupiter aligns with Mars . . ."

Benjamin brightened immediately and I breathed a quiet

sigh of relief. If "Age of Aquarius" kept his head from spinning, I'd gladly leave it on repeat for the rest of the day.

Carefully rolling him onto the center of my bed to wiggle his legs like a helpless turtle, I tossed my now-stinking shirt into the dirty pile and threw on a light-colored tank. I'd learned quickly that wearing black was the kiss of death if I went out in public with Benjamin. Might as well paint a target on my head and invite the pigeons to take a shit on me too.

"Did you ever think maybe it's not the song choice that's upsetting him? Maybe it's that lovely singing voice of yours." Phineas's ears flattened as he trotted past me to jump onto the bed.

"Who's my little man?" The unicorn crooned at Benjamin and then winced when a hank of beard became the baby's newest form of entertainment.

"Keep that up and you'll be a baldy chin," I retorted. "And I don't recall asking your opinion. Not that that's ever stopped you before, Talivar around?"

"Nope, burned the coffee again. Ran out to get more." A snort escaped him. "He's even worse at it then you are."

"Probably something about being a prince and not having to actually cook for himself. At least he's trying. More than I can say for you." I stooped to search for my Crocs, pushing through dust bunnies and clumps of what suspiciously looked like unicorn droppings. "Christ, Phin, use the toilet or go outside or something." I snatched my hand away.

"That's not me. I think you've got mice." His tone became wheedling.

"I'll bet. Just clean it up."

"With what? Gonna turn my tail into a broom?" The furred tuft in question flicked as if to make the point.

"I'm sure you'll come up with something. Besides, aren't unicorn horns proof against poison? Purifying water, that sort of thing? Surely something that can bring a dead man back to life can disinfect like Lysol?"

Aggrieved, he arched his neck in disdain. "I never said anything about dead people. And I've got limits, you know."

"Good manners being one of them." I found the Crocs and the diaper bag. "All right, time to go." I picked up a now-dozing Benjamin, swaddling his shoulders in a blanket and strapping him into the chest carrier. People tended to be drawn to his face before anything else, but no sense in tempting fate any more than I had to. Although I supposed Talivar could have put a Glamour on the wings. I would have to ask.

Hoisting his diaper bag over my shoulder, I turned off the iPod and headed through the kitchen. Sure enough, the scent of scorched mocha java blend was in full evidence. Strangely enough, Talivar refused to touch anything that came out of the enchanted fridge. "Only organic," he'd told me once, and insisted on paying for his own share of the groceries. I didn't care one way or the other since neither of us could cook worth a damn anyway. Burned was burned, so what difference did it make?

"I'm going to the Hallows," I called to the unicorn. "Tell Talivar if he comes this way."

"I'm not your answering service, you know. Prince too good to use a cell phone?"

"Technophobe," I said dryly. "Just do it, Phin. And stay out of my underwear."

"Like you'd know." I shook my head and left, taking the stairs with a careful touch on the rail and a death grip around the baby. I'd started taking my meds on a regular basis, and it had definitely made some improvements in the number and quality of seizures I suffered from. In the past, I had let the drugs slide more often than not, but with everything that had happened recently I figured it was only fair to give my body a fighting chance. It had been almost two months since my last grand mal, something that had probably contributed to Moira's decision to leave her child with me. Or perhaps it hadn't crossed her mind at all. OtherFolk could be horribly self-absorbed, and the Faery princess was no exception.

The early afternoon sun warmed my skin. It might have been early April, but a slight chill still clung stubbornly to the breeze. I paused to assess the garden. It had taken a little convincing on my part, but I'd gotten Didi to invite a few cousins over to help tend the flowers. The PETA pixie hadn't quite forgiven me for the loss of her wand, but Talivar had won her over with his self-effacing charm. The flower-Fae were tiny things, but most of them had potty mouths to rival even the most stalwart of sailors. Gave Phin a run for his money, anyway, and that was saying something.

They waved cheerily at me as I passed, blowing little kisses at the baby. He made grabby fingers at them and I whisked him out of the courtyard before he got any ideas. Cleaning squished pixie from his hands would undoubtedly lead to some awkward questions.

A casual peek into the Pit's front bay window showed everything as it ought to be. Which is to say, empty of customers and full of crappy used books, and happily so. It still seemed odd to me that a Faery princess would run a used-book store as a front to a magical marketplace, but I did actually enjoy working there. I'd temporarily closed it the last few weeks while I had Benjamin, but I still ran the Marketplace most evenings while Talivar watched over the baby.

Benjamin babbled in my ear when he saw the sign creaking in the breeze above his head, but I hurried along. I passed the Opera Alley and the renovated Waterfront Art Gallery, trying not to shudder at the familiar lettering. I'd heard it was under new management, but something told me it would be a very long time before I ever willingly entered the place again.

Being painted into a magical realm with your friends via the blood of a succubus will do that to a girl. Still, it *had* been Sonja's ex-TouchStone, Topher, who put us all there, so I couldn't exactly throw myself a pity party about it. Even if it had been under Maurice's command, knowing that the person you should have been able to trust most had murdered your sisters wasn't the sort of thing you wanted to brag about.

"Cute baby."

I glanced up from my inner waiting-at-the-stoplight-montage to see an elderly woman beaming at me. "Ah, thanks." I tightened my grip instinctively.

Her mouth broadened into a smile. Benjamin gave me a look that could only be described as alarmed, and I shifted him away from her, lifting him up slightly. Hollow boned or not, the kid was getting seriously heavy to be hauling around like this. If Moira didn't come back soon, I was going to have to invest in a stroller for sure.

"He's got your eyes, you know? That's how I can tell he's yours. So pretty and blue."

I nodded stupidly at the woman. When the hell was the light going to change? The mere fact I held a baby seemed to drive people to the most inane of conversations, but who was I to shatter the illusion? The fact that those were Robert's eyes, ice blue and intense, would mean nothing to someone who never met him, and the truth of the matter is that people say shit like that all the time just to be polite.

For a moment I was tempted to tell her I'd found him on a doorstep.

She seemed harmless enough, but I'd run into a number

of people that I once categorized as "harmless," several of whom had turned into anything but.

The woman continued to make faces at Benjamin. Inwardly, I sighed. No sense in tempting fate. The light changed and I made my escape as politely as I dared, losing us in a cluster of window-shoppers before I ducked around the corner to the hidden alley leading to the Hallows.

Sequestered neatly off the main drag of Portsmyth's pubs and nightclub district, the OtherFolk bar still remained one of the prime hot spots of the city. Its werewolf owner had worried that business might slow after Maurice's daemon attack, but the resulting notoriety had only earned him a more loyal clientele.

I tapped on the rusted metal door. "Meet me at the CrossRoads," I murmured, the Door shimmering in answer to the passphrase. A careful check of the alley showed nothing by way of hapless mortals, so I ducked inside.

Benjamin blinked at the silver sparkles, fingers rapidly opening and closing as he tried to catch them. One lit upon his palm, hovering for a moment before fading. He chortled and squirmed free of his blankets, tiny wings fluttering.

"That's new." Brandon grinned at me as I hastily attempted to wrap the blanket around the baby's shoulders again. This early in the day meant the Hallows was empty of patrons, but no sense in taking chances. Benjamin wriggled with pure enthusiasm as his wings beat lopsidedly. The werewolf snorted, his tongue lolling from the side of his mouth.

"Yeah, well don't make an issue out of it. I'm trying to keep it on the down-low." As the bartender, the werewolf knew more than his fair share of OtherFolk secrets. One more wouldn't hurt.

"Ah well, maybe I wanted to know how my favorite little angel is doing." Brandon winked at me in that half-flirtatious way that left me a little uncertain as to which one of us he was speaking to. But then, that was nothing new. Even newly TouchStoned, the werewolf had a tendency to hit on anything that walked through the front doors and was remotely female. I wasn't entirely sure how Katy could stand it, but then, I wasn't barely eighteen, blond, and drop-dead gorgeous, was I? I was twenty-seven, currently saddled with a baby, a live-in job, a horny unicorn, and a fridge full of almost nothing but bacon. Given the choice, maybe I *could* understand, though I had to admit the bacon thing was a real winner.

"Stinky and cute, just like you," I deadpanned, pulling a sweatshirt from Benjamin's diaper bag and slipping it over his squirmy little head. A thin rope of drool slid over my hand. "Napkin, if you don't mind." I glanced about the nearly empty nightclub as Brandon dug beneath the bar. I'd been here since the renovations were done, but only at night, when the place was in full swing. A little different to see it in the cold light of day.

Moira had paid for all the damages and it showed. Not that it had ever really been a dive to begin with, but the gleaming teak wood was obviously several calibers higher than what had been there before. The stage, the sound system, the polished granite bar—all of it was brilliant. Even the dance floor had been replaced, the scuffed boards now glittering with some sort of Glamoured marble. My eyes fell on it and I pursed my lips. New or not, if I stared long enough at it, I could almost see the blood spatters and that spot where I'd stepped on that daemon's brain . . .

"Did you get a chance to look at those latest letters, Abby?" Brandon's voice pulled me from my reverie with a little start. He handed me a stack of napkins, his eyes suddenly fixed on the bar. The words were casual, but the tone was bland. *Too* bland. Bastard wanted something.

"Out with it, wolf-boy," I said sourly, wiping at my

palm. "You only pretend not to care when you really want something. No, no." I moved an empty glass away from the baby. "Not for you."

"I'll take him for a while, if you want." Katy emerged from the lounge looking like a golden Venus, all dewy youth and fresh sparkles. She was wearing jeans and a cut-off shirt, her perfectly tanned abdomen displayed free and clear. I frowned at it. Almost damn near unnatural, given the season.

Or you're just incredibly jealous, given that the only tan you'll ever have will be made up of the shades of "pasty" and "freckled," I thought ruefully.

"Hey, Katy. Happy birthday." I smiled at her anyway. Not like she could help it, right? "And sure, think he's a little sick of me anyway." I undid the carrier and handed Benjamin over to her. He immediately began gurgling, another bit of drool falling on her shoulder.

"Just like every other guy who comes within ten feet of her," I quipped. "And you're tag-teaming me. So clearly something's up." Katy cooed happily at the little guy, walking him over to the stage so he could see the way the disco ball lit up. Despite my inner snark, I genuinely liked her. She had spunk where it counted and she'd certainly treated Brandon like a prince. Not always easy to do with someone who often resembled an anthropomorphic canine most of the time. Besides, being kidnapped by daemons together made for excellent girl-bonding.

The werewolf stared at me for a moment and then chuckled. "You know, you're not nearly as ignorant as you let on."

"Now you're flattering me." I sighed and crumpled the dirty napkin. "Gonna spill?"

"Well, we've been thinking—Katy and me, that is. Or really, this is Katy's idea mostly, but I think it would be a good thing." He paused, looking at me expectantly.

"Brandon, it might actually help if you *told* me what you wanted me for."

"Oh, right. Yeah. You know we started that TouchStone dating service."

"Yeessss." It was still in the early stages as far as I'd heard, but with everything else going on, I hadn't paid it much attention. TouchStone Contracts were usually overseen by Moira as part of her Protectorate duties, but for the most part I stayed out of anything to do with those.

I stared at him blankly, but the hairs on the back of my neck rose. In the past I had a tendency to ignore my instincts, but this time I had to agree with them. "And this involves me how?"

His ears dropped, that canine brow furrowing. "Well, you *are* a KeyStone, Abby. We were sort of hoping you might, you know . . . use your talent? We figured you might be able to help us match profiles better that way."

I thought of the one night with my ex-vampire lover, Jett, and shuddered. A mortal TouchStone usually had a written Contract sanctified by the Faery Protectorate to allow at least some level of protection, but even then things could be a bit unscrupulous. There had been efforts in the past to regulate it better, but the three Paths barely managed to tolerate each other on a regular basis without coming to blows, let alone come to an agreement where a ruling party determined what was "fair." Angels. Daemons. The Fae. For all their magical snobbery, they could be such assholes.

As a living KeyStone I had the rare capability to Touch-Stone OtherFolk on contact, which could lead to a number of unfortunate situations. Without an actual Contract, the boundaries of such a bond were nebulous at best and dangerous at worst. I knew where Brandon was going with this; I actually got a vision of an OtherFolk's inner personality upon creation of the bond—but that sort of thing took energy. Plus it was damned creepy. Not something I was willing to put up with simply to make life easier for people who couldn't even be bothered get to know each other first.

"Um, no. I don't think that's a good idea. For one thing, the more people I'm TouchStoned to, the more energy I end up expending. For another—"

"For another, Moira wouldn't allow it." Talivar drawled behind me, but there was an edge to his voice that I'd come to recognize very well. His fingers brushed lightly upon my arm, their heat marking me as surely as any brand. "And neither would I. Abby has enough on her plate without taking on another project, don't you think?" His gaze flicked to where Katy cooed at the baby, Benjamin's happy giggles ringing through the bar.

Brandon bared his teeth at the elf, ears flattening. "And maybe you should let her decide for herself, aye?"

I planted a hand on Talivar's chest before he could reply. "Dudes, can we save the pissing match for another time? Moira's not going to thank you if you start smiting the newly renovated dance club she just finished financing."

The prince shrugged, sliding a steaming cup of coffee toward me, the scent promising something with cream and caramel. "The final choice, of course, is yours. As your bodyguard, I merely thought to make my opinion known." He smiled at Brandon. "My apologies, lycanthrope."

The werewolf snorted and then shook his head, but the ears had perked up. "Yeah, whatever."

"Ah. The delicate male ego. So fragile. So infinitely pettable." Ignoring the way they both blinked at me, I pointed over to the stage where Melanie was tweaking her amp. "Now go bother your own TouchStone for a bit. Find out how much planning is left for Katy's party tonight. I'll join you in a minute."

Talivar grunted in assent, watching Benjamin for a moment before heading past the bar and beelining for the stage. I watched the prince's ass, simply because I could. There was something about that slim-hipped swagger that had my Lord of the Rings inner geek demanding some sort of fanservice. Preferably the mostly undressed sort.

Brandon yawned, leaning on the bar top. "I honestly had the feeling that you wouldn't, but Katy thought it wouldn't hurt to ask."

I slipped into a high-backed barstool and took a sip of my coffee. "Well, even aside from Talivar's input on the subject, it would have to go through Moira first. After all, she's made a few allowances for me, but given the trouble we had before, I think the Faery Council would really have issues with it. I mean, they totally freaked out when they found out I was TouchStoned to . . . Brystion."

I shivered. I'd been accused of attempting to overthrow the Protectorate in a misunderstanding of massive proportions and I had no wish to revisit the process. If I never saw the inside of a cell within the Judgment Hall again it would be too soon.

"I hadn't even thought about that," he admitted. "But, yeah, I guess I can understand." He brightened, cocking his head at me. "Well, if not that, how about a 'Dear Abby' column in our newsletter, then? Maybe take some of the pressure off you having to answer all these." He pulled up a new stack of variously shaped envelopes and I groaned.

"Seriously?" I fingered one that looked to be little more than a leaf stuffed in a conch shell. "Well, that one's different, anyway. Snail mail," I quipped, my lips curling at my own joke.

"They keep coming in. If we set you up with an actual column maybe people would understand it if you couldn't get to them all."

"Why me?"

"Why *not* you?" His gaze rested heavily on me. "You're one of the first mortal KeyStones that's shown up in a very long time. You nearly died to save the Protectorate."

I scowled at him, slouching on my stool. "The bad guy still got away and my friends were hurt. Hell, your bar was completely trashed. I'm not sure I see anything overly heroic about that." To be honest, I'd thought I'd been nothing more than a big coward for most of it, giving myself to the enemy like some kind of sacrificial lamb. "I should have acted faster than I did."

"You acted. That's more than a lot of mortals would have done." His long furry fingers toyed with the edge of one of the letters. "The fact of the matter is you're TouchStoned to one of each of us. Each of the Paths, I mean. There's something sort of disturbing and comforting about that."

"That's me," I retorted. "Like holding a .45 to your skull with one hand and offering you a lollipop with the other. And I'm not TouchStoned to all three Paths anymore." I tried not to flinch as I said it, leaving my tone as matter-of-fact as I could.

"But you were." He sighed. "That's not what I meant. I'm sorry."

I waved him off, shuffling the pile of letters together to shove them into the diaper bag. "Yeah, I know. And I'll think about it."

"All we can ask."

It wasn't entirely true, I didn't think. The asking. I owed him a debt for being there when I needed him, and for him not blaming me when Katy was hurt. It was still on *my* shoulders.

Talivar had his back to me as I approached the stage. His voice was pitched low, his head beside Melanie's. I hesitated. If they were in the middle of a serious conversation, I didn't want to be caught up in it. I studied my best friend for a moment, taking in the way her familiar curly red hair hung loosely over one shoulder, tangled in the hooks of her leather corset. Her eyes appeared troubled behind the purple tea-shade glasses.

The commonality of their forced TouchStone Contract was me, something I wasn't overly comfortable with. The fact that Melanie had been required to do it to save her fingers wasn't anything I was proud of, particularly given that I'd inadvertently put her in the situation that had injured her. As a virtuoso of unsurpassed skill, she was in high demand among the OtherFolk. Without the ability to play, she would have lost her livelihood for certain.

For the first time, I really looked at the two of them, wondering if they'd break the Contract, given the chance. There was a tenseness to Melanie whenever she looked at him, and the set of Talivar's shoulders didn't speak of anything calm. Melanie shrugged, her words increasing in volume.

"—but I don't really think I'm the one you should be asking. Moira would probably be a better—oh hey, Abby." Melanie's smile suddenly became forced. Talivar turned to face me and I coughed.

"I'm sorry. I didn't mean to intrude."

"Oh, don't worry," Melanie said. "We were just discussing some of the details of Katy's party tonight. The musical stuff."

"Something like that," Talivar muttered. I frowned at Melanie, not liking the lie, but I wasn't going to press. As I'd discovered, TouchStone Contracts were terribly intimate, and given that this was the longest one Melanie had ever had, there was bound to be some friction.

"Well, okay then," I said, a sudden perverseness making me want to call them on it. "What did you have in mind?"

The elven prince shifted uncomfortably, even as Melanie lifted her violin to her cheek. With a sonorous sigh, the

voice of the strings spun about us in harmony, the purity of
the sound echoing through the Hallows. From somewhere
behind us, Benjamin babbled in delight. I couldn't help the
smile creeping over my face, Talivar and I sharing a quick
glance.

Uncertainly flickered in his eye. "Abby—"

"What a lovely couple you make. I can see why she chose
you." I froze, the tone of the words slicing through our moment with all the grace of a thrown bag of garbage. The
music cut off, all three of us turning to face the newcomer. I
did a double take, recognition sliding into place. It was the
woman from the street corner.

Instinctively, I pulled away from Talivar, my gaze rocket-
ing to where Katy still held Benjamin. I stepped in front of
them, something about the woman making my hackles rise.
"And you are?" I kept my voice polite, but firm. After all,
this time I had friends at my back.

"Oh, that's right. I'd forgotten." Her teeth gleamed beneath rouged lips. She shook her head, and the Glamour
melted away in a haze of sparkles, revealing her to be one
of the elves, tall and pale, complete with the broom-up-
the-ass arrogance so common to their race. Gone were the
dowdy mom-jeans with their elastic waistband and her ap-
pliqué vest; her clothes became chic and silken to match the
dark lustrous waves of her hair. There was nothing grand-
motherly at all about the way her perfectly shadowed eyes
gleamed hungrily as they fell on Benjamin. "I'm Tresa. The
new Protectorate of Portsmyth."

Three

Excuse me?" I frowned at her, eyeing her Jimmy Choos with a hint of envy. "And here I thought the Devil was supposed to wear Prada?"

Talivar shifted to stand closer, angling his body so that it was in front of mine. Brandon perked up, sliding from behind the bar with a look that was more than a little unfriendly. His eyes flicked toward Katy, who was clinging to a suddenly silent Benjamin.

"I think you heard me," Tresa said coolly, her brow raised. "I was led to believe you were Moira's TouchStone. Are you not?"

"She isn't required to answer you." The shadowed lilt of Talivar's voice made me shiver beneath the weight of his words, as though he'd wrapped a cloak of regality about him. Not a bodyguard now, but a prince of the Fae, staring hard at one of his subjects.

Unfazed, Tresa shook her head, a sneer tearing its way across her flawless mouth. "I already told you. I'm the new Protectorate. And I don't take orders from the Crippled Prince."

Ignoring Talivar's black look, she dug into her satchel

and pulled out a scroll. She shoved it in my face. "This is the new Contract. I'd like you to look it over. If you agree with the terms, we can go ahead and get you signed up, hmm?" Her eyes glittered as she spoke and her pretentious questioning hum had me about ready to elbow her in the throat.

My hand didn't move from my side. "I'm not signing anything." TouchStone Contracts were tricky even at the best of times, but I couldn't remotely fathom signing one on some woman's random say-so.

She paused, something flickering across her face. Annoyance? Anger? I couldn't tell. Her smile widened into something feral and toothy, but I brushed it off. "And what about Moira?"

"Ah. She's rather indisposed, at the moment. Taking care of the Queen, I believe, the poor thing." Tresa looped her fingers through her hair, a smile playing about her lips. Beside me, Talivar made a strangled sound, his jaw cracking.

Self-righteous fury heated my cheeks. "Bullshit. There's no way she would have left her baby with me indefinitely."

"Not to mention Moira said no such thing to me when I saw her," Talivar growled. *"Yesterday."*

Tresa's eyes narrowed. "Indeed." Her mouth hardened as she turned to where Katy stood. A flash of fur from the bar caught my attention. Brandon stalked past us, moving with a deliberate swagger. A wolf on the prowl, but not panicked. Not yet.

"Enough of this," I said. "I'm not doing anything until I get confirmation from a third party." Benjamin squirmed in Katy's arms. I moved away from Tresa, my head doing a couple of quick calculations. "I don't suppose this is something you can determine?" I gave Talivar a tight smile.

He blinked at me. "I'm hardly going to be objective. As liaison, Roweena would be the best choice. No one would question her word," he added with an odd touch of bitterness.

I nodded. Roweena DuMont was the liaison between the Faery Court proper and the Protectorate's Council. Usually all official court business would come through her, although sometimes wires did cross.

"All right, let's see if she can't give us the scoop. I think our friend here is neglecting to tell us all the details." Tresa's eagerness to have me sign over the Contract had set off a series of small alarm bells. I might still be a bit wet behind the ears when it came to the OtherFolk, but as TouchStone to the Protectorate, I wasn't going to just roll over on this chick's assurance.

Talivar didn't answer, suddenly reaching out to push me behind him. The ghosted presence of a hand snatched at the back of my head. I rolled to my knees, his low-throated growl of disapproval echoed in Brandon's snarl. Melanie pulled me to my feet, her violin balanced in the other hand. "What was that about?" I snapped, peering around the bulk of his shoulder as a whimper of pain sounded.

"She was trying to TouchStone you," he replied pleasantly, tightening his grip on Tresa's wrist until she sank to the floor. "Weren't you, Tresa?"

She winced, but whether that was because of the thunderstorm in his voice or the fact that he was quite clearly grinding her bones together I wasn't going to guess. "Was not," she gasped. "Just wanted to give her the paperwork."

"By touching her?"

Tresa looked away, her mouth firmly compressed. Any sympathy I might have had for her dropped out the window like a sack of bricks. Hopefully attached to her head.

I crouched down beside her, anger clipping my words. "It doesn't work that way, you know. Not really. I have to allow it, and there's about a snowball's chance of that. Now, are you gonna play nice?" It wasn't entirely true, but hell, I hadn't quite figured out the exact mechanics. Didn't mean I needed to tell her that, though.

"Yes." She jerked her arm away when I nodded at Talivar. He stayed within easy reach, a flash of warning shining from his good eye.

"You were following me earlier. Why?" She blinked and I rolled my eyes. "Besides the obvious, I mean."

"I wanted to make sure I knew who you were. So that I knew who to offer the Contract to."

"Sure you did." She placed the scroll into my hand in answer, careful not to touch me. I unrolled it slowly even as Talivar moved closer to read over my shoulder. Tresa got to her feet, brushing down her skirt with exaggerated care, which I assumed was more to soothe her wounded pride than anything else.

Pushing her wayward locks behind a pointed ear, she let out a small sigh. Talivar frowned at the Contract. "Is this worded right?"

"Does it matter?" she snapped. And then she was moving toward Katy, her shoes scraping on the marble as she barreled her shoulder into the girl. Katy staggered, curling herself around the baby and twisting to take the brunt of it on her side. Benjamin let out a howl of protest, his cry becoming sharp when the elf woman reached around to snatch his leg.

Brandon was on them a moment later, savaging Tresa's thigh even as Talivar and I tried to get Katy out from underneath. I tried to pry Benjamin from Tresa's grip, her nails clenching hard enough to break the skin.

Talivar forced her arm back by inches, until Katy was able to scramble out of the mess. Benjamin whimpered, and I noticed blood streaking down his calf. "Stop, Talivar! Stop! She'll hurt him."

Immediately he tugged on the werewolf's ruff to halt his assault. The four of us panted, Tresa's blood pooling on the floor. "The Contract." She pulled Benjamin closer to her. "The baby for the Contract."

"It won't hold up if it's signed under duress," Talivar snarled. "Assuming we let you live that long."

Ignoring her wounds, she limped to the door, still clutching the baby. Benjamin's face was red with fury, a squall of righteous terror escaping him. Something unreadable passed through her eyes as she looked down at him. Muttering something beneath her breath, she stared straight at me. "Catch."

Benjamin flew from her arms, his mouth open in a tiny "o" of alarm. I moved to catch him, but Talivar was faster still, rolling with an inhuman speed to gracefully pluck his nephew from the air as though he were capturing a bubble. He assessed the child long enough to see that there were no critical injuries before shoving him into my arms. Tresa had already disappeared out the front door of the bar, a trail of crimson the only sign of her passage.

Talivar didn't hesitate to bolt after her, the door nearly rocking off its hinges from the force of his exit. I stared for a moment before Benjamin's soft snuffle brought me back. Quickly I laid him down on the floor, checking him over. Except for the scratches on his leg, which seemed mostly superficial, he looked okay. Cradling him against my breast, I rocked him until he quieted down. "There we are," I crooned at him, relief flooding my shaking arms when he rubbed his face against my collarbone. "Katy, you okay?"

"Yeah," she said as Melanie helped her to her feet. "Just caught me by surprise." She rotated her shoulder experimentally, hissing. "Think that's going to bruise, though."

Brandon nosed around the bloodstains on the floor. "I just got this bitch waxed too," he growled, his tongue lapping out to trace one of the puddles. His muzzle wrinkled in distaste. "Something not right about this. It tastes foul."

"I wouldn't know," I said, "not being a blood drinker and all."

He rolled his golden eyes at me. "Fae blood is usually sweet . . . sweeter than human blood, even. But this . . . I'm not sure she is what she says."

"Not the Protectorate, anyway." I exchanged a glance with Melanie. "Do you think Talivar should have some sort of backup? What if that's an ambush?"

"I'll make a few calls. She may go to ground here if she's hurt, but if she manages to reach the CrossRoads he'll need a tracker." Brandon snapped his chops. "I know a few of the best."

"She'll know where I live, I'm sure. She was following me earlier. Not that Moira keeps any secrets about who I am." I sighed at the thought of having to dodge potential assassins. Again. Part of my job was to be available to those OtherFolk who needed to get in touch with the Protectorate. Everyone knew I worked at the Pit and I lived above it. Perhaps Moira had been wiser than I'd thought to have Talivar stay with me.

Of course that begged the question of what I was supposed to do when my bodyguard was out chasing the bad guys. And what was I going to do with Benjamin? My own life I could risk, but an innocent? Taking him back to the apartment was not an option, particularly if Tresa had friends waiting for us out in the alley.

I turned to Melanie as Brandon started patting Katy down under the guise of making sure her injuries weren't serious. He was probably trying to cop a feel, but that wasn't any of my business. She wasn't protesting, anyway. "I'm going to need you to make me a Door."

Doors were magical conduits that led directly onto the

CrossRoads. Most were hidden and hard to find, but Melanie had the singular ability to create Doors wherever she wanted. Her violin was the key to it all. She told me once her soul was trapped inside the instrument and I believed her, even if she hadn't quite gotten around to sharing the entire story with me.

Some things were just too personal to talk about.

She nodded slowly, understanding in her eyes. "I can do that. Do you know where you want to go? If there's an existing Door nearby I can steer you toward it."

I fastened the carrier around Benjamin's legs. He gave me a sleepy blink, gurgling as he fisted his hands into my hair. "Yeah. This is beyond me. I *should* take him straight to Moira, but I've never been to Faerie . . . and I don't know what would happen if I just tumbled through a Door with a baby in tow." *Particularly a winged baby,* I thought.

"Next best option?"

"His father," I said, stroking the baby's head.

Melanie pursed her lips. "You sure that's wise? I mean, with Charlie and all?"

"What choice do I have?" None. Charlie hadn't been aware that her angel lover had been having an affair with the Protectorate, but no one had. The fact that Moira was also his boss at the time probably didn't make things any easier to stomach, but I wasn't going to punish a child for parental mistakes. And I couldn't judge it anyway. Relationships between near immortals were sure to be messy long term. Throw a mortal or two into the mix and a broken heart was bound to happen.

As you know, my inner voice pointed out. I scowled. My inner voice could shut the hell up, thank you very much. "I know she won't be happy about it."

"All right." She blew out slowly, lifting her magical violin to her cheek again. A momentary silence gripped the room as we watched her. I'd only seen her open a Door a few times, the last being when I was still trapped in Topher's painting, so my memories were a bit hazy. "I'll need a formal request from you to make this work, Abby."

"A request?"

"Yes." Her fingers swirled over the silver-gilt wood with the greatest care to caress the strings gently, even as her mouth twisted in a wry smile. "Funny thing about daemonic gifts, you know? They never quite work out the way you thought they would." Her eyes met mine, a glint of warning flashing in their emerald depths.

"You don't need to tell me." I snorted.

She stood up, the violin resting easily beneath her chin, the bow poised above the strings. "I've got the Contract with Talivar, so we're all set there, but I still need an exit. Assuming there's a focus of sorts nearby, there shouldn't be any issue."

"As close to Charlie's as you can get, then. I don't want to be wandering around the CrossRoads any more than I have to."

"There's an alley near Charlie's house. That should work."

"Nothing closer?" Not that I had any issues with walking anywhere, but the less I was seen, the better.

"Technically, yes." Melanie paused and eyed me sourly. "Your funeral." I retreated into the hallway with a last look at Katy and Brandon and then the music began. For a moment I could think of nothing else except those wondrous notes, wrapping around me and Benjamin, tickling my skin.

Benjamin squirmed, craning his head as though seeing something I could not, his mouth a perfect cupid's bow of delight. The edges of my vision hazed into a silver arc, Saint Elmo's fire sparking up the sides of the doorjamb like crystalline snowflakes. I glanced at Melanie, noting only the rapture on her face. Her eyes were closed with a hidden smile curving the pout of her mouth and her fingers flew over the strings, the bow swaying with a butterfly's ethereal grace. Her Doc Martens tapped out a beat beneath it to keep time as she followed a path I couldn't begin to understand.

"Now," she murmured, eyes snapping open. I followed the curt gesture of her head, turning to the shimmering Door that had appeared. Still, I couldn't keep that little sliver of ice from running down my spine as I stepped over the threshold. Traveling the CrossRoads had never been my forte. A moment of tingling warmth and then my feet landed upon the cobblestones. I caught the barest glimpse of it, long and silver and stretching out into the blackness and beyond, a sparkling river that led to nowhere. And then it was gone, and I found myself at another Door. I didn't hesitate this time, trusting that Melanie knew what she was doing.

I dipped my head, and the silver strands fell over me like gossamer spider webs made of crystal. Benjamin's breath puffed on my neck. "It tickles," I agreed, closing my eyes as the webs slipped past my face.

"What the bloody fuck?"

That didn't sound too good.

I blinked, a hairbreadth too late as the stinging slap of Charlie's hand blazed over my cheek. Eyes watering, I staggered, but the Door had faded behind me, and I found my-self pressed into a wall.

Not an alley. So not an alley. In fact, judging by the extremely pissed-off mien of the angel and the nearly un-dressed state of Charlie, I was about as far from an alley as I could get.

My funeral, indeed.

Four

"Remind me later to thank Melanie for being so succinct," I said under my breath.

"Remind me to smash that fucking violin over her head," Charlie snapped. "What the hell are you doing here?"

I searched out Robert in helpless plea. "We've got a problem with Moira." I dropped the blanket from my chest. "And Benjamin needs his daddy."

Charlie's head swiveled toward Robert, her cheeks flushed. "You promised me. You promised me this wouldn't happen. That you'd take care of it."

"Hey, I'm sorry to bust in on you like this," I said, rocking slightly to keep Benjamin from making things worse. His eyes were very wide, but I could see his lower lip starting to tremble. Another outburst like that and he was going to tip over the edge. "But don't blame the baby. And don't blame me either."

She turned on me, dark eyes burning. Without another word, she strode into the bathroom and slammed the door hard enough to rattle the walls.

Great.

Sure enough, Benjamin's face squinched up into an infantile ball of fury all his own. "Hush, love." I slid off his sweatshirt before pulling him from the baby carrier to lean him over my shoulder. Robert stared at me, ashen. "What is it?"

"Wings," he said hoarsely, unfolding his own with a little sound of anguish. "My son . . . has wings."

"Yes. They kinda showed up a few days ago, actually." I frowned. "Did you want to hold him?"

His eyes widened. "Can I?"

"Well, for shit's sake, I would hope so." Something uneasy pitted deep into the bottom of my belly. "You're telling me Moira's never let you hold him?"

"No." He stretched out his hands, the tips of his fingers trembling as they brushed the top of Benjamin's head, soft wonderment slacking the hard edges of his features. The baby hiccuped roughly, but the sobs paused as he looked up at his father. Their matching eyes flickered with a strange sort of recognition, almost as though they were measuring each other. It was eerie, and certainly nothing I'd ever seen Benjamin do before. Inwardly, I could only shrug. Maybe it was an angel thing.

"Take him." Without waiting for an answer, I handed him the baby, stepping back to rub at my now-aching cheek. For all her normally gentle nature, Charlie apparently packed a bag of hammers in her fist.

Robert sighed, nestling Benjamin into the crook of his neck. "My little lad." Benjamin sniffed wetly, nostrils flaring for a moment.

"Well at least one of us is comfortable." I removed the rest of the baby carrier, rolling it up into the diaper bag.

"I'm sorry about that, Sparky." The angel's mouth quirked as though he tried not to laugh, his pet name for me rolling off his tongue in a Boston accent. "She has a bit of a temper."

"So I've noticed. I didn't mean to . . . um . . . barge in on you guys like that."

"Of course not. You're not stupid." He frowned. "Had it been anyone else, I'd have slaughtered them where they stood."

Beneath the crack of the bathroom door a shadow paced, the movement punctuated by what sounded like a fist hitting the wall. "She seems pretty upset."

"I should go to her," he said, but he made no move to give me the baby. "She's still a bit touchy since . . . she was taken." Something hungry flickered over his face, and he froze, fingers cradling Benjamin's head as though he might etch the moment in his memory forever.

I wavered. Stupid or not, I had no desire to put myself between an angel and his TouchStone paramour, but it seemed a bit beyond the pale to hand a man his son and then take him back two minutes later. On the other hand, I'd just scared the shit out of my friend, and that was on me. I could hardly blame her for her reaction.

"Here." I stooped down and dug through the diaper bag for a bottle. "Go heat this up . . . it's about time anyway."

The Celestial stared at me, caught between hope and misery. "Go on." I nudged him. "Pot. Hot water. Test on the wrist. You can do this," I assured him. "After all, I can barely microwave a hot dog, and *I've* managed." My gaze edged over to the bathroom. "I'll try talking to her."

"All right." He folded his wings tightly against his back. "I'll be in the kitchen."

He disappeared, leaving a small puff of feathers behind, his bare feet making no sound. Strange to see such a quiet grace from someone with the muscular framework of a small bull. Yet he held his child as though carrying spun glass. This was the right choice, I decided. Whatever Moira's reasons for not letting Robert see his son, she hadn't seen fit to let me in on them. TouchStone or not, I wasn't a mind reader.

I cracked my jaw and shook off the last of the sting, carefully making my way over to the bathroom door. I tapped the knob lightly. "Charlie? You okay in there?"

"Go away."

"Listen, I know you're pissed, and I'm sorry, but I really need your help right now."

The shadow stopped pacing for a heartbeat and then started up again. "I don't care. Since when have you ever listened to anyone? Not that it matters. Everything seems to have worked out for the best for you anyway."

"That's not fair. You and Robert got all up my ass last time for not coming to you when the Protectorate disappeared. Made it plain as day that I wasn't worthy of the position. Which may or may not be true," I added. "But I'm here now and I'm asking for your help."

The door flew open, the violence of the breeze blowing the hair from my face. I took an involuntary step back. Charlie glared at me, her tear-stained cheeks glinting in the bathroom light. It hurt me to see it, even as she smeared the remainder of her eyeliner away.

"You have no right to ask me for anything." She pitched her voice low, husky with a sob that couldn't quite escape. "Haven't I given Moira enough?"

I flinched despite myself. She was right, by all accounts, but still. "I'm not Moira," I said, not quite daring to put my hand on her shoulder. "And I've never asked you for anything you weren't willing to give."

"You're her representative. It's practically the same."

"Is it?" I raised a brow at her and she flushed.

"Maybe not quite," she amended. "But still. The woman

had a child by my lover. And you *knew!* You actually had the gall to look me in the face and not say anything to me. Not a word, Abby."

"Would you have told me? If our positions were reversed? Would you tell me if Ion got involved with someone else? Had gotten." My fingers clenched at the thought. Hypothetical or not, I understood her emotions all too well.

She blinked at me. "What kind of question is that? Of course I would . . . but honestly Abby, why would it matter?"

"It would matter to me," I said, unable to keep the edge from my voice. "Though I'm not sure what you're implying."

"He's a daemon, Abby. Why wouldn't he stray?"

I bit down hard enough to draw blood on the inside of my cheek. "I'm going to pretend you didn't say that. And first of all, I didn't actually know anything about Robert and Moria until after I escaped with the rest of you. And secondly . . . well, shit. How am I supposed to get between my employer, her bodyguard, and one of my best friends?"

She scowled, pulling her robe from the shower hook, and slipped it on, crossing her arms over her chest. She leaned on the doorframe, about as convinced as a canary in a room full of cats armed with shotguns. "You should have said something."

"And you let Robert off the hook without a word? What kind of bullshit is that?" A soft wail echoed into the bedroom from the kitchen. The sound cut off abruptly, followed by a distant murmur from Robert. I relaxed again, rubbing my elbow.

"I don't know," she whispered. "I just . . . I just wish none of it had ever happened. I would have done anything for him. Anything." Her lower lip trembled. "But I couldn't give him a child. And I tried. God knows, I tried. And then that . . . bitch . . . comes waltzing in waving that baby in my face."

"I didn't know. None of us did." I sat down on the leather ottoman next to her bed. "But that's what I mean, Charlie. Would it have been any easier coming from me?"

"I don't know," she repeated, her voice numb.

"Listen, whatever you and Robert have to work out, I don't need to be involved. But I wouldn't have come here tonight if I didn't think it was important. Whatever your issues are with Moira—and I can't say I blame you," I hurried along as she drew herself up, "but the baby is innocent in this. Don't punish him for being here, okay?"

She stiffened and then her shoulders slumped. Sighing, she sank down to the floor. "All right. I'll try. Tell me what's going on and I'll try."

"Well, you're not going to believe this, but Moira's gone again." I held up a hand to forestall her questions. "Not like you're thinking. She was only supposed to be gone for a few weeks. A scheduled trip to Faerie to clear the air about her involvement with Maurice." She shivered at the name of the man who'd nearly killed us. Even eight months later, his name created a sickening coil in my belly.

Charlie let out a weary laugh. "I still have nightmares about it, you know. Being trapped . . ." She sucked in a deep breath, her eyes meeting mine. Out of everyone who'd been affected by Maurice's plan, Charlie had probably had the worst of it. Giving me a wan smile, she sighed. "So she's gone?"

"Still in Faerie, anyway. Some freaky ass Fae woman showed up at the Hallows today. Said she was the new Protectorate. She wants me to transfer my Contract to her. When I refused she tried to take Benjamin. Talivar's out hunting her down now."

She stood up. "Come on," she said grimly. "Let's let Robert know. He's going to want some input on this."

"Input, hell," I muttered, trailing along behind her. "I'm hoping he wants to smite the bitch."

"Charming."

"You haven't met her yet. She crawled so far up my ass I could have tongue kissed her."

"Kissed who?" Robert looked up from where Benjamin was nestled in the crook of his arm, his face filled with a calm I hadn't seen before. The baby burbled contentedly, eyes half lidded and lazy.

Charlie swallowed audibly and exchanged a very long look with the angel. "Do you think it would be okay if I held him? Not for very long."

I shrugged, mouth pursing. "Ask Benjamin. I tend to let him call the shots on holding rights. Seems to be a pretty good judge of character, if you ask me," I said, thinking of his reaction to Tresa. Maybe it was true what they said about babies and cats.

She approached Robert with a soft step and an extended hand, her eyes widening as she looked down at the little face, the tiny wings. "Oh, Bobby," she murmured. "He's beautiful."

"Sucker," I said, unable to keep the smile from drifting over my face. "He knows how to work a crowd," I warned her as Robert carefully placed him in her arms. She merely nodded, her eyes closing as she clutched Benjamin against her breast.

Benjamin squirmed and then settled, one hand aimlessly reaching up to twiddle her silver necklace, blue eyes somber. Robert stared at the pair of them for a minute longer and then shook his head as though to clear it. "Kiss who, now?"

"Tresa. She's the kidnapping, lying bitch who's apparently the new Protectorate," I said, struggling not to take a step backward. Gentle or not, the guy intimidated the hell out of me, and with good reason. "Moira's stuck in Faerie and her supposed *replacement* just showed up."

"You're joking." His hand twitched down by his hip, fisting into empty air when it didn't find his sword.

"Did you know?"

"What the hell kind of question is that? Of course I didn't know."

"I'm beginning to detect a pattern here," I said dryly.

"Well, why would she tell me?" He snarled at the refrigerator as though it might give him an answer. "I was demoted for not doing my job."

Charlie looked up from her cooing with a frown. "It wasn't your fault."

He opened his mouth but I stepped between them. "That stuff doesn't matter right now." Help or not, I didn't want to be stuck in the middle of a domestic spat. The fact that I was sort of the indirect cause of said spat didn't escape me, but I decided it wasn't worth pointing out. "Here's the thing. She wanted me to switch Contracts to her, and when I didn't move fast enough she attempted to TouchStone me directly."

Robert frowned. "That doesn't sound like a Fae at all. Something's not right here."

"No." Charlie paused her rocking. "Fae cannot lie, though they are duplicitous at the best of times, but it's not like them to force a mortal's hand like that."

"They haven't forced it yet," I reminded her, handing the Contract scroll to Robert. "What do you make of this?"

He frowned, gaze darting over the words for a moment before rolling up the parchment with a snap. "I'm no judge of these. It looks legit, but I wouldn't go by my word."

"No. In fact, I need you to call Roweena for me. Have her come to the Marketplace tonight. Hopefully Talivar will have found Tresa by then and we can get all this shit worked out."

Robert's eyes narrowed. "I want to be there. Ex-bodyguard or not, I think I've a right. If that . . . elf . . . attempted to hurt my son . . ."

Charlie flinched, burying her face in the thick thatch of Benjamin's hair. I turned away from the longing flashing across her features, tempered with a very old hurt. I suddenly felt like the proverbial fly on the wall and I shifted. This was not for me to see. "No," I said. "I don't think you do. And I don't want you to be there."

He drew himself up. "She's the mother of my child. The hell I'm going to let something happen to her again."

"Jesus, you're an idiot," I snapped, unable to bear Charlie's pain any longer. "Are all Celestials missing the compassion gene or is your thickheadedness a fluke? There's a bigger picture here." I rolled out my lower lip. "Who else besides us knows you're Benjamin's father?"

He shrugged, bemused. "I certainly never told anyone . . . other than Charlie. Hell, I didn't think Moira wanted me anywhere near him."

"Maybe she didn't. But why? She doesn't seem like the type . . . even aside from the . . . um . . . cheating thing." His face reddened, hands clenching harder. Stupid of me, maybe. "But that's my point. I'm not sure she even told the Queen who the father was."

"The general consensus was that it was Maurice," Charlie agreed with a soft voice. "But anyone who saw these little wings . . ."

"But those wings weren't there before. Until now, no one would have had any reason to doubt her word."

"And what, exactly, are you implying? You think she was ashamed of me? Of what we did?" Robert winced at his own words, giving Charlie an apologetic look.

"Well, *I* would have been." I fought the urge to slap him upside the head. "No, you asshole. I think she didn't want anyone to know. I think she thought something was going to happen to her when she went back to the Faery Court. I think she's trying to protect her baby."

"I don't understand. Why would she let people think it was Maurice's?" Charlie frowned.

"I'm not sure she did. Assumptions are what they are. Maybe she didn't feel like increasing the speculation. But if she didn't want them to know who the father was, what better way than to push him away? Remove him from her presence?" I looked at the angel. "And who better to protect him now, when things are suddenly starting to go wrong? Talivar said that the Fae don't acknowledge the fathers of their children. She could have said anyone was the father and the Fae wouldn't have cared. But I think *she* cares. Very much."

"All right. Then what will you do, now that you've given him to us? And know that angels take parentage very seriously, Abby," he added softly.

"What I always do. Wing it and hope for the best. I'm going to go to the Marketplace tonight and see if I can figure out what's going on, but I don't want the baby anywhere near me. Everyone knows I'm TouchStoned to Moira. I would imagine I might make a tempting target for anyone who wants to threaten her." I gave them a wan smile. "As you know. Otherwise, I think you should lay low . . . or at least not make any sudden changes in your behavior. I'm not sure I'd go out with the baby either. Not until I get back to you with more info."

"But what about food and a crib and all the rest of it?"

"I've got some stuff in the diaper bag, but yeah, I can send Talivar over with more." I pursed my lips at them. "Of course, that means he'll probably have to use your personal Door."

"Once," Robert agreed. "And he better call first."

"I think I can manage that. Although Phin might come to visit. He's become rather fond of Benjamin."

"All right," Charlie said. "So where does that leave you? You gonna try to use the Door?"

I shook my head. "No. Mel opened this one directly. I'll get lost if I try to find my way home alone. Safer if I just sneak out the back."

"There's a tunnel," Robert said with a grunt. "Installed a panic room under the floor after . . . after all the other stuff."

"Not a bad idea," I mused. Though where I'd put such a thing in my apartment was probably a moot point. Wasn't like I had the money to do that sort of renovation anyway. "All right. You guys hang tight, and I'll contact you as soon as I can."

Robert nodded gravely, leading me to the bedroom. He rolled the ottoman out of the way to reveal a trapdoor in the floor. "If you need me, call. Baby or no, I will not leave you without protection again."

"I will. Where does this go?" I eyed the trapdoor dubiously. There were probably spiders in there. I shivered.

"You'll come out two blocks past the bus station. There's a Glamour on the custodial closet. You should be safe there."

"Convenient."

"Never know when you have to leave town." He shrugged. "You ready?"

"Yeah." Pulling up the trapdoor revealed an inky black oubliette of a tunnel. Lovely. "Some of us can't see in the dark you know."

"Watch the steps," he called helpfully as I descended. "There's a railing there."

I grabbed the rail, thankful it seemed neither slimy or particularly spiderweb covered, letting it guide me downward and out. The passing of a breeze and a click above me told me he'd latched the door.

And silly me. I'd forgotten to ask Charlie about the ghost-whisperer thing. "Damn." I shoved the thought to the back burner. Ghosts could wait. I had answers to find, and probably little time in which to do it.

Good times.

Five

"You'd think this place would get some decent delivery service," Phineas grumbled from his place on the counter. My iPod cheerfully chugged away next to him. It was on a B-52's kick tonight, and the trend continued with a dance version of "Rock Lobster."

"You should have eaten earlier." Though in light of all that had happened today, Katy postponed her party, so our original plans for a grander dinner had gone right down the crapper. And Phin was right—for all that the Marketplace seemed to do such a brisk business, even the metaphysical pizza places seemed to have trouble finding it.

"Suck it up, buttercup," I added anyway.

The unicorn shot me a frosty look. "Keep it up and I'll take a dump in your bed."

"The hell you will. Besides, if Talivar ever caught wind of that you'd be out of those free breakfasts you're always moaning on about."

I frowned at my watch. It was just past midnight; Talivar was late.

I hadn't heard from the Faery prince except for a terse voice mail via pay phone saying he had caught Tresa and was bringing her to meet with Roweena. Given the lateness of the hour, we'd decided to have her confer at the Market-place, rather than trek down to the Judgment Hall. Roweena had agreed, since she had to verify the accusations before any action could be taken.

Before Phin could answer, Roweena DuMont stepped through the door in all her Faery glory, flanked by the angel brute squad. For some reason the Fae preferred Celestials for their muscle when in the mortal realm, and given the cannons on these guys I could see why. There was enough chiseled chin between the pair to make a sculptor weep.

She arched a perfectly plucked silver brow, her gaze trailing around the store. Although markedly one of the oldest Fae I'd met thus far, Roweena still had the nearly age-less face of most of her race. Only a few hints of her years marked her mouth, but there was a coolness in her eyes that bespoke of exceptionally tempered steel. Something I could appreciate, having been on the receiving end of her disfavor more than once.

The majority of the OtherFolk customers hadn't shown up yet, so there was ample opportunity for her to take it all in without interruption. Her gimlet stare lingered on the lush hardwood and the rows of shelves spread out in a graceful chaos of potions and books, charms and fetishes. The witch-lights danced along the ceiling like always, but that was a standard Faery trick so I didn't think she'd be too impressed.

"Interesting place Moira has set up."

"I just work here," I said.

A large leonine . . . something strode in, earning a blatant whistle of approval from the unicorn. She had the torso of a woman and the lower half of a big cat, and her rounded, furry ears poked out from a massive mane of golden hair. Whatever she was, she prowled through the aisles with a deadly grace, silent on enormous lion feet.

Of course, the effect was somewhat ruined by the fluorescent green T-shirt stretching across a rack of truly monstrous proportions; the words FUCK YOUR FASCIST BEAUTY STANDARDS stretched across her chest in a childlike scrawl.

"I think I'm in love." Phineas sighed. "Just look at those . . . those *haunches*."

I stared at him. "I should think you'd be a little small for her."

"Well," he retorted, waggling his beard, "you know what they say about size and what you do with it."

"You're being obnoxious."

He shrugged, his own tail twitching. "The wombat porn on the Discovery Channel isn't cutting it these days. I need to get out, be free." His eyes narrowed as the lion-girl slipped out the door. "Get some pus—"

I yanked on his beard so that he squealed. "Dude."

"Hmmph."

"Sorry about that," I said to Roweena. "He's not usually quite this bad."

"Oh, it's quite charming," she said dryly. "Definitely been an enlightening first visit."

"I thought you'd been here before."

"I stay out of Moira's way. What she does here is her business, as long as it doesn't encroach upon the sovereignty of the Faery court. That being said, I'm not sure the Queen would approve of the riffraff." She shrugged. "But I have no wish to get between Her Majesty and her daughter on this particular subject, even though I have no doubt that most of this is highly illegal."

My gaze slid away from my enchanted iPod and I coughed. Mixing technology with magic was mostly forbidden, but I'd accidentally managed to magic up the MP3 player shortly after I'd taken the position of Moira's TouchStone. The Protectorate had been amused enough to let me keep it, but I wasn't under any illusions as to what would happen if it became common knowledge. I didn't even know who supplied Moira with most of the inventory we received, but the really big-ticket stuff was in the back. I wasn't even supposed to sell it without Moira's express approval.

Roweena cocked her head at me. "Do you have the Contracts?"

I handed them to her, the parchment crisp between my fingers. "I don't suppose you know anything about what's going on. Moira didn't say anything to Talivar yesterday when he visited the Court, as far as I know."

"Word has been rather sparse of late," Roweena admitted. "Rumors of the Queen's health have not improved communications and things have become complicated with the Maurice issue. We knew Moira was going to testify, but the Court has been fairly closemouthed about the details. Security reasons, you understand." The elder Fae eyed the scroll with a hint of anger. "Just because they want to know how he did something doesn't mean they want the way he did it blabbed to the CrossRoads at large."

"Makes sense. So what is the protocol for switching my TouchStone Contract to a new Protectorate, assuming *any* of this is legit?" I asked Roweena, rubbing my temples in an attempt to ward off an impending headache. "Because I have to tell you, if Tresa is the new Protectorate, I don't think I'm interested in the job." Given the circumstances, I doubted it was even a remote possibility, but the Fae were fickle. If word came down from on high that Tresa really was the new Protectorate, there wouldn't be much I could do, even if her management style sucked. On the other hand, a lot of the Fae were nuts. For all I knew, kidnapping babies was actually how positions of power changed hands.

Roweena frowned. "That depends on if you were Contracted to Moira personally or to the position. Normally I would assume it was to the position. If so, transferring your Contract to the new Protectorate would be little more than a signing of new papers." Her mouth twisted. "And yet somehow I suspect things will not be so easy with you."

"Never are." I sighed. The door chimes rang again and I stiffened, feeling an immediate tension cutting through the room. "Ahh, the woman of the hour."

Tresa staggered through the doorway with Talivar looming behind her. Her dress hung from her thin frame, torn and filthy. The bite wound from Brandon lay gaping open in a clotted, weeping mess. Her eyes were dark and spiteful, swollen with rage. Nothing cowed about this one.

Talivar's gaze remained cold as he steered her further inside and shut the door. Judging by the scratches on his forearms and the abrasion to the right of his mouth, it was pretty clear she hadn't been easy to subdue.

The Celestials immediately took up a position on either side of Tresa, blocking any chance of escape. "She bites," Talivar warned them, shoving past her to reach my side. "All is well with my nephew, I trust?"

"A few minor cuts, but he's in good hands." I wondered if it would overstep my bounds to hand him a tissue so he could wipe his face. His jaw tensed beneath my observation and I decided against it, reaching out to gently squeeze his arm. "I promise."

Roweena made a questioning sound in her throat and I nodded at her to continue. I was more than ready to have this day over with. "Roweena DuMont," she said to Tresa. "I understand you have some news? Important enough to skip past all protocol and delve straight into the attempted kidnapping of the Queen's grandson?"

Anger flickered over Tresa's face and she bowed mockingly. "I'm sorry, milady. I know I was supposed to come to you first to relay the orders, but I was under a lot of pressure to secure the whereabouts of the Protectorate's Touch-Stone."

I let out a snort. The Fae couldn't lie, but I suspected Tresa was skirting awfully close to it. "If you're so sure of that, why were you so eager to try to TouchStone me directly?"

Roweena held up a hand. "Please, allow me to ask the questions, Abby. Court law demands it." She looked at Tresa the way one might stare at a wriggling insect. "Is this true?"

Tresa had the grace to look slightly abashed. "It is. Perhaps I was a bit too . . . eager to stake my claim."

Eyes narrowed, Roweena stared at the other woman until Tresa dropped her chin. The liaison unrolled one of the scrolls I'd given her. "What are the terms? Surely even you know the transfer of power cannot be done without the Court's sanction. Assuming what you say is fact."

"Of course." Tresa shifted uneasily, rubbing around the sore spot on her leg. "That one signifies the shift of the Protectorate's responsibilities to me, including all assets. At least on a temporary basis."

"Which means what exactly?" It hadn't actually occurred to me that I'd have to give up my apartment if I left the job, but the thought of having to live anywhere near this woman was abhorrent to the extreme.

"I get the bookstore, the Marketplace, a seat at the Judgment Hall . . . and you, of course." Her smile became sly.

"I'm not a piece of property," I snapped.

"Indeed." Roweena rolled up the scrolls with a precise hand. "I'm afraid I'm going to have to review this in more detail . . . and with the full backing of the Council."

Tresa's face fell. "But I thought the documents would be enough."

"Documents can be forged, seals can be broken," Roweena said sharply. "And given the recent history here, you'll forgive me if I choose to take the side of caution. Regardless of the situation, your methods leave a lot to be desired. Abby seems to be holding up well enough here on her own for the moment." The elf's eyes flicked toward me, a warning written in their depths. "And if I find you've played us false there will be terms."

"Yeah," I muttered. "Got all my bits and pieces lined up." A hint of smugness crept into my voice. "I guess you'll have to come back at a later date? Like, oh, *never*."

Tresa snarled. "I was told I should not wait. There is a vacuum here and we cannot afford to let it remain."

"I'm confused. If Moira is only supposed to be gone for a few weeks, why all the need for a change in power? After all, she *is* coming back."

"No," Tresa said softly. "Actually, she's not."

"Bullshit." Talivar's fingers coiled around the edge of the counter and I laid my hand on top of his as I spoke. "You're telling me she left here without her baby? Not a chance in hell."

"Why do you think I was following you today?" Tresa rolled her neck, ignoring my words. "Though I notice he's not with you now. Find a convenient hillside to leave him on? A hollow log, perhaps?"

"None of your goddamned business." The ache in my head pulsed, beating at my brain like a butterfly made of flames. "Enough." I closed my eyes against a sudden wave of dizziness.

"Abby?" Talivar's voice echoed from far away, fuzzy like he was shouting at me through a jar.

Well, fuck.

I didn't have much time to think about what had suddenly triggered my first seizure in two months, trusting only in the prince's arms as he caught me. And here I'd been doing so well.

The edges of the counter filled my wavering vision, the darkness sweeping over me in a pressing wave.

My legs and arms refused to move for what felt like hours, and then I was gasping, only aware of the floor against my cheek. Some kind soul had turned my head to the side in case I vomited and I mentally thanked him as I swallowed hard.

Something warm and wet slithered between my legs.

Jesus. I'd pissed myself.

I rolled over sluggishly, ignoring the way my jeans suddenly stuck to my thighs. Humiliation burned my cheeks as Phin nudged my face. "Get away." My limbs were anchors, pinning me to the floor. "All of you."

"Abby, I . . ."

"Go *away*, Phin."

"Is that a normal thing for you?" Tresa frowned, twirling a loose curl around a pointed ear. "Because if it is, I might want to rethink taking you on. Find someone a bit more stable. Nothing personal. I'm sure you understand."

She started choking, the last few words nothing more than a gagging noise. I blinked, realizing Talivar had his hand wrapped around her throat.

"I think you might want to rethink it too," he said pleasantly, his voice taking on a dangerous edge. "Nothing personal. I'm sure you understand."

"Let her go, Prince," Roweena snapped.

"Why?" He purred the word. "Seems to me a lot of our problems would disappear if she hit her head on something hard. Repeatedly."

"Because we need to investigate what's going on with the Court, sire." Roweena glared at him. "If she is what she claims and you kill her, you could potentially cause a political backlash that cannot be undone. Especially with your history."

He grunted something under his breath, leaning down to Tresa's face. "Piss me off again and I won't care what Roweena says. And neither will you. Crippled Prince or no, I am still of the blood and you *will* obey me. Abby is Moira's TouchStone. Not yours."

My inner voice let out a little montage of cheers, but the urge to get the hell out of here and into a shower overrode any attempts at would-be snark. "All right," I said, wincing at the way my words slurred together. "I think we're done here."

"Yes." Roweena tapped the scrolls on her thigh. "I will contact you shortly as to the veracity of these documents as well as requiring formal word from the Court. Surely a better replacement could have been found." She sniffed, the hair in her tightly wrapped bun looking even more severe than usual.

Tresa stumbled, rubbing her throat. "This is a mistake," she hissed at Roweena.

"I agree," Talivar said. "Yours." He crouched down to help me to my feet, head tilted toward the angels. "I want her taken into custody."

Roweena's mouth pursed as she weighed his words. "I'm sorry, Prince, but you know the law here. If she is Moira's actual replacement, then by detaining her we violate her right of rule. On the other hand," she added darkly, her gaze snapping to Tresa, "it would not be amiss if she would accompany me to the Judgment Hall. For her safety, of course."

Tresa's upper lip curled but she nodded.

"Until the morrow, then." Roweena bowed and gestured at the angels to follow her out the door, Tresa in tow. Phineas let out an aggrieved whinny and trotted off in the same direction. I hesitated, aching to call him back, but the words choked in my mouth, shame biting at my belly.

"When was the last time you ate?" Talivar steadied me by holding my elbow.

I struggled with the urge to throw him off. "A crappy grilled cheese a few hours ago? I don't know. It's been a bit busy today, if you haven't noticed." I rubbed my arm, not quite able to meet his eye. "I need to get out of here and take a shower. And I need you to take the crib to Robert's. It's late enough as it is."

Talivar frowned. "You took Benjamin to Robert?"

I nodded, my eyes drooping. "Seemed like the best thing to do."

"Fine," the prince said after a moment of tense silence. He tipped my chin up so that I was forced to meet his gaze. I caught a hint of sympathy and something else, but it was gone before I could identify it. "But we're going to talk about that later. And you *are* going to eat."

"Whatever." I waved him off as he attempted to escort me outside. It was a slow night at the Marketplace and I wasn't inclined to linger, so I simply turned the lock, watching the door flare into a silver nimbus and then disappear. Gotta love a storefront that can be closed via an interdimensional gateway. Cuts down on thieves, anyway.

Shivering, I hastened up the creaking wooden steps with a wrinkle of disgust at my weakness. Talivar's presence shadowed me from behind, but I refused to acknowledge it. There was an argument brewing between us—but damned if I was going to get into it before I got cleaned up.

The water sluiced over me, hard and fast and hot. The steamed tiles slid beneath my palms as I pushed against the wall, trying to drown the biting sting of shame. Inwardly I knew I had no control over the seizures, no control over their effects—not even the pills could guarantee me that. But still . . . of all the fucking times to lose it, why did it have to be in front of the potential enemy? Or future boss, I thought snidely.

My hands fisted against the wall, nails biting into my palms as Tresa's face loomed before me, the arrogant way her nose tipped up, the sneering pout of her lips. I wasn't even sure why I gave a shit about her, honestly—or any of the OtherFolk, for that matter. After all, I was 100 percent human and except for my KeyStone ability, I doubted any of them gave two shakes about who I was or what I could do, regardless of what Brandon had told me.

I shut the water off with a jerk, the pipes banging in heated protest, and stepped out of the tub. I had a new bruise on my knee from when I'd fallen and I couldn't quite help growling at it. After I'd first gotten out of the hospital two years ago, the seizures had been a more frequent occurrence, as were the injuries. Not counting the metal plate in my skull, I'd probably sprained both ankles and a wrist from falling because of the vertigo. It was a rare week when I didn't get to show off the battle scars from losing a fight with the floor.

Maybe that was the whole problem? Hanging out with the OtherFolk as much as I did, maybe I'd forgotten I was human and fragile comparatively. I sighed and combed through the tangled snarls of my hair, pushing the blue and pink streaked bangs out of my eyes. The mirror remained steamed up, but I still ran my fingertips over the scar above my left ear. I always did. It was a perverse little habit, but not one I seemed able to break.

I shook out the rest of my hair so it fell over the bare patch, threw on a robe and stepped out of the bathroom. Cool air snuck past me to chill my legs. Something about the silence struck me as odd and I couldn't quite put my finger on it. The kitchen was dark except for the gleam of the appliances.

Empty.

It was the first time I'd had my apartment to myself in, what? Eight months? I sighed, reveling in the fact that once upon a time I could have trotted around naked and not had to worry about elves getting their hair stuck in the blow dryer, or finding a unicorn underfoot. Or an incubus. Or a baby.

Out of habit I peeked into Benjamin's room, my heart skipping a beat when I saw his crib was gone. I could only assume Talivar had done as I'd asked and taken the baby's things over to Robert's, but then I'd hardly given him the chance to tell me, had I? I leaned against the door, something in my heart twisting as my gaze roamed over the now-empty shadows. My ears strained to hear the soft sound of Benjamin's breathing, and I rolled my eyes at myself.

He was with his father and that would have to be good enough until we sorted this whole damn mess out. Suddenly ravenous, I fixed a bowl of nachos, complete with salsa, queso, and a heaping dollop of sour cream. After a moment I grabbed a bottle of Bushmills out of the pantry. I wasn't usually a heavy drinker and it was never a good idea after a seizure, but after the shit that had gone down today I didn't care.

Settling in on the couch, I decided to really indulge and channel surfed until I found one of the anime channels, contenting myself for an hour of watching Alucard and Father Anderson shred each other into bloody bits. Eventually Talivar came home, clearly surprised that I was still awake at 3 A.M. I was nicely mellow, full of nacho goodness and half the bottle of whiskey, my head swimming with cartoon vampires and pleasant warmth. I patted the space next to me, shifting to make room as he eased himself down.

"Real vampires don't fight like that," I observed smartly. He grunted an affirmation at me, and I glanced over. The light from the TV played over the sharp edges of his face, illuminating the straight bridge of his nose and the faded blue of the delicate tattoos upon his cheeks. There was a grace in the curve of his spine as he lounged on the sofa, his legs bent carelessly so his knees sprawled outward, one hand resting on his thigh. The callused tips of his fingers were those of a warrior, but the elegant slant of his knuckles was pure royalty. My gaze lingered on his mouth, the whiskey making my cheeks hot.

On sudden impulse, I reached out to stroke the perfect seashell point of his ear. He stilled, silent except for a sudden intake of breath, his eye becoming languid and half lidded. The pulse at his neck jumped, ruining the effect.

"You do realize that's the elvish equivalent of cupping my balls, right?"

I jerked my hand away. I hadn't meant to be quite *that* forward. "Apparently my knowledge of basic elven anatomy is lacking," I muttered. "Sorry."

He kept his face steadfast on the TV screen, but his mouth twitched. "Something we'll have to remedy, no doubt," he said dryly, pulling the bottle of whiskey from between my knees. His eye rolled toward me as he took a swig. His lashes seemed impossibly long. "You should go to bed."

"Care to join me?" I leered, giggling as he coughed into his fist. The fact that I was half serious didn't occur to me until I'd actually said the words, even if it *was* a bad idea. After all, he was my bodyguard. And Moria's brother. And a Faery prince, for all that he seemed to have his own secrets about it. Still, given the way things were going, I wasn't sure it could be any worse. And I hadn't gotten laid since . . .

. . . since Brystion left.

The thought sobered me and I sighed. "Guess that's a no." I swayed slightly as I stood up and shut off the TV.

Staggering to the kitchen, I threw my dishes into the sink before finding my way to the hall. Probably would have a killer hangover in the morning. A few hours from now. Whatever.

"You didn't actually give me a chance to answer the question." Talivar emerged from the kitchen to lean against the door jamb.

A wave of heat flushed through my cheeks. "Erm. Was that a yes?" I couldn't help the wistful tone of my voice, though I wanted to retract the words immediately. Served me right for being such a lush.

"No." He stared at me a moment longer, something about him hesitant. One hand reached up and brushed the bangs from my eyes. "Ask me again when you're sober."

The floor shifted beneath me and wobbled forward. I caught his arm to steady myself, only to find myself pressed against the wall. "God, I'm a mess."

His mouth met mine for a surprised instant, pulling away before I had a chance to react. I caught a fleeting taste of warmth sparking against my lips. "I'm sorry," he murmured, his head lowering so that his hair fell forward to shield his eyes. His fingers stroked shyly down my cheek, sliding beneath to cup my chin, which I took to be an invitation of another sort.

I didn't wait to be asked twice, arching on tiptoe to find him again, the whiskey hot on his breath as he groaned. He trapped me against the wall, his arms bent on either side of my face.

"You don't seem that sorry."

"Mayhap I'm not," he agreed, coming up for air a moment later. "You just seemed so . . . sad."

"And the prescription for sadness in Faerie is kisses?"

A smile tugged at his mouth. "When you have nearly forever to live, lovemaking becomes a rather extended endeavor. Plus we bore easy." His hand slid down my neck, lingering where it met my shoulder.

I fought the urge to writhe beneath it, all too aware of the heat of his body. "You've got a strange way of saying no."

I said it playfully, but the moment was gone the second the words left my mouth. "Of course," he sighed, sliding to the other side of the hall, his own cheeks flushed. "You are right. Forgive me for overstepping. It *has* been a long day."

I sucked in a deep breath, trying to coax my pulse into something that didn't resemble that of an oversexed rabbit. A tiny part of me wailed that he'd actually retreated so quickly, even though it was for the best. "I know . . . you had to take pity. I get it. I'm sorry about snapping at you earlier." My fingers drummed against the wall, agitation and anger at myself playing a toccata on the doorjamb. "I don't like that she saw me like that. That you saw me like that."

He tapped his eye patch with a wry chuckle. "We all have our flaws. And there is no shame in what you cannot control."

"Maybe. I still feel like an ass, though."

He cocked his head at me. "Did you know you limp when you walk?"

I blinked. "Uh, maybe a little. Is that supposed to be a compliment?"

"Yes." His gaze strolled down my hips to my bad knee, pointing to it. "This one. It's not always evident, but there's a roll of your gait—here—and it smooths out so easily, almost hidden." He demonstrated, twisting his own knee.

"Is pointing out flaws a cure for sadness in Faerie too?" I arched a brow.

"You misunderstand me." He waved his hands at me. "It's the adaptation to the physical issues. Your body compensates for the loss of your ability. Here." He touched my hip and I shivered. "This sways out to make up for the way you don't extend the leg fully, for example."

"If you say so. But what's your point?"

"It means you don't give up. Despite your limitations, you continue to move forward." He smiled, skin gleaming in the dimness of the kitchen light. "You have the heart of a warrior. Don't sell yourself short."

I let out a mirthless chuckle. Being the only survivor of a car wreck that had stolen my mother's life and left me disabled was hardly anything to crow about. "Why did Tresa call you the Crippled Prince today?" I blurted out the words, the alcohol making me bold.

And stupid.

He stilled, pain glittering from that one brilliant eye before giving me a gentle push in the direction of my bedroom. His mouth twisted self-mockingly. "Good night, Abby."

So much for that.

I retreated into the quiet of my room, sparing a last look down the hall before I shut the door. Talivar had turned away, one hand grasping tight around his elbow as he strode to his own room. I exhaled sharply.

The elven prince walked with a limp too.

Had I been so utterly wrapped up in my own minutiae that I couldn't even see what was before my eyes? I mean, hell, I'd only lived with the man for nearly a year. Surely I wasn't as blind as all that?

I closed my door with an audible click and tumbled into bed. No doubt Sonja was waiting for me in the Dreaming, but I wasn't sure I had the heart for another training session tonight. It was nearly morning anyway. "Sorry," I said as I closed my eyes, though I didn't know who I was saying it to.

Six

Morning drifted over me too soon, punctuated by the blaring ring of the phone and the belch of a hungover unicorn. I blinked against the blurring ache of my head, eyes trying to focus as I rolled out of bed to snatch up the discarded robe from the floor. Not that I cared much about parading about half naked in my own room, but Phin was another matter. I narrowly missed tripping over him as he staggered next to my bed, the tuft of his tail a tangled, wet mess.

One of these days I'd remember to keep the cell phone within reach of the bed, but as it was I had to scramble through a pile of clothes. I'd tossed them in a heap in the corner as soon as I'd gotten into the bathroom the night before.

"Damn." The phone stopped ringing about two seconds before I found it, wedged into the back pocket of my jeans. I snapped it open and frowned as the call cut off.

"Who is it?" Phineas's rusty growl rumbled at me from a nest of my underwear on the floor. I shuddered. Guess I'd be doing two loads of laundry later.

"Roweena," I muttered. "But I wish she had better timing." I squinted at the clock, sighing when I realized it was only 7 A.M. "Christ. Do you think the powers that be would mind if I asked them to make sure the next apocalypse takes place later in the day? Maybe around teatime?"

"Good luck with that." He yawned, rolling onto his side.

I padded to the bed, tucking the cell phone neatly on the night stand. "And what is that smell?" I looked down at Phineas, my stomach tap dancing in revulsion. "You fall in the toilet again?"

His red-rimmed eyes remained a study in indifference. "Oh, so *now* you give a shit about me. How's that for fair-weather friendship?"

I bit down on my lower lip to keep from laughing at his hangdog expression. Normally I would have taken him seriously, but an inebriated unicorn is pretty damn funny, regardless of the situation. Inwardly, though, I was cringing because he was right. "I'm sorry." I crouched beside him. "I didn't mean to snap at you, Phin. Where'd you go last night?"

"Chasing a little tail of my own." He scowled, his beer-stained beard waggling at me. He let out a high-pitched giggle as he attempted to flick his own tail, watching it hang there in a sodden mess. "Little tail," he repeated, sneezing suddenly. I backed away. Last thing I needed was unicorn snot on my feet. "There was this . . . nymph? Undine? Oh, hell, I don't know what she was," he chuckled. "But she had the sweetest ass I've ever had the pleasure of—"

"More than I need to know," I said hastily. I'm not a prude by any stretch, but some things are better left to the imagination. I glanced down at him and shuddered. Or not.

He shot me a withering look. "Oh, please. You think listening to you and Brystion get it on was any bed of roses?" He reared up on shaky legs, prancing forward and swinging his hips, his voice a high-pitched falsetto. "Oh, Ion, I've never done it like that, you naughty boy! Maybe next time you can stick your hot man-rod up my—"

I poked him with a finger, watching impassively as he tumbled onto the rug, snorting in wild-eyed surprise. "You," I said sourly, "need to shut up. And get cleaned up. And do it now before you track any more filth on my floor." I headed for the bathroom, pausing only to grab a towel before turning on the hot water.

He grunted and shook himself, his legs wobbling as he followed me.

"Cheer up. I'll make you breakfast."

"You sure you're not trying to poison me?"

I rolled my eyes. "Fine. Have it your way. Canned spam for nummies. How's that?" Gingerly I picked him up and placed him into the tub. "I'll wash your mane in a minute."

"Whatever."

I retreated to the bedroom to give him a little privacy and find some clothes. A knock on my door and a muffled question announced Talivar's presence on the other side. I tightened my robe, suddenly shy. "I'm decent."

The prince popped his head around the corner. "Just checking to make sure Phineas was all right. He didn't look so good when I found him trying to climb the stairs."

"He's okay. Just dirty."

"Isn't he always?" I stared at Talivar for a moment, trying to decide if I should say anything about the night before, but he beat a quick retreat before I had a chance. I took it as a sign I should get dressed and forget about it. I'd had enough morning-after regrets to last awhile without bringing my roommate into it.

I pulled my hair up into a loose bun, the familiar sounds of a frying pan on the stove suddenly filling me with warmth. It would appear the way to my heart was through my stomach. Or at least the attempt, anyway.

Shrugging away the uneasy feeling of early morning phone calls, and trying to ignore the thought of breakfast,

I proceeded to lather up Phineas with a careful hand. He wasn't exactly a dog, and he wasn't really objecting, but it still felt a little odd to be washing him. The fact that he was humming "Pokerface" wasn't helping matters. "I'm not doing your privates. Those are up to you."

"Spoilsport." He grunted, ears twitching. "Though I probably wouldn't either, based on where they've been."

"Yummy. Now, hush up and let me finish." I rinsed out the last of his mane, wrinkling my nose at the wave of filth running down the drain. "Dude—when you go slumming, you really go *slumming*."

He yawned, shaking himself out as I shut off the water. "You have no idea."

Hastily I dried him off, setting him free on the carpeted part of the floor. Although it was amusing as hell to watch him skate over the bathroom tile, the unicorn could hardly stand up, let alone make it across the slippery hardwood of my bedroom.

He shook out his rump and winced, cocking up a hind hock to nose his underbelly. "I think I broke something."

I shuddered. "Do I need to find you a vet?"

He shot me an unfriendly look. "I overdid it is all. Not like I picked up a case of scabies."

"Well, it was an undine," I murmured. "Maybe it was crabs?"

The unicorn bared his teeth at me, whatever he was going to say interrupted by Talivar's polite cough. "Breakfast," he said mildly and disappeared again.

"Come on, Phin." I scooped him up and headed for the kitchen. "Let's go eat." I put him down in a chair, nosing over the plates of food. The unicorn's ears flattened as the ceramic scraped over the table.

"My head hurts," he moaned.

"And here I thought that horn could cure hangovers."

He blinked at me. "Oh, yeah . . . get me a glass of water, if you would."

Talivar dug in the fridge for a bottle, popping open the cap and handing to me. I poured it into a bowl, exchanging a quizzical look with the prince. He shrugged and slid it across the table to Phineas. The unicorn coughed and dipped his horn into the bowl, a little shiver twitching over his body as though he were shaking off a fly. A flash of silver burst from his horn and sparkled over the surface. He snorted, eagerly reaching forward to guzzle the now-milky liquid.

"That's the stuff," he burbled happily.

"Now that *that's* out of the way." I found my own seat and a plate of eggs. They were runny and half raw, but I gave Talivar a smile anyway. Points for trying and all that. "Time for food and tea and a game plan."

Talivar slouched in the chair next to me, casually lifting his bare feet to rest upon my chair's footrest. It was an oddly possessive move. It was also oddly sexy. His gaze lingered on me a half second longer than it should before his face turned down to his own plate, mouth twitching.

"Roweena called this morning, but hung up before I could get it." I took a bite of the eggs, trying to ignore the warmth flush that suddenly suffused my belly. "Suppose I'll call her back in a few, but I dunno. I don't want to be Tresa's TouchStone. If Moira insists on it, then I suppose I will— but only until another replacement can be found."

"Mighty generous of you," he said dryly. "But I can tell you now that if Moira had anything to do with this she would have told me. Believe me, you're far too important to her to leave blowing in the wind. If this is coming down from the Court, however . . . it would mean you've become a pawn, Abby. And pawns are rather expendable, if you take my meaning."

"Yeah. I know. Bacon's good, by the way."

He stabbed viciously at his own eggs. "You're changing the subject."

"You'll get used to it. And pawn or not, one thing I've noticed about dealing with OtherFolk is there are no guarantees." I fixed him with a glare. "About anything."

"There never are," he agreed, grabbing the teakettle to refill my mug with hot water.

"Besides," I added, swallowing another bite, "I'd think you'd be just as happy for me to break the Contract with Moira. After all, then you'd get to go home."

He looked at me blankly. "I what?"

I glanced down at my plate. "Isn't that what you were talking to Melanie about yesterday? At the Hallows? I mean, I'm sort of the only reason you were sucked into this whole mess. If I'm Contracted to someone else, that makes you free and clear, right?"

"Anyone ever tell you it's rude to eavesdrop?"

Phineas twitched, his ears flattening and then standing upright. "Do you guys hear that?"

"Hear what?" I frowned at him. "I think it's your hangover. Or maybe you farted?"

"No, no. The ambrosia did the trick on that end. But that ringing . . ."

Talivar went still. "I hear it too. Like a voice . . . or some sort of crying."

I stared at them both incomprehensibly. I didn't hear anything.

Talivar lurched forward, his head cradled in his hands as he pressed his fingers in his ears. "Oh, shit. Hold on to Phin. This is going to hurt."

I whirled, watching in horror as the unicorn reared, the whites of his eyes showing. The bowl flew off the table in a splash of silver as he lurched sideways, hooves drumming the side of the chair. "Phin!" I twisted out of my own seat to grab him, hissing when the horn's point gouged into my wrist. I retracted my hand, a thin red line bubbling up along the inner skin of my forearm. Shaking it off, I grabbed the larger of the dishrags to throw it over the unicorn's head, dodging another hoof as I managed to wrap him up.

A gagging noise erupted from Talivar. He was choking. Ignoring Phin's struggles, I bolted to the elf's side. "Seizures," I breathed. They were having *seizures*. "What the hell!"

Phin had passed out beneath my arm, legs dangling. I laid him on the floor as hastily as I could, pulling Talivar away from the table. "Hey?"

No response. Damn.

My arms slid beneath him and I yanked him from the chair as his feet kicked out wildly. I heard the shatter of the plates as the table upended, narrowly missing us both.

Focus, Abby. Get him on his side. Put something under his head.

The words were like a litany as I attempted to follow them. I knew what to do for seizures. After all, I'd certainly had enough of the damn things. But then, for all I knew he'd start floating or . . .

Or go completely apeshit . . .

I rolled out of the way as his body shivered, the magic of his Glamour melting away. I caught the quick glimpse of scar tissue along his neck, but didn't have time to pay much attention as he snatched at my arms. It took nearly everything I had to press him to the floor, his fighter's physique coming into play. Had he been cognizant of what he was doing he could have snapped me in two.

"Stop fighting me . . . you son of a bitch . . ." I straddled him, my knees on his shoulders, trying to release his hold on me.

In the distance I heard the phone ringing but there was

nothing I could do about it now. "Talivar? Wake up." My voice cracked beneath the strain and I knew I wasn't going to be able to hold him still much longer. He stiffened, neck rigid, and then his mouth slackened, arms dropping to his sides.

My own arms trembled, adrenaline surging through my veins with a vengeance. Ignoring the cramps of muscles that wouldn't quite relax, I crouched beside him to see if it started up again. But like Phin, Talivar now appeared to be sleeping.

Sinking onto the floor I took a haphazard look around my kitchen, barely noticing the way the tile was covered in a mess of cheese and eggs, grease and tea and shattered porcelain. Swallowing hard, I shut my eyes and breathed deep.

Calm. I need calm.

The phone rang again, echoed by a frantic pounding on my front door. "I thought I said I wanted to schedule the apocalypse for midday," I muttered, fighting the urge to slam my fist through something. Still shaking, I lurched to my feet, listening to Melanie's panicked voice shouting over my answer machine.

I found my way to the door, snapping it open to reveal a tear-sodden Charlie holding an unconscious Benjamin in her arms, the baby's wings sagging. "Oh, God, Abby. I took the Door here . . ." Her lower lip trembled.

Wordlessly I took the baby from her, my heart lurching when I saw his sagging jaw. "What's going on? Do you know?"

"Know?" She shot me an incredulous look, her mouth dropping as she saw Talivar and Phineas sprawled out on the floor. "Oh, shit. One minute I was feeding him and everything was fine . . . and the next . . . I don't know. He started choking. I thought it was febrile seizure or maybe an allergic reaction. Or I would have, but when he finally stopped shaking I went to find Robert." She swallowed hard.

"He's like them?"

Charlie nodded. "I couldn't move him. Couldn't figure out what to do. I tried calling you but you didn't answer and that's when I came over here." Our eyes met. "You think that Fae woman had anything to do with it?"

"It doesn't make any sense. They took Tresa into custody last night."

"So they did." Tresa's voice drawled at us from the doorway. I could only watch helplessly as the elven woman strutted into my apartment, rolling her hips. "About ready to sign those Contracts now? Because if you're not, I'm going to let them die."

Seven

"Touch them and I'll fucking kill you," I snarled, my hands gripping Benjamin tightly.

Her eyes rolled in disdain at Talivar's prone form as she brushed into the kitchen to inspect her handiwork, high heels clicking on the hardwood. "You and what army, TouchStone?"

"This one, you bitch." Before I could move, Charlie whipped out a black handled dagger from her pocket, the blade suddenly poised beneath the Fae's chin. Tresa's eyes widened as the edge touched her, but Charlie snagged the back of her head with her other hand to hold her still. A faint sizzle sounded from the tip of the blade.

Tresa whimpered. "Recognize that, don't you?" Charlie hissed. "Pure iron, forged from a fallen star and tipped with silver."

"Jesus, Charlie." Impressed despite myself, I still noticed the tremble in her hands as she held the blade to Tresa's throat. Iron could be quite deadly to the Fae, particularly in its pure form, although having a TouchStone often offset some of the effect. I didn't have anything like that around the apartment since I lived with one and worked for another, but I was beginning to have second thoughts.

"It was Robert's." Charlie's eyes rolled wildly at me in a mixture of panic and madness. "You think I'm going to let someone hurt me again? Hurt my family?"

"Not at all." I smiled at Tresa pleasantly. "And now that we're on more even terms, let me just tell you that I don't do blackmail." I took a step closer. "What the hell did you do? And where's Roweena?"

"And here I'd been led to believe you actually understood what you were doing. Roweena's hopefully taking a dirt nap somewhere." Tresa growled, her nostrils flaring when Charlie prodded her with the knife again. "I severed their connection to the CrossRoads. It's not a permanent effect." She nudged Talivar's leg before meeting my eyes, her gaze glittering. "Yet."

My brain settled into a strange calm, anger pushing away the fear once I realized they weren't permanently injured.

Yet . . .

"And you decided you'd take out the baby too? Or Moira's former bodyguard? Villain school must teach you to be very thorough."

"What are you talking about? The spell was only geared toward the people you're TouchStoned to. "

I raised a brow at her, shifting the unconscious baby over my shoulder. "I'm not TouchStoned to either of them. Hell, I'm not TouchStoned to Talivar either, for that matter."

A frown twisted Tresa's mouth and I caught the first hint of actual alarm flash from her green-gold eyes. "You're not?" My cell phone sang out. Quickly I dodged around the elf to get it.

"Abby? Abby!"

"I'm here, Mel."

"Do you know what's going on? I'm at the Hallows and

all the OtherFolk have just fucking up and passed out." She paused. "Hell, some of them were damn near foaming at the mouth."

"Same thing happened here," I told her. "Hold tight and I'll call you back. Is Brandon out too?"

"Yeah, but Katy's here with him."

"Good. Let me try to get to the bottom of this. If you see Roweena anywhere, let me know ASAP, okay?"

I shut my cell hard enough to shatter the buttons. "You stupid, stupid woman. What the hell was that spell you used?"

"I already told you," she retorted, irritated. "I shut off their connection to the CrossRoads. And I added a little bit of you into the mix, as an added bonus."

"The seizures." Charlie stared at me, a fascinated horror in her voice. "You gave them Abby's seizures."

"Got me," Tresa chuckled. "Although that part wasn't actually intentional. Just a rather interesting side effect."

"How long will it last?" I said softly, trying to decide if it would be worth it to try pounding her face into the floor.

Tresa bared her teeth at me. "Until you become my TouchStone. Otherwise the spell will hang on until they die." She looked at the baby thoughtfully and then shrugged. "Though it seems like there was a bit of an overlap. Well, no matter. Merely sign the Contracts and they should be rejoined to the CrossRoads, none the worse."

"Wonderful." I snorted. "Except you fucked up."

"Did I?" I thought I detected the barest undertone of doubt in her voice.

"Yeah. You just severed the connection on the Cross-Roads for pretty much every OtherFolk being in the entire city of Portsmyth."

The blood drained from her face. "I what?"

My inner bitch sang with glee at the whispered hoarse-

ness of the words. "I think you heard me. So good job, future Protectorate." My brain raced with potential ways out
of this mess. But first things first. "Keep an eye on her," I
said to Charlie. "I've got a few things to do."

Charlie nodded at the Fae woman with the single-minded
focus of a cat about to eviscerate a mouse. Carefully, I laid
Benjamin on the sofa, propping him in a nest of pillows. I
would have handed him to Charlie, but given her current
state I didn't want to risk it.

I stooped to pick up Phineas, stroking the top of his head.
The unicorn didn't stir beyond a light twitching in his upper
lip. I couldn't tell if he was dreaming or not. If it was a true
seizure it was entirely possible that he could hear everything
going on around him.

"I'm going to put you in my bed, Phin. If you can hear
me, I'm heading over to the Hallows. I'll be back as soon as I
can." Gingerly I stepped around the pieces of broken glass.
"What a fucking mess." No time for any sort of cleanup
now, though.

After I tucked Phineas in comfortably, I debated for a moment on how I was going to drag Talivar out of the kitchen.
It seemed terribly rude to leave him in a pile of runny eggs
and spilled milk, but he was a solidly built guy. No chance
of me picking him up. In the end I found an extra bedspread
and rolled him onto it. With a little extra effort I was able to
drag him into the bedroom.

Without his Glamour, my gaze was drawn to his scarred
neck and then further down his body. His shirt had torn during the seizure and I could see the marked flesh all along his
left side. The same side he limped on, I realized. The white
marks crisscrossed by his belly, disappearing along his hip
and further still.

"No wonder you understood," I murmured. The marks
of a warrior, indeed.

I told him the same thing I'd told Phin and then scratched it out in a note for good measure before tossing on a pair of jeans and a T-shirt.

"You realize, of course, that Talivar will probably try to kill as you as soon as he comes to," I snapped at Tresa as I shoved the broken crockery into a pile with my shoe.

"I thought of that. I'm not stupid, you know. And that's why when you sign the Contract, you'll see there's a clause in there that forfeits your life if I am killed."

Charlie stared at her. "That's outrageous."

Tresa shrugged. "It's part of what makes me so charming."

A thought suddenly occurred to me. "You said the spell was supposed to affect all those who were TouchStoned to me? Barring the fact that apparently nearly all the Other-Folk seem to have succumbed to it—did it ever cross your mind what would happen to Moira?"

Her eyes darted away. Was it an admission of guilt? Or something else?

"I think you're in a lot of trouble," I said softly, taking Benjamin into my arms and covering his shoulders with his blanket. "And I think me signing this Contract is the only way for you to escape alive. Once the Faery Court discovers what you've done . . ." I was bluffing, of course. I'd never seen the Faery Court. Hells, the closest I'd ever come to seeing even a bit of it were the Council sessions I'd been to at the Judgment Hall, and I wasn't entirely sure if that counted.

I turned toward Charlie. "You ready to go?"

She nodded, moving the dagger a few inches. "Yeah. If she tries anything I'm going to jam this into her."

"Fine by me." My friend's sudden bloodthirstiness was worrisome, but I'd deal with it later. And to be honest, I didn't much care if Tresa got a little cut up along the way. I gestured to the Fae to move in front of us, Charlie keeping the blade covertly pointed at her back.

"Maybe we should look at using a Door to get to the Hallows?"

"Seeing as we're holding her at knifepoint, yeah," I said dryly. "I'm for Keystone Kops and all, but I think we'd be pushing our luck parading her down Main Street."

Charlie grunted as we approached the gate leading out to the alley. A silver haze lit up the edges when she touched it and then faded away. She tapped the Door again, frowning when it flared up and then damped out. She did it a third time, muttering something under her breath.

"The Door isn't responding." Charlie adjusted her grip on the dagger. "It worked a few minutes ago."

"What do you mean it's not *responding*? Maybe you're not doing it right." Tresa shoved Charlie out of the way to stroke the gate with her own hand, watching impassively as nothing happened. Again. "I don't understand. I had all the calculations worked out."

"Forget to carry the one and the CrossRoads close? Remind me to stay away from Faery math."

"No," she said sharply. "There isn't a spell in the world that could just shut them down like that."

"Well, *something* did. And you're the only one I know of who's been dicking with it. So where does that leave us?"

She scowled at me. "Don't be stupid. Only the Queen has full command over the CrossRoads. At least this part of it," she amended glumly.

"And you think that's what she's done? Shut down the CrossRoads?" My heart sank down into the pit of my stomach at the thought.

"Yes. There can be no other explanation."

"Awesome. Looks like we're hoofing it." I glared at her. "Let's not have any funny stuff, okay?" Not that I remotely trusted her, but I suspected she wanted answers pretty damned badly. For the moment, we had that in common.

"My word on it," she said softly as Charlie tucked the dagger up her sleeve.

The three of us booked it down the main drag of Portsmyth. It was a Friday morning and normally things would have been hopping, at least for local hole-in-the-wall eateries or Opera Alley, or the other little shops, but a pall seemed to hang over the town.

To my great relief, the Glamour over the alley to the Hallows was still standing, its spiderweb softness tangible as we walked through it, swallowed up by whatever magics were still left. Quickly, I jogged over to the door to give the passcode, my breath becoming a quiet hiss at the chaos displayed before me.

A sudden flashback from the daemon fight eight months prior overtook me and I pressed myself against the wall in response, seeing the way the bodies overlaid each other. I shook my head to clear it. There was no blood here, no daemon mercenaries out for death. Just friends and OtherFolk, passed out on the floor.

And a fair number of them at that. I spied Brandon lying in front of the bar, his head cradled in Katy's lap, Melanie kneeling beside her. A flash of relief shone in their faces when I stepped across the threshold.

"Oh, thank goodness you're all right Abby," Katy half sobbed at me. "And Charlie too. And little Benjamin."

I looked down at the baby with a grimace. "He's like the others. When did this start?"

"About twenty minutes ago," Melanie answered quickly. "I'd just finished up one of my all-night gigs. We were wrapping up as per usual, and then suddenly all the OtherFolk started acting . . . off. Like you do, right before one of your seizures." She glanced at me. "How's . . . uh . . . Talivar?"

I frowned at her little hesitation, wondering if she'd seen

his scars. "Back at the apartment. He's a little scuffed up since he fell out of his chair."

"Good. I was worried." She sighed, thrusting her chin at Tresa. "What's her deal?"

"This is her handiwork." My fingers ground into my palms as the woman delicately strode between the fallen bodies.

"Where's Roweena?" I demanded of her again.

She waved me off. "I left the old bat stuffed in a closet somewhere so I could finish the spell. Of course, I had to hit her a few times . . . you know, to make sure she wouldn't follow." She chuckled. "Those angels were a bit on the slow side, let me tell you."

"One thing I'd like to know is how you did it," Charlie interjected suddenly, breaking up a delightful vision of me beating the bitch senseless. "You said you linked it to Abby, but how?"

Tresa's gaze dropped for a moment, something sly passing behind her eyes. "It was easy enough. I just needed a few small things. Hair, for example, snagged from the back of her shirt yesterday."

A cold shiver ran down my spine. What was that old wives' tale about keeping your nail clippings and the hair from your brush? I glared at her to cover up my agitation. "Well, it worked brilliantly. Now undo it."

"I'm not sure I can. I no longer have the power of the CrossRoads to draw from . . . and I don't have a TouchStone to augment the power needed." Something triumphant lit up her face.

"So find someone else. Surely there's some hapless groupie out there that's more than willing to temporarily let you set up shop inside their soul long enough for you to break the damn thing."

"It would be easier with you."

"Actually," Charlie said slowly, "I'm not sure Tresa *can* TouchStone you."

"And why the hells not?" the Fae snapped. "I Touch-Stone her, and become the de facto Protectorate, release the spell, and everyone goes on their merry way."

"Except that the CrossRoads will probably still be closed. You know, if *you* weren't the cause. Besides, the spell apparently causes seizures in all of the beings Abby is Touch-Stoned to, right?" A smirk crept across Charlie's soft face.

Tresa paused, her mouth shutting abruptly.

"Someone didn't think her shit through," I said in a sing-song voice, snorting at myself. "But hey, let's try that theory, shall we?"

"Are you out of your mind?" Charlie took Benjamin hastily into her arms.

"Well, we seem to be out of options," I said, a plan suddenly springing to mind. With the CrossRoads closed I wasn't sure if it would work, but a loophole was a loophole. As a living KeyStone I could circumvent the actual signing of any Contracts . . . and break it just as quickly. Distasteful in the extreme to think of bonding with the woman, but if got us off the hook without actually making her Protectorate? "I think it's time we called her bluff."

Tresa looked at me, an expression like that of a cat suddenly finding herself in a room of wingless canaries crossing over her face. "I've never done this with a KeyStone. I hope it's as good as they say."

"I hope you choke on it." I snatched her hand and squeezed it hard. I didn't have much time to experiment with the KeyStone aspect of my life, but I knew both parties had to be willing, even if that acceptance was on a sub-conscious level. I'd done it by accident a few times over the last few months, but for the most part no harm had been done—a couple of embarrassed smiles, a vision or two of some inner part of their essence, and an awkward parting.

The moment her fingers slid into mine, I opened the channel. I could only liken it to surfing the radio, searching for the frequency that would let me tune in to whatever stuff was made into her inner being. Sometimes it was instant, like with Ion or Phin—whatever it was about them that made them who they were resonated in me, and the response in both cases was instant and tangible.

This time, I wasn't so sure. Tresa slid by me, something oily about her essence, and I realized there was very little that could be construed as "likable." Certainly nothing I could sympathize with.

"You're going to need to open up a bit more if you want this to work," I ground out, the vibration of the touch causing my teeth to ache.

Her eyes closed, brow furrowed as though she were concentrating, and then suddenly I felt the bond snap into place . . . but it was dark. Furtive. Something about her hands . . .

. . . her hands were entwined about me, wrapping around my throat, clinging, choking, ensnaring me in the darkness. The green leaves shone brilliantly, living emeralds of delicate silk veins, but they were hiding something. A thick stench of rot and decay burbled just below the surface, thrusting its way into my mouth, coating my belly, taking root in my center . . . I tried to scream, but my mouth was full of leaves, overflowing with vegetation . . .

"No! No . . ." I lurched backward, slapping her hands as the vision invaded my mind. But the link still held, something black and hateful about it. "Break the spell. Fulfilled my part of the bargain." The words gasped out of my throat, burning as though she actually had been strangling me.

"Done," she hissed, teeth gleaming far too whitely. I staggered down to my knees, every nerve crying out with the sheer wrongness of what was going on, too stunned to do much more than watch as Tresa spun away, hands twisting in an intricate weave. Her hips gave an odd little shake and there was an audible crack. The spell breaking?

And then agony twisted through my limbs, melted the skin off my bones, sent me down into oblivion cursing the bitch's name and the foolishness of my own pride in thinking I even had a chance of fixing this problem . . .

Eight

"Abby? Can you hear me?" The voice wavered at me from a distance, like I was underwater. But it was a familiar voice, at least. Feminine. Soft. Trusted?

Yes, I decided. This voice I could trust. Of course, I also wondered why I always seemed to end up on the floor after blacking out so conveniently, though this time it didn't feel like a seizure. The voice asserted itself again, blending in with a cluster of others.

I cracked an eye, blinking into some semblance of focus. I was still in the Hallows—and there seemed to be more people awake than I remembered from before. A very good sign.

The ominous rumble in my belly was not.

Without warning, I gagged and rolled onto my side. Some-one thrust a bucket under my head, and I accepted it grate-fully, empting out the contents of my stomach with gusto. The slick taste of oil and bile remained, coating my tongue.

"Drink," I managed. "Water." I struggled to kneel, mur-muring a stilted thanks to whoever placed a glass into my hands. "This is getting really fucking old."

Melanie crouched before me, pushing the hair from my

face. "That wasn't a seizure, I don't think. It looks like you got caught up in the backlash of whatever . . . *she* . . . did to break the spell."

"Where is she now?" I swished the water in my mouth before spitting it in the bucket. "That's about the worst thing I think I've ever been through. Almost," I amended. Choking to death or not, I'd gladly take it a thousand times over having my mother die in my lap.

Melanie wrinkled her nose. "Ah. Well. I kinda knocked her ass out when you started screaming. With an ashtray. Don't think she's going to wake up for a while."

"Good for you," I said cheerily. "She deserved it. How about the others?"

"Look around." She took my now-empty cup and slouched on her heels. "Everyone seems to have come to."

I paused, suddenly aware of the low hum of voices. Rolling my neck so that it cracked, I peered around the room. The OtherFolk stood in small clusters, the Paths clinging to their own sense of familiarity. Daemon. Fae. Celestials. No chance of them working together yet, even bound to a common foe.

"They blame me, don't they?"

"Not your fault," Melanie grunted. "Blame the Fae bitch."

"The CrossRoads still closed?"

"Yeah. I can't even make a Door to anywhere," she said glumly. "Guess the Wild Magic depends on the CrossRoads as a whole to work."

"So what you're telling me is I'm stuck in a bar of OtherFolk who've just been gotten out of an extended set of seizures and now can't even go home?"

"That's about the size of it." Melanie nodded. "Charlie is watching Benjamin and Katy is with Brandon pouring everyone drinks. On the house," she added.

"Good idea." I wondered at the wisdom of having an underage teen serving the alcohol, but on the list of things to worry about it rated pretty damn low. "Although I'm guessing Moira will be footing the bill for it later."

"Probably." A ghost of a smile crossed over her face. "And Talivar called a little while ago. You should probably ping him back." She tossed me her shiny new iPhone. "He's got yours—he's out with Robert looking for Roweena now."

I started to dial, my gaze finding an unconscious and bound Tresa, laying haphazardly upon the stage.

Melanie's eyes hardened. "I don't think they've got anything particularly pleasant in mind for her when she wakes up."

"Watch me cry." I got to my feet stiffly, ignoring the rush of vertigo. I breathed a sigh of relief when Talivar's voice sounded at the other end of the line. "You okay?"

"As good as I might expect," he said dryly. "But we haven't found Roweena yet." He paused. "Did you see?"

"See what? Dude, I saw the seizure, but don't worry about it. Not like you haven't seen me at my worst, right?"

"I meant the scars, Abby." There was a world of hurt in that statement, but it didn't jive with the warrior mind-set of his. Hell, I'd always thought scars were signs of manhood, or some shit.

"I don't think they're as bad as you think," I said slowly. *Maybe it depends on how he got them.*

"And maybe it's none of my business," I muttered under my breath. I heard a muffled grunt in return. I decided to change the subject. "How's Phin?"

"He's fine." A flutter of amusement tinged the prince's voice. "I've got him in your backpack. He insisted on taking a pair of your panties as a security blanket."

I rolled my eyes. "Guess he's earned it." Although, how someone earned the right to roll around in my underwear I couldn't say, but he'd been through quite a bit, so I figured I'd give him a pass. Just this once.

"Melanie told me what happened. Are you okay?" A hint of reproach lingered in the question, and I couldn't quite keep a flush of shame from burning up my face.

"Yeah. I think so. I'm sorry. I had no other choice. She said she didn't have the power to break the spell otherwise. I'll end the bond as soon as she wakes up."

Silence met my words for a moment and then a soft sigh. "I know. I just wish there were some other way." His voice hardened with distaste.

I yawned, head spinning slightly. "We'd better figure out what we're doing fast, because I'm not sure how long I'm going to last." The energy it took to be a TouchStone was usually offset somewhat by the power of the CrossRoads, but without that particular safeguard, Tresa was going to drain me into the ground—and that wasn't even counting my bond to Phineas.

"Get rid of her. I'll come down there and kill her myself if you don't."

I glanced at the stage where the others stood guard. "Think you might have to get in line. But I see your point. All right, what next?"

"I think I can answer that," Roweena said from behind me. I lowered the phone, trying not to gasp. The liaison hobbled up to the bar, a frailty taking hold of her bones that had nothing to do with old age. She took the first drink Brandon offered, swallowing it in a single gulp before continuing, the alcohol dribbling out of one side of her mouth. The left side of her face drooped with an earthy haggardness about her features that hadn't been there before.

A stroke? A faint bruising shone beneath the translucent skin below the eye socket.

"Tresa has a lot to answer for," she said, her speech

somewhat slurred. "Heard from the Court before the Cross-Roads were closed." A chuff of disgust emanated from her chest. Her hand shook as she gestured at the room. "None of this . . . farce"—she spat the word—"is sanctified. A new Protectorate *was* dispatched . . . but *not* Tresa."

The others looked at each other for a moment and then back at the unconscious Fae, the curtest of nods ghosting over Brandon's face. Whatever the outcome, Tresa's fate had just been sealed, it seemed. And something told me there probably wasn't going to be much of her left to bury.

Funny thing, that. For all that the Fae seemed to easily betray us, or trick their fellows into submission, apparently fucking with the only way out of the mortal realm was a massive no-no. I would have to remember that.

"So, what is the word?" Melanie asked, crossing her legs from her perch on top of the bar. "Surely there's something that can be done? The Queen can't keep the CrossRoads shut forever. Can she?"

"Technically, she can." Rowena gave a one-armed shrug and dug into her pocket for a crumpled scroll. Pity rocked me to the core, watching the once proud woman try to un-roll it. It was on the tip of my tongue to offer her help, but Brandon met my gaze, a warning in his eyes. So I waited, letting the ancient Faery woman struggle her way through the remainder of her dignity, merely holding down the far corner of the parchment as she opened it, fingers brushing over the words.

I peered at the scroll, squinting at the fine spiderweb script, blinking as the words blurred and formed into some-thing akin to English. "Nice trick." I assumed it was the same sort of magic that was used in the Marketplace to allow me to talk to everyone. Scanning the scroll, I read it aloud, a coldness taking root in my gut.

> *Upon order of Her Highness, Queen of Elfland,*
> *Mistress of the Seelie Courts, Keeper of the Middle*
> *Path, all those found harboring the traitor Tresa ce*
> *Drindal will be imprisoned and tried in the Highest*
> *Judgment Hall and condemned to death.*

"I can hardly wait to find out what this means for me. After all," I said dryly, "I'm her TouchStone now."

Roweena stared at me, her right nostril flaring. "I will be forced to take you into custody. But with the CrossRoads shut down, the point is moot."

"Well, sure. But what else I was supposed to do? Let you all sit there in a coma forever?"

"And it's not like any of us knew," Melanie said. "We went on the information we had."

A sound of outraged agreement blared out from her cell phone. Startled, I looked down at my hand, cursing myself for being an idiot. I'd forgotten Talivar was still on the line. I jerked it up to my ear, wincing at the steady stream of profanities.

"—coming down there right now, Abby. Do not do *anything* until I get there." He'd hung up with a savage click before I could say anything.

"Talivar's coming with Robert," I said, ignoring Roweena's grunt. "Look, you and I both know that I did it to save everyone, so if I have to throw myself on the mercy of the Court for that, I will. But if you think for one moment that I'm going to let myself be executed for her, then you've got another thing coming."

"You cannot leave," Roweena said, staring at me with an iron will. "Not yet. Not until . . . she wakes up."

"Fine. I grok. You need a hostage, and since I'm now connected to the bad guy, I suppose it would be stupid of you to let me go."

Like they did everyone else . . .

I supposed the thought was uncharitable, but it still pissed me the hell off when I thought about how Topher had played everyone. And shit, as far as I was concerned, Maurice should have been damn near executed on the spot, but the Fae had decided he was worth more to them alive. At least until he told them how he managed to extract the life force out of the succubi.

And what happened if the Fae discovered that for themselves? I cringed inwardly. And if they figured it out and managed to use that knowledge to . . . do what? Torture daemons? Invade Heaven? I sighed. Just my luck to have been involved in the instrumentation of a potential metaphysical cold war.

Melanie pursed her lips as she slid off the bar. "Tell you what, how about I go wait for Talivar out front?" Our eyes met. "Might not hurt to try to calm him down some, anyway."

I nodded as Charlie approached us, Benjamin on her hip. Relief seared into my heart when he fluttered his eyes at me. For a moment. And then his mouth sprawled into a gaping tunnel, the first cry of outrage resounding through the room.

The cluster of OtherFolk glanced over at us, and not all of them in a particularly friendly way. Now that the immediate danger seemed to be over, the usual personalities of the Paths were starting to wend their way to the fore. Although I would have liked to think none of them would have hurt the child of their former Protectorate, I was also pretty sure that some of those daemonic types actually enjoyed eating babies.

. . . and now there is no Protectorate here. Not really.

No. Once the novelty of having Tresa tied up had worn off and the actual realization dawned that they weren't going to be able to leave set in, this was going to be a very ugly situation.

A grim calmness swept over me.

Focus on what you can change, Abby.

"I really think you should take him home, Charlie. He'll be safer with you there than in a bar." I gestured at the stage with my head. "Besides, the natives are getting restless. Without their Glamours to get them out of here, they're going to be a bit pissy."

"I think you're right," she said softly, holding Benjamin closer. He gripped her shoulder with tiny fingers. "I left all his things at home anyway." She turned toward Melanie. "I'll wait with you so Robert can walk me home." She said it casually, but a current of fear floated beneath the words. Ever since Maurice had taken us captive, she'd had a lot of difficulty going anywhere alone. I could hardly blame her for that.

Melanie nodded, shifting the violin case on her shoulder. "Think I'll take this along, just in case you pull a miracle out of your ass and the Doors are reopened in the next few minutes."

"I'll be sure to get cracking on that." It was better this way anyhow. Robert could be hotheaded at the best of times, and Charlie's agitation would only serve to stir him further. Better if he fussed over his son in private for a bit.

Roweena grunted in what sounded like a solid agreement as we watched their retreating forms. I gazed at the proclamation scroll. "Why did the Queen close down the CrossRoads?"

Her lips slapped wetly and she wiped at the corner of her mouth with the back of her hand, a grimace of distaste following behind. "Moira also fell . . . ill. The Seers were able to divine the nature of Tresa's treachery, although not the result. The Queen sent this last missive to me to inform us of her decision." She sagged, leaning against the bar. "More troubling is that she left no additional direction."

"Maybe she was busy getting her nails done." I slumped against the bar. "Seems awfully quick to jump from a possible crisis to just slamming the CrossRoads shut without even trying to find out why. I mean, hell, it was what, ten minutes after the seizures happened?"

"Our Queen is not one for trivial frivolities." She drew herself up stiffly, a semblance of her former self echoed in the motion. "Closing the CrossRoads would not have been an option if the reason behind it were not of utmost severity. It requires a terrible price." Her lips smacked shut. "But what that is I do not know, and that terrifies me," she said, swirling her glass of brandy.

"And what happens to you now? To the rest of the OtherFolk trapped here?"

"We survive . . . for a time. Eventually we will fade."

"All of you?"

"Those of us who are not TouchStoned. If we have a mortal soul on which to anchor, we can use that power to sustain us, but even that will only take us so far. Without the power of the CrossRoads to foster it, the Contracts mean nothing." Her mouth twisted, chin shaking; a guttering burble escaped the wrinkled depths and I realized she was laughing. "Unless we had a living KeyStone, of course."

"Gee. Don't let me stop you." KeyStones were normally sacred places where OtherFolk could gather without the need for TouchStones—the Marketplace was one, the Judgment Hall, the Hallows . . . but how long would they last?

Tresa stirred on the stage, her body shuddering beneath the ropes. I wandered in her direction, but kept my distance. Her eyelids fluttered, her head wrenching violently to the side as she began to gag. I felt a momentary flicker of satisfaction. The crowd of OtherFolk parted before me, but I pretended not to notice. I wasn't Moses and this sure as hell wasn't the Red Sea. I glanced down at the floor. *Yet*.

"What have you done to me?" Tresa croaked.

"Well, Melanie hit you over the head with an ashtray . . . and judging from the bruises around your neck, it would appear someone tried to strangle you after that. Not that I would have known," I added pleasantly. "Being that I was rather indisposed myself. You remember, don't you?"

"I am the Protectorate," she snarled. "You have no right . . ."

"They had *every* right," Talivar's voice crackled from the doorway, a bedraggled Phineas at his heels. Melanie hung behind him, her face unreadable. The anger burned from the prince like a firestorm and for a moment the room seemed to darken. He'd restored his Glamour apparently, the tattoos on his face stark against the unblemished skin. He stalked into the room, his limp suddenly terribly obvious. "And you *will* step down. The position was not yours to take."

"And yet, here I am," Tresa spat, wriggling precariously on the edge of the stage. She would roll onto the floor in a moment, but no one made a move to restrain her.

I met Talivar halfway and shook my head. "It's okay," I murmured. "We're all okay for now." He stared at me for a moment, his hair falling forward to hide the eye patch.

"I'm sorry," he said, taking my hand. "I should have guarded you better."

"Buck up," Phineas nickered, prodding me in the leg. "And stop wasting time making eyes at each other. We've got decisions to make. Or really, you do."

"It's like having Yoda for a personal assistant," I grumbled, letting Talivar's hand slip from mine. "And I'm not sure my opinion holds any weight here right now. After all, I'm sort of supposed to be arrested. Again. Consorting with the enemy and all that."

The unicorn stomped a hoof. "Bah. You're going to have to break that Contract."

"She can't do that." Tresa grinned. "I put a clause into it that ends in her death if she does so."

"And where are the scrolls?" He bugled in challenge. "When did Abby sign them?"

"I didn't, actually. How's that for a loophole?" I smirked, waggling my finger at her. "We did the KeyStone thing."

"Then any concept of a written Contract makes no difference in this case. Abby didn't sign it . . . therefore it is not binding," Roweena agreed, her eyes resting on me. "You may break it at will, without repercussion."

Tresa's eyes bulged. "No! You can't do that! I worked the spell to only be released when we TouchStoned."

"We did," I said shortly. "Just not the way you were hoping." The connection between us fluttered like a trapped butterfly. "I release you," I intoned, the ritual words stiff on my tongue. I twitched at the snapping of it, sighing when the essence of "her" drained away.

"Lying bastard," she spat. "He told me if I did this it would set him free."

The hairs on the back of my neck rose. "He who?"

"Who do you think?" Contempt rolled off of her in bitter waves. "Maurice, you stupid bitch."

Nine

I stared at Tresa, blinking stupidly. "Maurice? But I thought he was . . . being taken care of." Or at least that was what I'd been led to believe. Though why I expected anything resembling the truth from the Fae was beyond me

"They're taking care of him, all right." Tresa laughed. The sound was without humor, but a shivering edge of desperation rippled beneath it. An echo of darkness seemed to shimmer between us.

"He has a hold on you," I said sharply. "What is it?"

"He holds the key to my undoing," the elf woman said bitterly. "More than that I will not say. Only that by freeing him, I might have a chance at escape."

Talivar stepped closer to her, his gaze flat and dark. "You chose to align yourself with a known traitor."

"You know nothing. From where I stand, the Queen is the traitor." Her eyes burned with madness.

"Now I know you're crazy," I muttered, rubbing at the side of my temples. "Guess we just need to get the Cross-Roads reopened and we're good to go."

Roweena let out a weary sigh. "As per this latest Court mandate, Moira was removed from her position as Protectorate, but you still remain her TouchStone. However, with the CrossRoads locked down, we need to chose another Protectorate, if only to preserve what little order is left to us. Tresa is obviously unsuitable."

I shuddered at the thought of having to bond to yet *another* Fae. "What difference does it make? I mean, without the power of the CrossRoads, it's not like a Protectorate could really do anything anyway, right?" I frowned at her. "I would have thought you'd want the job. After all, you seem to be the next Fae in position to do so."

"If I must," she said after a moment of hesitation, "but as the Court Liaison, there may be a conflict of interest. I'm here to protect the interest of the Court above all else. I shouldn't even be thinking of undoing what the Queen has wrought."

"Oh, the humanity of it all." I sighed. "Surely the Council would want a say in it?" The local Council was made up of nine members of all three Paths and overseen by the Protectorate. They were supposed to provide balance and make sure each group was fairly represented.

"Assuming we could even find all of them in time?" Roweena shook her head. "The choosing of the Protectorate is a Faery matter only and should stay that way."

"Then what about Talivar? Honestly, doesn't he make the most sense? Related to Moira? Royalty? Fae? Hell, he's even already got a TouchStone." Melanie's brow wrinkled at my words. "We could just modify that Contract, couldn't we?"

There was an uncomfortable silence, the two elves not looking at each other. "I'm afraid that's out of the question, Abby." Roweena murmured. "Talivar is not . . . suitable."

"Fuck suitable," I snapped. "*None* of this is suitable." I turned toward Talivar. "Do you want it? As . . . whatever I am . . . I'm offering you the shot."

He looked at me gravely. "It would be my honor."

Roweena shook her head at me. "This is asking for trouble."

"Yeah, well, I get that you all have your little secrets, but unless you want to enlighten me on the red flag here, this is the best course of action."

"As you will." Roweena's eyes darted between me and Talivar before moving on to Melanie. "We will have to re-work the Contract, of course," she said coolly. "Unless Melanie wishes to remain his TouchStone."

Melanie shook her head violently. "No. I'm sorry, but I can't." She gave me an imploring look. "I'm sorry, Abby . . . but there are other things in my way that won't allow it. It would be a very, very bad idea."

I stared at her, watching as she nervously stroked her violin. It wasn't in me to judge, but for a brief moment I really wished someone else would step up to the plate here. On the other hand, she'd nearly lost her soul for me and it's not every day you can say that about a person.

"All right." I nodded at Roweena. "How long will it take to draw up an official Contract?"

"Normally, not too long—but this is getting a bit complicated. I will endeavor to have it to you tonight." Roweena straightened up. The effects of her injuries appeared to be fading, her words becoming less slurred. "And in the meantime, we can nullify the Contract between Melanie and Talivar. Thankfully Moira left it in the archives. Without the CrossRoads behind it, it won't be binding, of course, but it will go a long way. Come by the Judgment Hall this evening."

"I didn't think we could get in there with the CrossRoads shut."

"It's a KeyStone. Like the Marketplace. Like you. It exists under its own pocket of power. It won't last forever, of course—but think of it as a temporary generator. The Queen is the only one who can reopen the CrossRoads, and we have no way of reaching her—so this will have to do."

"Too bad cell phones don't work across planar dimensions," Melanie muttered. "This would be so much easier if we could text the Court or something: *Plz open XRoads. KThxBai.*"

Phineas shook his head, waggling his beard. "The Key to the CrossRoads could be used to open a Door, allowable for just such a purpose." His eyes darted to me, unblinking. "It was intended to be a fail-safe, should any be trapped on one side or the other."

Tresa rolled her eyes. "The Key? That's a myth, even for those such as us. After all, the Key hasn't been seen for ages. We have no idea where it's gone."

"Or what it looks like," Talivar added sourly. "Though there might be something in the library at the Judgment Hall that delves into it." He glared at her. "Not that anyone was asking you."

Roweena sighed. "Oh, it's real enough, I suppose. Or it was, once. But as to its location . . ."

"Missing talismans, this week only, on *Scavenger Hunts of the Magical and Fucked,*" I quipped. Not that I was planning on leaving that much to chance. I glanced over at Melanie. "I don't suppose you've seen Sonja around today?"

Melanie shook her head. "No. Why?"

I tapped my head. "Well, if I find her in the Dreaming, maybe she can get onto the CrossRoads from there? She could carry a message to the Queen. I don't think she uses a Door when she travels that way." I chewed on my lower lip. "Of course, if she's not around I suppose I could try to break through myself . . ."

She bopped me on top of the head. "Um. No. You can't go through Doors that way either. You remember what Ion told you? That whole thing about dying if your Shadow Self emerges on the wrong plane?"

"It was just a thought."

"Of course, that sort of begs the question. What if Sonja isn't there? Could you ask Brystion?"

I flushed as Talivar stared at me. "Erm. Yes, I guess I could. If he's there. Though it's not like we see each other much there. Like not at all, really."

"It's worth a shot," Phineas agreed. "I'm not sure how much luck either one of them will have actually getting into Faerie, but maybe they can pass along a message."

"Good enough." I looked at my watch. Even after everything that had happened it was only approaching noon. I nudged Talivar. "So now what, Protectorate-to-be?"

He frowned, and I could almost see the way the thoughts calculated behind his gaze. "First thing is to get . . . her"—he tilted his head toward Tresa—"situated in the Judgment Hall. I don't want her escaping. In fact, I want Robert guarding her. She is to have no contact with anyone. Understood?"

The last was said with a bit of an edge to his voice, and I could only wonder as Roweena finally bowed her head. "As you say."

"I'll call Charlie and let her know," Melanie said, winking our way. "Consider it one of my last TouchStone duties."

Katy approached us from behind the bar. "And actually, I was thinking maybe we should see about trying to notify any of the OtherFolk who might be stuck somewhere else. We had a fair number of people on that dating list—we can try contacting them. They'll be just as confused as we were if they all woke up from seizures."

I blinked. "That's actually a damn good idea. I hadn't even thought of that, but there's bound to be OtherFolk

unable to travel, especially if they've lost their Glamours."
I glanced over at Brandon. "Can we use the Hallows as a
base of operations? Maybe find a way to transport people
here?"

The werewolf sighed, his eyes suddenly twinkling as
he watched Katy. "Guess we'll find a use for that potential
TouchStone list after all."

Katy beamed at him. "I can borrow my mother's van."

"Shotgun," Melanie said as we shared a look. Katy could
be enthusiastic, but it wouldn't hurt to have someone a little
more knowledgeable about the situation tag along—and everyone knew Mel by reputation, if nothing else.

"Sounds like a plan." Tresa let out a derisive snort.

"If I wanted your opinion I would have given it to you," I
said sourly, somehow knowing whatever I did here, it would
likely come back and bite me in the ass.

I shoveled down the last forkful of my mac 'n' cheese, scraping the yellow cream off the bottom of the fast-food con-
tainer. "Stop hogging it all," Phineas whined, poking me
hard in the ankle.

"Belay that," I retorted. "Besides, it's all gone. There are
still some chicken strips left, though." He grunted what I
assumed was an affirmative and I tossed a few into his bowl
on the floor.

Talivar paced in the kitchen, his arms crossed. The
prince had cleaned up the mess from before in rather short
order after we got back from the Hallows, scraping the broken crockery into the trash without a fuss. He'd eschewed
the chicken when I bought it, so I didn't bother offering a
second time. "Are you sure you want to do this?"

"Do what?" I shrugged. "All I have to do is fall asleep.
It's not going to be a big deal or anything. What's the worst
that could happen? Aside from Sonja not being there."

"I mean about the TouchStoning thing. And me being the Protectorate."

"Well, sure. I mean, you fit the bill well enough. Unless there's something I don't know."

"Isn't that usually the case?" Phineas grunted at my feet, narrowly avoiding my kick.

I leaned in my chair, studying Talivar's profile as he continued to pace, one hand reaching up now and then to rub the back of his neck. His hair hung in a loose tangle about his face, the braids a tattered mess. "Care to tell me what this is all about?"

"Not really."

"Please. You've lived here for, what? Eight months? I'm pretty sure Moira wouldn't have dumped some sort of mass murderer on me, so what is it? Why do people dance around you like you're some kind of Fae leper?"

He stilled, his back to me, but he shuddered as though he was holding his breath. In an instant he had removed the hoodie and pulled up his shirt, giving me a glimpse of a flawless form. The muscles moved smoothly beneath the dusky skin, my fingers suddenly aching to touch his sculpted beauty. The T-shirt dropped to the ground like the discarded scales of a snake. And then the Glamour melted away and I froze.

Welts crisscrossed into the flesh of his back, working their way around his left shoulder, wending over his hip before dipping below the belt. He shifted so that he was turned partway to face me, unflinching as he allowed me to look at his chest, the white scars like a spider's web along the left side of his abdomen. His face remained mostly untouched, expressionless marble except for the barest of twitches in his right cheek. Slowly he removed the patch covering his eye, the puckered skin marring the perfection of his brow.

I thought he'd be done there, but a moment later and

he'd removed his jeans too. And hey, Talivar went commando. Who'd have thought? But he gestured downward and I could see the ravaged remains of his knee, the slightly shrunken thigh, ropey with scar tissue.

"Behold the Crippled Prince." He stared at me from beneath the shadow of his hair, daring me to react.

Beside me Phin let out a low whistle, but I ignored it. What sort of reaction was he going for? Shock? Surprise? Sympathy? The unveiling of one's scars could be terribly traumatic, but given the circumstances . . .

"Who did this to you?" I said finally, my voice steady, keeping my eyes upon his face.

"My father."

I raised a brow at him. "There's a whole lot more to this than just the normal sort of 'I accidentally drove Daddy's car through the garage door,' I'm thinking."

He grimaced as he bent to retrieve his clothing, carelessly pulling on the jeans. "You might say that."

"But why does that make you unfit to be Protectorate?"

"Aside from the fact that I committed regicide and patricide? Those inconveniences could so easily be overlooked, but for my physical flaws." At my questioning grunt, he shook his head. "In Faerie, only the most physically perfect of us may rule. We're considered to be representative of the land. A broken body indicates a broken kingdom. To lose a limb, or an eye . . . or both?" he said pointedly. "Well, there isn't much chance for me, regardless of how royal my bloodline may be."

"You killed your own father?" I debated taking a few steps back and then decided that would be asinine. There was a massive story here, but somehow I had the feeling I wasn't going to get a straight answer from him. Not yet.

"And quite rightly so," he said mildly. "The damage had already been done. I saw no reason for my sister and mother to endure life beneath his thumb." He rotated his hand. "So to speak."

"They don't seem to care about my scars that much," I pointed out.

"You're not Fae. Or in line for the throne . . . Frankly, none of them care."

"Ouch." Nothing like a little bluntness to make a girl feel good. "Most of my scars are hidden anyway. Except this one." In a show of camaraderie, I pulled up my shirt, exposing a silver oval on my belly. "I got this one for Moira, when Maurice tried to gut me through the painting."

A gentle smile crossed his face. "I know."

I touched the scar on my head. "I've always kind of wondered why they didn't try to heal the rest of me. The Royal Healers, that is. Seems like a bit of a waste, doesn't it?"

He shrugged into his shirt. "Why would they? You didn't earn the others while you were in Moira's service."

"Practical. All right then. So you've got some issues. And you have flaws." I smacked my lips. "I'm going to have to say, I don't care much. Just don't fuck up."

He blinked, carefully replacing the patch over his eye. "Is that all?"

"Yeah well, something tells me you're a fast learner. And it's only temporary, right? Until we get Moira back."

"Famous last words," Phineas muttered. "And speaking of, don't you have the Dreaming to get into? Succubi to chat up? Messages to pass along? Our asses to save?"

I glared at him, scooping up the remainder of the food. "All right, all right. I'm on it. As soon as I can fall asleep, anyway." I winced at the light streaming through the window. I always had a tough time napping deeply enough to get to the Dreaming, but I would try.

I headed for my bedroom, the unicorn trotting at my heels. On impulse, I looked behind me, my gaze meeting

Talivar's as he stood in the kitchen, watching us go. "Good luck," he mouthed, one hand sliding over his mouth as though he were going to kiss the palm. I felt the blush creeping over my cheeks, but said nothing as I carefully shut the door behind me.

Ten

The Dreaming seemed empty tonight. Dimmer maybe. I'd gotten here the usual way, but even my nightmares couldn't be bothered with me; the sharks kept their distance, dead eyes focused somewhere else.

Not a good sign.

Still. I was here, sitting on the front porch of my Heart. I closed my eyes, the breeze whispering its way through the darkness, tickling the back of my neck. It was always night here. I didn't know if it was my subconscious or the state of my mind, the inner darkity-dark reaches of my soul or what. There were times when I wouldn't mind a little dream sunshine, but I hadn't quite mastered the whole weather thing.

The iron gate was closed—the way I'd left it—but there was no sign of Sonja. Sometimes she would wait for me on the outside; sometimes she'd show up after the fact. I trotted down the stairs, the gate opening with a creak as I approached. "Sonja?"

I stepped out onto the path and eyed the road to the beach. The air felt damp that way, the taste of brine and death carried in the distant sound of the waves. I frowned, wondering how long I should wait. Perhaps I could leave a note? The thought of using a Dream Post-it struck me as funny, but I wasn't sure I had that option.

I kicked around the gate for a few moments more, my hands absently rubbing along the rusted frame as I glanced at the forest behind the house. Did Brystion know about the CrossRoads being closed? Assuming he was even here and not trapped somewhere on the other side like the rest of them.

The thought twisted harder in my gut than I expected it to.

"Fuck it." There were bigger things at stake here than my wounded pride. Sooner or later I was going to have to cop to the fact that I had actual responsibilities. I'd look for the incubus, and if he wasn't there I'd leave a note for Sonja . . . Ion . . . whoever happened to stumble through. And if there was no answer to that . . . well, then I'd just have to see about breaking through to the CrossRoads, Shadow Self or not.

My mind made up, I retreated into the house, happy enough to find writing materials. For all that Sonja claimed I could control this place, more often it controlled itself, weaving bits and pieces drawn from the memories I'd had when I actually lived here. The notepad magnet on the fridge was straight out of my childhood, right down to the torn cardboard backing, the words "Chopin Liszt" scrawled at the top, complete with a bust of each of the composers. Ah yes, family dorkitude, for the win.

It would be good enough, I decided, knowing I was stalling. "Time to man up, Abby."

Sighing, I slipped out the kitchen door and onto the patio, surrounded by a wild garden. What had started as a few small bushes had become a monstrous tangle of creeping thorns. It had grown up all around the house, soft and beckoning with roses.

I paused at the edge of the garden, the crickets chirping

cheerfully in the grass leading into the forest. Trees loomed on either side, hawthorn and ash and slender birch. A gentle willow beckoned me to sit upon a woven bench curling with vines and thick with wisteria.

My hand stroked the rough bark, the leaves of the tree tangling gently in my hair.

"It's very pretty, Ion. But I'm not here to play games. There's a lot of shit going down and I . . . I need your help." The words stumbled from my mouth, even as my ears strained for the sound of bells.

Silence.

I scowled at the bench. Eight months ago, the incubus had sought out the Protectorate, looking for help to find his missing sister.

He'd found me instead.

His accidental TouchStoning of me had led into an intimacy far greater than anything I'd been prepared for. In a fit of romantic pique I'd offered him the one thing no incubus could ever have—a Dreaming Heart of his own. Or at least a piece of mine. The offer had been given freely, without strings attached, and I had no plans to renege on it, but it still stung, knowing that he'd left me anyway.

"Evening, Abby." Bryston's whisper crept past me, the heated slide of his voice coiling like an ember in my belly, but the sharp nip of his teeth upon the back of my neck snapped me to reality quick enough. "Whoa there, Prancer." My head jerked up at the intrusion. Hurt flashed in his golden eyes for half a moment and then he gave me a tight-lipped smile.

He'd chosen to appear in his daemonic form this time and for some reason the intimacy of it wounded me all the more. His skin shone a luminous blue-black, the spiral markings on his flesh glowing with a silver light reminiscent of the CrossRoads. Great crystalline antlers burst from his brow as though he was the living incarnation of some ancient forest god. He should have seemed monstrous to me, I suppose, standing there with the lower half of a stag and the upper torso of man, but he didn't.

He never had.

Cupped ears flickered as he absently rubbed an antler on the willow, close to where I'd touched it.

"Marking your territory?"

"Maybe. Maybe I'm just stopping by to check on you. I don't know." One hoof stomped the ground. "Watching you, I guess."

"You do that a lot," I observed, trying not to do something stupid. Like throw myself into his arms. I'd forgotten how strong the pull between us could be. More the fool, me—though judging by the halo of gold in his eyes, he hadn't forgotten.

"Not as much as you might think." The long length of his tail twitched like a cat's. "Enough to see how your training is going."

"And? What do you think?" As much as I wanted to cut to the meat of why I was here, it was hard not to break away from the small talk.

He brushed by me, staring out into the woods as though he hadn't heard. "Does it matter?"

I bristled. "No, it doesn't."

He paused at the edges of the garden, head raised to sniff the breeze. "What I meant was that your performance in the Dreaming isn't really why you're here." The expectant hush of a required answer bled through the pronounced innocence of his statement. A warning lingered there too.

He'd once threatened to kill me if I lied to him. Even though I knew he'd never go through with it now, the implication that I owed him the truth was quite clear.

Which was a crock of shit as far as I was concerned. His

lies to me may have been born from desperation and not malice, but that hadn't made them any less devastating. I let the question hang there, my will clashing against his expectation.

"The Faery Queen has closed the CrossRoads," I said finally.

His head whipped back to face me. "She what?"

I laid it out for him quickly, his eyes narrowing as I chronicled Tresa's appearance and the seizures, the spell and Moira's disappearance.

"Well that explains that," he muttered. "If I've never expressed my sympathy properly for your medical condition, let me just say I appreciate it a bit more now."

"Where were you when it happened?"

"Here, actually. Or," he paused, "the Dreaming, anyway. Maybe not *here* exactly."

My lips compressed into a thin smile, trying to ignore the ache clenching up my chest. "Was she good?"

"She wasn't you, but she did well enough." The incubus coughed uncomfortably.

"Yeah, I don't think I really want to know." And I didn't. Far too much history here, but he had been the one to walk away. On the other hand, the guy had to eat and I couldn't resent that. Much. Just sucked that his methods of sustenance required some form of sex to work.

He let out a regretful chuckle. "And you? Sharing your bed with anyone else these days?"

"None of your business," I retorted tartly. Not really fair of me to snap at him given my own line of questions, but there it was.

"No, I suppose not." We stared at each other for a moment, then, a subtle longing urging me to step toward him. I grasped the corner of the bench to steady myself. He remained motionless except for his lion's tail, swishing in a lazy motion. Eventually he shuddered, shaking his body like a dog. "So, why are you here?"

"I—that is—we, were hoping that you might be able to help us get a message through to the Faery Queen. Assuming you can reach Faerie at all. We don't know how things stand there and Moira needs to know about what's going on with her son and Tresa, and all the rest of it."

His ears flattened. "No."

"Why not?" I grabbed his wrist, nearly gasping at the warmth coming off his skin. "We need you, Ion!"

He snatched his hand away as though I'd burned him. "What would be the point?"

"What's the matter with you?"

He frowned. "This. This isn't your job. Hell, if you're no longer required to be Contracted to Moira, why not let *them* figure it out?"

"Well, what else am I supposed to do? Sit around and watch everyone fade?" A ripple of frustration washed through me. "You think I could live with myself if something happened to Benjamin? Something I might have been able to prevent?" I tugged sharply on his ear when he refused to look at me. "And if I'd been so practical about Sonja when you came to me looking for help—is that what you would have preferred?"

His face softened, ears twitching as he crouched below the tree, cloven feet tucked beneath him. "No. I just don't get why it's always got to be you."

I sank to my knees beside him. "Question of the week. I'm a Dreamer, remember? A Dreamer and a KeyStone and now I'm going to be the TouchStone of the new goddamned Protectorate. Who else would do it?"

"It's a Faery concern," he pointed out. "And they're using you. And this . . . *Talivar* seems able enough. Surely there's another mortal who could take up the burden this time."

I cocked my head at him. "This isn't like you, Ion. Why does it matter so much to you what I do? I mean, other than the obvious?"

"What the hell kind of question is that?" he snapped, lurching to his feet. "You were my TouchStone, Abby. You think I want to see you hurt? Or captured? This bullshit with Maurice is *not* something you should be dealing with." He glanced down at himself. "And I can't keep rushing in to rescue you."

"Fine. Then don't." I struggled to my own feet, stung. "I'm sorry I even bothered asking. I'll just wait for Sonja. After all, you pawned me off on her once before. Might as well stay the course, right?"

He flinched. "I didn't pawn you off on her. At least, not intentionally."

"You know what they say about intentions, don't you? Keep in mind that if something happens to me, you'll lose this." I gestured around the garden. "And then what will you do?"

His ears flattened and he lowered his head, his hooves scuffing at the grass.

"I dislike arguing," he said finally. "And I dislike arguing over stupid things. And I truly dislike arguing over stupid things *with you*." His hand slid over my wrist, clawed finger glittering. "This is beyond us. Beyond you."

I flushed at his words. "And how would you know?"

"I know you, Abby. If I were blinded and deafened and crippled, I would still know you." He pulled back so that his eyes bore into mine. "There is no part of you that I do not know, save what bits you choose to hide from yourself. And those are enough." His tail lashed over the furred hocks, unable to contain his irritation. "That's why I suggested Sonja. I don't think she'd let any feelings for you get in the way of what you need to be taught."

"Noble of you, but too much booty call really shouldn't be an excuse."

His ebony skin grew darker still and I knew he was blushing. "When I see you here, standing in the Dreaming . . . I can think of nothing else. You shine so brightly and I am so utterly helpless before it."

My lips pursed. "I think you're full of crap. Whatever your issues are, they've got less to do with me than whatever you're afraid of."

Anger simmered beneath his suddenly coal black eyes. "You want to talk fear, Abby? You want to see what it is you haven't confronted yet? What you can't control?" He drew himself up, making a careless gesture with his wrist. The air around us grew frosty, the forest fading into silence.

Instinctively, I wrapped my will around the Dreaming, shielding like Sonja had taught me. Brystion let out a humorless laugh, snapping his fingers. Abruptly the darkness loomed around us, the familiar things of my Dreaming Heart shattered like so much dust. An arc of silver light encircled the place where we stood, the crescent edges of an ephemeral bubble cocooning us in a shield more powerful than anything I'd ever been able to make.

I peered into the void, making out small sparks of light in the far distance, fireflies winking in and out of existence. "What is this?"

"The Dreaming. All of it." Brystion's voice was without inflection, his face flat as he stared out into the distance. "Each ball of light is another Dreaming Heart. Sonja spoke to you of being able to travel between them, but you will never manage it."

"Thanks for the vote of confidence."

"Look." He inclined his head toward the front of the bubble. I followed his line, my knees wavering as a tooth-filled mouth brushed up against the barrier. It should have swallowed us whole, its gaping maw large enough to have driven a Mack truck through. The shadow of another one slinked past, dorsal fin cutting through the void with predatory ease.

It seemed my nightmares had taken on monstrous proportions again. I shrank back when another approached, circling twice before sliding into the darkness. "Could you make it past them, Abby? Could you allow yourself to be consumed for the chance at actual freedom?"

Wordlessly I shook my head, trying not to vomit. "I thought I was doing better," I said hoarsely. "Sonja never told me."

The shield faded into the darkness as the familiar surroundings of my Heart came into view. "You are, but you give your nightmares far too much power." He cupped my chin so that I was forced to stare into his eyes. "That shield is my payment for staying here, lest you think me merely a freeloading . . . parasite." Something sad crossed his face. "I always pay my debts, Abby."

Anger swelled in my chest, compressing on my lungs until I thought I might burst. "I didn't ask you to. I offered you this as a gift," I snapped. "How will I ever manage to learn on my own if you're always protecting me?"

"You're reckless," he whispered. "Heedless of your actions here. You think by just throwing yourself to the wolves you'll somehow master them."

"It worked before," I said, remembering the way I'd been swallowed up by the sharks in the painting. "Working" being the operative term. I'd survived, anyway.

"You were lucky. Very, very lucky." His fingers slid from my cheek, his golden eyes filled with regret. "But all the other Dreamers I've run into were already trained. I've never dealt with one that wasn't—or one so powerfully haunted by nightmares. I don't want to fuck it up."

"So what do I do?"

"I don't know, but I owe nothing to the Faery Court, regardless of their assumptions. And this mess is of their making."

"Then it's become my mess too." I straightened up. "And if you aren't willing to help us, I have to go. I've got things to do. A world to save. You know—the usual."

Without consent from my conscious, our fingers entwined as he stroked my wrist with his thumb. I ignored the shiver creeping down my spine, spurred on by a flood of memories. "I am sorry, Abby, but regardless of the situation I will not get involved this time."

I withdrew my hand from his, disappointment aching in my breast. "You do what you think best, Ion. So will I." Abruptly I turned and walked away. A jangle of bells sung out discordantly and I knew without looking that he was gone.

"Fuck love, anyway," I snarled, slamming the door to my house hard enough to make my grandmother's china rattle against the walls. Hastily I scratched out a message to Sonja with some details, hoping that she might take it upon herself to get the message out. Stomping through the living room, I grimaced at the sudden strength of the potpourri, thick with strawberries.

Mother.

"Not now," I sighed at it. I taped the note to the outside of the gate; with luck, the succubus would find it.

"Your brother is an ass," I said aloud to the paper, trying not to wince at the pain bubbling up behind the words.

What had I really expected? That he would just drop everything to help out his fellow OtherFolk? To help me?

Yes.

My hand drifted up to play with the amulet he'd put around my neck that last morning we'd spent together. In all this time, I hadn't bothered taking it off, though now it seemed like the physical reminder of a doomed memory. For a moment I was tempted to break the chain and toss it into the grass.

In the end, I let my fingers fall.

"Sentimental idiot."

I glanced up at the dusk-purple sky, willing myself to wake up. And then I felt myself falling, tumbling into the brightness of the sunlight of a golden afternoon and the waiting sheets of my empty bed.

Eleven

The Judgment Hall was an imposing sort of place at the best of times, but in the fading daylight, it took on an eerie "Night on Bald Mountain" vibe. It was Glamoured, of course, housed within the deep recesses of the run-down cemetery of Portsmyth.

Crumbling mounds of granite, cracked and gnarled with fading gray lichens, rendered this part of the cemetery ancient and untouchable, entrenched in a moldering loam of damp leaves and small prickly plants. Thankfully almost no one ever came here, save for the occasional art student or small-town historian.

But then, this particular Glamour seemed to work by making unaware mortals feel as though they'd stepped on an ant mound or a spider's nest, a creepy crawly sensation of hundreds of little feet skittering across a hapless leg. Visitors never seemed to stay long.

I shuddered. Even knowing it was there, I could still feel a tickle when I pushed through its gossamer strands. In the center of the cemetery a decrepit mausoleum stood watch beneath the shadows of a rotting oak, flanked by angelic statues with great sweeping wings.

Or so they appeared. The angels nodded briefly as I approached, Talivar keeping pace behind me by a few steps. His own Glamour was restored so the scars were gone, the pointed ears hidden. I caught a glimpse of what appeared to be pixies crouched on top of a pillar, arrows nocked at the ready. Guess the OtherFolk weren't taking any chances at potential invasion into one of their last remaining sanctuaries in the mortal realm.

I shifted my backpack, hearing a small grunt from inside. "Almost there," I told the unicorn. To the angels, I gave a friendly sort of smile. "Roweena is expecting us."

The angel on the left frowned, his aqua eyes darting between me and Talivar for a moment. He waved us in, the marble door shifting to let us through. The Glamour melted away as soon as we entered, leaving us standing in the long, stone corridor that led to the Council room.

Immediately my backpack started squirming and I set it down, releasing Phineas with a quick flick of the zipper. He snorted, shaking himself out. "Gods, I will never get used to being carried around like a lapdog. Humiliating."

"Kind of hard to be humiliated when you have no shame," I said.

"It's a gift. Come on and let's get this over with. I've got a date tonight."

I exchanged a glance with Talivar. "Anyone I know?"

"Doubt it. Hedgehogs aren't in your social circle."

"Ah." I paused, my mind trying to bend itself around *that* particular image. At least it wasn't with the lion girl. "Yeah. Okay. Just, um, be careful. Quills and all that."

The unicorn rolled his eyes at me. "Teach Grandma to suck eggs, why don't you?"

"A date actually sounds like fun. Though it's not really all that appropriate, under the circumstances."

"A date?" Talivar started down the stone hall, footsteps echoing with a strangely familiar ring.

"Courtship," Phineas sighed. "You're expected to spend money on the object of your affection and maybe they'll sleep with you in return."

Talivar eyed me appraisingly. "That simple, eh?"

"You've been here long enough. You tell me if you really think things are that simple." I arched a brow at him.

He let out a rolling chuckle. "They could be."

We passed several long sets of doors, the burnished wood and copper handles gleaming in the witchlight. I knew what the inside of the cells looked like a little too well, having once been an occupant for several hours. Only one door had a guard out front, Robert's familiar silhouette perched beside it, his wings tucked beneath a trench coat.

"Tresa inside?" I asked him, though I knew the answer.

"For the moment, though I half wonder if it might not be better for her to have an 'accident.'" He grimaced at me. "She has a wicked tongue."

"How's my nephew?" Talivar's posture suddenly went rigid.

The angel frowned at him. "Charlie's watching him. He's fine."

"Keep in mind this is only a temporary solution," the prince announced. "When we get things settled here, Abby and I will be taking him back."

"Uh. No." I caught Robert's momentary look of anguish and stepped between them. "I think he's fine where he is, Talivar."

The prince drew himself up. "I'm Protectorate. And more than that, I'm the boy's uncle. Robert can have no true claim on him."

"Think you're overstepping your bounds there," Phineas

said, waggling his beard. "You haven't become the Protectorate yet."

"Babies should be left with those who can best take care of them. Right now, that's with his father," I said.

"But according to Faerie law—"

"We're not *in* Faerie." I rolled my eyes.

Robert coughed. "Technically, the Judgment Hall is considered to be under Faerie jurisdiction, Abby."

"Whose side are you on, anyway?" I tugged on Talivar's sleeve. "Look, I understand you're his uncle and all, but let's be realistic. You gonna haul a baby around while we try to track down a way to open the CrossRoads? With the diapers and the milk and all that?"

He shot me a puzzled look. "Of course not. That's what you're for."

"I'm what?" My feet scuffed the marble as I stopped dead in my tracks.

"You're a woman. That's what women do," he continued, sighing with a wistful hum. "Service their men, raise their babies, trail behind us when we go off to war . . ." I made a choking noise. "I jest," he said dryly, the corners of his mouth twitching. "Besides, I've seen the way you cook. I'd starve if I were dependent upon you for my meals in the field."

"That makes two of us, then," I retorted, ignoring Robert's snort of amusement. Roweena gestured at us from the main doorway. She looked better than she had before, though given Talivar's earlier missive about physical flaws, I wondered if she was hiding her issues behind a Glamour as well.

I shrugged inwardly, not really one to judge. After all, I tried to hide the scar on my head often enough; I certainly had no room to point fingers. Behind me, the two men exchanged some sort of verbal He-Man mutters, but I didn't bother trying to listen in. "Contracts all drawn up?"

Roweena nodded, weary lines etched into her forehead. "Yes. Melanie is awaiting Talivar so that we may formally dissolve their Contract." Long-term Contracts had never been Melanie's thing. It spoke volumes to our friendship that she'd allowed herself to be shackled even this long.

I entered the hall, relieved to see it had a slightly more friendly appearance this time around. Of course, not being on trial for potentially murdering my friend certainly helped with that.

I spotted Melanie up at the dais, perched on the great stone table, her booted feet swinging aimlessly. "How'd it go with Sonja? Any luck?"

I shook my head as I approached, Roweena sliding beside me. "No. She wasn't there. I left her a note—hopefully she'll find it and be able to help us out."

Melanie raised a brow. "And Ion?"

I sighed, peering at my ragged nails. "Not exactly. I mean, he was there, but . . ."

"But he wouldn't help," Melanie said softly.

"I would have thought he might at least be willing to try. After all our history together and all." I swallowed down another wave of bitterness. "Self-absorbed prick."

"He's an incubus," Roweena said. "There's no point in hoping daemons will do anything but for their own reasons." Her shoulders slumped. "I suppose we might as well move along with this and concentrate on finding another way."

Footsteps from the doorway indicated Talivar's presence. He stalwartly kept his head facing forward as he passed me by, but his good eye slid sideways, winking when he met my gaze.

"So soon?" Melanie's mouth pursed.

"Not hardly," I snarled. "And no, before you ask, I'm *not*

sleeping with him." If he heard me, he gave no heed of it. I bent down to scoop up a wriggling Phineas, who was making quite the ass out of himself with demands that he be allowed to see.

"All right, then," Roweena said crisply, unfurling the first of the scrolls. "This is Melanie's Contract with Talivar. Do you both agree the Contract has been fulfilled, in as much as can be?"

Talivar nodded curtly even as Melanie smiled. "Oh, yes." She sighed, one hand running down the side of her violin case, her happiness at being released radiating from her in waves.

The elven liaison scratched out a few things on the parchment. "Both of you sign here . . . and here. And then I will stamp it with Moira's seal."

I debated pointing out that Moira wasn't technically the Protectorate anymore, but since the alternative was hauling Tresa in here, I decided it wouldn't really matter. Without the CrossRoads behind it, this was all just a matter of semantics anyway. The two of them quickly scrawled their signatures, Talivar's in sweeping, broad strokes, Melanie's in a surprisingly lovely script.

"Now, then," Roweena said, rolling up the scroll. "I'll put that one in the archives for later. In the meantime, I've gone over Abby's original Contract with Moira, as well as the forged documents from Tresa. Although her actions are woefully misled, we can certainly use the wording to do the transfer." She tapped her fingers on yet another scroll. "And I have done so. If you would care to look it over?"

I peered over the table, nearly butting heads with Talivar. He gave me a sheepish smile. I pushed back my bangs and resumed scanning. "None of the perks, it seems?"

Roweena shook her head. "Moira handled that side of things. I figured I would let Talivar decide what reward to give you for your service. But I wouldn't be too frivolous with the promises," she admonished. "It's unlikely any of them could be fulfilled until we get the CrossRoads open."

I nodded. "There's nothing I really want, anyway. Not at the moment."

Talivar shrugged, his eye resting on me with a curious bent. "I'll leave it open, for now, to be granted at a later date."

"Good enough." I took the quill from him, the callused edges of his fingers brushing mine. Exhaling softly, I signed my name. "Guess that's it then."

A little disappointing, really. When I'd signed Moira's original Contract, I remembered a bit of a magical spark as we finished. But with the CrossRoads closed, there was no magic. Sort of took all the fun out of it, really.

I looked at Talivar, studying the curve of his cheek. "I'm still a KeyStone, you know. We could do this for real, if you think that would be better."

The prince cocked his head at me, something unfamiliar passing over his face. "No," he said at last. "It would not be right."

Surprised, I withdrew my hand. "What's to be right or wrong about it? I just thought it might lend better credence to the whole situation. Make it more legit. Whatever."

"And that is appreciated," he said firmly. "But not necessary. It would not be fair to the others if I took advantage of that when they could not. If things take a turn for the worse, I may be forced to take your offer, but until then I'll stick with this."

I nodded. To be honest, I was a bit relieved, even though the less rational side of me raged at being rejected for the second time that day. And not even for anything romantic. "Oh for two," I muttered. "Fair enough. What's next?"

"Research," Roweena said, gesturing at several large tomes beside the scrolls. She stamped the new Contract with the Royal seal. "There, now. New Protectorate, bound to a TouchStone. One small thing in order, anyway." She picked up the first book, a solid, leather thing that probably weighed about twenty pounds. With a wan smile, she handed it to Talivar. "Your first duty."

She gazed at me apologetically. "Unfortunately, these books are in old Elvish, so I don't think you'll be able to help us. I don't actually think we'll find much about the Key, but perhaps there will be something else we can use."

"I could look at pictures," I offered, but even I knew that was a hollow answer. "I'll just wait over here." The two elves barely batted an eye at my words, already starting to skim the pages. The scent of book dust and crumbling parchment hit me full on, my nose wiggling against a vicious tickle.

"Almost like the Pit." Melanie chuckled. "You should feel right at home." The two of us moved away from the elves, planting our asses on the last row of marble benches. Padded cushions of emerald green lined the seats, but I got the distinct impression they were only there for decoration.

"Guess you must feel pretty good about getting that Contract lifted," I yawned. "Sounded like neither one of you was happy about it."

She frowned at me. "What are you talking about? "

"I overheard you guys talking yesterday. At the Hallows. I assumed he was looking for permission to break it?"

"Ah. Abby?"

"And Ion. I don't even know where to begin with that. Do I have 'Untouchable' tacked on my forehead today? I mean, I know we're a little awkward these days, but I at least thought he might be willing to try."

She pushed her violet teashades onto her forehead. "Guess maybe that depends on how you asked him. How did he look?"

"Well enough. He's been feeding, anyway." I couldn't

quite meet her eyes, but the jealousy flared to life beneath my breast.

"You miss him, don't you?"

"Yeah. As much as I hate to admit it." I fiddled with the necklace again, twisting the chain. "And for shit's sake, I know we only knew each other for a week or two—it's not like that's long enough to get to *know* anyone. Not really." I let out a sigh. "When he broke up with me he admitted that if he hadn't been attracted to the Dreamer in me, he would have let me die."

Her brow rose and she shook her head. "No way. I've known Ion a long time and I don't think that's true," Melanie said quietly. "He may be a bit confused as to how he feels, but deep down he's a good person. I truly do believe that."

"Got a funny way of showing it." On the other hand, the guy was keeping a shield around my nightmares, so there wasn't much I could say to that. Still, it sucked all the way around. First things first, though. Responsibility over love life and all that shit.

Her mouth pursed. "Talivar wants to court you, Abby. That's what he was asking me about yesterday."

"Court me?" I said faintly, some of his previous comments now making sense. "Ah. So he was asking your permission to date me?"

"Guess he thought it was common courtesy. He seems like a very old-school sort of guy. Very proper. He might even be good for you."

"Famous last words. And incidentally, I'm not sure there's anything old school or proper about dancing the Hustle at a Dance Dance Revolution competition."

She glanced over at him and giggled. "Where the hell did he learn that?"

I scowled at her. "I taught him a few weeks ago. Katy set up a disco dance-off in the back room of the Hallows. And before you knock it, he's actually pretty damn good." I shrugged. "Of course, it's the only dance he knows, but it was totally worth the price of admission."

She chuckled. "He's learning. Just decide what to do now that you know he likes you. I'd rather not see him strung along."

"Little fond of him yourself, aren't you?"

"Sure. As OtherFolk go, he's not that bad. There's something rather noble about him. Feels like he's been trapped in a shell or something." She smiled at me. "This has been good for him. We've been good for him."

"And you never thought to make a play for him yourself?"

"When was the last time you saw me with anyone that way? OtherFolk are strictly off-limits for dating material." I thought about that for a moment and realized she was right. In all the time I'd known her here, she had never been in a relationship with any of her Contracts.

"Why?" I asked bluntly.

"I hate mixing work with pleasure. And honestly, mortal guys are going to like me for who I am—not for what I am, or what I can do." She twiddled her fingers, not meeting my eyes. "I get tired of being treated as a commodity. And sometimes normal is nice . . . uncomplicated."

I watched the two elves across the way. Phineas was wriggling his way between them as they stared at the books. Roweena pointed at something and Talivar shook his head. His hair was tied back so it didn't drag across the paper, the torc at his neck gleaming like a vestige of his former royal glory.

"I don't know," I murmured finally, a flush spreading

over my cheeks as I remembered his mouth on mine the night before. "He's my bodyguard. Seems a little inappropriate."

"Well, technically he's your boss now, but yeah, I see what you mean." Melanie yawned. "Want to go get something to eat? I'm starving, and if they're going to be here all night, we might as well snag some grub. I'll probably need to crash soon anyway."

My stomach rumbled in answer. "Sounds good." We made our way up to the table. "Any luck? Mel and I are gonna go get a pizza or something."

"If by luck you mean 'shit out of,' then yes. And I'd kill for a pizza," Phineas sighed. "With sausage."

"We did discover some usefulness about the Key's properties," Talivar said. "The mechanics of it are quite complicated, but we do know that the Key has changed its form over the years. Makes it a bit hard to track down, though."

The unicorn wrinkled his nose, pointing at a small sketch in the corner with his horn. "Last time the Key made an appearance, it looked like this."

"And when was that?" I peered over Talivar's shoulder to get a closer look. The page was stained in places, the scrawling description nothing more than a faded script beneath a few small drawings. I frowned at them, a sick feeling bubbling in the pit of my stomach.

"Hard to say," Talivar mused. "The Queen's Steward isn't usually forthcoming about the whereabouts of our Faery relics, but it was discovered missing from the vaults about thirty-five years ago, maybe? Mortal years, that is. But it hasn't had a wearer for a very long time, even before that."

"Well," I said softly, my knees going weak as I studied the scroll, my finger delicately tracing the curved edges of the sketch with a sick sort of giddiness. "I don't think we need to worry about where it is anymore."

Four heads swiveled toward me as I caught myself on the edges of the table. "What are you talking about, Abby?" Talivar frowned at me.

I let out a hysterical burble of laughter as I reached beneath the collar of my shirt to pull out my mother's amulet. "Because I'm wearing it."

Twelve

If this is your idea of a joke, it's not very funny," Roweena said coldly. "Take it off so that I can get a better look
at it."

"I don't recall ever seeing that before." Talivar lowered
his head for a closer look. "Wherever did you get it?"

"I . . . um . . . it was in my mother's envelope. The one
the estate lawyer sent me. I've been wearing it since . . .
since Ion left. He put it on me, the, uh, last night he was
with me."

"Still carrying a torch, eh?" The unicorn stomped a hoof,
sniffing at the amulet. "Never saw it on you once. And I've
seen you totally naked, you know. When you come out of
the shower."

I shuddered. "Good to know."

Talivar held it gingerly between his fingers. "It's been
Glamoured."

"That makes no sense. I could see it just fine in the envelope. So did Brystion, for that matter."

"Maybe it only takes effect when someone wears it."
Melanie looked at the scroll where the sketch of the necklace
appeared. "Does it say anything about that here?"

Roweena snapped her fingers impatiently. "Hand it here. My old bones don't feel like moving."

"I'm trying." I tugged at the clasp. "It's not loosening."

"Let me," Talivar moved behind me, his hands brushing the nape of my neck. I flushed beneath his sudden scrutiny, the whole courtship idea making me strangely shy. "She's right," he said finally after a moment of fiddling with it. "It's not coming off."

"Well, isn't this just wonderful." I stepped away as Talivar dropped his hands. "And how the hell did my mother end up with this anyway? Assuming someone didn't slip it into the envelope later." I'd never seen the thing before it fell out of the envelope that morning I'd finally gotten the courage to open it. Certainly not around my mother's neck. But if it had been Glamoured . . .

Roweena limped closer, yanking hard on the silver chain, her hawk's eyes taking in the details—the silver filigree, the blue topaz stone, the crystal clasp at the tip. "It's not quite right," she said critically. "The archives are very specific. It should be glowing."

"I'll just click my heels three times, shall I?"

"It could very well be that it needs to be activated in some fashion. Perhaps we should try opening a Door with it. That is its intended purpose, after all."

"I tried going through a Door this morning and that didn't work. Maybe it's broken."

"There's a Door in the far chamber behind the altar," Roweena said. "Let's try that one. Its power might be activated now that you're aware of it."

For a moment I wished I'd just kept my mouth shut. After all, I'd quite possibly be slurping down a few slices of greasy pizza by now, and all the happier for it.

I stared at the plain opening Roweena directed to me to. "You sure this is it?" I held the necklace in my hands, cupping it beneath my chin. "What am I supposed to do?"

"Ask it to open?" Phineas waggled his beard shrewdly.

"Thank you, Captain Obvious." Feeling like a total ass, I stood in front the Door. "Open Sesame," I intoned, un-surprised when nothing happened. "Well, that was exciting. Any other bright ideas?"

"Hold it out to the Door," Melanie suggested. "Or stroke the stone, maybe?"

I did both, scowling when I was rewarded with a fat pile of nothing.

Talivar frowned at me. "Maybe it only works for the Fae."

"Feel free to try it, but unless you can get it off my neck, I think we're stuck."

Roweena shook her head. "No, the records are fairly clear. Only mortals may use it."

"Makes sense," Melanie added, her gaze darting to the amulet. "If the Steward is mortal, and the Queen's trusted . . . uh . . . consort."

Talivar gave her a wry smile. "It's a fairly well-known se-cret. My mother has always been rather careless about dis-playing her lovers."

I'd heard the rumors off and on, but my general un-derstanding was that the Steward of Faerie was actually the Queen's TouchStone. I supposed it made sense that it might become something more, given the closeness of their stations, but I still didn't get what it had to do with my mother.

I began to wonder at Talivar's father's motivations at beating the crap out of his son. Regardless of what the prince had told me about Faery parentage, I had a fair notion that perhaps it meant a bit more to some than he would have me believe. Not something I needed to press him on right this moment, however.

"Was there anything else in the envelope, Abby?" Phineas buried his face in another pile of scrolls.

"Like directions, you mean? Nope. There wasn't even any mention of it among the rest of the paperwork." I paused. "There was a key to my mother's lockbox, though. Back in our old hometown."

"Sounds like a road trip is in order." Melanie's eyes lit up. "Maybe there's a clue there."

"Sure," I retorted. "Let me just go pull up the Mystery Machine and we'll all pile in, right?"

"Katy has a van." Phineas looked up at me innocently.

"Katy's *mom* has a van," I corrected him. "And it seems a bit rude to commandeer it just so that we can—"

"Save the world," Talivar said softly. "Or at least, my people. Your friends. My nephew."

"Well, when you put it that way." The heat rose in my face at the subtle reproach.

"Here we go!" Phineas reared up suddenly, tapping one of the scrolls.

Roweena took it from him, unfurling it for a better look. "Ah," she said, her lips compressing. "He's right. There's a bit about how the necklace works. And it would appear you're stuck with it." Her clear eyes gazed at me coolly. "For life, in fact."

I let out a sharp bark of laughter. "Figures. I somehow get mixed up with a sacred Faery relic and it's broken." I tugged on it again, cursing my own sentimental heart. "Damn you, Brystion."

"It says here that it can only be removed upon the wearer's death," she continued as though I hadn't spoken. "And it is guarded by a powerful Glamour. This is obviously to protect the bearer—in this case, you—as it seems to be a reasonable assessment that you could be killed for it."

I paused, thinking of that last fatal night of my mother's.

If she had been wearing it that night, would it have flown off? Or did the Glamour fade with her death? I had no recollection of much of that night or the weeks that followed—the coma had seen to that, but no one had mentioned it to me afterward either. I said as much, pondering such an anomaly aloud. "But that still doesn't explain how my mother got it in the first place. I mean, if you're telling me the Steward was the last person to have it . . ."

There was an uncomfortable silence as my words died. I stared at each of them in turn. Melanie simply shrugged at me, but Phineas refused to meet my eyes.

"You know something," Talivar rumbled, one hand brushing over my shoulder. I stiffened despite myself, and the hand stilled, finally coming to rest at the crook of my elbow.

Phineas flattened his ears. For once he didn't appear to have a snappy comeback. In fact, he looked as though he'd rather be just about anywhere else. My eyes narrowed.

"It wasn't chance, was it?" I said softly. "You showing up when you did at the Marketplace?"

His azure eyes blinked up at me, deep and unreadable. "No." He shivered, as though suddenly deciding something within himself. "I was sent . . . I was sent to keep an eye on you. Not quite a guard," he added hastily as I exhaled. "More like a guide, to make sure you didn't get in too deep."

Melanie sniffed and his ears flattened further.

"Hey—I did the best I could," he snapped. "I wasn't supposed to let on I could talk, but you forced my hand when you started that Dreaming shit."

"You bit me on the ass. I hardly think that constitutes forcing your hand. Not that you actually have any," I reminded him, my knees buckling at Phin's confession. "It wasn't like I had much choice."

"What difference does it make?" Talivar pulled up a seat,

steering me toward it. I shot him a grateful smile as I slid into the sturdy wood frame. "I think the real question is who sent you? On whose behalf were you working? Moira's?"

"No." Phineas slid down on the table so that his front hooves dangled over the edge. He drummed them against the stonework like an irritated child. "I was sent by the Steward, as you may have guessed. He has a vested interest in you, I'm afraid, and a rather lousy sense of foresight at times."

A prickle crept over the back of my neck and I leaned forward. "Does he?" Bad enough to be so intertwined with the OtherFolk as I was, but the Steward? I frowned at Phineas, ignoring the strangled sound coming from Melanie. "That doesn't make any sense. I certainly don't have any dealings with the Steward, except for this damned thing." I pulled on the necklace again. "Hell, I don't even know who he is. And what does any of this have to do with my mother and how she got the Key?"

Something sad passed over the unicorn's face, as though he'd aged two or three lifetimes. Gone was the sarcastic, lecherous little beast, replaced by a mien of ancient weariness. For a moment I wished I hadn't asked, but there was no going back. The air stilled into something thick and cloying, the space narrowing down to only the unicorn and me. "He's your father, Abby."

I blinked. "He's what?"

"Bullshit!" Talivar exploded beside me.

"And just who is the Steward?" I sagged, my face suddenly numb in my hands, though I was pretty sure I already knew the answer. My father was still alive? And the Steward of the Fae? Had my mother known? My thoughts tumbled wildly, the words buzzing loud enough that I completely missed Phin's answer. "What?"

"Thomas," he said gently.

I chuckled, the sound sour in my mouth. Several thousand years ago, a certain Scottish bard stood at the CrossRoads with the Faery Queen and agreed to become her TouchStone—an act that shaped everything about mortal relationships with the OtherFolk from that moment on.

I'd always assumed it was a legend, or at least been twisted with time like so many other stories. Hell, once you've got ballads written about your exploits it's pretty much a given that something's going to be exaggerated about them. At the very least, I figured the guy would have died long ago—not been out fathering bastard children with unsuspecting mortal women.

"You're telling me that not only is my father still alive but he's actually True motherfucking Thomas? The original TouchStone? From that goddamned poem? Now I *know* you're full of shit."

"I can't lie," the unicorn reminded me, but his gaze focused on the floor again. "And he's the one who sent me here to keep an eye on you."

"How convenient." I shifted away from Talivar, not really wanting to be touched, even as I felt the oncoming wave of dizziness. A swelling tickle flip-flopped in my stomach and I swallowed it down, my throat constricting.

Choking on the taste of bile, I scrambled to my feet.

"Abby?" Melanie moved to steady me.

I shook my head at her. "I have to get out of here. Now."

"All right."

I escaped into the hallway, refusing to look at Phineas as I strode off. Fury raged within me at the thought of being betrayed. Again. Sure the unicorn couldn't lie, but he could clearly damn well omit stuff if he wanted to.

I brushed past Robert, trying to blink back a sudden rush of tears. The angel stared at me, moving as though to hold up my passage, but one look at my face and he stopped. "Abby?"

"Later." My feet moved faster until I was running. I burst through the doors, heedless of the statuesque angels or the pixies with their little elfshot darts. The leaves crackled beneath my violet Chucks. I was half sobbing now, the setting sun bathing the trees with a hazy crimson halo.

Should I be happy that my father was still alive? Angry because he'd abandoned me? Sad because my mother died alone? The emotional backlash swirled around me until I realized I'd made it down the cemetery path and was heading for Main Street. I caught a few concerned looks from others: a mother pushing a stroller, a man in a mustard coat, the shopkeeper in front of the farmer's market. I slowed down, furiously wiping at my eyes.

For a moment I debated leaving. Just catching a bus to somewhere. Anywhere. Finding a new place and starting over, far away from the OtherFolk. Melanie had always managed it well enough—at least before she came to Portsmyth. On the other hand, she had her violin and a musical talent that surpassed most virtuosos.

I had nothing.

Not even someone I could trust.

I stood on the street corner, unmoving as a wave of tourists rolled past me, sucking me into their midst in a rush of bodies. I wasn't going to go home. Not yet. I needed time to think. My stomach rumbled in protest. And something to eat. Moments later, I was safely ensconced in the rear booth of Gino's Bar and Grill.

The Rolling Stones blared from the jukebox in a tired, worn-out mumble. I barely noticed, keeping myself hidden from the front door. I pulled my hoodie over my hair and ordered a cheese-steak and a heaping plate of curly fries.

I picked at the fries when they came out, hardly tasting the bay seasoning, my fingers drumming on the table. I couldn't stay here all night, but at least it was out of the way.

"Mind if I sit down?" Talivar snagged the bench across from me.

"This isn't a date. You don't have to be polite."

"Thought I'd try." With a wry smile, he ordered a Sam Adams from the server, leaning back to sip it slowly. My cheese-steak arrived, but it stuck in my mouth like ashes. I chewed through it mechanically, finally glancing up at the prince.

"Why are you here?"

"Wanted to make sure you didn't do anything stupid."

"Like run out on you, you mean?" I let out a brittle chuckle. "You found me fast enough."

"I followed you. And duty is what it is." There was nothing mocking in his tone. He took another swig from the bottle. "But that doesn't mean it's all bad."

"I can't say I'm too thrilled with having a huge chunk of my life be nothing more than a lie. Not to mention Phineas knowing this whole time." I bit down on the sandwich savagely. "Where is he, anyway?"

"He went with Melanie. They're trying to find us a mode of travel to find your mother's . . . lockbox, is it?" He rolled his tongue around the unfamiliar word.

"Funny, I don't remember inviting any of you."

"The Key is too important for this sort of petty sniping," he said abruptly, nudging my knee beneath the table. The words echoed those of Brystion and I bit down hard on the inside of my cheek.

My lip curled. "Nice to see I fall into the commodity category for you. A means to an end."

"Not in the slightest. We're practically family, Abby."

I paused, an odd feeling bubbling in my stomach. "How so?"

"Moira and I share the same mother . . . but different fathers."

"You said you killed your father . . . he was the king, right? Then who was Moira's?" The answer snapped in my face, my mouth going dry. "Oh, Jesus. You're saying Thomas was Moira's dad too?"

He nodded. "Or so the story goes. Like I said, paternal rights are usually overlooked. And the Queen . . . well, she is the Queen."

I eyed him wryly. "If you can't keep it in your pants, keep it in the family, eh?"

"I'm sorry?"

I sighed. "Melanie. She told me what you asked her about the other night."

The Glamoured tips of his ears flushed scarlet. "Ah. I did not think she would break my confidence to you."

"Life's a bitch." I took another handful of fries. "Why do you want to court me? And is that even allowed now?"

"Brother and sister have married before in Faerie. In some times it was even expected. Not that it's anything I've ever aspired to," he added hastily at my offended snort. "In truth, I never expected to court anyone ever again." He tapped his eye patch. "Not since this, anyway."

"Perfection."

"And the lack of it," he agreed. "Elven women demand it."

I glared at him. "And so what, I'm supposed to grateful for the leftovers? What sort of pathetic suck up do you take me for?"

"No! I mean that you don't seem . . . preoccupied with such things. The fact that I might be of royal blood holds no weight with you, nor does the fact that I no longer have access to the crown." He set the bottle down, staring at me intently. "These things . . . they mean a great deal . . . to me. And we have things in common. Our scars, for example."

"And here I thought you liked me simply because we were friends." I threw down the rest of the sandwich, my appetite gone. "Not because you pegged me as some sort of . . . cripple." Shame flooded my face. "Here, we can make it just like a real date," I said quietly. "You can pay for my slop and I'll go powder my nose and forget to come back."

I stood up, not looking at the hurt expression on his face, knowing I was being a total bitch. "Enjoy the fries," I snarled, stalking out the door.

Thirteen

The headlights sped past the darkened windows in a blurry haze of bright shadows, the motion filling me with dread. Though it had been nearly two years since the accident, I still got terribly jumpy when I drove.

In the silence, I heard Phineas sigh, the outline of his white form curling up in the seat beside mine. We'd been driving for nearly ten hours, down through New York and over the Tappan Zee Bridge, onto the Garden State Parkway and through the faceless nothing of the New Jersey Turnpike, exits whizzing by us like the come-on of a cheap carnival trick. *Food! Rest! Six Flags!*

I rested my head on my knees, losing myself in Katy's cheerful chatter from where she sat riding shotgun. Given my options, I'd much rather have taken that spot, but I'd lost my license with the seizures and I figured the drivers should get the comfortable seats.

I stared out the window, trying to ignore the other two passengers, but the tension strained between us like a cord of miserable anxiety. Talivar had remained wordless, barely acknowledging my presence since he got home last night and found me packing. Our first real fight, I supposed. I'd

understood his points just fine. I just didn't fucking agree
with them.

I eyed the prince sideways, studying the quiet demeanor
of his face with each passing illumination. Was it being
a warrior that kept him so composed? It was as though he
merely bided his time, clamping down any emotions until
action was needed. My fingers clenched, unable to stand the
quiet between us.

It wasn't even due to whatever romantic notions he had
managed to swing between us so much as the fact that he
was my friend. And I'd lashed out again, like an idiot. I suppose it spoke volumes to whatever bit of friendship we had
that he hadn't packed up and left.

Like Ion.

I'd slept alone last night, my door shut to Phin and to
anyone else. In a fit of pique I'd revisited my Dreaming
Heart, on the off chance Sonja had stopped by. A quick
check showed my note still stuck against the gate. Not only
that, but my Heart was . . . empty.

Brystion was gone.

Sick to my stomach, I wandered the gardens and finally
into the darkness of the woods, but it was a void, the thick
flavor of his essence whisked away as if it had never been. I
couldn't tell if the shields were still in place, but no night-
marish visage stormed my Heart while I was there.

I ached at his loss, though the rational part of me argued
it was far past time. Still, I hadn't realized how much comfort I had taken in his presence. We had a history, if nothing
else. I'd left after only a few moments more, the wind in the
trees whispering in a hollow sigh. Out of a perverse need to
torture myself, I Dreamed a set of wind chimes into being
and hung them in the willow above the bench.

"Good-bye, Ion," I murmured. I woke up to my empty
room, blinking back a soft blur of tears. Pride kept me from

apologizing to the others, but it made for a cold bed and a lonely breakfast.

And I owed Talivar an apology, for certain. Instead, I clutched a battered paperback, willing my hands to still. Phin had been strangely quiet almost the entire trip. But now the unicorn was leaning up against the window, humming something beneath his breath, his tail swinging in time.

"'And she's loving him with that body, I just know it.'"

Melanie picked up the refrain, harmonizing on the chorus, quickly joined by Katy. I remained silent, not trusting my voice to interrupt this rather surreal and spontaneous outburst of Rick Springfield.

My phone vibrated in my pocket and I jumped, nearly dropping it. *Charlie* . . .

"Hello?"

"Abby." Charlie's voice crackled through the speaker, strained and weary. "Where are you guys?"

I gazed out the window. "Almost to Maryland, I think. We're getting there. Singing 'Jessie's Girl,' apparently. How are things going?"

"The OtherFolk are growing . . . restless." Her voice lowered a bit. "We're starting to get fights in the Hallows now. Robert is down there, breaking heads and trying to keep the peace as best he can, but it's a bad situation."

"I know. We're going as fast as we can. How's Benjamin?"

"No different really. I don't know."

"I should have TouchStoned him," I said, cursing myself for my stupidity. Not that I even knew if it was possible to TouchStone a baby, but I should have tried.

She paused. "Well, maybe, but what good would it do if Tresa's spell ended up causing some other mischief?"

"Speaking of which, how is . . . she?" I couldn't quite

bring myself to say her name, a wave of loathing dripping from the word.

"Still at the Judgment Hall. Still a complete bitch."

I grimaced. "All right. Thanks for letting me know."

She hung up and I relayed the information to the others. Melanie didn't say anything, but I could feel the clanking acceleration of the van, a subtle nudge in speed at my words.

I picked up my book, flicking the book light off and on aimlessly. Unable to help with the driving, there was little I could do save immerse myself somewhere else for a bit. The events of the last few days continued to roll through my thoughts over and over as I searched for alternate answers or clues in some distant memory.

My gaze slid sideways to where Phin sprawled over the armrest of the bench. Would knowing his true purpose have made my decisions any different? I bit down hard on the side of my cheek. Probably not, but at least I would have understood the stakes better.

After all, I had a sister now. An honest-to-God sister. Who just happened to be a Faery princess. My mouth twisted at the thought. Somehow being her TouchStone seemed a lot like a crappy door prize. Had she known who I was, that first morning when I entered the bookstore?

In either case, I wouldn't know until I found her again. For now, though . . .

The vampire raised his head, his lips lightly brushing the inside of her inner thigh, causing her to quiver in heady anticipation. Her skin burned with longing, limbs trembling in thwarted need. "Francois," she gasped, arching her back when she felt the skim of his fangs prick at the junction of her sex.

"Angel," he murmured against the taut flesh, the

heated velvet of his tongue lapping at the tiny wound, a
soft growl escaping him—

"Is this the part where he starts to sparkle?" Talivar
snorted over my shoulder. Not exactly a scion of pop cul-
ture, the elf still took a great deal of amusement at mortal
misconceptions.

"None of your business." I slammed the book shut, unable to halt the flush of heat creeping into my cheeks. "I like
smutty romance. So what?"

"Just filling in the blanks." He gave no outward sign of
acknowledging my rudeness from the night before, but the
tactical gleam in his eye suggested he was measuring me up
a little differently now. I wondered if I'd managed to squash
something good, or if I was going to be subjected to a more
traditional sort of hunt.

I shrugged, tossing him the paperback. "Knock yourself
out. If you need pointers or whatever, I can highlight the
good parts for you."

The tips of his ears pinked. "I assure you, I need no such
instruction." He paused and then opened the book, his eye
scanning the pages rapidly. His brow furrowed for a moment and his lips moved as though he were having trouble
understanding the words.

"It tends to get a bit euphemistic," I advised him. "Let
me know if you need a translation for 'purple-headed warrior' or 'gentleman's relish.'"

The prince sputtered for a moment and I felt the smile
creep across my face in return. Not quite all fixed. Not yet.
But a good step.

I resumed staring out the window. So many questions I
wanted to ask my father. Or even my mother, for that matter. Why had she kept him a secret from me all those years?
One more thing I'd probably never know.

The top of the manila envelope with the lockbox key tucked neatly inside mocked me from the unzipped pouch of the backpack at my feet. I had a sudden urge to open it and throw the key out the window, the weight of responsibility resting hard and sweaty on my shoulders. A natural leader, I wasn't.

I swallowed it down, hating the restless rush of anxiety that caused my knees to start shaking. What if the lockbox didn't hold the answer? What if the Key didn't work? My inner voice seemed strangely uncertain, and lent me none of its usual sarcastic comfort. Underneath it all was a soft sort of loss, wondering at the other secrets my mother had kept from me. Had she known what was there? Or had my father merely left her something for her safekeeping, under the pretense of coming back to get it?

"That's not even possible!" Talivar exploded next to me, shoving the book at Phin. "Is it?"

The unicorn squinted at the pages before giving the elf a sly look. "Maybe not for *you*."

"That might actually be a bit of a compliment, Phin." I gently pulled the book out of Talivar's hands. "Now, if you don't mind?"

"Suit yourself. Though I would have thought we might focus on something a bit more serious than reading about a vampire doing . . . *that* . . . to an angel." Mild outrage still tinged his voice.

I raised a brow at him. "And here I thought you were slumming for ideas."

His mouth pursed. "Oh, no worries on that account. Now that I know what sort of things you're into, I'll tailor my responses accordingly." His hand reached to gently brush my knee.

I opened my mouth to snap at him, the motion apprehended by Melanie's chuckle from the front. "What is it?"

"You two. It's refreshing."

"Do tell," I drawled. "Far be it from me to shed light on your only source of amusement."

"It's just sort of surreal to be driving down I-95 with you and an elven prince arguing like an old married couple in the backseat."

Phineas slid off the seat and reared up so that he was resting on the center console. "I could make it even more surreal, if you like." He leered.

"Don't press your luck." She pushed him out of sight. "I think Katy's mom would prefer it if we kept the seats dry. But you know what I mean." She glanced at me slyly from the rearview mirror. "Not quite like the romance books, is it?"

"Is that your way of telling us we've got more important things to worry about?" I sighed, crossing my arms as I shifted in the seat.

"That and I need to stop soon. Think I'm just about at my limit for driving today. I can find us an EconoLodge or something . . . unless you'd rather sleep in the van."

"I can drive another shift," Katy said. "But I wouldn't mind getting something to eat first. Something real." Her nose wrinkled at the crushed bag of Cheetos on the floor. "Something that doesn't taste like it came out of a zebra's ass."

"Speak for yourself. I happen to know some very nice zebras." Phineas sniffed the air. "I think I smell a White Castle nearby."

"Indeed." Melanie said dryly. "Let's see if we can't find one of those box motels and then we'll snag supplies."

I stretched out on the bed, watching Talivar pace. "You're restless," I observed, idly playing with a french fry. Melanie had found us a Motel 6 not too far off the interstate. We hadn't quite figured out what the sleeping arrangements would be, but at the moment we all sat in one of the rooms, scarfing down burgers and fries with abandon.

The prince flopped into one of the overstuffed chairs by the sliding door. "I am worried," he confessed, gazing through the slit in the curtain. "Things were in a precarious position when I left Faerie this last time. I am afraid for my mother's sake."

"Your mother?" Katy said, sipping her Coke. "Is that the Queen?"

I nodded at her, drumming my hands on the bed. "She's ill. And one of the reasons Moira was delayed."

Katy blinked. "I thought you guys had voodoo doctors or something for that kind of stuff. You know, like what they did for Abby . . . or Melanie's hand."

Talivar shifted uncomfortably, rubbing his bad knee. "You do not understand. The Queen is physically sound . . . but her mind . . ." He shook his head. "For the most part she is lucid, but these spells of—madness, I suppose—are occurring more frequently and for longer periods of time." His mouth compressed. "Our healers cannot cure insanity."

Melanie frowned. "Then what happens?"

"It becomes complicated." He rose and started pacing again, with the numbing repetition of a tiger trapped within a cage. "Depending on her supporters, it may be kept hidden for a while, but sooner or later it will come to light and she will have to step down." He stilled, staring straight at me. "And then Moira will be able to make her claim."

"It's not a guarantee, then," I mused aloud.

"There are never any guarantees. And there are some that may take her mixed blood into consideration as a negative."

"Whatever happened to that 'all children are sacred' mantra you've been spouting at me?"

He shrugged, a sheepish smile tugging at his lips. "Some become less sacred than others when it comes to succession."

"Figures."

"I need to get there as soon as I can—to support my mother—or to assist Moira in her claim to the throne, should it be needed." The prince's face smoothed out to emotionless blank. "I was a general in the Queen's army years ago. I have men loyal to me still, and they could help strengthen that claim."

Or help you plan a coup of your own. Something of my thoughts must have shown in my face because he stiffened, bowing to me formally, one hand upon his breast.

"I swear to you that I have no designs upon the monarchy," he said softly. "My vengeance has already been taken and I need nothing else." His gaze met mine. "And you have a responsibility as well, Abby."

"Responsibility for what? Aside from the TouchStone thing, that is." Katy frowned at him, stretching out a perfect set of tanned legs. "I mean, she's not part of any of this, right?"

"When a new monarch takes the throne, certain positions are usually . . . vacated." His pause made it clear that the concept wasn't always voluntary, but I had a good idea of where he was going with the thought.

"The Steward. You want to groom me for the Stewardship. Maurice had it pegged when he captured me in that painting. He said as much to me then, though he couldn't figure out the relationship between me and Moira."

The prince faltered a bit. "But you do admit it would make perfect sense." His brow rose. "You're family, after all."

"A family I know nothing about." I shared a wry smile with Melanie. "I'm a big believer in making my own family. God knows the one you're given isn't always the best. Besides," I added, "I know dick about being a Steward. Hell, I barely know what I'm doing with this Protectorate stuff."

Phineas coughed and I glared at him. "Plus there's the little matter of my father—and Moira's too, for that matter. If Thomas doesn't step down nicely, were you planning on taking matters into your own hands?"

Talivar blinked, suddenly horrified. "Gods, no. If it came down to that, I would see no reason for Thomas not to retain his position to help advise his daughter. On the other hand, he may choose to go with the Queen, should she officially retire."

I glanced at my watch, noting that it was nearly midnight. "Well, as much fun as I'm having playing the 'what-if' game, I think we could all use some sleep." Everyone stopped and stared at each other. "And I suppose that means we need to figure out who's sleeping where?"

"Katy and I will take the room next door," Melanie volunteered, innocently avoiding the eye-dagger I threw at her. "And Phin will come too. That will leave Talivar free to . . . uh . . . guard your body."

"Your funeral. Just watch your backsides. He bites."

Katy grinned. "That's okay. I'm still a virgin, so we ought to get along great." She reached out to ruffle his mane. "Right, Phin?" The unicorn shot me a look of pure terror, but I refused to have sympathy for him.

"Sorry. I'm thinking I could use a night without unicorn drool on my pillow."

"Eww. Seriously?" Katy wrinkled her nose at him. "There will be no drooling on pillows tonight or you're in the bathtub, got it, mister?"

"Kill me. Please." Phineas mouthed.

"What goes around, comes around," I said as they

gathered up the remainder of the food before retreating into the room next door. "Have a good night, you guys." I hid the smirk in my sleeve. "And good luck. You're going to need it."

Talivar snorted softly as I shut the door. "I'm guessing they've never been on the receiving end of his affections."

"Let's not spoil it for them." I chuckled. "Besides, Phin can't stand virgins. He might actually behave." There was a moment of silence then and an awkward shuffling of feet, and I sucked in a deep breath. "Listen, I wanted to say I'm sorry for . . . everything. The last few days—I've been a total bitch."

His mouth quirked up. "You forget—my mother is a queen and my sister is a princess. Bitchy women run in my family." He cocked an eyebrow at me. "Our family."

I shivered. "Yeah, you know, I'm not quite sure I'm ready to accept that just yet, so can we let that part go? Gotta give a girl a chance to get her head straight, you know?"

He gave me a rueful smile. "Of course. But nothing between us has changed—just the relationships of those around us."

"Yeah." I paused. "And I went to the Dreaming last night to see if Sonja had picked up the note."

"No luck, I take it? Judging by the long face, anyway."

"No . . . and Ion was gone too."

"Gone?"

"Yeah. I mean, he's always come and gone as he pleased. But I don't know. My Dreaming Heart was empty. Like he'd taken whatever bits of himself that had been there and removed them." I sighed, attempting to give him a smile that turned out like more of a grimace. "I'm sorry. I guess I shouldn't be so surprised."

He sat down beside me with an air of quiet melancholy. "I do not know all the details of your relationship with him, and I don't need to. But I do know that the man who left your room that morning was quite deeply in love with you."

I nodded, hurt making my face too tight. "I know. And I know why he broke up with me. But I guess I always assumed things might go back to the way they were. Someday."

"What good does it do to mourn him, Abby? Perhaps your disagreement the other night made it clear to him that he couldn't stay. To deny you aid and yet take up your hospitality—well, that's rude no matter what Path you hail from."

"Maybe." I yawned. "And maybe I should just go to bed. Hopefully things will look better in the morning."

"They usually do." He gave my shoulder a quick squeeze, the hand hesitating before stroking my hair. "I will not press my suit upon you if you do not wish it," he murmured. "But perhaps it is also time for you to move on."

My gaze raked his face, seeing nothing there other than his usual grave demeanor—but his eye burned with a sudden fierceness. Was he truly interested? Simply protecting the family name? I had a moment's hesitation, Ion's face blistering its way through my mind. I hardened my heart against it.

Talivar angled my head up, and I allowed him to draw me forward. Our mouths touched, a tentative question, answered in kind. Nothing demanding or insinuating—merely a gentle meeting. My hands roamed over the muscular curve of his shoulder, finding their own way to the loosely tied tail of his sable locks. I toyed with the ribbon, hit with the sudden impulse to set it free.

His kiss became insistent and the elf hadn't been lying about his mastery of this particular art. And yet he went no further than a soft probe of his tongue, lingering at the corner of my mouth.

My fingers wove through his hair, the bedraggled ribbon hanging on for dear life. A hint of mischief struck me and I traced the outer edge of his ear, marveling at its point. A moaning growl escaped him, captured against the side of my neck. He shuddered, pulling back with a gasp.

We tumbled to the mattress, a giddy excitement pounding in my ears. I let it sweep me away, ignoring the subtle differences between now and the last time I'd had a lover. No magical-induced lust here, just a flash of hands and fingers everywhere—sliding up my shirt, down his pants, tracing my hip, stroking his shoulders.

I'd closed my eyes when he rolled on top of me, the warmth of his body stretched out over mine. His hips nudged forward, sliding the length of his erection over my belly, the heat of it apparent even through the thick denim of his jeans.

I found his belt with little trouble, my breath coming in short pants as I struggled with the buckle. He let out a low moan, kissing a hot trail down my neck to my breasts. I froze as a sharp bang echoed off the shared wall between our rooms, followed by Melanie's voice raised in disgust.

The prince and I looked at each other. "Phin." I sighed, my ardor dropping like a thermometer in January. "Nothing like an oversexed unicorn to ruin the moment."

"Enough." He grinned at my utterance of disappointment. "I refuse to have our first time in this place of cheap bed linens and moldy bathrooms."

"Willpower of a warrior," I grumbled, my body not really caring about his sudden sensitivities. "And would you be so picky upon the battlefield?"

"This is merely a battlefield of a different sort." He tapped my nose in mock admonishment. "Besides, I suspect there may be a bit of an audience next door." He leaned forward to nip at my ear. "And I like my lovers noisy with their pleasure."

I flopped onto my side, ignoring the rising flush of my cheeks and the frightfully fast way I seemed to be breathing. I let my fingers drift over his hand, marveling at the way they slipped so easily between his, shivering as he raised them to his lips. "So what now?"

"So now we go to sleep," he said, a tinge of regret in his voice.

"That sucks." I let him curl around me, some unspoken agreement between our bodies allowing me to fit inside the protective curve of his frame. "However will you make it up to me?"

"I'll stuff you full of pancakes tomorrow," he said, capturing my mouth fiercely again. "And bacon," he added, before turning out the light. His head settled on the pillow next to mine, one hand draped over my hip. "And when things slow down enough, I'll make you a *very* happy woman."

"That had better be a promise," I whispered, fighting the urge to squirm against him. "Because I intend to hold you to it."

He let out a soft chuckle. "I'm counting on it."

Fourteen

I swirled up the last of my pancakes in a flood of butter pecan syrup and washed down the sugary goodness with a cup of Lipton, sliding against the seat of the corner booth. IHOP was apparently a swinging place to be this morning.

"Hey, don't be a bacon hog." My backpack rocked against my hip insistently. "Some of us can't look all human and shit." This last was directed at Talivar, of course, who was sitting directly across from me. He was Glamoured, as usual, his mortal semblance wrapped in a sweatshirt and jeans, the dark hair still tousled in a sort of bed-head chic.

Melanie sat beside him, half dozing over her third cup of coffee. "That piece of shit doesn't *deserve* bacon," she growled, cracking open a single bloodshot eye at the backpack. "Between the snoring and the . . . biting."

Katy shuddered next to me, heaping a huge dollop of whipped cream out of the way of her chocolate-chip smiley pancakes. "He didn't bite me, but he was in my suitcase. Rolling in my . . . my unmentionables. There's glitter everywhere."

"Rooowwwwrrr," came the purring retort from my side. "I like the lace. Too bad Abby doesn't wear any."

Katy made a face. "I can't believe you live with that."

"I did warn you," I said archly, taking another sip of tea. And then I jumped, the tea sloshing over the top of my mug to puddle on the table. I managed to muffle the yelp, shifting away from the backpack. "Bite me again and you'll be lucky I don't leave you in the Dumpster."

"At least I'd get something to eat there," the unicorn retorted.

"Fine." I carefully slid a slice of bacon off my plate, casually pretending to drop it on the seat. I unzipped the top of the backpack, narrowly escaping Phin's quivering nose as he thrust it through the tiny opening.

"Gimme." He lipped at the grease-laden strip.

"Don't make a mess," I warned him. "I'm not cleaning you up later." A soft chewing sound was my only answer. Something nudged my foot and I glanced up to see Talivar eyeing me slyly from across the table. The nudge became suggestive, a lazy stroke up my calf bringing a rush of heat to my cheeks. "Isn't it a little early for that sort of thing?"

"Did you get enough to eat?" His voice was innocent. Lazy. *Content.* I half hid a smile. Regardless of the lack of any true action the night before, he certainly seemed rather smug. I wondered at it, struck by a vision of a formal dining hall out of some fantasy book, imagining the courtiers flirting in such a way. How long had it been for him? And still, there was the underlying question beneath the question.

"Maybe." I dropped my eyes to look down at the dregs of my tea, pretending to ignore the soft rumble of his chuckle as he bent to finish his own plate.

"Nice to see you guys managed to patch things up," Melanie interjected dryly. "You sure you two don't want to be left alone in the booth for a midmorning quickie?"

"I think we'll manage playing footsie under the table,"

Talivar said, shouldering her gently. "Besides, we should probably get going, yes?" I sobered a bit at the thought, knowing this last moment of respite was over. At least bacon had been involved. Katy took one look at Melanie and sighed. "Guess I'll take first driving shift?"

"It's all yours." Melanie stood up to toss a twenty on the table. "Let's make some time."

The bank manager was tall and blond and had a smile that screamed "arrogant prick," but he settled down after my credentials checked out. He ushered me into one of those tiny windowless rooms meant for exposing secrets. It pressed down on me as I sat at the offered table. Like a funeral parlor, only with the cloying scent of money instead of embalming fluid. With a swiftness that belied his larger stature, the man reentered the room to place the battered box before me. "It's all yours," he said, retreating. "Take as much time as you need."

The door shut behind him with a gentle click. I could only stare at the box, the key trembling between my fingers. I resisted the urge to wipe my hands on my pants. What if the answer wasn't there?

"Then this would be a long-ass waste of a trip," I muttered, though in truth, I didn't believe that. At the very least, I might get a last bit of closure. Without pausing to think, I slid the key into the lock, the release switching with a snick.

Sucking in a final breath, I opened the box.

And found . . . nothing. I stared at the empty space, my mouth dropping before I slumped down in the chair in a wave of misery. All that for nothing, indeed. And even though a perverse edge of relief poked through my thoughts, it certainly wasn't anything I could admittedly hope for.

I ran my fingers inside the edges of the box as though

some mysterious bit of parchment might materialize between them, but was met with more of the same. Sighing, I struggled against the urge to pound the table. "Fuck."

Scooping up the box, I relocked it, poking my head out the door to gesture to the manager. Wordlessly, I watched him take it and disappear into the hidden bowels of the bank, a dull ache taking root in my chest. As much as I hated to admit it, there had been a part of me that had hoped beyond hope I'd find some lost part of my life nestled away in a secret corner.

Grimly, I left the bank, Melanie's questioning eyes following me as I approached. I brushed past her to crawl into the van. If I looked at her, I was going to cry. I didn't want to cry yet.

"Well?" Phineas tapped me with tiny hoof.

"There wasn't anything there," I mumbled, wiping at my eyes. "Not a damn thing."

"What do you mean? Surely there was something in the box?" Melanie turned from the front seat to face me.

"That's just it," I said, anger at the situation leaking into my words. "It was empty. Not even a photo or a postcard or anything." I stared dully at the unicorn. "Fool's errand." I yanked on the necklace with a sudden fury. "And this fucking thing is useless."

Katy gave me a sympathetic look. "Well, maybe it was a mistake? You know, maybe something was supposed to have been put in there, but your mom forgot?"

"My mom never forgot anything. I mean, shit, there wasn't even anything that would have been useful financially—no shares of stock, none of my grandmother's jewelry . . . nothing."

"But if she was wearing the necklace when she died, Abby . . ." Melanie let the thought trail off.

"*If* she was wearing it. What if she wasn't? What if this

is something else entirely?" I closed my eyes, the minutes ticking by in a haze of sunshine as I tried to figure out what to do.

"Take me to the cemetery," I said finally. "Might as well attempt to make peace while I'm here."

"You sure?" Melanie glanced at me, but whatever she saw on my face shut her up and she nodded, starting the van. Katy brushed her hand gently on my arm as I crouched there between the seats, sucking in air through my nose.

"Abby?" Talivar's voice broke the silence but I shook my head at him. It was all a little too much. The engine rumbled, the vibration shaking beneath my feet and I closed my eyes, letting the rhythmic sway of the van capture my attention.

"It's just past Williams, right?" Mel asked.

"Yeah, then the first left. It comes up pretty quick, though." I could picture it in my mind, the way the road ambled past the shops and the grocer's, a playground and an assisted living facility. And then, boom, there it was, nestled in a quiet crook of a street, all sparkling and granite. The headstones loomed, masking the fragility of the place—as if by asserting themselves so firmly there could be no denial of the final journey.

The gravel ground beneath the tires, popping against the rubber. I opened my eyes as Melanie slowed down, curving the van to rest in the flowered cul-de-sac. Katy squeezed my arm again. "Do you know which one is hers? Maybe one of us should go with you."

"I'll find it." I pulled the door open. Phineas's gaze sidled away from mine. "You're coming with me." My fingers slid through his thistledown mane, the muscles of his haunches bunching as I scooped him up. He squirmed slightly, but didn't protest. "We'll be back in a few," I told the rest of them.

Without waiting for a response, I tucked the unicorn beneath my jacket. The cemetery was empty and silent, and somehow I didn't think anyone was going to be looking too closely at what I carrying. I scanned the headstones, transported for a moment to that bitter day two years ago when I sat in my car in the rain, staring at my hands on the steering wheel. My fingers tightened in remembrance, relaxing as Phin let out a grunt.

Sucking in a hollow breath, I pressed forward, my feet carrying me to where I knew the site to be. The starkness of the shadows skittered over my skin, a crow's distant caw breaking the silence. I knew some people found cemeteries to be comforting places, but I wasn't looking for comfort at the moment.

"Why did you lie to me?" I glanced down at the unicorn, as though I might continue to deny where I was headed. *Ever the coward, Abby.*

"Technically, I didn't."

"You withheld information about who I was and what you knew." I ducked beneath the falling branches of a weeping willow. *Third row from the left and beside the second bench . . .* My aunt's voice wheezed from the lower levels of my conscious, where I'd so conveniently stuffed it.

"You let me think the TouchStoning thing was an accident."

He stiffened, and for a moment I thought he might try to wriggle free. "You never asked," he said finally, but I thought I detected a note of guilt in his voice.

"You never gave me cause to doubt you before. Don't do it again." I shook my head, mentally counting the tombstones, my gaze somehow getting captured on the little vases of plastic flowers, a handwritten note tucked beneath one with a childish scrawl. I swallowed past the lump in my throat. "You report to my father?"

"No. I wasn't supposed to interfere. Just observe."

"Even when I was trapped in Maurice's painting? I find that hard to believe. You know, given that two of his daughters were missing by that point." A thought struck me. "Does he . . . uh . . . have any more? Children, that is?"

"This isn't a conversation that's mine to be holding. I suggest you save these sort of questions for when you meet him. Assuming you want to, that is."

"Jesus, Phin. I don't know." Anger bubbled up in my throat. Ion had warned me, hadn't he? Hell, even Talivar pointed out that I was becoming a pawn for the Fae. It hurt beyond measure to think it would come from those who should have been protecting me.

"It's right there," Phineas said, his voice soft. I shivered inwardly, glancing over in the direction he indicated, though how the hell he knew where it was I couldn't have said. I wasn't sure I wanted to ask. But yes, there it was, a curving sweep of polished granite with a simple beveled edge. My mother's name etched beneath a single heart in a flowery script. *Jessica Anna Sinclair. Beloved.*

That was it. Nothing about being a mother. No solemn platitudes about God or an angel's grace. Just her name, and the respective dates.

I traced one hand on the outside of the stone, expecting it to be cold as my fingers feathered over the edge. I was tentative, suspecting it might bite, images of that long-ago night flashing through me over and over in a blur of lights and metal. Before I would have shut down, pushed the memories away, but I couldn't afford that now.

In the end, it was merely stone, nestled among a clump of decorative grass and a cluster of foxgloves.

I sank to my knees, barely noticing as Phin shook himself free. I couldn't remember who had made the arrangements, only that I had been told she was buried while I lay in my coma. I had assumed it would have been my aunt, but what if it had been my father?

"Did he love my mother?" The words were abrupt, as though I might swallow them if I didn't get them out. And really, what sort of question was that? How could he have? After all, my mother had barely mentioned him other than to tell my ten-year-old self that I did, indeed, have claim to such a mystical being as a dad.

Not that I'd even had so much as a picture. Nothing other than whatever strangeness I might have seen in the mirror, anyway.

The unicorn sighed, sitting down to lay his head upon my knee. "These are not my questions to answer," he repeated. "But I suspect so. As much as he might have been able to."

"I thought he was the Queen's lover?"

"Yes. But she has granted him certain . . . allowances." His cobalt eyes glimmered up at me sadly. "But he knew about you, Abby. That's why he sent me to watch you."

"Fat lot of good it did me," I said bitterly, inclining my head toward the stone. "Or my mother."

His ears flattened. "Don't blame me for that," he snapped. "Mortal foolishness took your mother's life. And even if I had been there, there's nothing I could have done."

I stared down at him. "I thought unicorns could bring someone back to life."

His upper lip wrinkled. "It's a bit more complicated than that. It's like a bee stinger. I only get one chance at it."

I blinked. "And then what? Your horn just falls out?"

A scowl crossed his face. "Never you mind. Here," he pawed at the cluster of grass in front of the stone.

I leaned closer, fingers pushing down the blades. A shiver ran through me at the metaphysical stickiness. A Glamour? Someone had put a Glamour on my mother's grave? I peered closer to the stone, blinking as the cobweb feeling fell away.

Beneath her name was a series of small pictures, similar to the little memorial settings I'd seen on other stones. Something told me these were a bit more permanent than pewter, however.

The photos were old and faded. Shots from my youth, then. Polaroids, maybe. The first was an image of my mother in her late teens—one I hadn't seen before—her hair falling in soft waves around her shoulders like sunlit honey as she sat on a fallen tree, her blue sundress lighting up her eyes. A distant smile flitted across her face, the expression causing an answering echo in my heart, knowing I'd caught myself with the same look numerous times.

I swallowed hard at the next one. My mother held an infant version of me in the crook of her arm, my tiny eyes dark with the secret wisdom babies always seemed to possess. What had I been thinking then, beyond the small cocoon of flannel blankets and the bobbed hat over my head? A funny half-smile curved up the edges of my tiny pink lips as we stared at something together, my mother and I.

And then the third picture came into view and I stopped breathing. *Him. My father?* I refused to give him the title of "Dad." The shot just held his face, blue eyes sparkling at some hidden amusement. His hair was an ash brown, loosely framing high cheekbones and a strong chin. He seemed young, but I'd been a TouchStone long enough to recognize the signs of agelessness when I saw it. There were eons of years etched in the faded crow's-feet at the edges of his eyes. Handsome and self-assured, for certain. This was a man who knew his charismatic power and how to use it. And yet, I hoped for my mother's sake that whatever affection he'd shown her had been at least somewhat honest. "Thomas," I breathed, reaching out to touch the image.

And plunged into an ocean of memories . . .

"*. . . who's my little princess?*" *I bounced upon my daddy's*

*knee, stubby fingers grasping a shiny yellow button on his shirt,
my infant voice shrieking with delight as he tickled my belly . . .*

*. . . I was being rocked into the darkness, the soft flannel of
his vest against my skin, the perfect tenor of his voice rumbling
through his chest . . .*

*. . . my parents kissing in the kitchen, the gentle sound of
laughter as I shoveled mashed bananas into my face . . .*

"I remember," I breathed, withdrawing my hand. "How
is that possible? What the hell sort of Glamour *is* this?"

"I don't know how it was done," the unicorn admitted.
"But I know that certain memories of yours were removed.
For your own safety."

"Of course they were," I snapped.

"He'd like to see you at some point."

"I'm sure he would. I wanted a pony when I was seven,
but just look at how well that worked out." Anger flooded
my cheeks as I focused on the picture of my mother and me.
Her free hand was raised up to her shoulder, as if to finger
something at her neck. A necklace? "Motherfucker."

I spared a quick glance behind me at the van. Talivar
leaned against the door, watching me gravely. He cocked his
head and I waved my hand at him. *Soon . . .*

"I suppose there's only one way to find out about this
Key thing."

"And what is that? It's not like you're going to be able to
send Thomas a message. Not with the CrossRoads closed."
Phineas flicked his tail as he stared at the pictures.

"No." I traced my finger around the portrait before facing the unicorn. "But I might be able to ask the previous
owner. After all," I smiled grimly, "she haunts my dreams
even still."

Fifteen

The creaking of the house echoed dully without Bryston's presence. But that was probably all for the best, given my mission. The overt sensual darkness that normally loomed seemed a shadow of its former self, and yet a faint pulse of his power threaded through me as I traversed the hall. I was surprised at the emptiness, but then perhaps I had not realized how entwined with my Heart the incubus had become.

I scanned the living room, but saw nothing out of place. My mother rarely made her presence known these days, though I suspected much of that had to do with Ion more than any desire of my unconscious mind.

We had left the gravesite and headed home shortly after my discovery. I'd kept the memories of my father to myself, as well as my potential plan for trying to discover more about the Key. Not because I didn't want to give the rest of them hope, but it seemed terribly cruel to dangle a possibility of success, only to fail and disappoint.

Plus, even I had to admit there was a certain flaw to the logic that depended on the nightmare-visage of my mother for the answers.

Katy had made the disappointing phone call to Charlie,

and a silent and solemn trip home was all that remained to us. Melanie and Katy traded shifts every few hours as we drove through the night, the urgency of our failure pushing them through their exhaustion. Given the late hour of our arrival, Melanie dropped me off at my apartment with Talivar and Phin, and I stumbled up to my room to attempt a Dream. I finally drifted off with my head in Talivar's lap, the unicorn at my feet.

And now I was here, drifting aimlessly from room to room in my Dreaming Heart, searching for the core of my nightmares. *Mother . . .*

I left the house, the rooms oppressive in the darkness. The trees pressed upon me, the scent of pine lingering when I pushed past the branches to the moss-covered steps and then to the gate.

My fingers tapped over the lock, the clank it made seeming somehow dull in the twilight. I stared out into the darkest part of my Heart, knowing the incubus had had his place out there in the grove, but I would not find my mother in his sacred shadows. A dappled road stretched out before me, curving past the gate to skirt the edge of the woods.

I followed the road, my feet bare upon the cobblestones. I walked cautiously, not really wanting to break through the Dreaming. After all, I'd done that once before, and without Ion to bring me back, I might end up trapped on the other side. I shuddered.

The path changed into something golden and I realized it was sand, the wind picking up briskly so that it swirled past my face. Grass crept over the edges of the road, sparse at first and then I sunk into the sand dunes, ripples rolling beneath my feet. A chill slithered over my skin, toes sinking into the fine grit.

The landscape changed again and I was walking on the sharp edge of a cliff, the sea below churning angrily. The foam gleamed beneath the shattered softness of moonlight, but did nothing to quell the sick roil in my belly. I knew this place. Knew the bladed shadows that cut through the waves with a deadly slickness.

I supposed I was safe enough, but I wasn't foolish enough to think I would stay here with the sharks down below.

I never did.

And yet, there seemed to be a hint of confusion in the way the silver dorsals split the night like metal sails. It was unusual for me to seek them out directly, I suppose. I sucked in a deep breath, and peered below, sharp teeth lost among the whiteness of the foam.

A crackling sound swept through the air from behind me. I didn't look up as her dry husk of a voice sputtered its question at me.

Why?

"I don't know," I said quietly, the way I always did. I never knew quite what she was asking.

"Why?" She whispered it again, a bony hand grasping my shoulder. I opened my eyes, clamping down on the terror lancing through my breast. I turned and there she was, brittle skin stretched tight over the remainder of her face, one eye nothing more than a milky white haze over a dull blue. The rictus of her mouth filled with only teeth, naked and gleaming in her pearled jawbone.

I exhaled in a choked sob, forcing myself to see her, the memory of that picture of her on the tombstone superimposing itself upon my vision. I shivered, gathering up my power, ragged as my control was. Brystion's voice danced in my ear, reminding me of what I was.

Dreamer . . . you have the power . . .

I blinked back the tears, blurring the scraps of honey-colored hair hanging from the naked skull and the shattered brainpan, pushing outward, stretching the bubble, willing things to be how *I* meant them to be. How I needed her to seem, whole and unflawed.

Her flesh rippled, a cocoon of silver enveloping the edges of her cheeks, as though I might knit skin and bone, muscle and sinew and delicate tissues, a hidden memory of the soul beneath.

"Why?" She breathed the word, but it sounded clearer this time, lips solid and plump. I glanced up as the halo of her eyes receded into the piercing blue of youth. A flicker of recognition sparked there.

And still I didn't know how to answer the question. Why was she there, in my dreams? Why had she died?

"I don't understand," I murmured finally.

"Why do you keep me here, Abby?"

Guilt tore at me, my knees shaky. "I don't mean to. I don't know how to let you go." The sharks circled below us, frenzied in a flash of whitecaps and salt.

"Ah," said the shade in a somewhat disinterested tone. "Mortal memories, made flesh for your amusement."

"No," I told her, swallowing hard. "That's not it. Or at least not what I intended." I reached out. "Mother?"

"As you remember me to be," she agreed, taking my trembling hand. The skin was warm and smooth, alive beneath my fingers. She rubbed her thumb gently over my palm in her old way.

"I remember this," she breathed. "I remember you." A frown slid over her face. "But I don't remember how I got here."

She paced away from me and toward the dunes, pulling me along. Her grip was surprisingly strong, constrictive. A niggle of warning brushed the back of my mind. *Careful what you invite into your Heart . . .*

And the truth of it was that this was *not* my mother. No

matter how much I might have wished it. She was merely a memory, a nightmare made flesh in my Dreaming. I pressed past the thought, unsure of how long I could hold her in this form.

"Why didn't you tell me who my father was?" I couldn't quite keep the brusqueness out of my voice; the strain of weaving the Dream to her image was making me weak. A thread of anger crept into the words, wondering at the need for such secrets.

"I didn't know, at first," she said simply, turning those brilliant eyes upon me. I fought the urge to pull away from her. There was no warmth of her previous existence within. "And then, when I had you, he left. It was to protect us, you see." Her voice dropped low, the way it had when she had something important to tell me. Odd. After all, it wasn't like anyone was going to overhear us, was it? Like whispering to someone on the phone while you're alone in your house. But I took the bait, anyway.

"Protect us?"

"From the Queen, of course. Jealous thing."

I stopped abruptly. "You knew the Queen?"

"Tom would never allow such a thing. But he knew the Queen wouldn't be happy if she discovered he'd gotten me pregnant. So he stayed as long as he could, but in the end he had to go." A sandpaper sigh escaped her. "I miss my Tom."

"And you were *okay* with this?" The mother I remembered had been gentle, sure, but never one to just let someone roll over her. For the life of me I couldn't imagine her doing anything so . . . so timid.

Focus, Abby . . .

And yet, what was I supposed to do? Come out and ask if dear old Dad had left her the Key to the CrossRoads? Assuming she even knew what it was. I wouldn't have hesitated if it this was my real mother, but a brightness sparkled

in the depths of her eyes with something far more predatory
than had been her wont.

I had to be casual about it. Careful. "I don't suppose he
left us a memento? You know, something for us to remember
him by? After all, I'd like to get to know my roots."

Her hand reached up as though to play with something
around her neck and I knew I'd hit on the right topic. "There
was a necklace. He gave it to me when we were courting. In
a small velvet box, if I remember . . ." Her voice became
dreamy, and I winced at the naked longing within. "Silver,
with a large jewel. He never did tell me what sort of stone
it was, and I could never quite figure it out. It seemed to
change from day to day. I meant to get it appraised once, but
I always seemed to get distracted."

The hairs on the back of my neck rose. Glamoured, of
course. I stifled a shiver. Whatever was going on here had
been a long time in the planning, leaving me and my mother
in the cross fire.

And it was seriously starting to piss me off.

For all that my father was supposed to have the gift of
prophecy, he would have a lot to answer for, assuming I ever
managed to find him.

"What happened to it?"

She frowned. "Funny that you ask. I could have sworn I
was wearing it . . . but I can't seem to find it. I can't imagine I
would have misplaced it like that. I loved my Tom, you see."

"Is this it?" I swallowed hard, pulling the amulet from
under my shirt to show it to her. Her fingers caressed it
gently, thumb stroking the stone with a hint of possessive-
ness.

"Ah, yes." She took a closer look at it. "It seems to be
broken. It used to sparkle like mad—a brilliant blue glow.
That's too bad."

My heart sank and I sighed, realizing I'd hit another dead

end. My heart twisted at the thought of raising her memory for nothing.

My arm brushed something cold and I looked up. We were standing outside the iron gates. They were closed and glittering with their own silvery light beneath the rust. The edges of my old home, my Heart, gleamed through the trees in the distance, beckoning to the soft comfort within.

"Won't you invite me in?" I glanced at my mother sharply, the wheedling tone very unnerving. I swallowed hard, a warning bell ringing through my mind. It was so tempting to let her pretend to be what she once was, but it would be a lie. A pleasant one, at first, but even I knew it would mean my doom. If I brought her shadow further in, I'd never be able to let her go.

"I might be able to fix your necklace if you let me in," she continued. "It's missing a spark."

The gate pressed into my spine. I'd retreated before her. *Giving ground,* my inner voice noted. A piece of paper flickered in the corner of my eye and I snatched it up. Something was scrawled on the back in Ion's neat script.

No regrets.

I crumpled the note in my fist, terror and sadness banding over my heart. "No," I whispered. "I can't."

"But you've brought me so far already," she persisted. Her hand tipped my chin up so that I was forced to look at her face, requiring me to deny her directly.

"It's as far as I can take you, Mom." Something hot blurred my vision, scorching down the side of my face. Her gaze became curious as she captured it, turning her fingers to peer at the crystalline softness of my tears.

"And yet you still weep," she said wonderingly. "Was it so very difficult, my death?"

"You wouldn't remember." The wind picked up around me, whispering its song of despair and I knew I wouldn't be able to hold on to the Dreaming for much longer. Without Ion here, I would plunge into nightmare. That I'd managed as long as I had surprised me as much as anything.

She stared off at something I couldn't see. "I remember a car and you. And then . . . nothing. And yet, here I am, day after day."

My knees started to buckle and I grasped the gate in support. The metal burned, lancing heat up my arm. Something fluttered to my feet in a golden heap.

Her hair . . .

Her grip tightened around my wrist, the knuckles suddenly brittle and pale. I knew before I looked up what I'd see, but I did anyway, trying to school my features into blandness at the balding head, the way the flesh sloughed off to reveal the moon-round skull, the mangled mouth, the dulling eyes.

"I remember," she sighed, leaning forward to brush my forehead with the remains of her lips. "Death is a funny thing sometimes, the way it happens. But it's not the going that's the sad part, Abby." She pressed something hard and gleaming into my hand. "It's the leaving."

I choked on a sob, the wind whipping around us with a sudden howl. I could taste the sea on it, echoed with a rotting odor beneath. My mother crumpled into a small pile of bones, my name nothing more than a dusty whisper as the gate opened behind me. Gasping, I tumbled backward, clutching my mother's parting gift as the Dreaming disappeared into a misty fog of dried leaves and darkness.

I clawed my way to the surface, coughing abruptly, to find Talivar lightly slapping my face. "Wake up, Abby," he growled, frustration sharpening the tautness of his mouth.

"I'm awake." I curled into a ball on my side, as he stroked the hair away from my eyes.

"You were crying."

"I found her." I curled up tighter, my hand clutched to my breast. "She wanted to come inside my Heart." My lip trembled as the tears began to spill again, the words rolling bitterly off my tongue. "I couldn't do it. Sonja and Ion both warned me against it . . . but it was so hard."

His thumb rubbed over my lower lip. "Brave warrior. You have the courage of a lion."

"I don't feel brave." I pushed down on the bed to sit up, exhaustion making my limbs tremble, hardly hearing Talivar's sudden intake of breath.

"Holy shit!" Phineas reared. "You're glowing, Abby."

"Not Abby. The amulet." Talivar reached gently for the necklace. In the dimness of my bedroom light, the jeweled center winked with a silvery-blue shimmer.

"She gave me this," I murmured, eying the crystal with a certain wariness. "I think it was one of my tears." It shifted in the twilight with its own inner brightness . . . now a sapphire, now a bloodied ruby, fading into a diamond . . .

I blinked at it. "Mom wasn't all that informative, but she did say it was missing a . . . spark."

"I suspect perhaps this 'spark' was inside you all along," Talivar said quietly. "You just needed to know it was there and have a way to draw it out."

"No." I twiddled the amulet between my fingers. "The magic was trapped between worlds. My mother died here, but my dreams were keeping some part of her alive. I had to let her go before it would work for me." My throat constricted against the truth of the words and I knew I would most likely never see her there again.

"Hell of a way to go about finding it." A sharp bark of hysterical laughter escaped me. "You'd think these mystical gewgaws would come with directions or something." I held the crystal up to the light, watching the play of colors scatter over my palm. "Never mind that. Do you think it will work?"

Phineas leaned forward to sniff it. His horn brushed the gem and a pure chime rang out. His ears flattened. "There's really only one way to find out."

I looked at the clock, sighing when I saw the time: 5 A.M.

Talivar pressed a kiss to my forehead. "Go on back to sleep. I'll contact the others and tell them we'll meet them at the Judgment Hall in a few hours."

I thought of that pile of bones outside the gates and shuddered. "I don't know if I can." I shook my head at them. "No, I've slept enough. Besides, the sooner we open the Door, the happier everyone will be." My eyes flicked to the window, the dim glow of false dawn hovering behind the blinds.

"Time waits for no man." I nudged him with my shoulder. "Or prince."

He eyed me gravely, a tight smile creasing his lips. "No, I suppose it doesn't."

Sixteen

My brother is an ass." Sonja rolled her eyes before hugging me tight. "And I'm going to slap him upside his thick head next time I see him."

"Thanks. I guess." Her wings wrapped around me briefly, tickling my nose with their softness. The Judgment Hall swirled around us with energy, a mass of tired bodies and anxious glances. I caught a few familiar faces in the crowd—Didi the pixie in Barbie pink, a pair of undines, a cluster of angels—visitors to the Midnight Marketplace and friends from the Hallows. Finding Sonja here to see me off was a nice surprise, though, all things considered.

She'd been caught in the backlash the same as the rest of the OtherFolk, but had been unable to make it back to the Dreaming without getting to the CrossRoads first.

"Stubborn prick always did need to figure things out for himself. But men are stupid."

My mouth quirked. "So you've said. Are you sure you won't come with us?"

"No. I've no dealings with Faerie and seeing as you've already got a way in, I think I'm going to sit this one out."

Her dark eyes became troubled. "As much as I hate that bastard Maurice for what he did to us, I'm just as happy to leave what happens to him up to Moira."

"I'm surprised you weren't called to testify as to what he did."

"I was. I didn't go." Her nostrils flared at my expression of surprise. "Don't judge me, Abby. The Fae may think they've got the right to demand their answers, but it's my people's blood that allowed it to happen. I don't want to know how he did it . . . and I don't want anyone else to either."

I looked at her pinched face and nodded. If things were different, I might have pressed, but we had bigger issues at hand and she'd clearly made up her mind.

"Sorry to interrupt, Abby, but it's time." Talivar tapped my shoulder, handing me my backpack. He gave the succubus a polite nod as I shrugged into the straps. I didn't have much in it besides an extra change of clothes and a few protein bars. Haute cuisine it wasn't, but I figured it would get me by for a couple of days.

"Good luck." Sonja brushed a kiss over my lips and slid into the crowd in a whirl of feathers. Talivar and Phineas flanked me as I strode toward the dais where Roweena currently held court, allowing my mini-entourage to push away the crowd with a flurry of tiny nips on the unicorn's part. Talivar stared down anyone foolish enough to stand in my way and that seemed to work just as well.

"Well?" Roweena got to her feet, a graceful swan among the masses.

"Is this all of them?"

"All who chose to come," she said, her eyes drooping in a weary acceptance. Underneath it I knew she meant that there were some who could not make it, given whatever state they were in, or some who just chose not to. And then there were the ones who were too weak to have lasted even the few days I had been gone. Some of their bodies had been brought over by van, their Glamours faded away like dying leaves; without the magic of the CrossRoads, all that remained were the fragile husks of their native forms.

"What do I have to do?" I fidgeted beneath the weight of stares upon me, eager to get moving.

"The Door beneath the Hill. It's a direct conduit for Fae royalty to our realm . . . and the one most likely to react to the Key. If we can keep it open long enough to let those who might choose to pass through to the CrossRoads, as well as messengers, that should work."

"All right." Melanie poked me in the arm, her violin case on her shoulder and a small rucksack falling down to her hip. "You ready?"

I shrugged, trying to quell the butterflies in my stomach. "You sure you want to come?"

"Are you kidding?" She smiled, tucking an unruly red curl behind her ear. "Besides, my feet are aching to move. That little road trip of ours sparked the urge to do some rambling. Might as well go somewhere I've never been, eh?"

"And if we all end up getting killed?"

She raised up a finger, her chin lifted. "To die would be an awfully great adventure," she quoted.

"As long as it's not your last."

"Ah well. Second star to the right and straight on till morning and all that shit. What about Benjamin?"

"Staying here for now." It had been a tough decision, but as terrible as it was to make, I couldn't see potentially walking into an OtherFolk mess with a baby. God only knew what we'd be getting into, or what we'd meet on the other side. I'd TouchStoned him this morning anyway, sealing the bond with a kiss to his forehead. I caught a fleeting glimpse of the world through his eyes, soft and hazy and full of milk and a contented belly and that was that.

He'd let out a gurgling laugh and yanked the hair stick out of my bun, but even I had to admit there was a little more color to his face. At least this way, I'd know he'd be okay, even if the CrossRoads only stayed open for a short while.

"If we can make it to Faerie safely, Talivar will send for him then, or go back to get him. If we're really lucky, Moira will be able to come for him herself."

Phineas prodded me in the calf with his horn. "Quit stalling, you two. Let's do this bitch."

"Aye, aye, Captain Small Shanks." I pulled the amulet from beneath my shirt, the glow illuminating everything nearby in a soft blue aura.

Roweena blinked. "Well, you managed to get it working, anyway. This might actually have a chance at success."

"Don't let your confidence in me get in the way or anything."

Talivar squeezed my hand. "Peace. And let me take the lead, once we get through the Door."

"All yours."

The elf had changed into an outfit I hadn't seen before, dark leather vambraces at his wrists and a thick vest over his tunic. His sword hung lose at his side, but now he also had a massive bow slung over his shoulder, a quiver of nasty looking arrows bristling at his hip. His hair was neatly braided and tucked out of the way. "It's like having my very own pet Legolas."

His mouth curled up in a private smile. "You have no idea."

I coughed suddenly, the four of us following Roweena through the inner workings of the Hall. The Door beneath the Hill was a bit of a misnomer as it was really embedded in the basement of the Portsmyth Catholic Church. An underground corridor connected it to the Judgment Hall, allowing OtherFolk on specific royal business to travel freely without the need for Glamours.

Behind us trailed the remaining OtherFolk. "We'd better not fuck this up," I muttered beneath their heated stares.

"What's all this 'we' stuff? Last I checked you were the bearer for the damn thing." Phineas trotted ahead of us a little faster, hooves tapping out a quick rhythm. Beside me, Melanie began to hum "We're Off to See the Wizard."

At last, Roweena stopped. The corridor split here, but the reason for the halt soon became evident. An elegantly carved Door arched to the left, Celtic knot work leafing the sides in silver-gilt intricacies.

"It's said these designs hold the secret to the CrossRoads themselves," Talivar mused, one finger reaching out to trace the pattern. "Though none of us has ever truly figured it out."

"Yeah, well, I'm gonna leave that up to someone else," I said.

Melanie coughed something into her fist that sounded an awful lot like "MarySue," but I let it slide. After all, she played a magic fiddle. Not like she had any room to talk.

Holding the amulet in my hand, I approached the Door, the stone shining with an even stronger light. Encouraging. The OtherFolk gazes hungrily strained toward me. I could hear Talivar snapping at them to get back, his sword humming as he walked a perimeter around our little group. Normally I would have assumed the Protectorate's word would have been obeyed, but the circumstances here were a bit strained, not counting the close quarters and the different Paths mixing together.

Behind him, Tresa sat in a cart drawn by an enormous white stag, its cloven hooves the size of dinner plates. And by sat, I meant she was bound and gagged for good measure. The Fae woman looked a bit worse for wear, her hair matted in greasy tangles, but I wasn't particularly heartbroken about it. Our eyes met and she sneered behind the gag.

I hadn't wanted to bring her along, but Talivar insisted we take her straight to the Queen. He knew his mother best so I couldn't see much point in making a stink about it. Anything to get this resolved faster was fine by me.

The Door began to vibrate, the stone arch shaking when I touched the carving. The stag bugled, and Talivar snatched at the harness, giving it a sharp tug.

"Open," I said hoarsely to make myself heard above the panicked cry from the rear of the crowd. Dimly I wondered if there would be reports of a low-scale earthquake in the papers tomorrow or some crazy story about the church collapsing upon a host of daemons.

I closed my eyes. Heat radiated from the stone beneath my fingers. A thread of power snaked through, golden and commanding. The Queen's? It was as though there was a veil between us, and my amulet poked holes through the seams.

Frantically the golden thread tried to sew up each pocket, but the faster I pulled, the sloppier the thread got. The veil bowed toward me, the power of the CrossRoads slamming against it like a silver river. Leaks dripped from the holes as I punched through, the magic pooling at my feet.

The golden thread spun faster, but it was already too late. I opened my eyes to see the Door glowing, silver and blue sparkles shining as it opened—only to be crushed into the side of the wall as the mob screamed past me a moment later, grinding my face into the carving. The breath rushed out of me in a whoosh as I struggled to regain my feet. Talivar shouted my name, and I caught sight of his head above the crowd. I pressed toward him, wincing as someone's hoof slammed down hard on my foot.

"Hold on!" I could see his mouth moving, but his voice was lost to the echo. He gestured wildly at me, his fingers pointing at my head. "—turn around!"

I barely threw my hands up in time to catch the brutal antlers of the white stag bearing down upon me, the traces half snapped from the cart. Tresa had curled into a ball, her hands still tied behind her as she tumbled into the side rail.

Abruptly the stag shook its head, snorting into my face, the whites of its eyes rolling madly. I winced as a prong cut into my palm, grunting when the deer plunged forward through the crowd, lifting me like a rag doll. I clung to my perch, trying to avoid having my legs trampled. I caught one last glimpse of Melanie, her jaw dropping before she disappeared from sight.

Everyone disappeared, for that matter, and I realized we'd entered the Door. The silver sparkles flew over us, stirred up by the churning of the hooves grinding into the CrossRoads. Where the fuck was the beast going? Did I just hold on and hope it stopped somewhere? Did I attempt to roll out of its way? Where would I even end up?

My arms burned with a dull ache from holding myself up for so long. "So much for a well-thought-out plan."

Here I was on the CrossRoads for the first time. For real. Alone.

Good times.

Before I could come up with any strategy that didn't end up with me becoming mincemeat beneath Rambo-Bambi's hooves, the stag stumbled. The slick road slid out from underneath us, and its antlers tore from my grasp as it sprawled onto its side, sending me flying into a moss-covered ditch. I attempted to roll without slamming my head into the ground. My bad knee wrenched hard when I landed, crack-ing with an audible pop.

The cart hurtled from the road and disappeared into the soft mist. Beside me, the stag chuffed, sides blowing hard. I skirted its lashing hooves; it couldn't seem to get up. My knee protested violently as I staggered to my feet. Limping, I gingerly circled the deer, keeping a sharp eye out for Tresa.

And then I saw the arrows.

Two of them—the fletching set with oily black feathers. *Talivar's.* One set in the rear flank and one further along be-neath the ribs. I wondered if it had nicked a lung. The stag's eyes had already started to glaze over, a sickly yellow foam pouring from its nose.

Poison? I retracted my hands quickly from the arrow. Not much point in trying to pull it out now. If it was poison, it was fast acting, and if there was any coating the outside of the arrow? No thanks.

The stag let out a shuddering sigh and went limp. A trickle of blood leaked from its mouth. I glanced behind the way we'd come, seeing nothing but darkness. Still. If Talivar had followed, we'd left him far behind.

"Oh the humanity." My backpack was a little shredded from when I fell, but still in working condition, its contents mostly unharmed. I pulled out Charlie's iron blade from where I'd tucked it and slid it into my back pocket.

She had willingly parted with it once I told her where I was going, though I hated the fact I thought I'd need it at all.

I hadn't told Talivar I had it. Undoubtedly he'd be in-sulted I didn't trust him to keep me safe, but here I was. Iron was often considered contraband upon certain parts of the CrossRoads, but to my knowledge there was a certain amount that sold under the table. TouchStoned Fae were able to resist it up to a point, but I was pretty sure getting caught taking it directly into Faerie wasn't going to make me any friends.

On the other hand, dying for a set of principles that weren't mine seemed rather foolish.

Like my last venture onto the CrossRoads, I could see nothing but shadows all around me; the light from the road was the only source of illumination. That, and my amulet.

I quickly tucked it beneath my shirt. With any luck the Glamour would still work, but no sense in taking chances.

Now what, Abby? Last time I was here I'd ended up in the Borderlands, which was a land between Paths. The denizens there held no allegiance to anyone, except maybe a high bidder, and this time I didn't have the others to save my ass. Best to stay on the road, and try to find my way to Faerie.

My knee screamed when I started walking away from the deer, heat swelling at the lower part of my thigh. A familiar sensation and one that usually meant a few days of keeping it propped up with a bit of ice, but there wasn't much chance of that here.

I retraced the way the stag had come, finding the spot where the cart had upset. Soft silver grass grew along the edges of the road, the blades flattened wetly against the ground, leaving me with little doubt as to why. The cart itself was only a few yards away. One wheel had been completely shattered.

There was no sign of Tresa save the tattered remains of her gag. I debated the wisdom of trying to track her down in the darkness. Uneasy, I retreated to the road, hearing the creak of something grinding into the cobblestones. A strange wooden caravan pulled by a set of pony-size elephants emerged from the mist; each carried the pink spiral shell of a snail upon its back.

I blinked. Mollusk or pachyderm? "Either way, double the trunk space . . ."

At the reins sat a wizened little man with a set of antenna sprouting from his head. A dark-eyed woman crouched beside him, their faces nothing more than a fat pile of wrinkles. They regarded me cautiously, stopping the wagon when they saw the stag.

The dwarf snapped his fingers and a third being emerged from inside one of the wagons. He only came up to my chest, but his face was that of a pig, his broad snout waggling comically. Tattered, dirty rags covered his feet. He grunted as his tongue slid from between thick lips to moisten his tusks.

"Dids ye kills it?"

"Erm. No." I shook my head.

"Steals it belike?"

"No. I just . . ." The words died on my lips. I had been going to say I'd found it that way, but the old adage about lying to the Fae held true. The Fae, even the lesser ones, assuming that's what these folk were, could taste lies as they were spoken. I didn't need to offend anyone yet. I gave the pig-man a weak smile. "It's complicated."

"Aye. I can sees that." He snuffled at the stag's body, coughing when he saw the arrows. "Ach. They've the swamp oil on them." His beady eyes roamed over me for a moment. "And yer name?"

"Ab—" I hesitated. Names were power here. Yet if the others came looking for me I would have to give them a trail they could follow. For a moment I almost said Bacon-hag, but given the porcine demeanor of my present company I decided against that.

"Ab?" His mouth bristles twitched.

"—sinthe. Call me Absinthe." It was lame, but maybe someone would figure out that Absinthe could maybe be short for Abby Sinclair. Probably not, though.

"Not much of a green Faery, are ye?" The pig-man chortled, ears flopping forward. "Ye can call me Jimmy. Jimmy

Squarefoot if ye like them proper sorts of manners. I can see ye have bloodies on yer hand."

I glanced down, surprised to see the dried blood on my palm. As though recognizing it made it more real, it suddenly began to sting. "Yes. I hurt it. When I . . . fell. Hurt my knee too." I lifted my pants leg to show the already bruising leg.

"Ach well. Ye are welcome to the back of the wagon there. We're headed to the Barras, if that interests ye."

I frowned. "Like the one in Glasgow?" I'd vaguely remembered hearing Melanie talk about it once when she'd done a musical tour of Europe, but other than that I didn't know much about it.

"Aye." Jimmy gave me a sly smile. "It's on the move, ye ken. Never in the same place twa', but all signs point in this direction." He craned his head behind him. "Now, hop on, Absinthe. We've a ways ta go, and 'tis not safe to remain in one spot long. Not with the daemons on the move."

I shivered. "Daemons?"

"Aye," he said cheerfully. "A whole damned army of them. They will nae bother us at the Barras, but better not to tempt fate, aye?" Something in his face made me wonder how much of that was true, but I wasn't going to get anywhere on my own with my leg the way it was. Besides, I didn't doubt Tresa was long gone—and if she decided to get reinforcements I wouldn't have a chance. Waiting for Talivar might be a better option, but if I could get to the Barras, I might even be able to get a message through to Moira.

I limped behind Jimmy to the wagon. He said something to the driver in a language I didn't recognize and the woman clucked at the elephants. Jimmy nimbly leaped into the bed of the cart to help pull me up. It was full of small mushrooms.

"Truffles." Jimmy snuffled them with a contented air.

I gently carved a place for myself, trying not to squash the spongy things. My eyes drifted past the white deer, and I shuddered at its rapidly stiffening form, great black stains on the snowy hide growing from where the arrows sprouted. Like some sort of evil plant. What sort of fruit would these bear? I half expected to see the body explode with maggots. I said as much to Jimmy.

He popped a truffle into his mouth, eyes closing in satisfaction as he slurped. "It's quite a deadly poison, that swamp oil, but nothing so vulgar as all that. There aren't many as would use it." He shook his head at me, giving me a sympathetic eye. "Bad business, this CrossRoad shite, that I can tell ye. Did ye get caught up in it, ye being a half-breed and all?"

I blinked at him. "A half-breed?"

Jimmy grinned, tapping his snout. "Finest nose in six counties," he said proudly. "I can smell the Glamourie on ye, sure enough . . . and yet, there's iron in yer blood. What else could ye possibly be?"

I schooled the frown on my face. Glamourie? Must be the necklace, I decided. He couldn't see it, but he could sense its magic. And there may well have been iron in my blood, but I wasn't going to enlighten him to the dagger in my pocket either. Omission didn't count as lying directly—Phin had taught me that much.

He grunted and offered me a truffle, which I quickly pocketed.

"For later," I told him. In truth I was ravenous, but I wasn't eating jack shit from anyone here unless Talivar said it was cool. I'd read Rossetti, after all. "I uh . . . don't suppose you know the way to Faerie?"

"Suit yourself." He popped another mushroom. "They lets me eat them as I like, since I'm the one what finds them for the trade. Not much of a wage, but it does well enough, especially these days. And aye, I know the way to Faerie. Not going there, I'm afraid."

"Is it very far?" I made a few mental calculations, though seeing as I didn't know how far I'd gotten being carried on the stag, it was a bit of a moot point. If I could get to some central location, maybe I'd be able to meet up with the others there. Maybe.

"Depends on how ye go. Shortest if ye take direct to the rough country, but there's boggles and Unseelie wights aplenty that way." He snorted at me. "And ye don't seem the type to be able to take care of yourself out there, begging yer pardon. Besides, the road to Faerie is damn near tight as a cork up a barrel bung these days."

I chuckled and Jimmy flushed. "I've got . . . family there."

He eyed me appraisingly. "Aye, I suppose ye might. Mayhap they'll let ye in." His gaze roamed over my clothes. "Though ye might want to consider a different type o' dress. The purists do not always take kindly to mortal trappings." His nose twitched. "And they willna like that bit o' iron on your person, whatever it be." I blushed and he laughed. "I may be old, but I'm no' daft, lass. Iron in yer blood ye may have, but not to that extent."

I pulled it out of the sheath, displaying it hilt down. Discretion might be the better part of valor, but I didn't need my newfound guide turning on me.

He whistled low when he saw the blade. "Me and the Tipperaries here don't mind it so much. We're of stronger stuff than those high Sidhe sorts, but if ye tries to enter Faerie carrying a weapon likes that, ye willna be making it back out again, if ye catch my drift." My dismay must have shown on my face, for he laughed again. "No worries, lass. The Barras are a good place to lose somewhat, and if ye let me do the bargaining for ye, we might turn enough of a pretty penny to buy ye rags worthy of your station."

I nodded at him. Not like I had much choice at the moment, and anything that would make moving through the CrossRoads easier would be a good thing. I yawned into my hand. "How long until we get to the Barras?"

"Ye've got time for a wee nap, if ye like. There's a bit of setup of the stall when we gets there, but that willna take too long."

"Good enough," I sighed, my head tilting down onto my backpack. Might as well catch a few moments of quiet while I had the chance. I watched the CrossRoads spill out behind us like a silver river of light, sparkles churned up by the wagon wheels until I couldn't fight it anymore.

"Wake me up when we get there," I muttered, my eyes drifting shut despite the creak of the wagon.

Dreamless, I slept.

Seventeen

Dozing in a wagon full of fungi must have been more restful than I thought, as the next thing I remembered was a hand on my shoulder gently shaking me awake. I blinked into consciousness, only to see Jimmy's snout quivering with an expectant twitch. "Aye, then, Absinthe. We've arrived at the Barras. Best watch your wee step, like. It's right barmy outside."

I poked my head out of the wagon, blinking at the mad rush of beings clattering by us. I'd thought the Midnight Marketplace was chaos, but this . . . this was pure anarchy. Tents of various shades sprawled haphazardly in every direction like a Renaissance Faire on crack, interspersed with wooden stalls and roving food vendors. Smoke billowed up in small pockets, advertising cook fires or blacksmiths, perhaps. Someone was playing a hurdy-gurdy nearby, and the music swelled through the roiling cacophony of conversation and laughter, creating a din of monstrous proportions. I gaped for a moment, trying to take it all in and quickly gave up. "'You'll not find a more wretched hive of scum and villainy in all the galaxy,'" I quoted softly.

Jimmy clucked at me. "Aye, it's a bit much if ye've never

seen it before, but if we can get ye dressed proper, ye'll fit in just fine. Though 'hive' is probably a good enough word for it, especially this part here."

"How long will you be here for?" A nervous tickle pulsed its way down my spine, a sudden longing to lose myself in the hustling crowd outside mixed with the need to find Talivar and Melanie.

"Some leave when they sells out. Some stay. I canna give ye a better answer than that, lass. What I can tell ye is ye've got to get your wee arse out of the cart." He winked at me. "We've 'shrooms to sell."

I slid out of the wagon, brushing a squashed truffle from my backside. My knee buckled and I propped myself against a wheel, frowning at my leg. "Betrayer," I accused it, swinging it in and out to test it, nearly kicking the little old wagon driver who had chosen to come around the corner at that moment.

His beetle eyes darkened and I apologized quickly, though I was pretty sure he didn't speak English. I sure as hell didn't speak bug, though, so I suppose that made us even. He clicked his mini-mandibles rapidly and made a shooing gesture.

Jimmy looked up from where he was tying up a cloth overhang above the lip of the wagon bed. "He thinks ye will attract the wrong sorts of attention standing there like at. Any chance ye can look a bit more . . . natural?"

"It's been a bit of an odd day," I said sourly, staring openly at a hefty gnome leading a string of clockwork chickens.

"Aye, well ye look like a bloody tourist. It makes ye stand out. Even more than your garb. Have ye got a hat? Mayhap if we covered your face up a bit . . ."

"I get it, I get it. And no, I don't." Scowling, I limped to the front where the elephants were tied up. They were certainly cute enough. Of course, they also stunk like the backside of an elephant, so it didn't take me too long to realize I didn't really need to hang around there either.

"I'm going to take a look around," I said to Jimmy. "Maybe I can find someone to trade that blade to."

"Dinna wander far, Absinthe. There's slavers about as well, ye ken? If ye look like easy pickins, they'll pluck ye right up. Of course, ye are taller than most," he admitted. "Should not be too hard tae pick ye out o' a crowd o' crows. I'll catch up with ye in a moment."

"Lovely. I'll stay in this main row, then." Not that it was a row so much as a series of gutters, loosely linked by mud and horseshit, scattered tents and awnings perched in a multihued riot of colors. It was as though someone had vomited a bag of Skittles into a cow pie and then tossed a bouquet of roses on top of it to cover the smell.

Wary of what would surely be an excellent place for pickpockets, I gripped my backpack tightly and limped down the first row. Now that I'd gotten my bearings I could see that although there was quite the mishmash of OtherFolk here, they tended to cluster themselves by type. Jimmy and his fellow compatriots were squarely centered in what appeared to be bug central.

Bulbous eyes, chitinous shells, segmented antennae— everything from boy-size cockroach men to ladybug girls to pixies with butterfly wings. And Jimmy was right. I did pretty much tower over everyone. Of course, I also had to quash the urge to crush half of them underfoot. Humanoid or not, my first instinct was to stomp the unholy bejesus out of anything with more than two legs.

That or scream like a little girl.

Neither of which was going to get me anywhere. I browsed the various clothing vendors, watching with fascination as silkworm women spun their thread directly onto the looms. A maggot shyly held out a fragment of the silk so that I could touch it. I rubbed it between my fingers, strangely tempted. What would such a dress be like? Would Talivar like it?

I flushed as the thought crept through my mind. *Foolishness,* I thought. *Plus silk is a bitch to get the wrinkles out of.*

"If ye had the time and the money, ye could buy a bolt of it," Jimmy observed from behind me. "And then we could take it up to where the high folks do their buyin' and get them to make ye something nice. Seein as ye have neither, I'm afraid we're stuck with something more practical."

"Practical means boring." I sighed, my hopes of a real princess dress dashed. "And I don't really have time for this anyway."

The pig-man squealed with laughter. "Practical means sturdy and well made, lass. Ye dinna need glass slippers to prance in shite."

I glanced down at my mud-spattered Chucks. "No, I guess not. Where to, then?"

Jimmy snuffled into his sleeve. "We best heads down to the Lower Crescent. There's them what might take that wee dagger off ye, and won't tell tales about it neither."

An uneasy feeling threaded its way through my gut. "And what to people do with these types of weapons? I don't want to be providing ways to . . . kill."

"'Tis your call, of course, lass, but looking as ye do, it's quite probable someone's going to challenge ye and takes it. Might as well get somewhat for it, aye?" He eyed my leg with a worried frown. "And I think we might get ye a bit of a stick too. Ye can use it to walk and to bash someone over the head with."

He slowed his gait so that I could keep up with him, pausing here and there to wave at various vendors, friendly greetings passing back and forth with ease. Regardless of the language, bargaining was pretty much the same no matter what. I even found that I recognized some of the merchandise. At least if I got stuck trying to buy something here, I might actually have a clue about what a fair price would be.

The rickety stalls took a darker air, the cheerful little bug town slowly disappearing. Furtive looks and murmurings dominated the row. The colors bled dark and rich with a hint of seduction, but I could nearly taste the scent of decay beneath it all, like an overripe fruit. Probing too deeply here would surely reveal an underbelly of massively seedy proportions.

"So, Jimmy, why so eager to help me out? Not that I'm not appreciative," I said hastily, trying to cover up my own discomfort. If I was talking I'd look like I fit in, right? "I'll admit I wasn't really expecting more than a lift."

"Ah, well, ye have a touch of destiny about ye, lass." He tapped his nose gently. "I can smells it, ye ken? But to be honest, I was hoping ye might use your connections."

I stared at him blankly. "My what?"

"The Sidhe," he said impatiently. "There's a lot of bad blood between them and the lesser Fae these days . . . and with the CrossRoads shut down, there's many of us with family stuck on the other side. The pointy-eared gits won't tell us anything. Not to mention the lack of income. If ye truly are a changeling of the Sidhe . . ."

"I don't understand. There certainly seems to be a brisk business going on here, if the crowd is anything to measure by."

His snout wrinkled at my words. "Aye, but when the Queen banished us all from Faerie proper, it put a damper upon our way of life, if ye take my meaning. Not all of us enjoys sleeping on the road." He gestured at the hive. "Those wee silkworms, for example. Used to spin the very silk the Queen herself wore . . . but now?"

I frowned at him. Had Talivar known about this? Surely if the Queen were that mad someone would have stepped in and prevented her from doing so? My silence must have stretched on too long because he shook his head a moment later. "I'm sorry, lass. I forgot you're new to it all . . . but just, if ye could . . ."

"I'll speak to Talivar." I said the words without thinking, my mind still wandering over the possibility that the prince could have known and not done something about it. Or even Moira, for that matter. "When I see him again," I added lamely.

Surprise flickered over Jimmy's face. "Ye know the Crippled Prince? Truly?"

I swore inwardly at my stupidity. Nothing like giving away your hand before you've seen the ante. "Um. Yes. I guess so." I neglected to mention that he was sort of my not-by-blood-half-brother. And maybe my almost boyfriend. "Is that an issue?"

"I would use caution about where ye tossed that wee bit of information about, lass."

"I'm his TouchStone, actually. I was . . . trapped here." Technically not a lie, since without knowing where the other Doors where, I had no real way of getting back.

"Aye, well, then that changes things," he murmured, glancing down at my knee before taking my wrist in a meaty hand. The heavy knuckles were gnarled and broad, as though he spent a lot of time . . . *rooting*. "Come on."

Bemusedly I limped behind him, letting him lead me through the crowd. "Changes things how?" I said aloud, my other hand sliding to where the dagger rested in my pocket. Not that I had any intention of actually attacking anyone, but I wasn't planning on letting him possibly lead me to the slaughter either.

Run-down stalls of rotting wood and old cloth lined our

path. Someone had thrown down a series of thick planks on top of the filth in the gutter, a fact I was terribly grateful for. Bad knee or not, I'd take a little pain over slipping in shit any day of the week.

A goblin woman in front of us carried a slim basket full of blackened fruit, jewel-red juices leaking from the sides like blood. Jimmy nudged me when he saw me staring and I adopted a bored mien as he led me deeper down the row, taking us through a maze of twists and turns until I couldn't tell which way we'd come.

My heart started beating a little faster as visions of being shanked for my shoes crept into my mind. "Where are you taking me?" I dug my heels into the slime-covered walkway. Jimmy didn't answer, raising a finger to his snout.

"This way." He released my hand, gesturing at one of the faded tents. A small bamboo fountain trickled aimlessly in front of the opening, its green sprouts looking terribly out of place. "Someone here who can help you find your way . . . and maybe do somewhat about your leg."

A frown tugged at my lips. "I don't understand."

"The Crippled Prince has many allies here," he admitted after a moment. "And I owe him money from the last time we played cards."

I nodded gravely. The repayment of debts was taken very seriously among the Fae, and I knew I'd have to be careful of my words. Pulling the tent flap open, Jimmy slipped into the darkness and tugged me behind him.

The strong scent of ginger struck me hard, burning in my nostrils as I blinked through a wash of tears. Beside me Jimmy wheezed. Small wonder, given how much he'd gone on about how strong his sense of smell was. Why he wasn't crouched on the ground crying was beyond me.

My eyes adjusted to the shadows, finding solace in a few burning candles perched on a low table, the wax tapers dripping onto the tent floor. A hiss of fabric called my attention to the woman kneeling behind the table. She stared at me with a porcelain smooth face, her eyes crinkled with soft laughter. Fine red hairs upon her fox ears captured the flickering light, outlining them in a halo of gold. A kimono of brilliant buttercup silk was wrapped around her shoulders, a white obi belted at her waist. Kitsune, I observed from the hint of a white-tipped tail trailing behind her.

Jimmy coughed hard, his piggy eyes streaming. "I've brought ye a guest, mistress. She's one of Talivar's. I've got to go." He gave me an apologetic shrug. "Allergies."

The fox-woman smiled, lips closed. "I'll see to it, Jimmy." The words rang out in a crisp tone, clearly not meant to be defied.

Jimmy coughed again. "Luck," he whispered and slipped out the front of the tent before I had a chance to ask him anything else. I felt a momentary sense of panic, wondering if I'd be able to find my way back to the wagon.

"Sit," the fox-woman commanded, one delicate hand sweeping out toward a square pillow opposite from her.

I weighed my options for a moment and then carefully sank into the pillow. We sat there in silence, the minutes ticking by. Outside, the sounds of the busy street faded until it seemed as though the world had shrunk to only this little space. The candle flame guttered and I noticed a steaming cup of tea directly in front of the woman.

"I would offer you some, but you would not drink it." She picked up the cup with both hands and sipped it slowly.

I raised a brow. She was right on that account, anyway. "No."

"Why have you come?"

"I should think that was rather obvious," I said dryly. "Seeing as you know Jimmy brought me."

Her eyes flickered with impatience. "Why are you here?"

"What is your name?" I countered. Quid pro quo and all that.

"Kitsune is what you named me in your mind. That will do for now."

"That is what you are, not who." She remained quiet, sipping her tea as though I hadn't spoken. I ground my teeth together. "I'm stuck," I said finally. "I don't know how to get home and I don't know how to get to Faerie. I've got . . . a message for the Queen."

She let out an eerie bark of laughter like a fox yipping and the sound sent a shiver down my spine. "The Queen, is it? I do not think you will find what you are looking for there."

"Maybe not," I said, unwilling to mention much more. It wasn't her business anyway. Something warm brushed my face and I glanced down to see that a small cup sat before me now as well.

"Drink," Kitsune insisted. "It's a healing tonic. Very strong medicine."

"And what? I become your slave for the next two hundred years? I don't think so." I pushed the cup away gently. "All I want is to find the Crippled Prince."

She stared hard into her cup. "Are you sure that is all you seek?"

"Of course not," I said wryly. I didn't like the way she was twisting the request. "Besides, what difference does it make? The prince, a way out of here, and a chance to find the woman who betrayed us. That's all I seek right now." My thoughts tumbled over an image of Ion for a moment.

Kitsune reached down at her side and pulled out a small spool of red thread. "Destiny weaves as it will and the path to your goals may not be as direct as you'd like."

I huffed a sigh and pushed to my feet. "Esoteric words of

wisdom don't impress me. And I've had enough of destiny to last the next few lifetimes, so you'll forgive me if I decide I don't want to be a part of it."

"You cannot outrun what is faster than you." She thrust the spool into my hands. "When you leave here, simply roll the thread upon the ground and it will take you to your heart's desire." At my snort of disbelief, her ears flattened. "No one will bother you if you follow the thread. Interfering in another's destiny is . . . unwise." The last part was said with an exceptionally feral grin, her teeth clipping hard upon each word. I caught the faint outline of a fox muzzle overlapping her mouth, nearly superimposed upon her face, but it was gone before I could truly see it.

"And why would you do this? Help me, that is? Color me skeptical for not believing you're doing this out of the goodness of your heart."

"There are some here who would see the Crippled Prince upon the throne. Whether that is good or bad, I cannot say but I do recognize the Key when I see it, and I would not have it fall into the hands of someone who might force the issue." Her golden gaze dropped to my neck and my face flushed. "It's not nearly as well guarded as it ought to be," she said, her eyes suddenly sly. "It could be that you're not its true mistress."

"Nothing I wanted to be," I agreed. "And I thought Talivar couldn't rule?"

Kitsune folded her hands neatly upon her lap, seeming to diminish before my words. "It all depends on which kingdom you speak of. As you will, then. May you find what you seek."

I clutched at the spool and gave an awkward bow, unsure what else to say. When I looked up, a large vixen sat where she'd been, the grin still pasted eerily across her lips. She let out a soft yip.

"That's what she said," I muttered, emerging into the relative hustle of the Lower Crescent. The lingering scent of ginger chased me up the row like a mocking roll of laughter. I shivered, clutching my backpack a little tighter. At least it masked the fetid odor of dung.

I glanced down at my hand with the thread. Now or never I supposed. I stopped, waiting as a daddy longlegs shuffled by, ridden by a pair of pill bugs. Feeling like a complete ass, I took the end of the thread and tossed the spool onto the ground.

Where it did nothing.

"Fabulous." Soft snickers came from the nearby stalls. Fuck it anyway. I'd find my own way to my destiny . . . whatever that was. Unless the spool was insinuating that it lay here, but judging by the way some people seemed to be packing up I had to wonder. "Just get me out of here," I said finally, blinking in surprise when the spool jerked upright and began to roll forward.

Still holding the end of the thread, I limped behind it bemusedly as it picked up speed and disappeared into the busy crowd, slicing through the earth like a crimson sash. I hoped no one would step on it. Before long I was back where I started, but the spool didn't stop there, slithering down row after row until I began to suspect it was toying with me.

I let out a snarl, frustration tensing my jaw. For a brief moment I wished I was still TouchStoned to Brystion. The incubus had always had a major talent for finding me before. I could have sat in that 'shroom cart all day and waited for him to sweep me into some sort of gallant rescue.

"Waste of time wishing for nothing," I said to myself. I leaned heavily on my good leg, resting beside the last of the stalls. The thread was leading me toward a steep hill. A string of horses was tied to a series of poles below, surrounded by a primitive paddock. I was no judge of horseflesh, but even I could recognize the sleek musculature shivering between the glossy coats as the sign of what could only be magnificent animals. I gave their backsides a wide berth, even while admiring the curved haunches and the smartly polished hooves.

"You've got to be shitting me," I said when the last of the spool ran out right before I reached the horses. Surely I wasn't supposed to just steal one and Lady Godiva my way out of here?

"Brilliant creatures, aren't they?"

I stiffened, glancing up in surprise to see Tresa standing beside me. She'd found some new clothes, or at least a new cloak, the sable wool wrapped tightly around her shoulders. She still looked the worse for wear, I noted with a tinge of satisfaction as I took in the tangled mess of her hair and the swelling bruise on her chin. Her cheeks pinched inward when she saw me looking. "I owe you for that," she murmured, rubbing it with a self-conscious glare.

"Don't flatter yourself," I snapped. "You're the reason we're all in this damn mess."

She let out a humorless chuckle. "Am I? It was not my idea to shut the CrossRoads down, nor mine to banish the Lesser Fae from Faerie. Ask your precious prince to tell you about the true extent of his mother's madness. If not for *her*, none of us would be in this mess."

"I doubt you've made things any better." Reservation gnawed at my belly. She still seemed far too rational to be some mere revolutionary.

"There's a war coming," the Fae woman continued, "and there's not a one of you who will be left standing by the time it's through."

"And I'm sure once Maurice gives you whatever he promised you this place will become a land of sunshine and happiness, right? Lollipop guilds and all? You're the one who's mad if you think that asshole will give you anything other than a quick death."

She looked away. "He has my son."

Sympathy struck me at her words, but something still wasn't adding up here. I understood the mama-bear concept fine—after all, if someone were to take Benjamin, there probably wasn't much I wouldn't do to get him back—and that was before I knew I was actually related. But still. "So you decided to betray your people? Besides, last I heard Maurice was still in prison. How could he have taken your son?"

Her head snapped up, her nostrils flaring. "Do you think I lie?"

"You can't lie. I get that, but you sure as hell can choose not to answer an entire question. I call bullshit. Why not go to the Queen?"

"You understand nothing," she said bitterly, going very still. "There's still time. Give me the Key and I may be able to right things. Maurice would take it as a trade, I'm sure of it."

My hand touched the amulet as though to reassure myself that it was still actually there. "I can't. Even if I wanted to, I couldn't. It won't come off." Something I was terribly grateful for at the moment. The thought of Maurice with such a talisman didn't bear thinking about.

Her mouth tightened. "Pity." She moved forward, her feet squelching in the mud, though her limbs were shadow-swift. I spun, wincing as her fingers snagged my hair. I swung wide with my fist, the sting of my knuckles acknowledging that I'd made contact. My knee screamed in rebellion and I knew I wasn't going to win this. Time to regroup.

Ducking into the herd of horses, I slapped them on the rumps as I passed, narrowly avoiding being kicked.

"You can't outrun me," Tresa jeered, sliding between their legs.

"No," I agreed. "But they can." The piebald mare in front of me reared when I jerked hard on her lead rope. Tresa chuckled.

"Foolish girl. You think the Sidhe leave their pretty ponies tied with anything so mundane as mortal rope? It cannot be undone by any save the owner."

Well, shit. I tugged again on the rope. The knot certainly looked as though the slack would simply fall out, but it remained steadfast. The mare snapped at me, her ears slanted back. "Hell with this." I whipped out the iron dagger, half intending to throw it at the woman.

A roan stallion began to buck and I heard shouts from up on the hill. I glanced up to a cluster of elven men running toward us. Tresa continued to advance, pulling a stout walking stick from beneath her cloak.

On impulse I slashed at the rope attached to the mare, blinking as it began to smoke. A moment later there was a snapping sound. The mare wheeled and took off, her unshod hooves making dull thuds as she galloped away.

"Iron to break a Glamour," I breathed, rushing to cut the other ropes. If nothing else, I could cause a distraction, but best case I might even manage to ride one out.

Tresa snarled at me when she saw the dagger. "Cheater," she hissed.

"Yeah, well." I cut through another set of ropes. "I don't pretend to be anything else." By now, the horses were a squealing mass of rolling eyes and heaving sides, clearly uncomfortable at having two random strangers weaving between them. A stallion nipped Tresa hard on the forearm, and she let out a high-pitched scream.

"Abby!"

Talivar? I swung toward the voice, my knees going weak with relief as the prince vaulted over the outer fencing. I waved frantically at him as something slammed into my shoulder. Off-balance, my arms windmilled and I fell to the ground, Tresa pressing me facedown into the dirt.

I scrabbled in the mud, pulling my good knee up beneath me to try to roll out from under her. One arm wrenched free and snatched something soft. Her hair? Without thinking I yanked hard, concentrating on causing pain as opposed to any sort of logistical tactic. My eyes rolled sideways between the rush of horse legs, catching no sign of Talivar. A sizeable crowd had gathered at the edges of the paddock, looking none too pleased at the situation as several of the horses barreled through the gate and up the hill.

"Thief!" Tresa called suddenly. "Horse thief! She's cutting the ropes with an iron blade!"

An angry rumble started up and I began to struggle in earnest. Tresa alone I might be able to escape, but a furious mob of Fae were another thing altogether.

Did the Fae hang their horse thieves? I had no doubt I wouldn't get much chance to explain myself. Tresa disappeared into the dust, ducking beneath the wheeling punch of an elven blacksmith. "Good enough for the goose and gander." I jerked back as fire lanced through my fingertips. Someone was grinding my fingers together. The knife fell from my hand as I tried to roll away, wriggling out of another's elf's grasp.

Not fast enough.

Immediately, my arm was jacked up behind my back, my legs swept out from under me.

"Stop moving," grunted my captor, bending my wrist to emphasize the point. I bit back a yelp and did as I was told, turning my face so that I wasn't breathing dirt.

"Let her go," Talivar commanded, striding over to where I lay. He yanked the other elf off and gingerly helped me stand.

"My lord, she was stealing the horses."

"She was doing no such thing," the prince snapped, wrapping his cloak around me, his leather armor creaking. "The lady is my TouchStone and will not be treated as a common criminal, is that understood?" His eye narrowed when he saw Tresa struggling in the arms of two other elves. "That one, however, is another matter."

Tresa jerked her head upright. "Sanctuary," she cried, her eyes glittering with desperation. "I call sanctuary."

"And I deny it," the prince said, gesturing at his men to tie her up.

"Sanctuary here is not yours to grant or deny, my lord prince." Kitsune's words swept past us like a breeze made of iron. "As well you know." The others parted for the fox-woman, standing aside and lowering their heads as she passed, her tail swaying gracefully.

"She's a traitor to the realm, and has conspired to harm my sister's child."

Kitsune waved her hand at him impatiently. "And what concern is that to me? How quickly you've forgotten the rules, Talivar." She reached up to pat his cheek. "It was not so long ago when you claimed the same."

He exhaled slowly. "No, my lady, and I was grateful for your protection."

"Would you have me deny another's?"

Tresa smirked at this, pulling her arms free as Talivar nodded toward his men.

"No." He turned to Tresa, his face impassive. "Should you enter Faerie proper, your life is forfeit to me."

Tresa spat at the ground. "It will never happen. The land itself has cast me out." She raised her wrist to reveal a gaping wound, blood pulsing beneath a pustulant scab. "The thorns contain a slow poison . . . as you know," she added slyly. Talivar's jaw twitched at her words and I took his hand.

Kitsune raised a finger. "We're not done here yet. I require justice for the loss of my horses."

Shit. "But I didn't steal them."

"And yet, they are gone. Released by you."

"Some destiny," I muttered, but I couldn't fault her logic. I *had* cut them free. Didn't mean I wanted to die for it.

"The prince, a way out of here, and a chance to find the woman who betrayed you." Kitsune cocked her head at me. "Isn't that what you asked for?"

"What bargain did you make, Abby?" Talivar stared at me.

"She gave me a thread. A red spool of thread. I was supposed to follow it." I flushed. "What the hell else was I going to do?"

"Argue later," the fox-woman said with a sigh, clapping her hands twice in rapid succession. Immediately two dapple gray horses appeared from the remainder of the herd, flanks gleaming with sweat. Kitsune's mouth twitched. "I offer you this choice, my prince. Consider it an opportunity to assuage your potential losses of today."

Tresa's eyes narrowed. "You've granted me sanctuary. I'm not under his jurisdiction anymore."

"No," Kitsune said sharply, her ears flattening. "Now you're under mine. And you chose to attack this woman in the midst of my horses, leading to their escape."

"But—"

"And what is it we're doing here?" I interrupted, confused. Was I going to be dragged behind them?

"Each of you shall mount one and head off in different directions." Kitsune's smile turned feral. "Whichever of you the prince chooses to pursue, he can keep."

"And the other?" I was almost afraid to ask, not daring to look at Talivar. It was a shit decision to have to trade me for his enemy but that didn't mean I wanted the alternative either.

"Belongs to me, of course. A pity you didn't drink the tea when I offered it. Then I would be honor bound to seek recompense for the attack upon you." She yipped in that high-pitched bark again, laughing when the men lifted a panicked Tresa toward the first horse. The elf coldly stared at the fox-woman as she seated herself with as much dignity as she could. Kitsune turned to me. "I'll allow Talivar to do the honors."

He sighed, cupping my chin so that he could meet my eyes. "I will find you, Abby. I promise. Can you ride?"

"Uh, no. Not since the pony ride at my seventh birthday. Where are Mel and Phin?"

"Safe enough. We'll meet up with them later." He gave me a tight smile and a leg up onto the beast. I barely had time to settle myself before Kitsune let out another barking laugh.

"Off you go."

"Off I wha—" I tumbled forward, my mouth full of horse hair. I snatched at the mane, my hands wrapping around the horse's neck even as Talivar slapped it hard on the ass.

The horse snorted in surprise. I let out a warning shout, every bone in my body rattling as we barreled through the crowd. My legs slipped out sideways and I narrowly avoided cracking my nose when it jerked its head up.

Mud spattered my thighs, flung up by churning hooves. How the hell did one steer a horse without a rope or reins or what have you? I vaguely remember something about using your knees, but a squeeze of my shoes against the heaving sides rewarded me with a snaking neck and a snap of teeth at my calf.

I clenched my jaw and clung as tight as I could as the Barras retreated rapidly from view. I caught the silhouette of the other horse disappearing into the shadows, Tresa's form clinging like a burr. I eased my aching butt up a little higher. We were moving into the trees now. Branches and twigs snarled past me to catch in my hair and Talivar's cloak.

I could see no hint of silver ahead, no sign of the Cross-Roads. I pulled on the horse's mane, but it merely snorted and plunged deeper into the forest. Brambles and ferns, massive mushrooms and towering oaks whirled by.

"Goddamn but you're a bony thing," I said, wincing as my pelvis ground into the protruding withers as it leapt over a streamlet.

"You're not exactly a basket of fruit either," the horse—a mare, I assumed judging by the voice—sniffed.

Given everything that had happened so far today, I decided it wasn't worth being surprised that I was riding a talking horse. "Erm. Hello?"

"*Now* she decides she wants introductions. I hope like the hells you can swim."

"Couldn't you just slow down? I'll jump off if that makes it easier for you." I glanced down at the forest floor, ignoring the thought of what might happen if I landed on my bad knee. I blinked. "Did you say swim?"

"Yeah. And you can't jump off. Not until I allow it."

"Um, you wouldn't happen to be a kelpie, would you?" Kelpies had the pleasant distinction of taking their riders to the nearest body of water and then tearing them to shreds. Which would be the utter height of irony, but I almost didn't have the energy to laugh.

"If I were, do you think I'd warn you?" The mare made a noise that sounded suspiciously like an amused chuckle. She shook her head, dancing away from a cluster of thick bushes blooming with brilliant azure flowers. The Glamour melted from her body like mist, revealing a coat so black I could have sworn the color would have smeared onto my hands. Her neck curved toward me and I could see the lantern-glow of golden eyes.

"Ah," I said weakly. "That would make you a—"

"Puca," she agreed. "And I'm supposed to dunk you in the nearest pond and then gallop off, laughing madly." She made a sort of equine shrug. "Sorry to say."

"And you were in with the horses because?"

"I was there to guard the others," she said dryly. "Glamoured to look like a normal Faery horse. But here we are." She sniffed the air suddenly, blowing hard. "And here we go."

Before I could formulate a reply, we hurdled down an embankment so steep I thought she would summersault us the rest of the way, my body crushed beneath her weight. Abruptly we stopped . . . or more to the point, the puca stopped. I continued my trajectory ass over elbows and straight into a large pond.

Sputtering, I flailed madly, the shock of the water sucking the wind out of me. Stunned, I sank down into the murk for a moment, the brush of something slimy jerking me back to myself.

"You could have least picked something warmer." My teeth chattered as I sloshed toward the shore. At least the fucking thing hadn't been too shallow. Spitting out a clump of duckweed, I peeled off Talivar's cloak, throwing it into the bushes with a twitch of disgust. Damn thing was coated in slime. I glanced down. As was the rest of me, including my beloved purple Chucks. "Dammit."

The puca eyed me balefully, shaking herself like a dog. "That's that, then."

"Shouldn't you be off cackling somewhere?" I shot her a sour look.

She let out an eerie whinny that *did* sound a bit like maniacal laughter and stomped her hooves in the mud a few times. "Okay, propriety has been satisfied." She lowered her head to nip at a fern.

"Those are poisonous to horses, you know." I kicked at the bracken, squeezing the dirty water out of my hair. I should have been pissed that I was soaking wet, but to be honest, I was just so horribly tired. I could have been naked by this point and don't think I would've minded, as long as I wasn't riding a horse, being slammed into the dirt by crazy elf chicks, or half gutted by a stag.

"Not really a horse," the puca pointed out, continuing to browse.

I picked through my thoroughly saturated backpack, wrinkling my nose as I assessed the damage. At least the protein bars were wrapped up and therefore safe, but the rest of it was probably ruined. I sank onto a tree stump, my feet squishing inside my shoes.

So here I was. No knowledge of how to get back. No dry clothes. No iron knife. I peeled the wrapper of one of the protein bars and wolfed it down with a vengeance.

The puca's ears cupped toward me. "Anything good?"

I took another bite. "What do you care? You dumped my ass in a puddle. You think I'm gonna give you my food?" I shifted, my knee protesting. Hell, most of my body protested. I suspected after the day's activities I was going to be covered in bruises later, but for now it was probably better not to look.

For that matter, judging by the way the sun was beginning to set it wouldn't be too much longer until nightfall. The idea of passing the night in the mud wasn't all that appealing to me either. "Stumble around in the dark or wait around for something to come eat me?" My limbs shook with a rush of cold. If I didn't start moving around I was going to stiffen up something awful.

The cloak still hung from a low branch like some sort of puppet Dementor. I wasn't going to put it on just yet, but maybe I could use it for something else later. Groaning, I got to my feet. "Don't suppose you can point me the way we came? Aside from up that massively steep hill?"

The puca flicked her tail. "There's actually a path over past those trees. You'd probably have better luck there."

"Maybe it will take me to the CrossRoads?"

She shook her head. "Doubtful, but at least it will be even footing."

"Fair enough." I limped through a small forest of cattails. I'd heard you could roast them and eat them, but I was still wary about the food here.

There was a sudden flapping of wings and a breeze past my head. Startled, I ducked, glancing up to see an ebony eagle soaring past. "Shapeshifter," I said. I'd heard pucas could take multiple forms, but I'd never seen one at the Marketplace to ask.

My feet rolled out from under me, the ground suddenly giving way as I stumbled forward. Swearing at my own idiocy, I bent to tie my shoe and froze. It hadn't been mud I'd slipped in.

A female body lay in a grotesque sort of repose against the moss, her corn-silk hair a stringy mess. She was elvish, the long lines of her form indicating a warrior of some sort. *Or a messenger.*

A leather satchel hung at her side. My upper lip curled in distaste as I lifted the flap, carefully pulling out a few pieces of parchment. Holding them up to the dying sunlight, I realized they were in Elvish, the ink somewhat smeared from the damp, but I recognized the Royal Seal from the Contract I had signed earlier with Talivar.

"Moira's real replacement. I'm sorry," I said softly, kneeling at her side. A closer inspection of her head showed a scrape of blood and a shattered skull. A faint odor of decay arose when I attempted to inspect the rest of the satchel, but an additional search revealed only what appeared to be a few personal effects, including a tinderbox.

I wavered for a moment, exhaustion lancing through me. The woman wasn't going anywhere, but I didn't want to leave her there either. Burying her was out of the question. She was . . . evidence. Talivar would need to see her, if nothing else. Distaste at the thought rolled over my tongue, a chill taking root in my bones.

"Right, then." I fingered the tinderbox. It wasn't a Bic, but maybe I could manage to make it work. After all, how hard could it be to make a campfire?

Eighteen

Numbly, I sat as far from the corpse as possible, shivering as the night's chill descended upon the pond in a fine mist. The tinderbox had been a complete and utter failure. I'd managed to get a few sparks out if it, once I'd figured out the striking mechanism, but my fingers continued to fumble in the waning light until I could barely see what I was doing.

"Fuck it." I rocked back and forth with my arms wrapped around my knees for warmth. If my clothes hadn't been damp, the air would have been tolerable, but for the moment it sucked mightily.

I curled up on the tattered remains of Talivar's cloak, desperately wishing I could take off my shoes. On the other hand, if something came up and I needed to run, the last thing I wanted to deal with was stepping on something thorny. Thus far, except for small rustlings, the night had been quiet. Occasionally soft, glowing lights sparkled in the distance—small will-o'-the-wisps, perhaps, enticing me to follow.

At one point, the whispered strains of music trickled through the trees, echoed by the beckoning gleam of a bright, warm fire. My eyelids drooped even as I started to get to my feet, the urge to be warm and safe overtaking everything else. My foot stumbled over the dead woman's satchel and I sank to the ground. Abruptly the light disappeared, the music cut off, and I knew it had been just another Faerie trick.

Once I caught the chime of bells, and my heart lurched, Ion's name dying on my lips as a little pixie fluttered by carrying a cluster of bluebells. She eyed me curiously, her wings that of a great luna moth. Miserable, I laid my head on my knees, closing my eyes. Where the hell was Talivar?

"Absinthe?"

I let out a muffled shriek as a calloused hand slid over my mouth.

"It's me . . . Jimmy Squarefoot." The pig-man raised his head, releasing me gently. "I've found her," he shouted behind us.

I whipped around, nearly sobbing with relief as Talivar emerged from the shadows of the wood, a small ball of witchlight at his head. The silhouettes of other elves followed behind him, about twenty or so, and a few horses as well. Coughing, I staggered to my feet. "Talivar?"

Swiftly, he crossed the remaining distance, catching me gently around the shoulders. He began to pat me down, his fingers tracing through my hair and over my face. "Are you all right? Are you hurt?"

My voice was somehow stuck in my throat, a great lump making it hard to swallow. "I'm okay. Just wet and cold."

"That damnable puca."

"The Protectorate," I mumbled, pointing where she lay. "I found her. Tried to use her tinderbox to make a fire, but I . . . I couldn't get it to work." My head swirled, my legs swaying from underneath me. Talivar caught me and supported my weight on his strong side.

I heard Jimmy Squarefoot snuffling at the ground. "Aye, she's the right of it. Fae woman and foul play, belike. I can smell the blood."

Talivar turned abruptly and carried me over to where a white stallion stood, the reins held by what looked like a squire. I shook my head at him. "I can't ride anymore. Not tonight."

He pressed a gentle kiss to my lips, setting me down in the soft grass. "Give me a moment to set things to right and we'll get you taken care of." He dug into a pouch at his side to pull out a silver flask, uncorking it. "Here. Have a drop or two of this."

My hands trembled and I gasped as liquid fire pooled in my belly. Coughing at the bitterness, I stared up at him blearily. "I'm sorry you couldn't go after Tresa."

"We'll find her, but Kitsune will have her way of it first." He patted my head and then strode to the dead Protectorate, crouching for a better look. Moments later, he ordered the others to build a litter. I closed my eyes, taking another sip of Faerie firewater, listening to the glorious sound of people moving around me.

One of the elf women knelt beside me, her cool hand on my forehead, but I found I didn't have the strength to do more than peer between cracked lids. She made a tsking noise, jabbering something in her language that I didn't understand. When I didn't answer, she said it louder, the inflection making it out to be a question. Talivar replied shortly, his voice terse, but whatever he said must have made sense to her, for she nodded and patted my cheek before withdrawing.

The flask slipped through my slackened fingers, but I didn't care much. At some point I must have dozed off because when I came to, I was moving again. Or really, the horse was moving. I was arranged carefully in front of

Talivar, my head lolling against his chest, the dark scent of leather pressed against my nose.

I mumbled a question at him, blinking owlishly into the darkness. He chuckled softly. "I've sent the others to Eildon Tree. They're going to wait for us there tomorrow."

I frowned. "How come we're not going there? Are Melanie and Phin there too?"

"Yes, but I want to get you warmed up first. There's a hot spring a little ways from here—it's rich in healing minerals. Jimmy said you hurt your knee." He tapped it gently and I shuddered.

"No magic healers in your band of merry men?"

He sighed. "Not as of yet. A lot has happened since you left us this morning, Abby." His arms tightened about my waist. I was vaguely aware of the fact that I must have smelled like swamp water and ass, but he didn't seem to notice. "War is coming," he said softly. "There's an army of daemons camped outside the gates of Faerie, or at least the beginnings of one."

I jerked up, nearly tumbling us from the horse. "What? And you left Mel out there by herself?"

"Calm yourself." He patted the horse's neck as it danced sideways. "Things are done a certain way here. The protocols in place insist they give us time to respond to their demands." His tone became dry. "Besides, Moira is currently trying to broker some sort of deal that will allow this all to end peaceably."

I snorted. "What do they want? Besides world domination, I'm assuming."

"Maurice."

"Fucker gets around, doesn't he?" I rubbed my face wearily, fingers running through the gunky edges of my hair. "So let me guess—we give them Maurice and they agree to walk away?"

He grunted in affirmation, his hips moving subtly to
nudge the horse a little faster as we turned down what looked
like a deer trail. "Not too long now."

The statement was unnecessary. I could smell the scent
of the warm waters from here. He dismounted, sliding off
the horse with practiced ease. My feet squelched when he
set me down in the clearing. With a gesture, the witchlight
followed us as he led me past a cluster of small boulders.

"Are you sure we have time for this? I mean, shouldn't
we be getting back to the others?"

He shot me an amused look. "We've time enough, like
I said. And this is a place of healing." He yawned. "Been a
rather long day for me too."

Groaning, I could only nod my head at him. "Don't suppose you brought any food?"

"Of course." He placed one hand on my hip, gracefully
steering me to the edge of the largest hot spring. "Here, go
ahead. Get undressed and get in there. I'll fix us something
to eat and set up camp."

Wordlessly, I shucked off my disgusting shoes and sodden jeans. I could hear the creak of the saddle as Talivar
undid whatever supplies he brought with him. Above me,
the witchlight gently illuminated the water, showing the
spring to be softly rounded and not overly deep, although
I would easily be able to immerse my entire body into it. I
dipped a toe into the shallows, nearly weeping at the sensation of warmth sliding up my calf.

Quickly, I shed the rest of my clothes. I hesitated only
a moment when it came to my underwear. I'd seen him,
hadn't I? Fair was fair and at this point I would have happily
paraded around the Judgment Hall naked if it would have
gotten me a beer and a bath. I spared a quick glance behind
me anyway, but the prince was busy setting up a small fire.
With matches, I noticed wryly.

My panties went the way of the rest of my clothing. A heartbeat later I was gingerly immersing myself into the steaming spring. I hissed as the water hit the cuts on my legs and arms, yelping at the brush of my backside against a heated rock. Apparently I'd fallen harder than I'd thought.

I tipped my head to let my hair float about me, the warmth seeping into sore muscles until I became boneless. "I think I could stay in here forever." I massaged my bad knee between both palms.

"There are times I've felt much the same," Talivar said, crouching beside the edge of the spring. He handed me the flask again and I took a grateful sip, sighing as it slid through my veins until my head swirled. "Feeling better?"

"I'm warmer, anyway," I said dryly. "If just as wet." His mouth twitched and I flushed as I realized what I'd said. Scowling, I stoppered the flask. "How's the food coming along?"

"Nearly done. It's simply a little stew." His gaze roamed over me and I resisted the urge to cover myself up. "I've even got some bread." A minute later he was back with a small blanket and two bowls, a handful of rolls, and a few wooden spoons. My stomach roared to life at the scent and I eagerly snagged a bowl. "It's not bacon," he admitted with a wry smile, "but it should do to fill your belly."

"After the day I've had, it could be cheese-flavored sawdust and I'd eat it," I said between bites. "I wasn't sure what was safe to eat in Faerie, honestly. I didn't want to risk being caught up in sort of magic bullshit spell for the sake of an apple." The stew was thick and mildly spicy and tasted utterly divine. "And here I thought you said you couldn't cook."

"The key thing about Faerie gifts is the intention. Same with food. If you can trust the giver, then there's your answer. If you see me eating it, it's probably safe." His mouth pursed self-deprecatingly. "And this is about the only thing I can make. A few years in the army and one quickly learns that the cook pot is really just another word for catchall."

"Still good." I scraped the last of it from the bowl, licking my fingers before devouring the roll. Beside me, the elf ate quietly, his shoulders sagging as he leaned against the boulder. "What time is it? I've completely lost track of anything."

"Time runs a bit differently here, but I'd say it's probably about nine in the evening as you would tell it."

"Feels like I've been awake forever." I took another swig from the flask. "And no offense, but I'd rather ride to Faerie naked on your horse than wear those shoes again."

He set down his bowl, toeing off his own boots before stretching lazily, humor flicking about his face. "Tempting as it may be to see you try it, have no fears on that account. Becka gave me some of her clothes for you."

"Becka? The elf at the clearing?"

"Mmm," he grunted. "She's a soft-heart where I'm concerned. When I told her you were my TouchStone, she insisted that you be dressed as befitting your status."

I rolled my eyes, unsure if I should be insulted or not. Heaven forbid they take pity on me simply because I was cold and wet. "Whee, I'm chattel." I drifted into the center of the spring, dipping my head beneath the water.

"Don't judge us too harshly," he said reproachfully.

"Well, you have to admit most of you are pretty stuck up." I fluttered my fingers at him. "All that mysterious 'can't tell you for your own good' crap." Tresa's words of revolution and Kitsune's warning echoed in my mind, but that could wait until I was dry.

He stared at me, a long, slow smile curving his mouth. "Let me join you and I'll tell you anything you want to know."

"You just want an excuse to come ravish me. Or is that going to be your way of making today up to me? Tell you what though, if you are planning on soaking in here with me tonight, you'd better do it fast. I'm starting to prune."

He removed his vest, shedding his tunic and the vambraces in a few easy motions, the trews following in short order. He let the Glamour fade away, leaving him naked and vulnerable.

The witchlight pulsed once and then dimmed, leaving his scarred body softer, the silver strands of tissue seeming that much more terrible for the beautiful flesh that remained. His chest and abdomen were firmly muscled—not with the overindulgent ripples of a bodybuilder, but with the lean hardness that comes from rough living.

Prince or not, Talivar clearly had not basked in the ease afforded to his station. Wordlessly, he slipped into the water, ripples disturbing the surface. "I used to come here a lot," he said finally, easing himself deeper until the water was level with his chest. His face became grim, his fingers brushing over the wounded eye. "My father would allow no one to heal what I'd suffered, but neither would he allow me to seek solace elsewhere. Once the damage became permanent, he no longer cared what I did."

His gaze met mine, something terribly lonely passing between us. "Here I could at least be alone and lick my wounds, as it were."

I cocked a brow at him. "And you never brought a lover here? Because I have to tell you, you've managed all the moves pretty damn well." I gestured carelessly at the blanket. "Food, alcohol, campfire. A convenient lack of clothing. One might almost think you planned it this way."

A sheepish smile chased away the hurt of those distant memories. "Yes, well, I used to have quite a few lovers . . . before." He shrugged. "Not so much, these days."

"Pity," I murmured, floating toward him.

He reached out, taking my hand. I let him pull me closer, catching the question in his expression. I barely thought about it. After all, I owed nothing to anyone anymore. I bobbed up against him, pressing a soft kiss on his neck. "I don't suppose you brought any . . . uh . . . protection? I seem to be clear out of pretty much everything, at the moment."

He sucked in a breath at the touch of my lips, sighing when I withdrew. "Back pocket," he muttered hoarsely.

"You dog," I teased, "you *did* plan this." I glared in mock offense, laughing when he kissed my shoulder apologetically.

"Not quite the circumstances I was expecting, but Phineas did mention it as something of a necessity," he admitted, something heavy and hungry flaring to life in his mien. "You'll have me, then? For tonight, at least?"

I decided I wasn't even going to begin to wonder in what world my potential lover exchanging sex advice with Phineas was a good idea. I stroked my finger across his cheek in answer before sliding it into the water to trace wet circles upon his chest. He captured my hand, kissing it hard before sliding the tip of my index finger into his mouth. Pleasure arced from my wrist to my groin, a jolt of pure lust tightening my breasts.

He hummed softly, the vibration tingling through me. "Let me look at you for a moment," he whispered as I moved to take the length of him into my hand.

I stilled, his lips brushing my cheeks before firmly taking control of my mouth. His tongue flicked hard against mine, probing in a silent dance. I wondered at it, this hunger of his. If he'd truly been as shunned as he'd suggested, it had probably been quite a while, indeed. I could only imagine what it would be like, to be nearly immortal, without even the comforting touch of another. Not to mention love.

His fingers bit into my hips with a sudden desperation, sliding behind and beneath to cup my ass. I whimpered but remained still, giving him the opportunity to explore me at his will.

This too was a form of healing, perhaps.

When he bent to suckle my breast, I met him halfway, my body straining in the darkness. I became acutely aware of his breathing, punctuated only by my sudden gasp and the flat, wet sound of his tongue as he lapped at my nipples. He bit them gently, rubbing his face along the soft curves.

My hands snagged into his hair, finally setting it free from its braided confines. It cascaded through my fingers, silken as rabbit fur. It took on a bluish hue beneath the witchlight, gleaming as it trailed at the surface of the water. One hand snaked around my waist even as he tipped me back, supporting my head with the other.

"I'm sorry I didn't find you sooner." He leaned forward to kiss the largest bruise on my shoulder.

"The spa treatment makes up for a lot. All I need now is the happy ending." The vibration of his laughter rumbled deep in his chest, pulling an answering flutter from my heart at the sound. The light reflected from the water and played over his face. I caught a glimpse of the man he'd surely been before—the hint of boyish mischief about his eyes, the slightly impudent nose, the quick-to-smile mouth . . .

He lifted my chin so our eyes met, something dark and far more primitive burning within. And then the moment was gone, and his tongue was plunging into my mouth, rocking in time as his cock slid softly against my belly.

"Not yet," he growled, my legs sliding up to encircle his waist. I nipped at the delicate arch of his ear. He let out a husky groan and his teeth grazed my neck, his hips nudging insistently. With a grunt, he lifted me from the water, draping me so that I half lay upon the blanket, the bowls scattering into the grass.

His erection jutted up from a dark nest of curls and I murmured an encouragement, taking his finger into my mouth with a teasing swirl. He sucked in a ragged breath and slid his lips down between my breasts and below, lingering at my belly, pausing to kiss each tiny bruise along the way.

"So gentle," I murmured. By the time he reached the juncture of my thighs, I was squirming, raising my hips to find his mouth hot and wet and waiting. Without further request, he slung my ankles so they rested on his shoulders, his tongue delving deep. Cupping my ass, he tilted me up, my hands fisting the blanket as I let out a strangled cry.

He chuckled. "I'll make you sing for me yet, Abby." He swept over my clit even as he spread me wider, one finger trailing over the sensitive flesh.

My back arched, heat skittering up my belly. Impatient, I began to thrust against him, only to have him hold me still. I tugged on the length of his hair, clenching down on his finger with my inner muscles. He let out a groan in response. I smiled for half a moment and then all thought fled as he renewed his assault.

By this point I was drumming my heels upon him, my voice nothing more than guttural moans. My waist moved in rhythm with his tongue, each velvet stroke taking me to the edge, only to have him pull away at the last moment. "Please," I whispered hoarsely.

"As my lady commands." He smiled, suckling hard at my clit, even as he crooked his finger to strike that perfect spot within my core. I bit down hard on the blanket, my focus on the way everything bore down to that single point of pleasure. The orgasm rolled over me, six months of celibacy exploding in a single moment of violent ecstasy.

By the time I was cognizant of anything other than the blood pounding through my ears, I realized Talivar had moved up to lie beside me, kissing me softly along the jaw. "Thank you," he murmured, capturing my mouth with his own.

"Don't you have that backward?" I nuzzled his chin, my lips curving into a sated smile at the prickle of facial hair. "After all, you did all the hard work. All I had to do was lie here and think of England."

His good hand stroked lazily down my rib cage. "It's good to know I'm not as out of practice as I thought."

"Mmm . . . no. That was rather masterful, if I do say so." I nudged him, suddenly aware that he was still pretty damn aroused. "And you're not done yet, right?"

He snorted softly, one hand digging through his bunched-up trousers. "No . . . but I might need a little help. We don't exactly use these in Faerie." He tossed me the foil package with a shy grin. "Plus I thought we might move a little closer to the fire."

My hips swayed with a languid sort of grace as we retired to the tent he'd set up, a new energy thrumming through my veins with each step I took. In the back of my mind I ran through a number of scenarios about the wisdom of getting involved with an OtherFolk lover.

Again.

Given, our circumstances were not the best, but when would they ever be? I was lonely, I realized with a jolt—and had been for quite a while. Talivar burned with a hunger borne of solitude longer than anything I'd probably imagined.

I stroked his cheek, my thumb sweeping over his eye patch. "When did this happen?"

He shrugged, one dark brow rising. "Two hundred years ago, give or take a decade. I tend to blur out the more unpleasant memories."

"Understandable." I paused. "You realize the others are going to talk."

"Let them." He traced my lips with his fingers. "I'm tired of being alone, Abby."

He allowed me to draw him down, my arms about his shoulders. For the first time, I truly looked upon him as simply a man, as though those last few words had shredded the remnants of the veil he wore. No longer a prince or a Protectorate, a crippled elf or a tired warrior. Only Talivar.

Only us.

"Guess we can be alone together, then." I tore open the foil packet, extracting the condom with as much decorum as I could muster. Now that the hot and heavy moment had passed, I had to admit it was a tad awkward to be showing a nearly immortal elf the basics of birth control.

He caught my eye as I fumbled with the tip and we laughed, his hand catching mine to help me unroll it over his cock. "I think I get it." He stared at it bemusedly and then shook his head. "Mortals are such strange creatures," he said, his tone mournful.

"Practical," I reminded him. "We're practical. And prepared." Keeping one hand on his cock, I stroked him in an easy rhythm, letting him tumble me to the floor of the tent.

He stretched out over the length of me, his hips already teasing my thighs apart. "This part I remember." His words were muffled against my mouth as he kissed me again.

I had no answer save what my body could give him, my limbs shuddering with pleasure when he thrust his way inside. He lay still for a moment, his forehead resting on mine, and then he began to move in a circular motion. My legs crossed behind him, my hands entwined in his hair.

Lost in the soft sounds of our breath, the quiet moments between sighs, the half-sobs of pleasure and the tail end of lust, I passed my first night in Faerie, naked beneath a starless night, wrapped in the arms of a Faery prince.

And I was not alone.

Nineteen

Morning broke upon us with a rolling mist, a hushed whisper of things to come. Talivar rewarded me with a sleepy smile. The naked vulnerability of the night before had fled in the early hours. I returned it with a shy smile of my own, suddenly very much aware that I didn't have any clothes to cram into.

His mouth pursed at my sudden discomfort, and he curled himself around me to rest his head on my shoulder. I went limp, the heat of his body sliding into mine. Slowly I shifted my hips, wincing when they ground into the hard earth below the tent. "Guess I'm not used to roughing it," I groaned, rubbing a sore spot on my thigh where a rock had apparently decided to nest.

He kissed the nape of my neck. "Next time will be in my bed," he promised, snaking his hand down to give my ass a tiny pinch. "Much more comfortable for these tender bits of yours."

I flicked his ear. "I suspect I've got a reasonable excuse."

"Mmmph. Maybe." He traced his fingers over my hip in small circular patterns that I suddenly found rather mesmerizing. They stroked teasingly over my rib cage, settling on the curve of my breast. My hand rested on top of his and I rubbed my thumb over his knuckles, coming to rest on a small notch right below the center of the middle finger of his left hand.

On impulse, I lifted his hand to my lips to kiss it. He shuddered, wrapping me tightly in his arms. I turned to look at him. "Don't," he whispered, his voice husky.

"You okay?"

The brush of his lashes fluttered like a trapped butterfly against my neck and I wondered at it until I felt the damp warmth of tears. "This was . . . unexpected," he said with a rueful laugh. "I received that scar nearly two hundred years ago, and yet you bring forth those memories with such a simple gesture."

"Do you want to talk about it?" I wasn't sure how wise it was to probe, but I knew perfectly well what it was like to have one's emotions fester.

"It's a complicated story. One better left to later, I think." He propped himself up on his elbow, turning me so that we were face to face. "Or at least on the road."

"You know, I hear that kissing is the way to cure sadness in Faerie," I said archly. "Are you sad, Prince?"

"I just might be," he murmured, letting me pull him down, his mouth brushing against mine for a long moment. "And we had better stop, lest you tempt me to waste the rest of the morning."

I reached around him to find his shirt. "Let's start with clothes first." I yawned, draping it over my shoulders. He stretched out with the easy grace of one who is used to casual nudity. His gaze roamed over me, apparently pleased at my state of undress. With a regretful sigh, he rose and exited the tent.

The campfire had burned out during the night and I wandered over to poke at the embers with a stick. "No warm breakfast this morning, I guess."

"There's a bit of bread and cheese left in my pack," he said absently, bending to check the stallion's hobble. I took the opportunity to check out his ass, flushing at the score marks on the left cheek.

"Guess I got a little enthusiastic."

He looked up at me with a sly grin. "These are not the sort of scars a man minds bearing, Abby. I'll wear them with honor."

I rolled my eyes. "No one else will see them."

"Maybe not, but they'll see that." He gestured at my neck.

I craned my head down, unsure of what he meant until I caught the barest hint of purple just below my collarbone. Hickeys. The dude had given me hickeys. "How old are you?" I scowled, drawing the cloak tighter.

"It's the sign of a good night," he told me, the grin growing wider.

Shaking my head, I stalked over to his pile of belongings. "Where are those clothes you were going on about? I've got things to do."

Laughing softly, he procured the promised dress, a lavender confection with a fitted bodice and an ebony skirt. I wriggled into it, gazing hopelessly at the extra ribbons. Coughing his amusement into his hand, the elf swiftly tied the stays. "It suits you," he mused. "Perhaps it needs a bit extra for the hair, but either way, it's a vast improvement over muddy jeans."

"Something tells me the fashion police aren't going to be bothered with a poor little mortal like me."

He eyed my necklace carefully, his mouth tightening. "They'll bother with the Key, for sure. We'll need to make certain that's out of the way. Even with the Glamour."

He thrust on his trousers, belting them up so they slung low over his hips. He finger-combed the tangled mess of his hair, grimacing when he hit a few knots.

"It's going to take forever to braid those. Maybe I shouldn't have undone them." Chagrin blossomed in my cheeks. "Do you have a comb?"

He dug through another saddlebag, pulled out a silver-tined comb and handed it to me with an amused look, sitting cross-legged at my feet. Hesitantly, I ran it through the upper half, trying not to catch the snarls too hard. "I can see why you keep it bound as much as you do."

A chuckle escaped him and then he paused. Retrieving a dagger from his belt, he held it out to me, hilt forward. "Cut it off," he said.

I blinked at him. "Cut it . . ."

"My hair. I want it shorter."

"I didn't think the Fae did the haircut thing much."

"We don't. Royalty in particular," he added. "But maybe I'm tired of pretending to be something I'm not."

I looked at him doubtfully. "Rebel, rebel, your face is a mess." I gestured at him to turn around. "How short do you want it?"

He shrugged. "It will grow back. Whatever looks good to you."

"Oookay." I grabbed a hank, slicing through it carefully. It was a hack job, to be sure, but by the time I was finished, it reached to just above his shoulders, part of it hanging at a slant to frame his chin. "There. It should be a bit more manageable now, I guess." I rubbed my finger over his jawline, the rough hair prickling my skin. There was a reddish hue to it that didn't quite match the rest of him. "You know, I didn't think elves grew beards."

The tips of his ears pinked slightly. "Most can't. Has to do with certain bloodlines and the fact that some of us are a bit more refined than others."

"Is that what you call it? Refined?"

"Something like that."

I brushed my lips over his, lingering for a teasing moment. "Well, I think it suits you just fine. Your transformation to rogue pirate is complete."

He tucked the loose strands of hair behind his ears and rewarded me with a rakish leer. After worming into his tunic, he began taking down the camp, carefully binding up the loose hair I'd cut.

"I'll burn this later, but we need to make up some ground today. My men will be waiting at Eildon Tree. It's a central location and a good place for us to go over our plans. Plus it's neutral ground."

I frowned at him. "You're talking about the original Eildon Tree? The one from my . . . father's poem?"

He paused and then let out a sigh. "I keep forgetting you're not really one of us. Yes. Eildon Tree is the site of the original CrossRoads. Where Thomas made his decision to go with the Queen. The birthplace of TouchStones," he added, reciting softly:

> "Betide me weal; betide me woe,
> That weird shall never daunten me."
> Syne he has kiss'd her rosy lips,
> All underneath the Eildon Tree.

I shivered, wondering how deeply my own destiny was tied to this place. My hand found my necklace, rubbing it between nervous fingers. "Were the other Doors opened? When I went through yesterday?"

"No. After you were carried away, it was utter chaos. I damn near had to kill a few of them to let Melanie and Phin through with me, but the Door shut shortly thereafter. She still can't use her violin to open anything."

"So what happens if the Queen doesn't reopen the Cross-

Roads? We can't abandon everyone we left behind. Benjamin—"

"I know. If nothing else, I'll have you reopen that Door a
second time and we'll lead them home that way." His hands
fisted as he tightened the saddle's girth about the stallion.
"But if it comes to that, Abby, we're going to have far bigger
things to worry about than a mere rescue."

"War?"

"I don't know. Gods save me, I just don't know."

The horse's gait was swift and smooth beneath us, hooves
thudding into the dirt path. I sat pillion behind Talivar,
trying not to embarrass myself too badly. With my skirts
bunched up past my knees, I imagined it wasn't the most
romantic thing to look at, but a damned sight easier to throw
myself off the beast if it came to it. Plus, as much as Talivar
insisted I wouldn't be a distraction to him, the way he suddenly couldn't seem to stop touching me indicated otherwise.

Not that it had been anything other than mostly polite,
but at times it was as though he were a dying man newly
introduced to water. And so his flesh drank me, the constant
contact a balm to whatever drought remained within his
soul.

I'd decided that if we were actually going to get anywhere
today, I had better content myself with being the medieval
equivalent of a backseat driver. I draped my hands loosely
about his waist.

And what a difference a mostly full belly and a quiet
night had made. It was hard to stay too grumpy once the sun
came out and burned away the fog. Thick forest melted into
soft fields bursting with primroses, dewdrops scattered like
diamonds.

I hugged Talivar closer, marveling at it all. "Is it always like this? This sort of wild beauty?"

"In places. Some of it is not quite so lovely. Most of it is dangerous." We rounded a bend, coming across a small encampment nestled in a grove of young trees. Clusters of fresh-faced children waved to us from atop their wagons, gesturing at us to join them. A long table sat in the center of the camp, covered with food. My mouth watered.

"I think I smell bacon." I sighed.

His chuckle was without humor. "Take my hand, Abby."

Confused, I slipped my hand into his. A scrape of some-thing metal against my skin and I realized he'd slipped a ring on my finger. "A little soon to propose, don't you think?"

"Look again," he said softly. "But do not react."

I glanced over my shoulder, stifling a gasp. The children's smiles had turned pointed and feral, their teeth sharp. They pointed at the table again, but now I could see it was covered with rotting vegetables, moldy bread, and fly-encrusted . . . something. Beneath the table, what had been flowers was now a pile of bones, stripped clean and broken open, skulls of either mortal or Fae grinning in welcome.

"Jesus," I whispered. I looked at the field we'd passed through moments ago, shuddering at what was clearly a marshy swamp, cool puddles of stagnant water and dying vegetation.

"They lure in the unwary," he said. "Those who cannot see through the Glamour are easily trapped."

"Why do you allow it? Can't your Queen do something?"

"And what would she do? They have a right to live ac-cording to their nature. As long as they are not in the king-dom proper and she doesn't have to look at them, anyway."

"Then why are they out here—instead of the Bar-ras? Jimmy said the Queen had banished the Lesser Fae." I frowned as I said it, an unpleasant thought crossing my mind. "Or are you telling me the Barras is really some sort of Fae concentration camp?"

"The explanation becomes complicated. Long ago, my people were split into two kingdoms. You might know them as the Seelie and Unseelie Courts?"

"Yeah." In the old tales, the Seelie Court was supposed to have been made up of the "good" Fae, although I had the distinct impression that "good" really depended on one's definition. The Unseelie Court was the yang to the Seelie's Court's yin, and primarily consisted of the less pleasant denizens of Faerie.

"The short answer is that the Barras is actually the remnants of the Unseelie Court. They're forbidden to have their own kingdom longer than a day in any one place, so they're constantly on the move."

I chewed on my lower lip, Tresa's cry for sanctuary suddenly making sense. And Talivar had claimed the same once? "And they retain their sovereignty? When did they dissolve as a Court?"

"Yes," he murmured, his thumb rubbing against the scar on his finger. "And about two hundred years ago." I bit back the last of my questions, something in his voice indicating that I was treading dangerous ground. That he'd had something to do with it was more than clear, as was the fact that he didn't want to talk about it.

Fair enough, I supposed. For now. I spared a last look behind me, trying not to shiver at the narrowed eyes following our progress. The longer I stared, the less like children they were, their forms becoming gnarled and stooped, skin saggy. One of them bared her teeth at me. I returned in kind, suddenly tired of the intimidation factor; she did nothing but turn away eventually. Sour grapes that she wouldn't be dining on my mortal flesh, perhaps.

And then there was that matter about the Key. I said

nothing about the necklace, but something told me that there were plenty of folk willing to take me down at a chance to control the CrossRoads, seal of royalty on my finger or not. Abruptly I switched the subject. "What about the body of the Protectorate?"

"She was taken to the Tree as well. We will investigate as to how she died, but in truth it only proves that Tresa was clearly an imposter."

"Well, duh," I said dryly. "She said Maurice has her son, but didn't get into the specifics."

"Motive," he agreed, "but not one we'll be able to prove unless we find the boy—and she must still answer for her treason. Better to blame Maurice, as he surely has his finger deeper in this pie then we know."

At that we both went silent, my own thoughts lost in what was coming. The web was becoming increasingly tangled the more I tried to unweave it. The only real question was what we might find in the center.

Eildon Tree was less about an actual tree than it was a central space, I discovered. Not that there wasn't a tree there, but for some reason I imagined it to be something monstrous, filled with tangible power.

But it wasn't.

Ancient and gnarled, for certain, and covered in small white blossoms, the Eildon Tree was wrapped in quiet humility, and an ethereal vibration that seemed to emanate from its branches. I could feel it drawing me in, my limbs trembling in response. Talivar glanced down at me, eye filled with a gentle amusement.

Here is where it all began, my inner voice said, filled with a quiet awe. *Your history starts here.*

With my father. My mouth went dry at the thought, almost seeing it before me—the Scottish bard taking solace at the tree's roots, the music of his lute so utterly heartfelt as to draw the attention of the Faery Queen herself. What would he be like?

My stomach churned, each new question beating at my brain like a butterfly made of velvet nails. My legs shook as I slid off the horse, heedless of Talivar's helping hand. The silken blades of grass sprung beneath my naked feet as I staggered over to the tree, my hand already reaching out to touch its smaller branches.

The sound of humming washed over me. *Earthsong,* my mind named it, though I had no recollection of the word. A moment later found me kneeling, my face pressed into the bark of one of the larger trunks of the hawthorn. Abruptly, I plunged into a hazy swirl of visions, as though I stared at a multifaceted gemstone, thousands upon thousands of images superimposed upon themselves in a blur of faces and movements. My emotions turned inward, spiraling from great joy and terrible sorrow, uplifted into a gentle hope for the future, my brain short-circuiting at the myriad possibilities.

"What is this?" I said finally, my voice a husky whisper. I caught the impression of amusement from the tree, though that seemed impossible.

Talivar crouched beside me, one hand upon my shoulder. "They say when Lucifer left the heavens, God was stirred to tears and this is where they fell. She holds all knowledge of the past and future within her branches. She's the one who gave your father the gift of prophecy."

I pulled away from the tree, the music dimming into something less overwhelming.

He chuckled softly at my expression. "I grew up playing beneath it. Its song doesn't sing quite so loudly to me these days. Or perhaps I have grown used to it. Mortals have forgotten so very much," he mused, his voice dropping low. "Do you understand what we fight for now? We are its guardians and its keepers. Regardless of what happens with the Queen or Moira or even your father, Abby . . . this is what is important."

I only nodded, a lump swelling in the back of my throat making it hard to breathe. For an uneasy moment I wondered if this was how the Queen convinced Thomas to go with her.

Answers would hopefully come in time and until I met him, what was the point of speculation? A crimson fluttering caught my attention. "What is that?" I pointed at the silk rag knotted elegantly on one of the branches.

"A wish." Talivar got to his feet, pulling me up beside him. "People come here to make requests of the Tree. Wishes and hopes and dreams, each represented by a piece of cloth."

"Everything here is about wishes," I said sourly, thinking of my own Contract with Moira. I supposed I'd lost that particular benefit when I'd signed on with Talivar. "Do they come true?"

He shrugged. "Some do. Some don't. The Tree keeps her secrets." I took a closer look and realized the Tree was covered in them, in all different cuts and quality. Some were quite new and others twisted, thread-worn and nearly disintegrating in the breeze. I resisted the urge to touch one.

Dreams were sacred and I had no such illusions of what they might mean to others. On impulse I tore a piece of the underskirt of my dress, knotting it tightly around one of the other branches. No wish sprang to mind, and I let the cloth slip from my fingers to blow with the others. "Just in case," I said to the bemused prince, pushing the hair from my face. "What now?"

"Our camp is past the crest of the hill. Gives us a good view of the land, so to speak." His fingers wove through the tree's lower branches for a moment. "No one would be so crass as to actually pollute this place with an army." His face became grim. "Not even the daemons."

"I hope you're right," I muttered. I waited for him as he retrieved his horse, letting it trail behind us as we started the climb. The hillside was more of a gentle slope, but I leaned on Talivar anyway, my knee still aching from the day before.

Not that it mattered anyway. I cocked my head, recognizing what sounded like the chorus to Wolfmother's "Joker and the Thief" wafting on the breeze. Nothing serious, then—Mel was merely playing for an audience as opposed to rousing the troops to war.

My mouth curved into a grateful smile. At least one thing was still right in this world. If she could continue to play music, things couldn't be quite so bad, could they?

Talivar was now in deep conversation with what looked like an elvish scout standing sentinel, his chain mail glittering in the sun. Below us a series of tents were laid out in layered semicircles, a large pavilion set up in the center of the farthest ring. It wasn't enough to be considered a full army, but clearly the Fae were at least attempting to make show of their force without escalating into something more.

Clusters of elves in pale armor dotted about the camp, everything a flurry of metal and horses, campfires and messengers. And sure enough, I could see Melanie's familiar form standing in a loose circle of warriors, her bow moving madly upon the violin.

Leaving Talivar to his own devices, I limped down the slope. Melanie paused when she saw me, her face splitting into a wide grin as she wrapped up the song with a flourish. Bowing to the small crowd gathered before her, she quickly bundled the instrument into its case before heading toward me, the two of us falling into a friendly embrace. "Where's Phin?"

She rolled her eyes, linking her arm through mine. "Think he talked someone into carrying him around. He got stepped on during the stampede and he's milking it a bit." One brow rose when she saw my neck. "Nice to see you had a good night."

I scowled at her. "Yeah, you could say that. Sorry we didn't meet up with you earlier, but I was really dragging when Talivar and the others found me."

She sobered. "Yeah, I saw the Protectorate when they brought her in. They've got her wrapped up on one of the wagons. I suspect they would have burned her body by now, but . . ." We walked in silence for a few minutes, my skirt swishing through the long grass. "It looked like someone beat her head in with a rock or something. Primitive."

"Well, something tells me Tresa doesn't exactly fall into warrior category. But anyone can pick up a rock and chuck it. Maybe she got lucky. Or hell, for all we know there was some sort of intricate setup and someone wants us to *think* it was simple." I shook my head. "I didn't get that good a look at her honestly—she was half in a pond when I found her and it was pretty dark. Plus I was trying not to freeze my ass off."

I gave Mel the rapid-fire account of what had happened to me, leaving out the more intimate bits of the evening. She glanced up to where the prince still stood, gesturing madly at the encampment. "What the hell happened to his hair?"

"Had me cut it for him this morning. Not sure what that was all about."

She shrugged. "I'm sure Moira will love it . . . Not."

My heart beat a little faster at the mention of the princess. *Sister,* my inner voice said gleefully. "Is she . . . um . . . here?"

"Yeah. She's been going back and forth all morning between here and the daemon encampment on the other side of the valley. Doesn't sound like it's going too well." Her gaze flicked toward my neck. "They know it's here, that the Key is awake. They want Maurice for sure, but they want that too."

"They do realize they can't use it themselves, I hope."

"Maybe not, but how hard would it be for them to find a mortal willing to bear it and do their work for them? It's not like you can't be killed." Her voice became distant, quiet beneath the weight of her own memories. "We're moving into dangerous territory here, Abby. Unless the Queen re-opens the CrossRoads, I think some serious shit is going to go down." She stopped, resting her hand on my shoulder. "And we're going to be in the thick of it. Again."

"The cake is a lie," I intoned gravely.

She stuck her tongue out at me. "It always is. But we need to be a bit more alert to what's going on this time." Her mouth curved into a wry smile. "There's science to do."

"Well, the first thing I want is shoes," I said, wiggling my toes. "As much fun as this is, I find I run a lot better when I'm not worried about stepping in horse crap."

"I've got an extra pair," she offered. "Probably the fastest thing. I'm next to Moira's tent." She pointed to the largest tent beside the pavilion, gauzy with pink and cream cloth, a set of royal pennants snapping briskly beside it.

"Nice and simple," I quipped. "I like it. It's got that whole Barbie's My First RPG Campaign thing going on."

"Did Talivar take you to see the Tree?"

"Yeah. It kind of freaks me out, honestly. There's a part of me that wanted to throw myself down and never move again."

"I often wonder how much history would be changed if it had been me, instead of Thomas. Or someone like me," she added hastily, kicking the ground roughly. "Though I imagine the end would be the same, either way. Perhaps the

King would have ridden by instead . . . or maybe I would have chosen a different path."

I gave her a sideways look. "Look, I know you've got your thing going on with the Dev——"

She raised a finger to my lips. "Don't. Not here. To say the name draws attention, and that's the last thing we need."

"One of these days you're going to have to give me the whole story." I paused as she ducked into her tent, a simple muddy brown thing. Next to Moira's monstrosity, it looked a bit like a squashed mushroom, but Melanie had never stood on ceremony about such things before. As far as I knew, if it kept the rain off her head, she was pretty good about sleeping anywhere.

She emerged a few minutes later with a pair of socks and leather boots. They didn't match my dress in the slightest, but they didn't have heels either, and that more than made up for it. I'd had visions of stumping through the field, sinking into the ground every few feet. Plopping down on the ground, I slipped them both on. A bit of a tight fit near the toes, but nothing I couldn't put up with for a few hours.

"Right here is good, ladies." I glanced up to see Phineas being carried upon a velvet cushion by a set of bored-looking serving girls. One of them gave me a long-suffering sigh as they set down the pillow and beat a hasty retreat.

"I hope you weren't too rude to them, Phin." I propped myself up on my elbows, poking him with the toe of my boot. He made a big show of struggling to his feet, limping over to me.

"Be nice. I was stepped on. Nearly broken beneath an ocean of clumsy feet. Battered by a wave of idiots. Crushed—"

"—by his own overbearing pride," Melanie interjected.

"If you'd stayed by me instead of running off, none of this would have happened."

I picked him up and put him in my lap. "What about your horn? Can't you heal yourself?"

"I was saving it for you," he said sourly. "We didn't know if you would even still be alive after that damn stag took off with you." He butted my belly gently, resting his head in the crook of my elbow with a sigh. "And there's no panties to roll around in."

"Guess you're out of luck then," I sniggered. "I'm not exactly wearing any at the moment either."

"Well, isn't *that* good to know," a dark voice purred behind me. I froze, closing my eyes against the sound.

"Ion."

Melanie bit her lip. "I didn't know he was here until a little while ago," she said miserably. "I was trying to come up with a way to tell you."

I struggled to look up at him, watching as his boots came into view at my side. I quelled the rush of nervousness that threatened to spill from my mouth, but I couldn't quite help the guilty flush from rising into my cheeks. He was in his human form this time, wearing his old trench coat. The curved perfection of his mouth turned down he approached. The fall of his midnight hair framed the high cheekbones and familiar line of his jaw. I sucked in a ragged breath, the ache of seeing him here as opposed to the Dreaming making his beauty that much worse.

He crouched beside me, one hand tipping my chin up to look at him for a long moment, without a hint of gold about his fathomless eyes. Anger and embarrassment roared to life within me, but I stared him down, refusing to give him the satisfaction. He took my hand, his gaze lowering to rake over the love bites at my neck, his elegant fingers stroking Talivar's ring.

And then he released me, standing swiftly to walk away.

I would have known that easy saunter anywhere, but I also detected a stiffness in his posture that made a lie of it. What had I had been expecting? Hell, for that matter, what right did either of us have to expect anything at all?

Twenty

Talivar led us into the no-man's-land between the two encampments, Melanie and me striding behind him. Phineas was still in my arms, lolling over my shoulder like some kind of big baby. The only reason I even allowed it was because it hid the way my hands were shaking. That and he'd healed my knee with that magic horn of his. As paybacks went, this wasn't too bad.

We were flanked by twelve elven warriors that I could see, their swords drawn loosely at their sides. I suspected there were quite a few others obscured from my vision, arrows nocked at the ready if this should turn out poorly.

Of Bryston, I had seen no other sign. Talivar had taken one look at my face when he found me a short time later, his mouth twisting as Melanie told him the incubus was also in the camp. He'd given me an awkward kiss on the forehead and murmured that I shouldn't worry, but something in his expression made me wonder if he'd already known.

But no time to worry about that. My personal fuck-ups were going to have to wait until we got through the daemon business.

Moira stood outside a small silver tent halfway between

the camps, a white flag fluttering in the wind like a lady's handkerchief. Wearing a resplendent dress of pale green and gold, the princess was the epitome of grace and beauty, her hair twisted in a series of elegant braids. In the distance I could see the black smoke, ugly and shadowed, rising up in a sea of oily canvas. The daemons had quite clearly made themselves at home.

Talivar stepped forward first, placing a kiss on both of Moira's cheeks. She frowned when she saw his shortened hair, but said nothing. The glance she sent my way probably meant there was a long discussion in my future. I opened my mouth, not sure of what I would even say, choosing to set down the unicorn instead. I took a hesitant step toward the Faery woman.

An uncertain smile crossed her lips. "Sister," she said finally. "It is good to see you, thus."

The silence stretched out into a chasm and I finally waved her off. I had my own questions, but they would have to wait. "We don't have to go there yet," I said, noting the momentary relief that flashed in her sea-green eyes. "Perhaps I should meet . . . our father first?"

She let out a small laugh of genuine happiness. "I'd forgotten your mortal sense of practicality. It's refreshing."

"Like a cold beer to the face," I muttered. "What do we need to do here?"

And just like that the tension broke, the five of us retreating to the small canvas shelter, the tent flaps folded open. "The daemons will not back down," she said regretfully. "It's a matter of saving face now. Regardless of whether the Queen's in the wrong or not, we cannot afford to bow down to the whims of Hell simply because they wish it. As it stands, she will only release the CrossRoads if their army retreats. The daemons insist they will only retreat if she releases the CrossRoads . . . and so here we are."

"And if you hand over Maurice?"

"It amounts to the same thing." She shrugged, face hardening.

Talivar shook his head. "And I assume he has given us no more information?"

Moira stilled, her gaze dropping down to her feet. "No. And every time he is called upon by the Council, his claims become more and more outrageous." Her nostrils flared, and I wondered what sorts of things he had insinuated about her. Somehow I suspected having one's dirty laundry trotted out in front of the entire Court was trumped by knowing your parents were getting an earful as well. "He is determined to make the entire thing a circus . . . and we are merely puppets to dance at his bidding."

"So why not kill him and get it over with?" Melanie wondered aloud. "I mean, if he's not going to talk, why not take the dog and pony show somewhere else?" She fixed her green eyes on us. "Like the afterlife."

Moira sucked hard on her lower lip, glancing at Talivar. "How much have you told them about Mother?"

"Enough," he said hesitantly.

Melanie and I exchanged a look. "You think Maurice has something to do with her . . . illness?"

Moira exhaled softly, her normally smooth face flawed by a deep wrinkle at her brow. "He has insinuated as much. The Court is losing patience and they are inclined to execute him for his crimes." She shrugged helplessly. "But she is my mother. And so I am here."

I sobered at that. If it had been my own mother, would I have done any less?

She gazed up at me, the ache of loss cutting deep. I reached out to grasp her hand, her delicate fingers twining tightly through mine.

Talivar hovered behind me for a moment, arm sliding

around my waist and the three of us stood there for a span of heartbeats. I closed my eyes as he rested his head upon my shoulder, his forehead pressed into Moira's.

Family.

My heart jolted at the thought. It wasn't unpleasant, simply a venture into the unknown. Phineas let out a polite cough at our feet. "Not to interrupt the whole kumbaya vibe you've all got going on, but maybe we ought to can the love-in for the moment. There seems to be a contingent coming our way."

Abruptly, we pulled away from each other, though Talivar's fingers lingered in my hair. Beside me, Melanie made a slightly strangled sound, whipping her violin from its case in a matter of seconds. Curious, I glanced up to see three daemons bearing down upon us.

Two of them were hooded and cloaked, their faces masked within the shadowed darkness of something akin to black burlap. But the one in front looked like the lead singer of a J-Rock band. The low-slung leather pants would have given Brystion a run for his money in the smexy brooding department, but the sleeveless shirt and the laced arm-socks that reached midbicep catapulted him straight into visual kei. His bangs alone were a peacock's tail of spikes that defied explanation, the rest of his artfully tousled hair cascading down his back in a hue of extravagant greens and purples. The effect was offset by a great cape sweeping behind him in an ebony wash of feathers.

I couldn't quite help the slow whistle from escaping my pursed lips. "Who's the glamurai?"

"Fallen angel," Melanie noted, her voice trembling. "Soul eater."

I blinked. "Like from Death Note?"

The daemon raised a sardonic brow at me. "Not quite." He turned to Melanie, his expression unreadable. "Not yet.

I was a sin eater once. Do you remember which of your sins I was forced to consume?"

"Pride," she confessed bitterly. Her foot started tapping in time and before I could ask her what she was doing, a hideous screech rang out from her violin. Aghast, she stopped, the bow hovering inches from the strings as she stared at it in horror.

"That's a bit against the rules, isn't it?" The daemon gave a curt bow to Moira, his almond eyes lighting up with amusement. "Guess it's a good thing Mumsy hasn't re-opened the CrossRoads yet. The Wild Magic is warped, I'm afraid. A bit hard to tap into its power when the flow is being blocked at both ends." He focused on Melanie, reaching out as though he might stroke the side of the violin.

She neatly sidestepped him and he chuckled. "Our Master wishes you to know He thinks of you often. Anytime you'd like to come home, merely say the word."

She retreated another step and I moved in front of her. Phineas's horn flared with silver light at my feet. "This is not your domain, *lapsus*."

"It's not yours either," the daemon said pleasantly as he crouched to look at Phin. "It's also none of your business." His eyes slyly roamed up Melanie's body. "None but hers and mine. Pity about your wrist, little bird. I heard we almost had you a few months ago."

I grabbed her arm, holding it through a rush of tremors. "This has nothing to do with why we are here," I snapped.

He paused, his face puzzled. I held myself steady beneath the icy brilliance of his gaze, willing myself not to flinch. "No," he agreed, staring at my neck, "but I think you are." He withdrew to stand with his little group, inclining his head at Moira respectfully. "It would seem I underestimated you, Princess. For here you have collected the surest single way to rule all of the Paths. . . . Our lovely Door

Maker"—he gestured to Melanie—"and now, the Keeper of the CrossRoads."

"You can see it, then?" The words fell from my mouth before I could stop them. Talivar let out a hiss.

"No, but I can bluff pretty damn well. And now you've confirmed it," he added slyly. "Might want to make sure you're well guarded. Hate to see you lose your head over such a bauble."

Talivar tensed behind me, but before I could do anything Melanie let out a soft sigh of reproach. "Nobu." Just a name, and yet the air seemed to vibrate with the roll of the syllables, a distant echo of power pressing behind the words.

The daemon stiffened, his eyes narrowing. "You dare?"

"Put it on my tab," she snarled at him. "I'm damned anyway."

"You always did have balls, Mel." He reached out to tap her teashades. "Someday I'm going to ask for these back, you know."

"Yes. But not now."

His hand lingered in her hair for a moment, stroking down the corner of her jawline before tipping her head to the side to expose the silver mark there. Melanie tended to rub it when she got nervous, but I'd never really thought about it. Until now. "Does it still burn?"

She glanced down at her feet. "Every day."

"Good." He straightened, releasing her. "What does thou wish of me?"

Melanie bit her lip, her eyes darting between me and the two elves. "Leave. Now. Take all of those daemons and go back to where you came from."

"Can't do that, sweetheart." A thin smile twisted his lips. "My orders come from higher up than you, I'm afraid. The most I can do is retreat for a short while."

"How long?"

The daemon paused. "Three days I can grant you. If in that time no other bargain has been struck, we will be forced to come and take what is ours." His gaze rested upon her with something like regret. "Including you."

"What are you doing?" I hissed at her.

"Done." Retreating a few steps, she picked up her fallen violin case and fled toward the cluster of tents behind us. The guards separated like a ripple of water, allowing her to pass.

I moved to follow her, but Talivar's hand on my wrist halted me abruptly. He shook his head. "Wait." I shut my mouth against the questions bubbling up, the grimness of his tone the deciding factor in my sudden lack of curiosity.

Moira's nostrils flared. "So be it. In three days time shall our factors meet again to discuss the terms, whatever they shall be. Until then, we ask that you quit the field."

"Agreed." Nobu nodded briefly at each of us in turn, his upper lip curling at me. "And don't let me catch you using that little charm to wander where you shouldn't be," he added, pointing at my neck. "Or our bargain will be nullified."

Before I could answer, the cloak exploded into a set of midnight wings, launching Nobu skyward like a Satanic peacock. The other two daemons shrugged at each other and bowed to us before trudging back to the daemon camp. A tad anticlimactic given their companion had just made an exit straight out of an anime, but at least they were gone.

"I don't trust them." Moira tucked a stray lock of hair behind her ear. "They've given us their word, but they'll twist it, for certain."

"I don't get it . . . what did Melanie do?"

"Names have power," Phineas said, turning in the direction Melanie had gone.

"It's part of the bargain she made," Talivar added, giving my hand a squeeze. "You've a power of your own, to command such loyalty from your friends."

My face flushed hot. "I would never have asked her to do such a thing."

"No," he agreed, his face softening. "And that is why she did it."

I clung to Talivar, the horse moving beneath us in a rhythmic trot that threatened to vibrate the teeth from my mouth. In front of us, Moira led the procession of elven nobility to what I could only guess would be the Faerie kingdom proper. I twisted Talivar's ring, remembering some of the more ancient tales I'd read in the Pit. Would it be real? Or would it all be a Glamour, the castle stones merely mud-covered walls and beds of leaves, wretched Fae groveling in the dirt? I hesitated to ask, not sure I really wanted to know.

Melanie's last actions continued to hammer through my head, distracting me from my internal angst. A quick glance found her trudging behind the procession, Brystion at her side. My heart skipped to see them both together, though they'd been friends far longer than I'd known the incubus.

And who do you ride behind? I wondered. *What do you owe him, when he left you?*

"What a fucking mess."

Talivar cocked his head toward me. "It could be better," he admitted. "And the incubus . . . complicates things."

"But it shouldn't. I'm not here for him. I'm here for you and for Moira. He and I have a history, it's true, but that's for us to work out."

"Moira said he came here upon your request, but that the Queen insisted he stay to state his testimony against Maurice." His mouth tensed. "I'm not sure he was given much of a choice. He has offered his services to us should we need a daemonic liaison in the meantime."

"So I'm an ass twice over," I muttered. "Once for asking him to go, and once for . . ." I paused. For what? Betraying him?

"Do you regret last night?" Talivar's voice was gentle, a soft hush intended only for my ears. I could detect a subtle note of resignation behind it, as though he'd already made up his mind to be rejected and was steeling himself against it. A rush of anger heated my face.

"No," I said fiercely. "And I would not regret it if it happened again."

The tips of his ears pinked. "He was a fool to let you go."

I shrugged. Ex-boyfriends were always a touchy subject, but this was a powder keg of emotions threatening to explode. I hurried along, searching for a safer topic. "I'm more worried about Melanie right now. And Benjamin."

"We must see to the Queen first. If she can reopen the CrossRoads, that will enable us to move between worlds much faster. I'd rather have Robert bring the boy directly to Faerie, instead of being forced to travel to Eildon Tree if you have to open the Door locally." He gazed out to where the daemon camp lay. "Regardless of his parentage, the boy is a prince of the Fae and an heir to the throne. We can't risk it."

I peered around Talivar to watch Moira ride. Her seat was easy and graceful upon the white mare. Was she thinking about her baby? Robert? Or was everything in her head coolly assessing what was to come, full of treaties and political backlash? Clearly my newfound sister was made of stronger stuff than I.

And still, there was Melanie. Incubus or not, she and I had to talk. I didn't mind secrets, but there was so much more going on here than I knew. "How much farther is it?"

"A few miles, by your reckoning. Where are you going?"

I'd already slid off the horse, making sure to land on my good knee. Pulling out my skirts, I gave him a small smile. "I've got some things I need to discuss. I'll catch up with you later."

He frowned, glancing behind us and then nodded curtly, trotting off to ride beside his sister. Standing to one side to avoid being trampled by the rest of the procession, I let the other horses pass, overwhelmed for a moment by the prancing hooves and the shining armor. The elves were nothing if not beautiful. And yet, what price did they pay for it?

I spotted Melanie walking a short distance from the rest of the wagons. Ion sauntered a few paces behind her, his face thoughtful. Girding my mental loins, I headed toward them, one hand shielding my face to avoid the dust kicked up by the horses.

"Coming to mingle with the commoners?" Bryston asked, arching a brow when I started coughing. "Careful. It's a bit dusty back here. All that filth we're coated in."

I shot him a dirty look and motioned to Melanie. "Can we talk? Alone?" I pointed toward a small outcropping with a few moss-covered stones jutting up from the ground. "Come on, we'll sit over there."

She looked up at me miserably, her eyes red. She'd been crying. "Jesus, I suck." Scowling at the incubus, I waved him off, tugging gently on her arm. "Go on. We'll catch up with you later."

"Not hardly, Abby." Bryston curled his upper lip. "Go do your girl thing over there if you have to, but I refuse to simply walk away and leave either of you unprotected. I'm surprised the prince allowed it, frankly. What with you two being so important and all."

"*Now* you care." I ignored the barb and led Melanie over to the rocks, finding a seat on the largest one. "Besides, we've got an accord of sorts. Surely there's honor in that, even among daemons?" I arched a brow at him.

"You tell me. I only happen to be one." Without waiting for a reply, he marched several yards away to lean lazily against the golden smoothness of a nearby beech, his dark eyes gleaming as he watched us. I turned my back on him.

"You gonna tell me what all this is about? I know you've got your secrets with the violin, but we can't go into this blind . . . or at least I can't."

She pushed the hair out of her face, tucking the flyaways beneath her bandana. "It's complicated." She rubbed at her neck, lingering on the spot Nobu had exposed.

"Isn't it always?" A halfhearted chuckle escaped her. "You don't have to tell me all of it if you want to wait until we're somewhere more private."

"Ion already knows the story," she said wryly. "After all, he was there." She slid the battered violin case from her shoulder, popping it open to reveal the instrument in all its silver-hued glory. The sunlight played upon the bridge so that the colors seemed to ripple beneath it.

"I was TouchStoned to Nobu once." She said softly, stroking the strings with callused fingers, sadness lingering about her mouth as she said it. "Before I came to Portsmyth. I was stupid and arrogant and I thought I could bend the world to my whim." Her lips pursed. "I was a better musician than he was, but not by much."

"And modest too," I added with a small wink. I tried not to look over at the incubus, but curiosity burned within me. I'd known they were close, but it was irritating to realize he knew such an intimate part of her that I did not.

Her gaze became distant as she watched the caravan trundle past. "We wandered from place to place, playing for our supper. They were good years. And then I had to go and spoil it all by trying to take on more than I could handle."

"So how does the violin come into play? Or is this the part that gets complicated?"

"Yeah. Did you know the Devil has a violinist for a TouchStone?"

"Erm. No. And you're being awfully free with that name now, aren't you?"

She shrugged. "Nobu knows I'm here, so He knows I'm here. Nothing I say or do at this point will change that."

I wondered at her nonchalance, but decided it wasn't worth pointing out. The tremor in her voice was more than I felt like rubbing her face. "So. TouchStone?"

"Yeah. In a nutshell, I challenged him for a chance to win an instrument that would allow me to open Doors to the CrossRoads with the Wild Magic. Seems simple enough, except for the part where I lost."

I blinked at her. "You lost?"

"Mmm. On a number of fronts." Her fingers curled around the neck of her violin. "Turns out it was more of an audition than a challenge, if you catch my drift."

A terrible thought crossed my mind and I stared at her in horror. "Christ, you're not *His* TouchStone are you?"

"No. Not yet." She rubbed violently at her neck, craning her head to show me her silver violinist hickey. "The Devil's mark. Nobu was forced to kiss me there to seal the bargain when I lost, but he absorbed the sin of my arrogance in doing so." Her gaze flicked to Brystion, her eyes glazing with unshed tears. "My soul was forfeit by all rights, but Nobu traded himself for me. The joke was on me, of course. Even though no one else can play the thing, I can't make Doors for myself either."

A lightbulb went off in my head. "Hence the short-term Contracts."

"Yeah." Melanie fumbled in her pocket like she was looking for a cigarette. "I can't really trust anyone for very long.

The OtherFolk, I mean. They all know I can open Doors and almost all of them want full control of that. I did the Contract with Talivar for you . . . and because I didn't have much choice if I wanted to play again."

I flinched inwardly, glancing down at her wrist. No sign of broken bones now; the flesh was soft and supple. Our eyes met, regret and courage sliding between us without another word. I rubbed my own knee in sympathy. There was obviously a lot more to this story than she was going to go into, but I had enough for now.

"Seems like he still cares about you. Maybe there's a way to make it right." I nudged her gently, wrapping my arm around her waist. She rested her head on my shoulder.

"If he does, it's nothing I deserve. Besides, the moment I agree to my end of the bargain, he'll be set free." Her knuckles whitened. "I'm nothing more than a cowardly, selfish bitch."

"Makes two of us," I murmured. "We should start a support group where we write sad poems in our journals about it." She sucked in a shuddering breath. It wasn't quite a sob and not a laugh, but it was better than nothing. I gestured at the incubus. "He can be our dark and smexy mascot of broodiness."

He raised a brow in my direction, but there was a hint of amusement about him as he spoke. "My life's aspiration, clearly. And we should probably get going. Wouldn't want to keep the Queen waiting."

"Eh, I've always rather enjoyed being fashionably late." I picked up the violin case for Melanie, giving her a hug before clambering off the rock. "I feel like we should be leading a procession in, Pied Piper style."

"I know just the thing." A hint of her old self peeked through her eyes.

A moment later the first bars of "Safety Dance"

hummed from the strings. I bit my lip trying not to giggle. Together the two of us broke out in lopsided chorus as I twirled about her. Ignoring the stares of the elves, we strutted up the center of caravan, Bryston trailing behind us bemusedly.

Twenty-one

The castle rose up in the distance, ensnared within the hollow heart of a massive tree. Or maybe the castle was the tree, carved into the very bark like some sort of living sculpture. I wasn't sure what I had been expecting. Something out of Camelot, maybe. Towering spires of pearlescent ivory and frosted sugar–pane windows. But the wild twining of the tree trunks suggested a different story altogether, its dark and feral beauty threatening to swallow me up into a prison of sap and rotting vegetation.

Melanie and I had woven in and out of the procession with various levels of nervousness and hysterical laughter. At one point we were joined by Phineas, who insisted on reciting bawdy haiku. Still, it was my only defense mechanism left, the knowledge of what was at stake taking root in my mouth until my tongue was only a desiccated lump. And now, here we were, approaching the very heart of Faerie itself.

Around me, the elves shed the visage of their Glamours, taking on a wilder countenance of their own, everything about them sharper and paler, the magic nearly seeping from their skin. My eyes blurred with it, and I felt as though

I were an elephant shuffling through a bounding herd of deer.

Before long we were at the front of the procession, the line halted at the massive gate of thorns barring the path. Talivar and Moira dismounted from their horses. If there was any sense of impatience about them, I couldn't tell, my vision lost in the appearance of the nearly four-foot-long spikes blocking our passage as far as I could see. The elves both seemed taller than I remembered, with eyes slanted high and wild. Talivar's hair had come loose and the tattered edges of my amateur chop job framed his face in a dark tangle.

I didn't quite look at Melanie, but her presence at my side was a welcoming shadow of mortality. I would have hidden in it if I could have. The weight of Faerie pressed upon me with a terrible certainty.

"The Queen has sealed the entryway," Talivar said, his voice soft. "A sacrifice is required to pass."

"That sounds reassuring," I muttered, getting awfully tired at the Fae woman's paranoia. Maybe it was unfair considering her kingdom was about to be invaded, but all these little trials seemed like a big waste of time given our own situation.

Moira gave me a wan smile. "It requires a drop of blood from each person who passes." Her eyes flicked to where Brystion stood. "Although it would normally not allow the passage of daemons—"

"My blood has already been tasted by the gate," the incubus said brusquely. "It knows who I am."

"Of course." To me and Melanie, she gestured at a tiny thorn midway up the first branch, very much like where a lock might be on a normal door. "Simply place a finger here and the gate will allow you to pass."

"If I fall asleep for a thousand years, I'm counting on one

of you to come to the rescue." I'd intended it as a joke, but the elves merely stared at me as though it might very well be an option. Shuddering, I watched as one of the elvish guards stepped forward and removed her gauntlet, her hand nimbly snaking forward. She didn't even flinch as the thorn pricked her and I began to wonder if this was merely a formality after all. The thorns parted to allow her passage and she slipped easily through the curving vines without even snagging her cloak.

I glanced down at my own dress and shook my head. If I didn't manage to somehow trip over my own feet and hurdle headlong into the thing it would be a small miracle. I allowed myself to be jostled aside as the body of the dead Protectorate was brought through, her shrouded form a clear reminder of why I was there.

Don't be such a pussy, Abby. I straightened, watching as the cart was allowed to pass without incident. "She has paid her price," Melanie murmured beside me. She bound up her violin in its case as we waited. "I'd rather not see what happens if I get blood on the wood."

"Probably a good idea." Phineas nudged me with his horn. "Pick me up. I can't reach the thing."

"Guess the Fae don't believe in pet doors."

"Everyone's a comedian." He scrambled into my arms when I stooped down. "See if I do you any favors later on."

Stretching out a dainty hoof, Phineas scraped his foreleg on the thorn lock, hissing at the streak of scarlet marring his perfect white coat. I followed suit, refusing to be cowed by a giant plant.

As my finger brushed the point, I stiffened, the pain sharp and sudden, lancing down my arm. Immediately a burning heat swelled along my fingers, a deep pull as the thorn absorbed the blood. I had the distinct impression it would happily suck me dry if I continued to stand there, and

I jerked my hand away, surprised at how deep the point had gone.

Clenching my hand into a fist, I shifted Phin in my arms, the vines slithering open to reveal a tunnel. I smiled at Talivar, trying not to let my uncertainty show. "I'll meet you on the other side." I could feel Ion's eyes burning into my back, but I resisted the urge to look at him, ducking under the brushy overhang.

It went quickly, the thorns parting as I stepped forward and then closing at my passage. In the murky depths I saw the white gleam of bone, an empty grin of a skull hanging upon a thorn like a teacup. "Looks like someone didn't have permission." Phineas's ears flattened. "This place always gives me the creeps."

"I'm surprised they're even afraid the daemons could get through, frankly. Faerie seems to have its own protections."

He gave an equine shrug, nipping at my bodice. "Fire still works. As do chainsaws," he added. "Or iron. The advances of your world have changed the balance among the paths. It makes them uncomfortable."

"I'm just the messenger." I hopped over a large root, my boots grinding against the bark. "But I guess I can understand it. Suppose they haven't brought in firearms yet?"

He snuffled into my shoulder. "No. They don't work too well here. Something about the firing mechanism doesn't allow for them. Yet."

"Small favors." Up ahead, a burst of light signaled what I could only assume was the exit. Sure enough the vines split open and I emerged into a large clearing, the other elves standing at attention, their crystalline gazes spearing me. I blinked at the rush of sunlight, and carefully set down the unicorn.

A heartbeat later revealed Brystion shouldering his way through the hedge, his dark eyes finding me almost immediately. My heart lurched at his beauty, but I told it to shut up.

"Why can't I quit you?" I muttered. For all my fine words to Talivar, the truth was that I wasn't over him.

As though he could sense my thoughts, the incubus approached me, his face unreadable. "Did it hurt? Getting pricked?"

Volumes of innuendo in *that* particular statement.

Before I could answer he took my hand, turning it over to run a careful finger over the now-clotting wound. "Shall I kiss it and make it better?" He raised it to his lips, his gaze never leaving mine as the faintest hint of gold flared to life around the dark pupils. I willed myself not to react, but a small whimper escaped me anyway.

"Why are you doing this?"

"Because you're taken," Talivar said coolly, brushing a stray leaf from his shoulder. I jerked my hand back, flushing hot. The elven prince stepped in front of me. He and Brystion were nearly the same height and the two men sized each other up with a simple nod.

Brystion snorted. "He's only using you. The Fae are good at that, I've noticed."

"I was there the morning you let her go," Talivar retorted. "Why shouldn't I retrieve what you so casually threw away?"

I bristled. *We are so not going there.* I debated shoving them apart but the memory of getting clocked upside the head last time I attempted to stop a fight between Paths was still a tad fresh for my liking. The fact that the incubus had been part of that little throw-down too wasn't lost on me either. I gave both of them a hard look, finally tossing my hands up in the air.

"Let's make this simple," I snapped. "I'm done with

both of you. Think you all can stop thinking with your cocks for thirty seconds now?"

Melanie and Moira had emerged from the hedge by this point, both of them giving us puzzled glances. I shrugged and stalked up the path that appeared to lead to the castle.

A strangled snort sounded from behind me, but I didn't bother turning around. Fuck them both if they couldn't get their heads out of their asses long enough to work together.

Of course, I wasn't entirely sure where I was going, but I wasn't going to let a little thing like that stop me. Glancing over at the nearest guard, I inclined my head politely at him. "Care to escort me to the palace? I believe the Steward is expecting me."

The guard gaped at me for a moment and then Moira cleared her throat. "Indeed," she said dryly. "Methinks cooler heads might prevail." Snapping her fingers at her brother and Bryston, she gave them a withering smile. "You two go on ahead and let the Queen know of our arrival. See that Abby and Melanie are given rooms in the royal wing." She paused, her teeth snapping shut. "Next to mine."

The men exchanged an abashed look, Talivar bowing to his sister. "As milady commands," he said formally. Something hardened in her eyes, but she said nothing, watching impassively as he mounted his white stallion. Sparing me a sideways wink, the prince galloped off, the thud of his horse's hooves clattering in the distance.

"Suppose I'm walking," Bryston noted.

"It will be good for you." Moira's voice remained icy. "Mayhap give your head a chance to cool. I will not have infighting among my allies, incubus." Her gaze flicked to me. "Regardless of where their affections may lie. There are far more important things at stake."

"Of course, Your Highness." He sketched a quick bow of his own before sauntering up the path, hands shoved into his pockets.

I stifled the urge to sigh. "There are times when I really dislike men."

"Being so highly sought after is a great burden, to be sure." Moira arched an amused brow at me. "And I fear it will only get worse as we get closer to the palace. Courtiers are not always known for their discretion. Despite the oncoming war, you will be considered fair game, especially as you rather publicly gave up your claim on either man."

"But why would anyone care?" I already knew the answer as the words fell from my lips. KeyStone. Keeper of the CrossRoads. Steward's daughter. Princess's sister. Lover of the Crippled Prince. So many titles . . . and not a single one really belonged to me. I twisted Talivar's ring upon my finger, feeling as though the vines of the hedge were strangling me, even so.

"What about her?" I punched Melanie lightly in the arm. "She's the one with the magic violin."

"I've got my own problems." Melanie gave me a wry smile. "At least it won't be boring."

Moira's mouth pursed. "With you two, it never is."

We walked the remainder of the road to the palace. Time may have been of the essence, but I suspected Moira wanted to give Talivar a chance to warn the Steward of my approach, the presence of the Queen notwithstanding. The princess had assured me that a hot bath and clean clothes would be provided, along with a small meal before we were presented to the Queen.

"Things run at their own pace here," she murmured. "And protocol is almost always followed, regardless of the rest of it."

I nodded. Truth be told I would have loved a nap. Something warned me that I would need all my wits about me in this place. The road was deceptive in length, a twisted, windy thing, overgrown with gnarled roots and creeping moss, bloodred mushrooms and crystalline flowers in the softest hue of azure. Before and behind us remained the guard, but it was slow going with us occasionally forced to march in single file around a particularly large tree. And yet somehow it all felt empty, the air still and stale.

As if the magic was fading.

My thoughts wandered to the Barras and the massive wave of transient Fae there. The Unseelie Court was considered simple and callow and feral to the elves, perhaps. But Jimmy Squarefoot surely had not been, even with his fearsome appearance. And Kitsune had her own graceful sense of judgment and honor.

The Fae, I realized, were racist. At least the elves, with their need for beauty and perfection. What fate, then, to one who didn't meet such stringent requirements? It didn't take me long to realize Talivar's appeal to the lost Unseelie kingdom . . . the outcast prince, a friend of royal blood, and a possible way home.

"I would have thought there would be a more straightforward way to get there. Doesn't it seem dangerous to have the main road so overgrown?" Melanie ducked beneath the branch of a low-hanging willow.

"That is precisely the point," Moira said. "Natural defense such as this give us time to prepare and are often much easier defended. Besides, the forest around us can be quite deadly given the proper motivation."

I thought about the table of bones from this morning and shuddered. "No doubt." I debated the wisdom of pointing out that by shunning the lesser Fae from the inner sanctum of their kingdom, the elves may have removed one of their internal ways of defense. In the end I bit my tongue. I was the stranger here, after all.

We rounded the last bend and the palace proper came into view. As we approached, I could see that while the inner sanctum did appear to be rooted directly in the base of the tree itself, the palace extended behind it for quite a ways. Spiraled staircases wove up to the taller branches, cleverly notched into the bark. I could only imagine how easily archers might hide deep behind those leaves to let fly a rain of arrows. Death from above, maybe.

"It's impressive, in a retro-Lothlorian sort of way," Melanie said. "But it seems like it would be easy to . . . I don't know. Set it on fire?" The princess stiffened and Mel backpedaled. "Well, it *is* made of wood. I was just assuming that it would . . . um. Burn?"

"The tree drinks from an aquifer," Phineas piped up before Moira could draw herself up any further. "It runs far below ground here, but its natural magics have infused the bark with powers of regeneration. Not that it hasn't been tried before," he added beneath his breath.

"Legends say we are merely fallen angels." Moira's eyes stared off into the distance as though she were someplace else entirely. "We cannot return to Heaven, but neither do we belong in Hell. Living in the trees reminds us of this—halfway between the earth and sky." She winked at me. "Or perhaps we just like the view."

"I'll bet Benjamin would like it. Leaping from branch to branch like a little bird?" The image pleased me and I could only hope the boy would get a chance to do so.

Moira's face became troubled. "Please, Abby. Don't speak of my son here. I want him beneath notice. As long as he is safe, that is all that matters—but I do not wish Maurice to discover more than he already has."

I bit down hard on my cheek. "Sorry." Moira ignored me,

her attention drawn to the sudden appearance of Talivar, striding from the main doors of the hall. Exasperation bit deep into the lines of his face and I wondered if he and the incubus had already managed to get into it again. Not that I'd seen Ion since he'd wandered off either.

"We have a small problem." The prince took Moira by the arm. "The Queen has insisted on seeing Abby now. Maurice is before the Council again."

"This is about me giving testimony, isn't it?" The blood drained from my face as I set Phineas down. Sure, I wanted to see the bastard gutted for everything he'd done to me and my friends, but to do so here, where the chances of me screwing something up were so high seemed ludicrous.

"I'm afraid so," Talivar said grimly. "I had been hoping to get you prepared to see her first, but it looks as though she'll have her way. She is not having one of her better days, Abby. Try not to anger her, if you can."

"What the hell kind of advice is that?"

"The best I can give you right now." He ducked his head to kiss my cheek, his voice dropping low. "Be cautious in your words. Maurice has his own supporters among the court, although they may not always be obvious."

"Great. No pressure or anything."

Phineas prodded my shin with his horn. "Stop whining. It's unbecoming."

"Like I have anyone to impress?"

"Your father, for one," he said, his tone gentle. "Let's not melt down in front of the family."

My anger drained away at the thought, leaving behind only a hollow weariness. "Fine. Let's get the gawking over with. Then maybe I can get something to eat." My stomach rumbled at the thought, but at this point it was probably better that it was empty. Nothing like vomiting on the Queen's ruby slippers to make my humiliation complete.

I let Talivar slip his arm into mine as he escorted me up a set of limestone steps, bleached soft and white and overhung with ivy. My hands shook and his fingers tightened around my elbow, somehow managing to steer me in the right direction without making it look like he was helping.

I glanced behind me to see Melanie and Moira bringing up the rear, Melanie peering about her in a strange fascination, as though she were writing music in her head. Maybe she was.

Moments later we were whisked down a series of hallways, all within the inner reaches of the tree. Light slanted from above through a canopy of soft leaves, bathing the floor in tiny pools of gold. My heart lurched as though it meant to take flight through my mouth.

An intricately carved set of wooden doors opened as we approached and I had only a moment to notice they had the same sorts of markings as the stone Door at the Judgment Hall. I swallowed hard, barely noticing the wall of courtiers lined up on either side of the throne room. I had a vague approximation of a multihued explosion of silks, the aching beauty of the people around me nearly overwhelming.

A page announced us by name, but I ignored it as Talivar led me down the steps into the throne room. My focus narrowed on the curved, crescent stone table, so much like the one in the Judgment Hall, except this time there was actually a full contingent of elves filling the seats, each one attired in lavish dress and a bland expression. Before them was the Petitioner's chair.

There I met Maurice's beetle-bright eyes, steeling myself against the sly smile creeping over his face. His wrists were bound in front of him, but I didn't take any solace from that fact. Anyone who'd ever been in his presence surely had to know it was his silken viper's tongue that was the real threat.

I had the sinking feeling we were playing straight into his

hands. At the very least he appeared to be enjoying my discomfort immensely.

The throne itself was carved directly into the tree, burnished to a soft golden color, smooth with the passing of more years than I could probably count. It sloped with great curling armrests, living vines bursting from the seat like a waterfall of greenery. Tiny pink roses dotted the edges.

Upon it sat the Queen of Elfland, cross-legged and regal. And bored as hell.

Her eyes glittered as her gaze raked across me. A feral intelligence lit up her face, and she shifted upon the throne, the porcelain curve of her calves peeking from the tattered shreds of her dress. Pointed ears, draped with rings of gold, thrust up from the riot of honey-blond curls piled upon her head.

She pitched up when she saw us, crouching so that she was balanced on the balls of her feet and cradling her head in her hands. "Naughty," she muttered. "Naughty, naughty lover to have betrayed me so."

Talivar stiffened and I risked a glance to see an echo of pain ghost over his face. It was bad enough to have your mother go slowly insane, I supposed, without watching her drag an entire kingdom down with her. He bowed, indicating that I should do the same. I attempted an imitation of a curtsey I'd have done on stage in my former ballerina days. The effect was probably ruined by the combat boots, but I wasn't going to beat myself up for it.

"Might I present my TouchStone, Your Majesty. I believe she may have information pertinent to your investigation." Talivar gestured to Moira, who moved to flank my other side. "We also bring word from the daemon encampment, which we would discuss with you in private."

The Queen stared at us, an odd wash of emotions playing over her face. Looking at it from her perspective, I had to admit it might be a touch unnerving to see the three of us together. That her children chose to stand by my side was no mistake, and bolder than I'd have liked, given the sudden rush of voices that sprung up through the room.

"Well, it's clear she's one of *yours*, Tom." The Queen was clearly unhappy at no longer being the center of attention. "I'd know the shape of that mouth anywhere." She licked her own lips suggestively, the red edges like overripe strawberries.

A flash of movement caught my eye as a man entered from a side chamber near the throne, wearing a simple robe that channeled only a touch of understated nobility in comparison to the peacock gaudiness of the others.

My father.

My head hammered with a rush of those forgotten memories as I drank him in, from the tousled brown hair loosely bound behind him to the piercing blue eyes, the gentle slope of his face, and the angled chin. The strong nose. The sad smile when his gaze found mine.

Maurice made a self-satisfied cough. "Well, that's one mystery solved. Pity I wasn't aware of it when I took you, Abby." His eyes narrowed. "Things would have turned out much differently if I had, but that's quite the little group you've assembled behind you. Elven prince and princess. The Door Maker. Rumors of a certain amulet at your neck. One might think you're planning a coup."

There was another murmur at that, but Moira had already turned toward him. "Your words are not needed, traitor. Still your tongue."

"I have earned the right to be heard, as well you know, lover. How's our son, by the way? I can't help but notice he's not with you. I do hope the poor lad is okay. What with all those strange seizures going around."

I opened my mouth to interject, but a warning squeeze

from Talivar stopped me and I bit down on my lower lip instead. Maurice chuckled, the sound rippling like ice water down my spine. The Queen's eyes narrowed. "Did you know your pet daemon is here too, Abby darling? I heard he broke your heart. Pity." He raised his bound hands in front of him, one finger pressing into his lips. "Say, isn't there a daemon army camped out by Eildon Tree? Convenient."

The throne room exploded in an uproar, accusations being thrown in all directions. I shared a panicked look with Melanie, trying to measure how quickly I could get the hell out of the room, when things immediately quieted down. The Steward calmly walked toward the Council, one hand held up.

"Peace, friends," he said, his voice ringing over the crowd with a tone of warm finality. I frowned, the soothing cadence of his words sinking all around us like raindrops on a pond.

If I'd had any doubts that this was the True Thomas of legend, they were gone now.

"I do believe our guest has overstayed his welcome once again." Thomas gestured toward a smirking Maurice. "Perhaps it would not be amiss to see him to his cell while we sort out these grave accusations he puts forth." A hint of mockery lingered on the word "accusations" as though one would have to be mad to believe them. Awkward chuckles emerged in response, but I caught several courtiers exchanging glances of dismay. Maurice supporters, perhaps?

The Steward gestured to a pair of guards standing on either side of Maurice, indicating they should escort him away.

Maurice said nothing, but his eyes sparkled with glee at the interruption he'd made, laughing to himself as he was led out of the throne room. I sighed with relief that I wasn't going to be made a spectacle of this time when I caught sight of the Queen, still sitting upon her throne.

She tilted her head at me as though nothing had happened. "What do you do?"

"I'm sorry?" Talivar coughed at my bluntness and I flushed. "Your pardon, Highness. I'm not sure I understand the question."

Her lip curled, a flash of pointed teeth showing. "What art do you perform? Are you a bard, a teller of tales, a juggler? Surely one of Thomas's get would be blessed with some sort of talent."

"I'm the TouchStone to the Protectorate of Portsmyth, Highness."

"Do not mock me, mortal." She snapped her fingers, rising to her feet to descend from the throne. "And do not make me ask you again. What are you?"

"I used to be a dancer."

"Used to?" Her brow arched. Pushing Talivar out of the way, she circled me critically.

"I was . . . injured." I kept my eyes down, though some part of me burned to look at my father, to will upon him the knowledge of what he'd left behind. But there was a tiger in my face and it would be folly to ignore her. "I am no longer able to perform in such a way."

"Pity. I prefer songs and poetry to anything else." She frowned, pulling at my skirts. "Where is this injury you speak of?"

My face burning, I exposed my leg, demonstrating its hypermobility. "I'm a bit messed up in the head too," I added, revealing the scar on my skull. "It sometimes affects my balance. And I have seizures."

That drew her up short, Talivar's warning shake coming a few seconds too late. Her gaze darted between me and Moira and I realized I'd made a terrible mistake. Silence filled the room as the others made the connection.

I was Moira's sister. I had seizures . . . something she had also recently suffered from. Such a lack of perfection would clearly make her unsuitable to rule. That the OtherFolk of Portsmyth had suffered even as their Protectorate had was irrefutable proof of the bond between ruler and land. Suddenly the Queen's refusal to reopen the CrossRoads made a hell of a lot more sense.

Bad enough she suffered her own mental illness, but to have it appear as though there were a genetic pass-down of physical instability? There was clearly a shrewdness to her methods, an instinctual need to protect her daughter despite her madness.

Moira's face paled even as the Queen let out a low hiss. Even if it had been caused by a spell, the very perception that the princess suffered from such an ailment only lowered her status in the Court's eyes.

Inwardly I cringed as I geared up to throw myself under the bus. "Moira's seizures are not of her making," I said, inspiration striking in the form of a half-assed explanation that actually made a strange sort of logic. Quickly, I explained Tresa's deception, aiming my words more at the court than at the Queen herself. "When the spell went off, only those I was TouchStoned to were to suffer the same." I paused, sparing a glance at Moira. "My belief is that because Moira was Protectorate, my seizures were given to all those beneath her protection. A sort of retroactive backlash of my own physical flaws."

Talivar stared at me in a sort of what-the-fuck admiration and I shrugged. "You have to admit it makes sense."

"But you are no longer my daughter's TouchStone?" If my explanation confused her, she didn't show it, her only focus on that of Moira's good name. The Queen leaned close, her scent thick and cloying and dank with an underlying sweetness, as though she no longer bathed but merely tossed on a spray of perfume.

I nearly gagged at it as Talivar caught my hand to hold me still. "No, Your Majesty. Due to the . . . situation . . . we were forced to transfer the title of Protectorate to your son."

Her eyes dropped to the ring still on my finger and she laughed, a brittle hiss. "A crippled TouchStone for a crippled prince. How fitting."

Anger flooded my limbs as Talivar stiffened, a red haze of fury filling my vision. "The hell with this. You—"

The blow came at my face like a bolt of lightning and I flinched, stumbling from an impact that never came. The Queen's fist slammed into Talivar's open palm, the prince staring at her impassively. The Queen blinked in surprise at her son's sudden movement of open rebellion.

"Not her," he snapped. "Hit me if you must, but not her—"

His words cut off with a stutter as her hand cracked against his face. "Take your whore and get out of my sight."

Moira rushed to her mother's side, sending Talivar a warning shake of her head. "Come, Your Highness, let's get you back to your rooms and cleaned up. Perhaps a spot of tea? We'll look at the roses in your garden."

The words nattered past me, their rhythmic and weary cadence suggesting they had been repeated many times in the last few weeks. I glanced up to see my sister and my father gently whisking the Queen from the hall.

Talivar sighed, the sound washed away by the conversation of the courtiers. As though released into mobility at their Queen's absence, the men and women seemed to sag, though they studiously attempted to ignore my presence with all the subtlety of a shoe in dog shit. The gossip would be damned good.

"Well, that could have gone better."

"It could have gone worse too." The prince rubbed his cheek with a wince. It had already started swelling from where his mother's rings had grazed him. "She's never been violent. A few more outbursts of that caliber and we're going to have a real problem."

"I suspect Maurice is counting on that," said Phin. "He couldn't have been any more obvious about his baiting if he'd painted a sign on his chest."

"*Real* problem? If that little scenario doesn't constitute a real problem, I don't know what does." I gestured at the throne. "I don't understand why *any* of them are still following her commands at all. She's nuts."

"Creatures of habit," the prince said. "Thousands of years of rule are hard to break. We've grown complacent, blindingly following protocol beyond reason."

Melanie shifted her violin on her back. "What about the CrossRoads?"

Talivar nodded, staring where his mother had gone. "The Steward is who we really need to talk to right now, but he'll have to wait until my mother is settled first. Sometimes she requires him to play for hours after one of these episodes. It's the only thing that calms her."

"Well, if it helps any, maybe I can take over for him? If it's just about the music. I've been told I'm not too bad," Melanie said dryly.

I fidgeted, discomfited in my own skin and tired of being observed like some sort of trained dog. I was done with jumping through hoops. "Well, I could use a bath. And something to eat before I fall over."

"Of course," the prince agreed, pausing when a page dashed up to hand him a message before hurrying off again, his little feet slapping hard upon the floor. Talivar grimaced. "Seems my presence has been requested a bit sooner than I thought. Let me find you a guide to your rooms."

Phineas shook himself out. "I know the way."

"Do you?" Talivar frowned. "I don't remember ever seeing you trotting down these hallways before."

"You weren't looking properly," the unicorn said cheerfully. "And I didn't say I traveled using the hallways. No fear, though. If I can figure out which end means business on a hedgehog, I can find a couple of bedrooms." He lifted his nose. "Gotta follow the scent of panties."

The three of us gave a collective shudder. "I think I just threw up in my mouth a little," Melanie grumbled.

Talivar lifted my hand to his lips. "Were we not in the throne room, I'd send you off with something a bit more intimate. But I will come to you as soon as I can."

"I'll be waiting."

He bowed again and disappeared down the same corridor his family had taken.

For once, I would have liked things to be simple. With a sigh and a sinking heart, I followed Phin down the hallway, his hooves tapping in time like the beginnings of a dirge.

Twenty-two

I emerged from beneath the steaming water with a sigh, rolling my head on the edge of the copper tub. Blissful quiet hovered about the room—my suite of rooms, in fact, which had been set up adjacent to Moira's. Melanie's were on the other side of mine, a shared door allowing us to move between them.

Evening sunlight swept in through an ivy-latticed window, the wood polished to the same burnished glow as the throne room. It should have been wondrous and relaxing, but given my earlier impressions I couldn't help but feel I was a bird in a gilded cage.

Of Talivar and Moira there had been no sign, although a crystalline invitation from the Queen was delivered to my rooms shortly after I'd arrived. Dinner and dancing. Like I was on some sort of hellish cruise ship. What was a mere daemon invasion against an evening of profiteroles and petticoats? A wretched giggle exploded through my nose, bubbles swirling in response.

Not like I had anything to wear anyway. The lavender dress was travel worn and dusty and probably not appropriate. Hell, what difference did it make? The Queen was insane and wearing rags. Me showing up naked would probably be an improvement.

I wiped a weary hand over my eyes at the futility of it all. And yet I couldn't help but see Talivar there, unflinching as his mother slapped him, and continuing to offer her support. No wonder he couldn't find a wife. Even if they managed to overlook his physical imperfections, there wasn't a woman in the world who'd want *that* as a mother-in-law.

Pulling the stopper from the drain, I swung my legs out of the copper tub, sighing when my feet touched the thick lambskin carpet. I toweled off quickly, pulling my hair up into a loose bun. A glance in the standing glass mirror showed the flare of bruising at my neck and I traced my fingers over them, my face flushing hot. Whore, indeed.

"See something you like?" Bryston purred at me from the windowsill.

Startled, I nearly dropped the towel before descending on him. "What are you doing here?"

"So glad you're happy to see me," he retorted dryly. "And obviously I climbed up the window trellis." He flexed his fingers.

"Multitalented, just like I remember."

His eyes sparked gold, but he merely pulled himself through the sill, crouching on the ledge with a lazy curl of thigh.

"Why are you here, Ion?"

"You should know. Weren't you the one who asked me to come?" A rueful smile crossed his face. "Despite my better judgment, it would appear I can deny you nothing. Though I hate to say I told you so."

"No, no, go ahead. Tell me what an idiot I am for getting us all involved in this Spectacular Craptacular production. You did warn me, after all."

"I seem to recall warning you about a lot of things," he pointed out. "And that's never stopped you before."

"That's not what I mean and you know it." I scowled, hugging the towel a little closer. It wasn't like he hadn't already seen me in all my glory, but I wasn't too eager to be strolling around with all my bits and pieces showing either.

His face softened. "I know." Uncoiling from the ledge, he strolled over to the bed, one finger sliding along the bedpost. I exhaled sharply, remembering what it was like to have all that muscular perfection stretched out on top of me, the way he'd bitten my neck, licked my shoulder . . .

Perfection.

I shook my head, amazed at my own gall. Talivar had no such recourse, beyond Glamour. I shut my eyes against the imagined hurt.

"You shouldn't be here." My voice was strangled. "Please go."

He exhaled, the sound puffing against my ear. "Are you sure that's what you want?" One hand slid over my shoulder, a miniature explosion of heat prickling my skin.

"No," I admitted. "But you don't get to do this, Ion. You left me. Swore up and down that you couldn't be what I needed. That you wanted more for *me*."

"And you think Talivar is it?"

"I have no idea. It may be something. It may be nothing. But guess what? It's none of your business. That's what letting go of someone means." I sagged onto the bed. "And I've got too much going on right now to have to worry about . . . this. Us. Whatever."

He stared out the window. "It's funny. I never thought I would be jealous of an elf."

"Whatever happened to all that stuff about how you wouldn't grow old with me or give me kids or the rest of all that shit you were too presumptuous to talk about with me?"

"You'd have the same age problem dating the prince."

"Yeah, I suppose so and that's a right bitch, but thus far he's made no assumptions. For all I know we'll merely have a nice torrid affair and then he'll settle down with a lovely Faery lady and that will be that." I paused, wondering why that idea bothered me so much. "I mean, shit. You and I . . . we had a week or two, tops. And the sex was great. I can't deny we had a connection, but what was it based on, really? Did you ever think that maybe the reason I was so attracted to you was because I'm a Dreamer? You're an incubus . . . it would make sense for me to—"

His finger found my lips, shushing me with a single motion. "That was the point I was trying to make before."

"But you never even gave us a chance. How was I supposed to get to know *you*?" I frowned at him. "Maybe that's the real issue. Talivar's been with me for nearly eight months now. I do his laundry sometimes, for Christ's sake. Even if he wasn't interested in me, I'd still know him better in some ways. At least the mundane ones," I added. It was hard to completely argue the point with the incubus who'd lived in my head for nearly the same amount of time.

He raised a brow and for a moment the edges of his skin went blurry as he shifted. I blinked. He'd become an old man, crow's feet and tired mouth, sagging ears and hollowed cheeks.

"Kept the full head of hair, I see."

"Vanity," he retorted. "It's my only vice." He twitched again, the haziness melting away, returning to his normal state. He reached out to stroke my cheek. Against my better judgment, I let him, my face sinking into the warmth of his palm.

A sad chuckle escaped me. "You know, I can't tell if you're here because you still think you love me, or simply because you can't stand to see me with someone else."

"What if it's both?"

"But nothing's changed. Sure, it's great you can take on the semblance of age, but it's not real. How are you going to feel when I'm forty-five? Fifty-five? Where will we be when I'm seventy and drooling with saggy tits and a flat ass?"

"You don't get it. It's never been about what you look like." He pursed his lips, kneeling beside the bed, but didn't touch me. "It's the Dreamer in you that I love. The physical part of it, your age, your weight . . . none of it matters." He tapped my forehead. "It's all about this."

"Then why leave me in the first place?" I punched him in the shoulder, anger and hurt warring with the sudden urge to pull him onto the bed. When he didn't answer, I shrugged. "Well, I still meant what I said—there's too much going on here right now. And regardless of what's happening between me and Talivar, I'm not going to rub you in his face like a dog. He doesn't deserve that." I cracked a small grin at him. "You're a complication I don't need, Ion."

His eyes flared gold. "Touché," he murmured. The silence stretched out between us and I became terribly aware of how dark the room had become. The sun had set fifteen minutes ago.

"Aren't we supposed to go down for dinner or something?"

"Or something. Though with Melanie here we might actually get some real music. Thomas doesn't play in public often anymore—the Queen is too jealous of his attention to allow it."

I shook myself. "That's right. You don't know, do you?" I gave him the quick and dirty version of my history, revealing the necklace, my new relationship with Moira, and that I did, in fact, have a father.

When I was done, his gaze rolled down to my necklace for a moment. He began to laugh. Ripples of amusement rolled off of him as he sagged onto the bed, his entire body shaking with it. My own lips twitched in answer and before I knew it I'd joined him, the absurdity of our entire situation finally bubbling up in torrid waves of hysterical giggles.

Wiping at my eyes, I held my stomach when it began to ache. "God, I'm so fucked."

His mouth pursed. "You could be." And then I was in his arms, and he was kissing me, the tension between us released in a blistering wave. I let it sweep past me for a moment more, our tongues probing hard and fast. My towel was half undone, falling open as he ground his hips against my belly.

I broke away from him, my body sighing in protest, and I had to wonder at its own sense of moral ambiguity. After all, I'd made love to Talivar the night before and here I was attempting to make the beast with two backs only a few short hours later . . . with my ex.

The incubus groaned, taking the moment to plant a soft kiss beneath my right breast and sucking hard. "There, now," he said, his eyes flaring with satisfaction. "Marked as mine."

I rolled my eyes at him. "Ion, there's like ten of them down there. It's not like anyone else would know."

A feral grin curved his mouth. "I'll know." He stood, carefully replacing the towel across my chest. "Shall I see you at dinner, then? Perhaps you might save a dance for me."

"Assuming I can even find something to dance in, yeah. I guess." I hesitated. "And, um . . . thank you for coming. I'm sorry it's become such a cluster."

"I find the towel rather charming." He smirked, and I half debated throwing it in his face, but that clearly wasn't the right response. "And I *never* mind coming, Abby."

"Get out." I pointed at the window. "And try not to

break anything on the way down. I suspect the Fae won't be particularly sympathetic to your cause if I'm forced to call a healer."

He blew me a kiss and slipped out onto the trellis with a rustling of leaves. I fought the urge to watch him climb down and lost, feeling like a whorish Rapunzel as he disappeared into the darkness and out into the garden.

A scratch at the shared door had me wrapping the towel a little tighter. "Yeah?"

"Abby, it's Mel. Can I come in?" The door cracked open as she peered into the room. "Decent?"

"Eh. Sorta. Haven't figured out what I'm supposed to wear yet." Of course, I'd sent away the serving girls or ladies' maids or whatever they were the moment the bath water was hot enough. Maybe that's how it was done here, but extra people poking at me make me nervous.

"Did you look in the wardrobe?" Melanie rolled her eyes at me and made a beeline for the great hunk of furniture, ignoring my gasp of surprise. Great sweeps of emerald cloth crossed behind her shoulders, somehow giving her a plunging neckline *and* a scooped back. A delicate tattoo of spiraling thorns crept over her right shoulder blade. "Gee, there's almost enough cloth dragging behind you to make you a real dress."

She shrugged. "I think I put it on upside down, but I don't really care." She kicked out her feet to reveal her calf-high Doc Martens still in full effect. "I'm not dancing in these anyway. Besides green with red hair . . . it's such a cliché."

The door to the wardrobe opened with a welcoming creak, a light cedar scent drifting from the darkness. Melanie made a little noise and pulled out an elegant sapphire dress.

I looked at it dubiously, feeling the cloth with a curious finger. "It's the right color, anyway."

Melanie made a scoffing sound and yanked the towel from me, ignoring my protests. "Nice hickeys," she noted dryly, throwing the dress at me. "Go try this on—we're gonna be late."

I grumbled something rude to her, but wriggled my way into the gown. Surprisingly it fit well, the bodice tight but breathable, the skirt falling just below my knees. "It's a bit conservative, don't you think?"

"Compared to what? The piece of shit I'm wearing? Sure, I suppose so. Actually, it's a bit like a ballet dress, don't you think?"

I eyed my reflection. "Could be a little poofier at the top, maybe, but yeah. I guess so." I twirled about for a moment, watching it flare out to expose the lower half of my thighs, a ghost of a memory settling over me. "All I need are some pointe shoes."

"Hmmph. Ask and you shall receive." Melanie opened up a box to reveal a matching pair of ballet toe shoes.

"Gee, this is a bit much don't you think?"

"Maybe it's a magic wardrobe?" She waggled her fingers mockingly. "As you can tell, I'm clearly the Faery harlot of the night."

"They're even the real thing." I rapped my knuckles on the stiff base before glancing down at my feet. "I don't know if I even have the calluses for this sort of thing anymore." A year ago, two years ago, I'd had the ugly, blistered toes of the professional dancer. I'd barely even had toenails on my left foot.

A few years of inactivity hadn't quite fixed them, but they weren't the tattered mess of before, I realized with a pang. Battle scars of another sort altogether. "I'll put them on, but I don't think I'll be wearing them for very long." I slipped into them, wrapping the ribbons around my calves. "I look ridiculous."

"Actually, you look a lot like your old self." A soft smile touched her lips. "It's nice to see, Abby."

I pliéd carefully in fifth position and then rose to pointe, a lump in my throat as my body remembered its former glory. My knee held up surprisingly well, but even I knew not to be fooled by that. It had gotten stronger over the last year, but not enough to convince me it would ever truly heal.

Still, I couldn't quite help circling my arms before lifting my bad leg behind me as I shifted into arabesque and then leaned forward into penché. My lower back shrieked in protest and I grasped the bed for support, sucking in a deep breath. My legs strained with muscles stiff from disuse, and if my former teachers had seen it I would have been scolded into next week, but the old spark of excitement burst into my veins, as though I would simply turn and pirouette into the past. And yet I held myself quiet, finally exhaling myself into first position, my leg lowering and sweeping into fourth.

Melanie applauded with a cheeky wink. "Brava!"

I let out a gasp as my arches started to cramp and I shook my head, sinking onto the bed to untie the shoes. "And that's enough of that, I think. Fairy tales are lovely, but I don't have time to break these in. Halfway down the hallway and I'd be leaving a bloody trail a mile wide."

"That's a tasty thought." She dug in the wardrobe again and flushed out a pair of strappy sandals that would be far easier on my feet. "Look at it this way. At least they weren't enchanted or something. It would really suck if you were forced to dance yourself to death."

I rolled my eyes at her and attempted to do something with my hair.

At least that was something I remembered how to do.

There was a beetle swimming in my soup. At least it was round and had legs. Beyond that I wasn't going to look too closely. I wasn't going to eat it either, so I carefully shoved the bowl toward the edge, leaving the spoon untouched. I didn't know if it was a mistake or a joke or what, but it was *not* going in my mouth.

My stomach rumbled in protest and I snagged a roll from a nearby woven basket. Bread was usually safe, right? I nibbled at the crust, watching Phineas demolishing his own bowl of soup with sloppy gusto.

"Eww," I cringed as he licked his lips.

He snorted disdainfully. "Suit yourself, but jewel beetles are a delicacy here. Besides—" He crunched down on something hard for a moment, rolling it around on his tongue. Spitting gracelessly into the bowl, he gestured at something winking in the milky liquid. "If you do it right, you get to keep the jewel when you're done."

I shuddered. "No thanks. You've got a leg sticking out of your mouth, by the way."

His tongue swiped it away. "I'd forgotten how nice it is to be pampered." I wasn't sure if he'd been given a set of rooms of his own, but wherever he'd been, they'd certainly cleaned him up. His coat shone almost silver and the dandelion fluff of his mane puffed out like a resplendent cirrus cloud.

"You drool on my pillow and molest my underwear, Phin. What else were you hoping for?"

"True enough," he said thoughtfully. "Plus I get to look at your boobies."

"Be still my beating heart." I slouched in my chair, weariness overtaking me again. We were seated in what could only be described as a great hall of some kind. Much larger than the throne room had been and decorated with pale white marble. Above us the branches had been pulled back to reveal the night sky, glittering balls of witchlight pulsing like iridescent disco balls. I'd been shoved out of the way into a convenient corner, farthest away from the long table where the royal family was ensconced. Their voices were low and unheard over the din of the other diners.

I couldn't really blame them for putting me here. When my name had been announced with Moira and Melanie, my elven escort blanched and quickly dumped me as soon as he could. Obviously everyone had decided I was out of favor with the Queen. Not much point in risking another outburst like this afternoon, after all. On the other hand, it allowed me a singular vantage point where I could observe the comings and goings of the others undisturbed. The Queen herself had not arrived until I'd been seated, Talivar trailing behind her.

She had changed from her dress of rags into a soft silken gown of amethyst. The simplicity of it displayed the beauty of her race to alabaster perfection. My father escorted her easily, dressed in a tartan. I blinked. *Well, he was Scottish, after all,* my inner voice reminded me.

Even if they probably hadn't worn kilts in the 1300s, I reminded it. Still, he cut an exceptionally fine figure and I couldn't help the little dose of pride warming my chest when he nodded at me. Of course that was tempered with the disappointment that our little reunion apparently either wasn't going to happen or was guaranteed to be strained and awkward.

Talivar frowned when he saw where I was, mouthing an apology at my raised brow.

"Don't be too hard on him. His mother has his balls on a string. If he gets too uppity people will think he's planning an uprising." The unicorn's ears flattened and he sniffed the air. "And to be honest, the way things are going, I suspect there are some here who would be all too happy at taking him up on it."

"As long as the Queen doesn't try to hit me again," I said, rubbing at my lip self-consciously. "And do we really have time for this? I mean, it seems like a bit much to be wining and dining inside Tolkien Central, when the CrossRoads are in shambles and an army is banging on the front door."

"No," the unicorn agreed. "We don't. And that is troublesome. Clearly the Queen is in mental distress. If they cannot get her under control soon, there's going to be a shitstorm of massive proportions."

I thought about the Barras and the lesser Fae there, outcast and rather tired of it. The Crippled Prince would certainly have a backing from that particular faction anyway. And given what happened in the throne room today, it was obvious Maurice would be more than willing to take full advantage of any conflict.

Moria sat next to her brother, of course, swathed in something that could only have been described as a Glinda the Good Witch getup, a huge crystalline and white silk monstrosity that could have hidden an entire Lollipop Guild beneath it. I suspected its formality was more to make it appear as though at least one of the royal family could affect some modicum of decorum. All she needed was a giant bubble. Melanie had taken one look at her in the hall and immediately began humming the refrain to "Defying Gravity."

Melanie had been seated closer to the royal table than I, but every once in a while our eyes would meet and she'd discretely make a rude gesture, forcing me to bite my lip to keep from laughing.

I shook my head, watching as Thomas attempted to get the Queen to eat. I twiddled the spoon between my fingers. "I can't even begin to understand how Maurice or Tresa fit into this equation."

Phineas shrugged. "Probably wasn't that hard to convince someone it was worth the risk. Anyone with eyes can see things are pretty fucked here. What better way to save his skin than to have them waste time with an internal struggle."

"Or a civil war," I said under my breath.

"That too."

A murmur of voices rippled through the room and I glanced up to see Talivar striding toward my table, wearing a lightly ornamented lawn shirt and dark trousers. The simplicity of it was massively appealing given the excess all around us. Behind him, the Queen's eyes narrowed as he took the seat directly across from me.

"Ignore them," the prince said. "They're nearly all idiots anyway." His gaze roamed hungrily over my face, taking in my dress with a spark of interest. "Did you pick that out yourself?"

I shook my head. "Melanie found it in my wardrobe. Figured it was what I was supposed to wear."

"Well, mayhap you'll favor me with a single dance and then I'll whisk you to my bed. I find these things so tiresome." His lips brushed my forehead, laying claim to me before the remainder of the room. The whispers became sharper and he chuckled. "I am sorry about this afternoon."

I waved him off. "I just want to get things done here and go home. And I was hoping I might actually meet my father, instead of being treated like some sort of pariah . . ." I shook off the rest of the words with a sigh. "Aren't you supposed to sit up there?"

"Probably. But I'm not some lapdog they can trot out every time they feel the need to show the others how punishment has its own rewards . . . or whatever such bullshit Mother feels like spouting tonight. Besides, if they're going to insist on treating me like some sort of exile, I might as well give them the satisfaction of acting like one."

"This seat taken?" Bryston's midnight voice fell upon me in a rolling wave. Without waiting for an answer, the incubus took the chair to my left, ignoring Talivar's raised brow. The incubus smiled slyly when I shot him the hairy eyeball. "Might as well make things interesting."

"Yeah, well keep your 'Plus Five to Sexterity' vest to yourself, eh?"

Phineas rolled his eyes. "At least let me have dessert before you make me lose my dinner." And indeed, a moment later we were all served plates of a sugar-encrusted confection, drizzled with a sweet sauce of chocolate and caramel. I groaned as I took at bite. At least the Fae got this much right.

The rest of the meal itself was quite pleasant from a culinary standpoint, though being trapped between the two men appeared to be a little less fun. Talivar occasionally nudged me with his foot, sliding it up my calf, even as Brystion appeared to use every excuse to jostle me with his elbow.

The third time I nearly dropped my fork I gave them both a look. "You know, if it's a threesome you're looking for, perhaps it might wait until we've got a little more privacy." I yawned. "I find public orgies to be a bit on the boring side these days."

Talivar pursed his mouth even as Ion arched a brow at him, the two of them sharing a look that was entirely too conspiratorial for my liking.

"Don't tempt me." Ion fluttered his lashes.

I flushed. "I was joking."

The incubus winked at me. "So was I, but it's fun to make you squirm." A fuss from the main table caught our attention. The Queen started to scratch at her arms again, shifting aimlessly in her seat. I frowned. If she was constantly doing that it would certainly explain the rags.

Talivar followed my gaze with a pained smile. "It happens more and more," he admitted. "It used to be once in a while, but these days . . . She would probably be happier naked, and I'd be inclined to allow it, except she's been scratching at her skin too. The healers have to work with her every night to remove the damage."

"And if it becomes permanent?"

"Then I suppose one of our questions will be answered. Music distracts her. Thomas spends a good deal of his time in her private quarters keeping her from making a bigger spectacle of herself than she already has." I heard the gentle reproach in his voice and I tamped down the bitterness in my throat.

"So what do we do?"

The elf paused. "If we cannot convince her by tomorrow evening as to the severity of our situation, Moira and I will take steps. I'll need every bit of your support, should we attempt it. Thomas has agreed to meet with us first thing in the morning."

Beside me, Brystion eyed the prince disdainfully. "Why is it that you put so much of your burden on Abby? Hasn't she already done enough for you?"

Talivar's jaw tightened and I put my hand in his to give it a squeeze.

"Ion, chill. If you aren't going to help, then be quiet."

"So quickly you pass me over," he retorted. "After all, I'm here by your request."

"After you said you wouldn't help." I shut my eyes and counted to ten. "Yeah, okay. I'm sorry. You guys don't exactly make it easy. There's enough ego between the two of you to sail to China on."

"That's your style though," Phineas added, his mouth still full of icing. "Long, lean, hardheaded, and thick skulled." I threw a spoon at him, but he ducked it narrowly, letting it bounce harmlessly to the floor.

Talivar opened his mouth to say something, but the words were drowned out by the sudden sound of music. The opening bars to what suspiciously sounded like Led Zeppelin's "Kashmir" spun out from Melanie's violin. Too busy with our verbal sparring, I'd missed Melanie's invitation to play, but now I could watch as she stood unobtrusively in the far corner, the acoustics bouncing the notes in a choral harmony.

Normally she would have taken to the center of the room, or even wandered about, but I suspected she was only trying to distract the Queen without becoming a target for her jealousy. The Queen's eyes were half lidded, but her hands remained in her lap, the frantic rubbing of her arms stilled.

I resisted the urge to say something about music and the savage beast when I saw my father's face. A terrible pain resided there and I could see the way his fingers twitched. How much of himself had he given up for her? How much had he given up for my own mother? I turned away before the rawness of it could delve any deeper.

Slowly, some of the other courtiers took to the center area, attempting a polite semblance of dancing. Having seen what elves were capable of in the Hallows, I couldn't quite keep the distain off my lips. It was so . . . empty. Joyless.

Ion caught at my free hand, his eyes glowing gold. "Dance with me, Abby."

Talivar glared. "I believe Abby promised me first."

"I think I'd almost rather do the threesome." Luckily I was saved from hearing the response when a masked courtier approached our table with a quick bow. He was dressed in a typical hose and tunic getup, simply cut in basic blues and greens but well made, his red hair hanging loose at the shoulders. Although his face was hidden by a feathered monstrosity, his eyes were kind and beckoning, without a hint of seduction.

Refreshing.

"If the lady would be so kind as to honor me?"

I weighed my options for half a second. It was an easy out. Chickenshit, yes, but that was nothing new. "Delighted," I murmured, ignoring Phin's snicker.

I let the courtier take my hand, not looking at either of my would-be paramours, but I could feel their gaze upon me as I stood. Judging by the steadfast simplicity of the other dancers it would be unlikely to present that much of a challenge for me, even if I didn't actually know any genuine Faery waltzes. I could do a basic box step in my sleep, gimpy leg and all.

I snuck a peek at the Queen, but she was ignoring me, her attention still steadfast upon Melanie. The courtier bowed with an elegant flourish and led me forward, my feet slipping into their old remembered grace.

I tried to engage him in a bit of small talk, but for all his quiet demeanor and decent footwork, there wasn't much to be said and I soon found myself extraordinarily bored.

"Cutting in," Brystion said brusquely, tapping my escort on the shoulder. "You're embarrassing yourself." He brushed the elf out of the way to take his place.

"And what would you know about it?"

"Dream-eater," he pointed out dryly, spinning me out and then recapturing my waist. Without missing a beat, Melanie slid neatly into a tango, an odd hint of Lady Gaga's "Bad Romance" lurking beneath the chords. Figured. The violinist studiously ignored my strangled motions at her.

Brystion's eyes bled gold, his mouth kicking up to reveal a gleaming smile. "I know quite well what you're capable of." His hip nudged mine, one hand sliding down the small of my back.

"And here I thought you were going to wait until after all this was over." Of course, I had to admit it was nice to have someone lead who knew what he was doing. I glanced over at where Talivar watched us, his face growing stony. "One dance each and then I'm done."

"Fair enough." He nuzzled my ear, his mouth sliding into a crooked grin as Talivar approached us. "Catch," he told the prince, turning me forward into Talivar's arms.

The elf swept me to the center of the room, and if he didn't have Ion's dance moves, he was certainly attempting to make up for it with enthusiasm. He dipped me low, his hair brushing over my collarbone before planting a soft kiss at my throat. A moment later and he'd handed me over to Ion, a hint of his own private amusement sparkling in his face.

Better than a fistfight, anyway. Back and forth the three of us moved, each man taking a turn to woo me in his own way. My body vibrated between them, the heat of their hands burning up each bit of skin they touched . . . this one blatant, that one subtle, both possessive, until I found myself nearly wedged between them.

The music had become more seductive and I was vaguely aware that I was causing quite the spectacle. Melanie had stopped watching us at least; her eyes were half shut so that I knew she was off in her own little world. The Queen . . .

Well, she stared openly, her lips curving into something expectant and cruel. Was she hoping Talivar would fall? My father had risen from his seat, something pained on his face. I caught a glimpse of him beating a hasty retreat through a smaller doorway that I hadn't seen before.

I twirled away from both men, feeling very much like the swan egging on her suitors. My knee began to protest as each took a hand to lead me back onto the dance floor and I gave them a smile.

"Gonna have to rest, guys. Leg isn't going to hold out

for much longer." A flicker of chagrin sparked in Talivar's face, echoed in the way Ion's eyes darkened. A slight tremor of disappointment wormed its way through me. No sense tempting fate—and having a seizure here wouldn't help me any in the respect department.

Carefully they escorted me toward our table, neither one appearing to want to relinquish his claim. I sighed inwardly as Melanie began playing something Celtic, the sprightly notes fading away into the background. This had been fun, but the potential for hurt feelings was rather high and I definitely didn't want to deal with that yet.

My knee ached and I wanted the chance to have a little quiet time to myself before tomorrow threatened to blow up in my face, as it was undoubtedly wont to do. My fingers slipped from their hands as I slouched in my seat, my feet continuing to tap out a beat in counterpoint. Phin had disappeared into the crowd while I was dancing, and the three of us sat in an uncomfortable silence for several minutes.

Finally I bent to remove my shoes, the arch of one foot burning. I wiggled my toes experimentally, but I suspected a good soak would be in order later if I didn't want blisters. I glanced at the royal table. My father was still gone, and Moira had left as well. Talivar frowned when he saw where I was looking.

"My mother should not be alone. Will you wait for me here?"

"Actually, I was wondering where that doorway leads." I pointed to the one I'd seen Thomas retreat to.

"The gardens. Normally they'd be full of trysting lovers and the like, but the Queen has forbidden any such frivolities." His mouth pursed as he looked at me. "Pity."

"Thomas went that way. I thought maybe I could get a chance to talk to him. Alone," I said, giving them both the eye. The last thing I needed was an audience for this. Some potential failures needed privacy.

"Of course." Brystion slid to his feet smoothly. "Perhaps another time?"

"Yeah. Actually, I want you with us in the morning. The only way we're going to solve this mess is if we work together." I looped the straps of the sandals together so I could carry them and reached out to squeeze his hand. "If we can put the rest of it behind us for now?"

The two men nodded at each other. It wasn't quite a truce, but at least maybe they wouldn't be publicly sniping at each other either. Together they escorted me to the alcove that led to the gardens. I descended into the shadows of the stairs, Melanie's music chasing me downward with an odd sighing melancholy.

Twenty-three

The soft grass soothed my aching feet as I tread carefully through a gentle maze of rosebushes. The light and sounds of the ball scattered upon the grounds from above me, but it seemed more intrusive than anything else. The path wended this way and that, becoming a spiral twisting in on itself. Ancient oaks dotted the landscape with bark as smooth and fine as paper. I began to feel inordinately foolish when my father didn't magically materialize before me, but I wasn't sure why.

After all, it wasn't as if he knew I was here. After a time the silence began to weigh on me and I debated heading back to the ballroom when I heard a soft hiccup. I froze, the rhythmic sound making me hesitate. Shit. For all I knew my father was out here "entertaining" some sort of tryst of his own. Uncharitable maybe, but it's not like he'd been overly faithful. Both Moira and I were proof of that.

The hiccup became a sob and I peered around the edge of the rosebushes, the sandals slipping from my fingers.

My father sat on a stone bench, his arms around Moira, tucking her close to his chest. The Faery princess clung to him, weeping as though her heart was breaking. Whatever else I'd thought I was going to do or say tonight flooded hotly into my chest in a flare of jealousy until I could barely breathe.

Thomas made a soothing cluck at her. Unable to watch anymore, I fled.

I slumped in a small crescent-shaped nook off the main garden path. I'd found my way to the stairs leading to the ballroom, but I continued to wander until I discovered a quieter spot. A pool of water bubbled nearby and I availed myself of it, dipping my sore toes into its coolness. After a while Phineas stumbled upon me and curled up at my side, half dozing with his head upon my lap.

Something hot slid down my face, the salty tang of my tears brushing against the chapped dryness of my lips. I didn't begrudge Moira her moment with our father. Heaven knew she had more than enough on her plate. It was even gratifying to see she wasn't quite as stoic as I'd thought. Made her more human, I guess, though she didn't show her mortal heritage that I could tell.

Still, the little girl inside of me couldn't help but wonder why I'd been overlooked so easily. It was petty. I'd never had a dad before—it was silly to lament his absence now, but it didn't stop the hurt.

A soft brush of fabric alerted me that someone approached, but I didn't bother to lift my head. Easier to sit and wallow.

"Abby?" I stiffened at the light Scottish burr rolling over my name.

My father. True Thomas of Ercildune. "What do you want?" Bitterness tasted like ash on my tongue.

He made a hissing sound in his throat, carefully picking his way around the rocks of the pool to lay my discarded shoes next to me. "Do you have any idea how proud I am of you?"

Now I did look up. "Picked a fine time to tell me." His brows were drawn tightly, sadness etched upon his face, but it was the familiarity of his features that drew me more than knowing he was upset. Mirror images reflected within myself, but I didn't care anymore.

"I know I have not earned your trust or your sympathy, but I ask you to hear me out." Crouching beside me, he dipped one finger into the pool, watching as the ripples widened.

"The way you heard Mother out when you left her? Left us? My entire life has been a lie. I don't even know who I am."

"I have never regretted anything so much as leaving you," he said softly. "Necessity compelled it."

"Did you ever think Mom might still be alive if you had stayed with us?" My throat swelled up as I choked on the words. I hadn't wanted to lash out like this, but I seemed unable to stop it now that the target was sitting directly in front of me. "I might never have been in that accident. I would still be a dancer. I wouldn't have seizures. And I sure as fuck wouldn't be *here*!" I winced at the sound of my own voice.

"I know. And I am truly sorry, Abby."

"That and a quarter will buy me a bag of chips," I snapped. I wanted to get up and pace. Unbidden, the tears came again and I glared at him. "This is all your fault."

He flinched this time, but did not dispute it, and that pissed me off even more.

"Your mother knew who I was when we got involved," he said finally. "And we both agreed it would be for the best if I left."

"Best for who? Mom never told me anything about you at all. Just that you loved me." My lips compressed. "I didn't even have the memories of that much."

"I wanted to protect you and your mother, and the Queen

can be terrible in her fickleness. My time with you was coming to an end. I hid your memories because I didn't want you looking for me."

My fist slammed into the ground. "Then why did you even have me? If you love the Queen so damn much, why toy with my mother? Why cheat?"

He sighed, shifting uncomfortably. Probably not the easiest thing to discuss with one's offspring, but I wasn't sure I wanted to consider him family. If this was the sort of thing it got me, I'd be better off the way I was before.

Alone.

"You can love someone and not like them much," he pointed out. I waited, but he chose not to explain further. "Every five hundred years or so, the Queen allows me seven mortal years. I will fully admit, my eye does wander from time to time. I find that the longer I remain here, the more I crave my mortality."

"Nothing like sowing your magical wild oats."

"In a manner of speaking, perhaps." He shrugged. "Nothing usually comes of such unions. I didn't stay with anyone long enough for that to be an issue."

The thought sickened me, imagining that I had other brothers and sisters possibly roaming the world, or multitudes of cousins, all left behind on the whim of an insane Queen of another world.

"But your mother was different." A gentle smile drifted across his ageless face. "Not since my Janet was alive so many years ago had I been so taken with a woman." He fixed me with his eyes. "I did not *want* to leave you, Abby."

"I think you're full of shit," I said thickly. "Talivar said the Key to the CrossRoads went missing about thirty years ago. I think you foresaw the need for it and went out and knocked up some mortal woman to use it as an excuse to leave it with her. Breeding your own savior, as it were."

He choked out a breath. "'The daemons made us an offer that would offset much of this, Abby. But it's not one I want to contemplate. Can you blame me for trying to find another way?"

"I don't understand any of you. Your grandson is trapped in the mortal realm. There's a goddamned daemon army waiting to invade your lands. Your Queen is mentally ill, and you've got what amounts to a rival faction just itching to get her off the throne. Why wouldn't you at least think about it?" I glared up at him. "And I don't know what's going on with the whole Unseelie Court issue, but their banishment has clearly had a detrimental effect here. This whole place is dying all around you and you don't even see it. You're so focused on the Queen, there's no room for anything else."

A faint smile crossed his face. "For someone so young you've certainly grasped the situation rather wholly. Almost."

"It's a gift." At least I had something to focus on other than my own self-pity. And he was answering my questions.

"So I see, but there's a bit more to it than what you've said. To be honest, I'm not sure the daemons really care so much about getting Maurice as they are set on reclaiming a foothold here."

"Why would they want one?"

"We're halfway to Heaven, I suppose. What better place to possibly stage an attack from? Closing the CrossRoads was merely an excuse for them, but what they really want is for us to reinstate the Tithe."

I frowned. I knew the stories of the Devil's Tithe had centered around the Fae kidnapping a mortal for seven years of bliss, only to hand him over to the Devil at the end of that time. And in return, the Fae got to live daemon-free.

"I was under the impression that was no longer done."
An icy ripple skated down my back at the thought.

"It's not. Since the formal establishment of TouchStones,
the balance of power shifted." He laughed ruefully. "I suppose that was my doing."

"How very generous of you." I was still trying to wrap
my head around the fact that this man and the one whose
shirt I'd mouthed the buttons on as a baby were the same
person.

"You're a stubborn wee thing, I grant you." He paused
before getting to his feet. "And if I was not so forthcoming
with you before, it was because I had hoped to spare you
this. Not everything that I foresee comes to pass, Abby. You
have a rare talent. I would not have had that be the price for
your admission into this world."

"All I want is to figure out what the hell is going on, fix
it, and get out of here." He had the grace to look chagrined
at least, so I chalked up a point in his favor. "You're the
Steward. If the Queen can't run this place, then you should
at least advise her to step down and let Moira take over, or
something. For all the tales, I find it a bit disconcerting that
the Sidhe seem so spineless. I mean, why did she shut the
CrossRoads down in the first place? Seems like a bit of an
overreaction."

"I will not have you slander the Queen in my presence,
daughter or no," he snapped.

"What's to slander?" I retorted. "She's a like a child, running her little tea party into the ground while the big bad
wolf stands outside getting ready to piss on the gates. And
the rest of the pigs are sitting here in their house of straw
playing canasta. What's it going to take for you guys to get
out the bricks?" My voice dropped lower. "I know you've
been here for a long time . . . Dad. But don't let a sense of
immortality wrap you in complacency. Another few blinks

and I'll be gone . . . what service will your memory give you then?"

A silence borne of history crept over us, a chasm of old hurt and regret so deep it would probably never be filled. Regardless of what Ion had spoken to me of living forever, I knew now that I would never take it. Immortality clearly made people lazy, and taking others for granted was nothing I wanted to be remembered for.

"Perhaps you are right, lass. It has been a long time since I was truly mortal. I've forgotten how things used to be. Mayhap we all have. I will think on what you've said. As to the CrossRoads . . . aye. The Queen's delusions grow stronger every day, no matter what we do. Her closing them was a mistake, one that only continues to escalate. She claims it was an instinctual reaction to the pain of her child, but she can't seem to let it go."

"I can't help but notice there's no mention of her closing them when Talivar was hurt," I said quietly. "Don't think about this too long." In truth I was amazed at my own gall for telling him how to do anything, but a gleam of amusement lit up his eyes as he looked at me.

"I've strong daughters, apparently."

I stared down at my feet. "Not always strong enough."

He squeezed my shoulder. "I must see to the Queen for the evening, but tomorrow we will meet to plan our course of action. For now, though, the hour grows late and I must take my leave." His mouth twitched. "Talivar seems rather taken with you. It's good to see."

Unless your other paramour is a sex daemon. I had nothing to say to his comment, so I let it go, giving my father a wan smile.

"Tomorrow, then."

"Aye," he said, bowing slightly. "Tomorrow."

I watched him go, walking the neatly trimmed path with quiet footsteps before giving Phineas a nudge.

"For someone who can't keep his mouth shut at the best of times, I notice you were rather quiet there, Phin." I tugged on his beard.

"And what would I have said? I'm not crazy enough to get between estranged relatives, even on the best of terms." He huffed, his ears flattening. "Nice segue way into the *Three Little Pigs,* by the way."

"Nice change of subject. And no, it wasn't. I don't have any right to say anything about how they do things here, Phin. It's like an elbow trying to tell an asshole how to take a shit."

He sniggered. "Guess so. But the brick thing was pretty apt. Things have been falling apart here for a while. Maybe this is the shakeup they need."

"Yeah. Now all we have to do is see if they're gonna build houses with them . . . or chuck one at the Queen's head."

"What a charming mouth on you, little whore. Not even here a day and you're already cozying up to my consort. Plotting to overthrow me, perhaps?" The Queen's icy, mad-swept voice rushed into the little grove, her dress hanging off her shoulders in ragged pieces. I jerked my feet out of the water, attempting to put as much space between me and the wild-eyed woman as I could. She laughed bitterly when I craned my head past her to look for my father.

"Thomas is somewhat blind when it comes to me, even should I be standing beside him while he passes by in the darkness. Easy enough to escape the watchful eyes of those who don't truly wish to see." Her nails raked across her arms, leaving jagged streaks of crimson behind.

I moved to take her hands, forgetting who she was. "You'll hurt yourself." Beneath my fingers, her skin was smooth and ice cold. Something pulsed over me, an electric rush of energy freezing me in place.

"KeyStone," she hissed. "And she has the Key. Wherever did you get this, little whore? I see my consort has been even more naughty than I thought." Pinpricks vibrated like thousands of tiny ants. From a distance I could almost get a sense of her mind, her thoughts beating against my mind like a butterfly trapped in a jar.

She was trying to TouchStone me.

. . . I plunged into darkness, the weight of years beyond measure pressing upon me like the endless depths of the sea . . . the glittering silver of the CrossRoads filling me to the brim, the magic swirling, pushing against my very skin as though I might burst open with it, spilling my guts like a ripened fruit . . .

I gritted my teeth and fought as hard as I could. In the past I'd had to at least allow it on some level, but the Queen's power was tainted by an insanity I couldn't comprehend.

"No," I croaked. "I will *not* do this."

"What else can I do?" she whispered. "How else can I protect my lands? The daemons will not rest until they have them, but I cannot free the CrossRoads until Moira is safe. She's only a little girl." Her maddened gaze focused on me. "Who would stoop to hurting a little girl? Can you help me?"

"I thought that was what I was trying to do." My knees buckled beneath the strain of holding her back, her power assaulting me a second time.

Phineas bolted upright and nipped the Queen hard in the ankle. She shook her leg like a dog in a trap, sending Phineas sprawling.

"Don't let her," he wheezed. "She'll kill you."

"Sorta figured that out, thanks."

Already she was turning toward me, her fingers reaching. No choice for it then. I bum-rushed her ass, landing hard enough to knock the wind from her. Admittedly not the smartest thing in the world, but I'd take it. She gasped, her eyes rolling into her head as she tried to bite me. "Now what?" I looked over the unicorn.

"Stuff her mouth with something, I don't know. Gag her?"

"Dude, I get caught doing that . . ."

"You want to find—" But whatever else he was going to say was lost when the Queen bucked up, raking her nails across my shoulder.

"Fuck it," I snarled, tearing off a strip of her dress and shoving it into her mouth. She bared her teeth at me, but at least it kept her occupied enough to stop from trying to curse me into oblivion. I attempted to kneel on her shoulders, dimly hearing Phin say he was going for help, and then I was barreled ass over elbows into the ground.

"What the hell are you doing?" My father loomed over me, shaking with rage.

"She tried to TouchStone me," I sputtered, pulling a cluster of desiccated rose leaves from my mouth.

He went to his lover, gently cradling her head and removing the makeshift gag. Her eyes glazed over as she looked him, her limbs beginning to shudder. "Leave us," Thomas said harshly, not looking at me.

"But—"

"Leave. Now," he snapped.

I couldn't quite bring myself to apologize. The cuts on my shoulder began to sting fiercely. I doubted she was practicing much personal hygiene these days, so I would have to clean that out for sure. Carefully I crept around the prone form of the Queen, Phin trotting at my heels.

I didn't look back.

The water splashed over my face, washing away the sticky feeling of tears, dirt, and blood.

Bleary, I peered in the mirror, blinking when I saw the leaves in my hair. "I haven't had nearly enough to drink to look this awesome." A rough patch at the corner of my mouth confirmed I'd broken a bit of skin when I'd hit the ground, but it didn't feel too swollen. At least I was back in my own room, though.

"You're telling me," Phineas proclaimed from my bed. "What a cluster."

"Eh, provided the guards don't come knocking my door down tonight, I'll settle for crashing." I yawned, cringing when I used a dampened linen towel to wash over the cuts the Queen's nails had left behind. "This had better not scar."

"If it still hurts in the morning I'll heal it for you. Might lead to some awkward questions, otherwise."

I yawned again, slipping easily out of the now-completely-destroyed ballet dress. "Whatever. I'm going to throw on a shirt and pass out. Worry about it tomorrow," I mumbled, stumbling into the wardrobe. No shirts, but I did find what was probably a chemise. It was soft and long and that worked just fine. "Good enough."

I glanced over at Melanie's door, grateful she'd been asleep when I poked my head into the room. Unusual for her to turn in so early, but it had been a pretty long day for her too. Couldn't blame her if she wanted some quiet.

A soft knock at the door jolted me to awareness. Guards? *No. Guards wouldn't bother knocking.* I hesitated, not sure I wanted company.

"Abby?" Talivar's muffled voice sounded from the hallway and I relaxed.

"Come in."

I emerged from the wardrobe, shrugging into the chemise as he strode in, dressed in a more casual set of trousers and shirt. His shorn hair was tousled in a rather alluring fashion, but I couldn't even come up with the effort of leering at it.

He blinked at me. "What the hell happened to you?"

"You don't even want to know. Ask me in the morning." I picked out another leaf from my hair, smiling when our fingers entwined. His other hand tipped my chin up toward him, his lips brushing over mine tenderly.

"Mmm," I sighed. "That's the way to end the night. Start the morning? I don't even know what time it is."

"Guess I missed out on my chance for a good night kiss, then." Bryston yawned from the windowsill, rolling a bottle of wine between nimble fingers. His eyes were dark as he watched us, but there was a hint of mischief about his mouth.

Startled, I pulled away from Talivar, though he kept his hand locked on mine. "Uh. Yeah? That is . . ." I shook my head. Why was I going to apologize? "Never mind. I'm too tired to deal with this now."

Talivar released me, his gaze flat. "My apologies. I didn't realize you were expecting someone else."

I rolled my eyes. "I wasn't expecting either of you. I certainly didn't *invite* anyone, if that's what you're implying." Inwardly, I sighed. Maybe this was the part where I went and poured water all down the front of my chemise to distract them with the medieval equivalent of a wet T-shirt contest?

The incubus nodded at my hair. "I thought he was supposed to be guarding you. Maybe you need to find a replacement for the job."

Talivar snorted. "Like you, perhaps? Wouldn't that be convenient?"

The pillowy softness of the monstrous four-poster bed beckoned to me. I pointed at both men. "Tell you what, gentlemen, I'm going to excuse myself completely from this conversation. Stay or go, but I'm going to bed. If either of you wake me up, I will shove a pillow so far up your ass you'll taste feathers." I blinked sweetly at their blank stares and extricated myself to crawl beneath the covers.

There was a silence as the two men quietly sized each other up. Phineas jumped off the bed. "Too many dicks on the dance floor," he muttered, heading for the shelter beneath the mattress. Not that I blamed him.

The sound of heated whispers had me cracking an eye to peer at the elf and the incubus, locked in a dispute that seemed to involve a lot of hand gesturing. Much of it pointing in my direction. I decided I didn't care. A moment later I heard the cork of the wine bottle being pulled and the clink of glasses. At least it wasn't being bashed over someone's head.

"Enjoy your newfound bromance, boys," I mumbled and drifted off to sleep.

Twenty-four

I shifted my legs to curl into the heat coiled around the curve of my spine, a hand gently rubbing my hip. I exhaled and sank further into the mattress. Outside, a dove cooed mournfully. I supposed it was morning, but I wasn't willing to open my eyes and verify that yet. Everything was deliciously warm and soft.

Playful fingers stroked my head, twirling the loose strands of my hair, even as a third hand splayed against my belly. Dimly, I realized that was one hand too many. I cracked an eye; the soft light of dawn streamed in through one window to bathe the bed in a soft haze. Frowning, I tried to remember what had happened the night before. I'd gone to bed, right? Right.

Which begged the question of why there were multiple uninvited bodies pressed up against me. I lifted my head and took a long, leisurely look at my bed. Blinked. Shut my eyes and lay back down.

I was on my right side, Brystion spooning me from behind. Talivar lay on his back in front of me, my left leg sprawled somewhat indecently over his hips. That they were both still fully clothed was at least some comfort that

I hadn't done something foolish. The fact that my chemise seemed to be riding dangerously high on my thigh was not.

"Okay, then. When does the orgy start?"

"Don't think that was part of the bargain," Ion whispered in my ear, nuzzling the sensitive spot right behind it. "Maybe you're dreaming," he added slyly.

"Mmmph," I grunted. "While I can't deny there's something appealing about being sandwiched between the two of you, if this were a dream you guys would be naked." Which was true. But on the other hand . . .

"Shush," Talivar murmured. "We'll talk about it later. Go back to sleep. There's still time yet."

Time for what? I tucked the covers around me as best I could, the subtle shift of our bodies making room for each other as we readjusted ourselves. I sighed and let consciousness slip away again, safe within my cocoon of sheets and sleep.

When I awoke several hours later, I was alone.

Phineas and I sprawled out on the grass in Moira's private gardens, looking up at the sky, mostly under the assumption that food would be arriving shortly. Or so Moira had assured us when she found us wandering the hallway outside her door.

Of my would-be suitors there was no sign other than the empty wine bottle on the mantel. I'd found a new dress in the wardrobe, though I suspected it was more of a shift than a proper dress. I'd have given just about anything for some pants, but apparently those were in short supply. For lying around in a garden, it worked.

"And they drank *all* the wine?"

"Yeah," the unicorn snorted. "One minute they were bitching at each other about which one was going to guard you and then Brystion decided he didn't want the bottle of wine to go to waste. Next thing I knew, they were sitting in front of the fireplace swapping stories. Go figure." He cocked an eye at me slyly. "You probably don't want to know what the stories were about, though."

I shuddered. "No, I don't think so. Odd, though. I thought this was the part where they had a duel over me or something. Fought for my honor. Fairy-tale shit."

"Fairy tales are overrated. Besides, that would have ruined the illusion when they started making out . . ."

"They *what*?" A possible variation of that image seared into my brain and refused to leave.

"Oh, yeah," Phineas yawned. "They couldn't keep their hands off each other. Surprised it didn't wake you up. Especially when Talivar dragged out the assless leather chaps and started riding the incubus around like a pony."

I scowled at him. "I think someone's been reading too much yaoi."

"Maybe. But the look on your face is pretty priceless."

"I thought you couldn't lie."

"Lie, no. Exaggerate the hell out of something? Absolutely."

"Whatever. Let's just call waking up with them as unexpected and leave it at that."

Melanie glanced over at us from where she sat cross-legged on a blanket. "I think it's cute. And refreshing. Better than the usual chest-beating and knuckle dragging thing." She flopped down beside us. "Wow. Faery grass is wicked soft."

"I'll be sure to take pictures for you next time."

She sniggered. "Is there going to be a next time? You're a bit more liberal than I thought, Abby. Good for you."

"Mmmph. Where the hell is breakfast?"

"We could always head down to the main hall," Melanie suggested, patting her belly.

Phin and I shared a look and I shook my head. "Yeah, you

know what? I think it would be best if I avoided the court
stuff as much as possible from here on out."

"This have anything to do with that scrape on the side of
your mouth?"

"Yeah. And I want to wait until Moira gets here before I
talk about it."

Melanie nodded, pulling her violin from her case to run
through her scales. It said something about our friendship
that she was willing to let it go, and I was grateful for it. A
few moments later she had already moved into a soft version
of *Canon in D.*

"Music to brood by," I quipped, as the incubus ambled
his way toward us through Moira's solarium.

"Sleep well?" Ion's dark voice rumbled, one brow arched
suggestively. Without waiting for an invitation he stretched
out beside me with his arms behind his head.

"You would know. Where's your partner-in-crime?"

He shrugged. "I'm sure he's off doing something noble
and princely. Seems the type."

"Maybe he's getting breakfast." Phineas rolled over to
shake himself.

"Gods know I could use something to eat." Bryston
nudged me. There was something suggestive about it, but
the golden flare of his eyes bespoke something a bit more
serious.

"Ah." I flushed, suddenly understanding. "What about
your TouchStone?"

"She was short term," he said softly, staring up at the sky.
"They all are. Besides, without the CrossRoads open I can't
manage to make it into the Dreaming anyway."

"I didn't realize things were going to get this messy."

His mouth quirked into a half smile. "Of course you did.
With you, the shit doesn't just hit the fan, it coats the walls."

"And isn't that a lovely image." I fingered the folds of the gown. "Look, if we can't get this stuff figured out in the next few days, I'll see what I can do."

"Generous of you. But I think we'll have bigger problems than that. You've become a target, Abby."

"Getting a bit slow on the draw, aren't you? I kind of figured that out yesterday."

"I'm serious," he snapped. "Don't let a few kisses from a prince fuck with your head. This isn't some sort of Sleeping Beauty bullshit. I *will* take you out of Faerie if this doesn't resolve soon."

I flinched beneath the reproach. "I know. And I'm doing the best I can." I glanced up to see Talivar approaching us with a small basket. The prince frowned when he saw Brystion, but whatever he was going to say was lost when I noticed the small figure beside him. "Jimmy!"

The pig-man gave a little grunt, which I took to be of good humor when his mouth split into a broad grin.

"You have a visitor," Talivar said, setting the basket beside me. "Sorry I'm so late. I found him outside the main gates, seeking an audience with me."

"Just a wee bit o' an excuse," Jimmy mumbled, his ears pinking. "I knew they wasna gonna lets me in so easy to see ye, belikes." He paused, beady eyes glancing down at my dress, his snout quivering wetly. "And I brought ye a wee bit of something too. Though maybe ye do no' need it so much now." Pulling off his shoulder sack, he rummaged through it for a moment, clucking in satisfaction as he pulled out a large bolt of silk. "A gift from the silkworms."

I smiled, genuine happiness flooding my chest as I took it from him. "I'll have something made up with it as soon as I can," I assured him, strangely touched by his gesture.

The prince opened the basket to reveal a cluster of soft biscuits and a bowl of fruit. "There's meat and eggs to be had, but I couldn't carry enough up here for everyone." His

mouth pursed as his gaze slid to Jimmy. "And under the circumstances . . ."

"I get it." And even *I* would feel a bit odd downing a
plate of bacon in front of Jimmy. I snagged a biscuit, tossing
another into Melanie's lap.

"I'll have the servants bring up the rest of it," Talivar
said. "I hadn't realized you were all planning on breakfast-
ing out here until Moira informed me."

"Speaking of which, where is she?"

"Attending Mother. The Queen apparently had some
sort of shock last night after I saw her to her rooms."

I stopped chewing and swallowed hard. "Yeah. About
that."

The prince frowned. "Is *that* what you meant last night?"

"Yeah. She found me in the garden after I talked to my
father and, uh . . . tried to TouchStone me." I winced, ignoring Ion's low whistle. "It didn't go well."

"Especially when Abby linebackered her ass into the
dirt," Phin said with a cough.

"You attacked my *mother*?" Talivar stared at me, his
mouth gaping.

"Not by choice," I retorted. "Would you have preferred
it if I'd let her suck me dry after I became her TouchStone?
Though I don't think she cared for the gag much."

Brystion made a little gesture with his hand. "Shit. Fan.
Splatter."

"Ha-ha. And now you know why I didn't want to talk
about it."

Jimmy shifted uncomfortably beside us. I clenched the
cloth he'd given me and got to my feet. "Excuse me a moment, guys. Think I'm going to do something with this."

I started toward the solarium and waved at Jimmy to
follow. The pig-man hesitated, but shuffled behind after a

minute. Not that I didn't trust him exactly, but I suspected there was going to be a discussion or two about to happen that I didn't really want to be involved in. Not one he needed to be privy to, anyway.

"Sounds like ye've been busy," he mused, his broad feet slapping loudly on the wood floors as we made our way to my room. "Kitsune asked me to send word along as well. She hopes ye've found what ye seek."

I frowned at him, opening the door. "I suppose I could better answer that if I really knew what that was."

He grinned up at me. "Aye, she said as much"

"And Tresa?" I laid the silk bundle carefully upon my bed, smoothing out the wrinkles. "Is she still . . . there?"

"Oh, aye. Kitsune has her coming and going to lay attendance as quick as she snaps her fingers."

"I'm surprised she'd let a viper like that so close. I wouldn't trust her, that's for certain." I bit down on the inside of my cheek.

"I canna say what Kitsune's motivations are, but it seems to be having a bit of a benefit, so that's something." His snout twitched suddenly. "Odd. It smells of poison in here."

"Huh?"

"'Tis an odd scent, to be sure, ye ken. I thought I smelled it in the hallways betimes when the prince led me here. Odder still to find it in your bedroom, aye?"

My blood ran cold as I looked at the empty bottle of wine on the mantel. I snatched at it and held it out to Jimmy. "Is it coming from this? Talivar and Brystion drank it last night."

"Nae. Good vintage, mind, but that's not it." His piggish eyes blinked nervously as he snuffled around the room. "There's somewhat blocking the scent of it . . . it's been hid verra well." His gaze fell on my discarded gown from the night before. "There."

"My dress? I have a poisoned dress?" I frowned at him. "But I feel fine. Are you sure?"

He tapped his nose. "This doesn't lie. Somewhat's amiss." He dropped to his hands and knees, his knuckles bending to support his weight. It would have almost been comical except for the circumstances. "Sweat," he grunted. "Rocks, and leaves and growing things, soup and . . . a unicorn . . . and here," he squealed triumphantly, shaking his head so that his big ears flopped forward.

In his hands he clutched the small bit of the cloth I'd used as a makeshift gag for the Queen. Maybe it had caught on my dress in the struggle? "Are you sure that's it?"

"Aye. Taint of spider poison sure enough. But it's a strange thing. Usually poison is coated on something, ye ken . . . and there's old sweat exuded upon it, but the poison smell goes deeper than that. Almost as though it was woven into the very fabric itself." He licked his tusks curiously. "Seems like an awful amount of trouble to go to poison ye."

"Poison you?" Moira stood in the doorway, her face a thundercloud. I tried not flinch beneath the steely eyes as she stared at me. Obviously she'd been let in on the little powwow of what went down last night. Talivar loomed behind her, face unreadable.

I shook my head at her, taking the scrap from Jimmy and holding it out to her. "Not me. Your mother."

"That's ridiculous. The Queen's clothing only comes from the finest of weavers. She's the only one allowed to wear this type of silk."

"Then it would make it rather easy to poison her with it, wouldn't it?" I pointed out.

"But to weave all her dresses from it? It takes long enough

merely to collect it—let alone make it something she could wear. If there were that much poison on it, the seamstresses would be affected." She gingerly rubbed the scrap between her two fingers, delicate brow furrowing.

Jimmy sniffed the air as she took it. "Bristlefangs. From the northern reaches. Not an easy place to get to, but their poison glands go for a pretty penny in the Lower Crescent. The scent isn't strong enough for it ta' be the entire cut o' cloth . . . but perhaps every few bits of it?"

My brain seemed to have disconnected itself as the pieces started to finally snap into place, the Queen's crazed behavior suddenly making a hell of a lot more sense. "And . . . um. How deadly is this poison?"

"Well, if ye was to get bit, it's pretty fatal . . . especially for you mortal types. The silk, though . . . I don't know. I imagine it might be a little slower acting. It drives ye mad, ye ken?"

My eyes met Moira's horror-stricken face and she let out a soft gasp. "That's why she's been scratching at herself. Why she's been tearing at her clothes all this time. Somehow her body knows . . ." Her mouth became grim. "And we've only been making it worse, forcing her to wear it."

Talivar thrust out his lower lip thoughtfully. "And if this poisoned spider silk came from the Barras? Kitsune will be implicated, you realize."

Jimmy backed up a few steps. "Ye canna' mean that. I know things are a wee bit rough between us these days, but she wouldna' stoop to poison. Not like this."

"Then someone wants you to think it," I said softly. "To create more conflict, distracting us from the real issue." I gave Moira a hard look. "Just how involved was Maurice when he was here as your TouchStone?"

The princess crossed her arms against my question.

"He had the illusion of immortality during his time with me. A chance at power should I become queen. There are those here who would not be averse to helping him in this, even under these circumstances." Her mouth compressed. "Some feel as though my mother has retained power too long. That Faerie is starting to suffer beneath her rule. That perhaps the power structure would be different if she had not chosen . . . Thomas."

Her face became troubled and she turned to her brother, handing him the bit of cloth. "Take this to Thomas and explain to him what has happened. But be discreet." Her eyes darted to Jimmy. "At the very least we can get my mother dressed in something other than what she has."

I scooped up the silkworm cloth from the bed. "I know this was a gift, but if she fights you on wearing anything other than silk, at least we know it's not contaminated."

Talivar nodded gravely, gathering it beneath his arm. "We will need to burn all of her clothing."

"But that's evidence," I pointed out.

"Evidence we might never want to come to light," he countered. "An extended illness we can explain away. To admit we let our own mother be poisoned before our very eyes?" He shrugged helplessly. "This is a very fine line we must walk, Abby. Assuming Thomas even believes it."

Jimmy tugged on his sleeve. "I'll go wit' ye, lad. He canna' fault my nose for finding it, aye?"

Moira nodded and the two of them left, Jimmy trotting comically beside the prince. The princess shook her head.

"I don't deserve him, you know. My brother. Anyone else would have blamed me for what happened to him, but he never did."

"Blame you for what? I thought his father was involved."

She sank onto my bed. "Yes. That is the gist of it, but there were rumors in the court that Talivar's injuries were caused simply to strengthen my own claim to the throne. By all rights, he should be next in line, but . . ."

"It's a stupid fucking rule," I said, my frustration at the political situation boiling to the surface.

"I agree." She swished her feet against the bed like a child. "It's why I brought him to guard you, you know. He's never been the same since it happened. I thought by giving him a purpose or by getting him out of the palace for a while, he might start to focus less on what he lost." A sad smile curved the corner of her mouth. "It's not nearly enough and it never will be, but thank you for all that you've done for him."

What the hell had he been like before I met him? From the way people went on about it, perhaps Talivar had been far worse off than I'd known. Anger rippled through me again. Despites all its beauty, there were some very ugly sides to Faerie.

"I'll bet. Funny how much concern you seem to have over someone you've essentially tossed by the wayside simply for having physical flaws." I tapped my own head. "I'm surprised you can stand to be around me, frankly."

"I do not make the rules, Abby. This is who we are as a people and I cannot change it. Not yet." She sucked in a ragged breath, frown lines creasing her perfect brow. "First things first."

"Can't you force your mother to abdicate the throne to you, then?"

"We could try, but that wouldn't solve the issue of the CrossRoads being closed. That's too deeply entwined with her own magic at the moment. The only way to force her hand would be to kill her . . . and I'm not ready to do that."

"And what about your son?" I cocked my head at her. "Do you sacrifice one for the other?"

She flinched. "It's complicated."

"No shit. If it weren't for me TouchStoning him, he might have faded by now. He still might. You might want to consider trying to 'convince' her a little harder."

"I'm bound by protocol. I've done what I can."

"Then I guess we'd better find someone a little more willing to draw outside the lines," I told her. My sympathy only went so far, and I was tired of letting my "destiny" spin me wherever it would. "Your world needs you—hell, your *son* needs you—and you need to stop hiding behind the old rules of what 'used to be,' and start living in the now. This isn't some Faerie legend of old."

"And what would you propose?" Talivar asked softly as he leaned against the doorway. His hands were empty, so I could only assume he'd found my father, though I didn't see Jimmy with him. Perhaps the pig-man had remained behind to speak with him; how Thomas chose to handle that bit of information was his business.

"Well, first I'm going to go eat the rest of my breakfast because I'm starving." I fingered my necklace, yanking down on it so it bit into my neck. "I imagine it might be faster to get to the Barras via the CrossRoads, don't you think?"

Moira stared at me. "You can't possibly be thinking about asking the Unseelie Court for help?"

I shrugged. "The irony of it all is that if you all hadn't banished the Unseelie Court or destroyed it or whatever you all did, you would have probably discovered the poison a lot sooner. And if you think about it, a united front of both Courts might be enough to give the daemons pause." My gaze rested on both of them for a moment. "We have two days left. I don't think your mother is cognizant of what she's doing anymore. Kitsune has the one person who might be able to get us some real answers."

The prince shook his head. "I don't think Tresa can come

back here. If what she said before was true, the hedge condemned her for a traitor when she left the first time."

I bit the inside of my cheek, my short-lived TouchStoning experience with the woman suddenly making a bit more sense. The thorns had been what I'd seen when our bond had formed. I snapped my fingers, shuddering at the memory. "Tresa told me Maurice has her son. If she can't come here to testify, perhaps he can . . . if we can find him."

"That's a big if, Abby. Assuming we even find him in time."

"Best plan I've got. Unless you can think of something else. Like strangling Maurice into a confession, perhaps?"

"No." Moira sighed. "As satisfying as that would be."

"So . . . breakfast?" Talivar reached for my hand.

"Abso-freaking-lutely," I muttered, as my stomach growled. "Priorities, people. And then we're going to go save your kingdom."

Twenty-five

The Door opened faster this time, the Key bending to my will easily. I would have thought the Queen's power would have been stronger here in Faerie, but it seemed as though the CrossRoads liked the taste of freedom I'd given it earlier. As I snipped through the last of the golden threads, the power eagerly rushed forward, the Door glowing with a silver light.

"Think that's it." Talivar's hand steadied me at my elbow as I released the amulet.

We were standing in an empty part of the castle, this Door apparently left to extreme disuse in the dusty room of some forgotten elven noble. The prince had assured me that there were many such Doors in the castle, but the less a Door was used, the less likely it was to be found. Easier for sneaking out of the palace, anyway.

I glanced behind me as Talivar took my hand to lead me through. Melanie, Brystion, Jimmy, and Phineas followed suit, although Moira had elected to stay behind. Just as well since she'd been less than impressed with my plan; more to the point, she could easily distract the Queen from what we were doing.

Bryston's gaze burned into my back, but he made no move to claim my other hand. Also just as well.

The coldness of the silver enveloped us, plunging our group into a moment of darkness until the familiar silver cobbles of the CrossRoads materialized beneath our feet.

"How far are the Barras?" I asked Jimmy as he shuffled toward the front of the line with a quivering snout.

"Not too far. Kitsune has decided to move to a more sheltered area for a bit until some of this other stuff blows over."

"Wise of her." Not that I could blame her, really. Holding fast until the major players showed their hands was probably the best way to go. Foxes were known for their cunning, after all.

Still. If things were coming down to some sort of internal revolution , I wasn't exactly sure I wanted to be smack in the middle of it. I said as much to Talivar and he chuckled.

"In the old days, warring factions would have terrible battles, and at the end of the day all of the wounded would be dunked into one of the larger healing pools." A soft snort escaped him. "And then, of course, we'd get up the next day and do it all again."

"It's a wonder you got anything done," I said. "Seems like a stupid way to fight a war."

"Aye. These days we prefer to settle things with hurling matches." He winked at me. "Just think, with you and Melanie here, we've got enough for a full team."

I smiled weakly. "You know, somehow I don't think I'm up for that this morning."

"We need a mortal for each side, even if you all you do is sit there."

"I'll pass. Besides, I think we have other things we're supposed to do today. Save the world or something, right?"

"Or something." He sighed. "I owe Kitsune a very great debt, Abby. I would prefer it if we stayed on her good side."

Sanctuary.

I left the word unsaid, but it didn't take much to start connecting the dots. At some point, Talivar had felt the need to claim protection from the fallen Unseelie Court. Whether that was before or after his scarring was the real question, but he'd been dancing around the subject for days now. As curious as I was, I couldn't see pressing the issue.

Behind us I could hear Bryston and Melanie speaking softly. The rhythmic rise and fall of a question. A terse answer. A pause and then an awkward laugh. And all around us, the wash of silver dust floated as we trudged along in the dark.

"So what was up with this morning?" I asked the prince.

"Mmm. Call it an insurance policy."

I cocked a brow at him, catching the barest flush at the tip of his ears. "An odd way of paying the premium."

"I notice you haven't asked the incubus about it."

I shrugged. "I *know* what his motivations are."

Talivar's flush grew darker. "It's difficult to explain. It has been an exceptionally long time since I was found worthy of a rival. And while I cannot say I necessarily welcome competition for your affections, just know how grateful I am to have been afforded the opportunity." He paused. "However things turn out between us."

Our fingers entwined briefly before he strode forward to catch up with Jimmy. I looked at Ion and Mel, catching the flicker of interest in the incubus's face. He inclined his head graciously and I turned away, not sure of what was written on my own expression to warrant it.

Our approach to the Barras was preceded by very little fanfare, though this time my ears caught the sounds of the upcoming settlement without much trouble. I had expected things to be a bit more subdued under the circumstances, but excitement pattered through the crowd. Runners dashed this way and that, black banners flying at every corner. Music and laughter still filled the air, but the punctuated raucous cries of the vendors had taken on a brittle edge of anticipation.

I had the feeling that weapon sales had probably skyrocketed, particularly anything made of iron, but I kept my suspicions to myself.

Melanie tugged on my arm. "Not so sure about the presentation, but at least it sounds like these guys know how to party."

"I'm just waiting for the White Rabbit to run by shouting 'Down with the bloody Red Queen!'"

She sniggered and Talivar shot me a sour look. "That would be my mother you're talking about, you know."

"The Red Queen?"

"Close enough." His mouth twitched. "Even if it's sort of true."

Ion eyed the goings-on with strange expression. "If I didn't know any better, I'd say they're gearing up for an extended campaign."

Talivar shook his head. "They cannot involve themselves in an official capacity."

The incubus let out a chuff. "Who's going to stop them? Your mother? It looks like they're going to stake a claim *unofficially*, one way or the other." His eyes narrowed. "They'll be open for bargaining, Abby. It will be to our advantage, but be careful what you promise."

"Not really an issue. I don't have anything to bargain with. Besides, I'm not interested in playing Storm the Castle."

"We're not storming anything," the prince said. "Let's try to stay focused, shall we?"

And then there was no more time for talk as Jimmy led us

through the cavernous maze of tents to the Lower Crescent, straight to Kitsune's tent. Tresa was kneeling outside, her head bowed. A red thread ran from her neck and into the tent.

I shivered. If Talivar had gone after her instead of me, would this have been my fate? Tresa looked up as we approached, snarling when she saw me. "My mistress bids you enter," she coughed out.

"My thanks," Talivar said formally, pushing back the flap to gesture the rest of us through. The ginger scent rushed out and Jimmy paused, his eyes watering.

"I think I'll just waits out here, if ye dinna' mind?"

Phineas shook his head, his nostrils flaring as he entered the tent behind me, the dark warmth enveloping us. "Jesus, that smells obnoxious."

"But I like it," Kitsune said calmly from where she was kneeling beside the low table, dressed in a sanguine kimono. Her dark hair hung plaited like a liquid black river over her shoulder. Her lips parted into a wide grin, the candlelight glowing eerily upon the smoothness of her face. "And that is all that matters."

Talivar knelt before her, inclining his head. "Of course. And thank you for granting us audience. We apologize for the informality of it, but we have a need to speak to Tresa."

Kitsune's grin became wider and she tugged on the red thread attached to her wrist. "My handmaiden? I should thank you for the gift, my lord prince. She has been a delight to train. Haven't you, pet?"

"Yes, mistress." Tresa crawled in through the flap, keeping her eyes fixed on the floor.

"There, now, ask what you will of her. But mind she belongs to me," Kitsune warned. "You may not undo this binding until I cut it."

Tresa raised her head, hatred burning deep within her

eyes as she stared at me, but there was a definite tremble in her limbs whenever she looked at the fox-woman. "I will not talk," she said finally. "There is no need. After all"—she let out a mirthless chuckle—"you cannot hurt me more than Maurice has."

"My kingdom is under rather dire straits at the moment. There's not much I wouldn't do." Talivar pulled out a piece of one of the Queen's dresses from a pouch at his side. "We know about the poison, Tresa."

The blood drained from her face. He'd been bluffing, of course . . . aside from the Protectorate issue, we didn't know for certain she was directly involved, but her reaction made it certain. She looked away, her eyes going dull. "You can't prove anything."

"We don't have to," I said. "All we have to do is parade our evidence in front of Maurice during the hearing and let him know you told us everything." A part of me felt like a total piece of shit at making her squirm—after all, she was trying to protect her family, the same as I was. On the other hand . . .

"If I were free I'd tear out your heart," she snapped.

"If you were free, you'd be dead," Talivar said bluntly, his voice simmering with a dark promise. "The thorns would have seen to that."

Kitsune chuckled. "Ah, yes. Nasty business, that poison hedge. Easy enough to heal if you know how." Her hand swept out to grasp Tresa's arm, sliding back the long sleeve to reveal the newly pinked flesh. "It was a deep infection."

"Thank you, mistress," Tresa said, her eyes dropping low again.

I gave the fox-woman a shrewd look. "And could you heal poison from spider silk? Long-term exposure to it?"

"I might." Kitsune's grin disappeared. "But I would

need access to her body, or someone else who's been exposed to it to the point of sickness to figure out the antidote. And there are no terms I could think of that would grant me that level of access to the Queen." Her ears flattened. "And no reason for me to either."

"Never mind all that," Melanie said to Tresa, her face thoughtful. "What do we need for the high ground here? What's going to get you to give us the information we want?" I eyed her bemusedly. Never one for confrontations, Melanie would usually rather make a bargain to get her way. Most of the time, it worked.

Tresa let out a desperate laugh. "My son, of course. He is innocent in all of this. A child." Her nostrils flared out in a shuddering sigh. "Rescue him and I'll tell you anything you want to know. I can give you proof that the daemons are backing Maurice's actions." Her gaze met Talivar's, but there was nothing sly about her now. No bargains save what she was offering. "Grant me this and I'll even tell you the antidote for the poison."

A terrible silence gripped the room, the tension between Talivar and Kitsune wire-tight as they exchanged a glance. It wasn't hard to tell what the answer would be.

"Where is your son?" Melanie asked it simply and without preamble.

Tresa's face fell, her eyes rolling wildly. "I don't know. Maurice took him."

I frowned at her, something not quite right about the story. "He took your son, for no reason at all?"

Her limbs squirmed as though she might try to scuttle from Talivar's sudden scrutiny.

"Did the Queen take any interest in my plight when she cut off all contact with the lesser Fae?" Her head whipped toward Talivar. "Did any of you? I was a seamstress before the silkworms were no longer allowed to sell to me. I made the cloth for those fancy dresses the Queen wore. We had a good life, my Timan and I."

"And as soon as it went sour, you decided killing your liege was the thing to do?" Talivar's face had gone blank, his eye narrowing.

"I didn't intend to kill her. Just make her sick enough that she would step down. If trade were to be reopened between the Courts, I'd have my livelihood back. Maurice discovered my duplicity but kept his silence. In return, I agreed to help him." She shook her head. "Your capture of him merely slowed things down, but much of this was set in motion a very long time ago. When the poison did not progress as fast as he wanted, he decided I should take over the role of Protectorate to keep you in the dark. If I could take Moira's child from her, I was to do that as well. I balked and Maurice had his daemon mercenaries take the boy in return for my continued compliance."

I exchanged a glance with Talivar, exhaling softly. "Full circle," I murmured. "What will you do, Prince?"

"I should think it would be fairly obvious," Phineas piped up from beside me after a few moments of silence. "Rescue the boy and we've got some bargaining power. If we can prove they instigated all of this through Maurice, they'll have to back down. The moment the Queen releases the CrossRoads, it will loose the Wild Magic and you'll have the ability chase those daemon fuckers off your lands." The unicorn coughed as he looked at Brystion. "Present company excluded, of course."

"Of course." Brystion cracked me a private smile. "Though the description is still rather apt."

I rolled my eyes. Incorrigible bastard. Even if it was true.

"So what now?" I began. "We've only got, what? One more day until we have to give the daemons an answer . . .

or Maurice. That's not much time to find a kid who could be anywhere."

Kitsune frowned, glancing at my neck. "The Key could be used."

Talivar shook his head. "How? We could wander the CrossRoads for days trying to find him."

"The Key can do more than randomly open the Doors to the CrossRoads," she said, eyes never leaving mine. The ginger scent grew sharper. "The wearer can direct where the Door should exit—even if they do not know exactly where that is."

"What are you talking about?" Talivar stared at her.

"It's an older power, to be certain—and not one that is widely known, but some of us have seen it used in such a way."

"Guess you really can simply walk into Mordor," Melanie observed dryly.

"Indeed. The Key can only use existing Doors, but more important, Abby could indicate where she wants to go and it would take her to the closest Door there is, thereby skipping the CrossRoads altogether. In this case, perhaps a description of the boy would suffice."

Bryston let out a low whistle. "No wonder they locked that shit up in the vault. Rather convenient of you to drop this information *now,* don't you think?"

She shrugged. "If we are truly going to remove the daemons from Faerie, then why not?"

"I will not allow it." Talivar paced about the tent. "We could end up straight in the middle of their army. There's still a chance we can avoid war. If we get caught blitzing into their territory, that's completely gone."

"But we've got a truce with them for the time being," I tugged on the necklace, wishing like hell I'd known about this sooner. I could have left anytime I'd wanted.

Bryston let out a humorless laugh. "And you think

that would save you? A truce that you've just broken?" An exasperated grunt escaped him when he saw my look of confusion. "Right now everyone is on even terms. The CrossRoads are closed—no one is moving around easily. But if the Queen were to start using the Key to potentially launch an attack directly at the daemon camp? Even if that wasn't your intent, you'd still be thought of as spies. I don't think even your current elevated status would save you." He paused, his face going flat. "Assuming they didn't force you into working for them first."

Not entirely sure if I was mad or not for considering the idea, I asked Tresa for whatever detail she could provide on her son's whereabouts. His age. What he looked like. His clothes. I tried to image it in my head. "And what if I can direct it so that it doesn't open directly into the daemon camp?"

"It's a thought, but there will still be traces of the Cross-Roads at the site. There's no way around that," Phineas said, nudging me hard. "But it may not matter in another day or so anyway."

My gaze fell upon Melanie. Intent was so important when it came to the OtherFolk. I worked the amulet between my fingers. "The daemons are expecting us to try. Our bargain will be null if they catch us. That's what Nobu said."

"Well, that makes for an easy answer, then," Melanie said mildly. "We don't let them catch us."

The air stilled around us, sticky and hot and thick enough to choke on. The ginger scent suddenly disappeared, leaving us with only the wicking smell of candle wax. Kitsune sat up very straight, her ears flattening. "You realize that if I allow you to leave from here, I implicate myself in this?"

"I suspect things are already past that point." Phineas rubbed his horn on his rear hock in irritation. "After all, why suggest the idea if you didn't want to be a part of it?"

"Clever thing. I will require your word," she said to Talivar, her voice abrupt and clipping. "For the love I bear you, cousin, I will allow this thing to happen, but I want assurances that you will use your influence to see our Court reinstated. Thus our debt will be settled."

He stiffened. "I have no way to undo what the Queen has wrought, but should it fall into my power, I will do so."

"Then that will do, Prince. There is a Door beyond the edges of the Barras that you may use. I suggest you choose your companions wisely," she added. Her dark eyes remained coolly steadfast, but I caught the sly smirk on her lips, nonetheless.

Melanie stirred beside me. "Well, I'll be fairly useless without the Wild Magic. And strategically speaking, if you get caught . . ."

I could see in her face that she didn't want to go. It stung, but I couldn't blame her for being afraid. As shitty as things were, walking straight into the lion's den held far more implications for her than it did me.

Talivar shared a glance with me and nodded. "We don't want to risk both of you. And should the daemons find you there, I'm not sure Nobu will be able to keep them from taking you."

"And Abby's chopped liver, right?" Ion snapped. "Once again, you call upon her to do your dirty work."

"What other choice do we have?" The prince made a little sound of frustration, his hands balling into fists. "If I could take the Key from her and use it myself I would do so. But I can't. So suck it up and shut up."

The incubus drew himself tall, eyes flashing, and for a moment I could nearly see the punches about to be thrown.

"Fine. But I'm coming too." His mouth twisted wryly. "After all, having an actual daemon in your party can't hurt. A distraction, if nothing else."

It was said off the cuff, but I could hear the promise beneath the words. Come hell or high water, he would take me out of Faerie if things went badly. If Talivar understood the warning behind it, he said nothing.

I crouched down to look at Phin. "And you?"

"I'm not exactly built for covert operations, Abby. All things considered it's probably best if I don't know the details of what happens. If I don't know about it, I can't give you up. I can't lie, you know." He gave an equine shrug. "Open the Door to the CrossRoads proper and I'll escort Melanie to the palace. That way she'll be able to feign ignorance as well."

"Mmph. Guess that leaves the three of us." I sighed. "I don't want to involve anyone else from the Barras."

"Assuming I'd even give my permission. And I wouldn't." Kitsune folded her hands into her sleeves. "This is done solely on your head."

Tresa had remained huddled by Kitsune's side during our conversation, her face turned down. The thread around her throat tightened, the flash of her pulse a rapid staccato. She didn't deserve my sympathy, but still. "I would ask that the boy's mother be allowed to choose."

"Gracious of you," Kitsune murmured. "Though your trust is misplaced. She has the power to undo her bonds and, as of now, she is not worthy."

Talivar pulled on my sleeve, ushering the others through the tent flap. "Let's go, Abby."

I spared a last glance at the two women. Kitsune made a sign of farewell with a graceful hand. And then I emerged into the relatively fresh air, the chaos of movement around us a confusing blur.

The others waited outside, their faces sober. I sucked in a deep breath of air. "All right. Let's do this."

✳ ✳ ✳

The sparkles subsided as Melanie disappeared through the
Door and a dull ache tightened in my chest. It wasn't in me
to ask her to come with us, but I wished she would. I let out
a sigh as Talivar gave my hand a squeeze. "It's time."

No more stalling then. I grasped the necklace and placed
my hand upon the Door. It was made of bamboo and woven
reeds, but the carvings were the same, even if the whole
thing had a bit of a collapsible feel to it. As escape routes
went I suppose it made a lot of sense, especially given the
transient properties of the Barras. But without the power of
the CrossRoads to bring it to life, it lay just as motionless
and dead as all the others.

The amulet flared as I touched it, illuminating us in that
same blue glow as before. Dimly I wondered if the Queen
could feel me here. Did it hurt? Would it alert her to what
we were doing? The thought twisted uncomfortably. Time
to move.

As the veil unraveled, I concentrated on Tresa's boy.

. . . *a lad of about fourteen years . . . small boned and delicate . . . a half-breed with slanted eyes and olive skin . . . a scar
upon his forearm from when he was a child . . .*

"Timan," I whispered, the veil shuddering in response
as I tried to formulate what I wanted. Close, but not too
close . . . preferably without walking directly into danger . . .

A vibration ran through me, the Door uttering a chord
that saturated into my bones as I willed it to open. Likely
exits flipped through my consciousness, even as myriad possibilities of potential outcomes skittered across my mind.
But which one to take?

"There," I gasped, trying to hold them still. "This is the
one."

"You are sure?" Ion spoke it as less of a question than
a comment, but I gestured at him and he took my hand to
lead us through . . . and into a grove of tall trees thick with

golden-veined leaves, glowing with their own soft hue.

Talivar blinked in surprise. "The Halcyon Forest. These are sacred trees. The daemons should never have made it this far." Beneath my skin, the magic continued to thrum faintly.

"I can reopen it," I said. "It's almost like I'm tethered."

"All right." Talivar adjusted his quiver, loosening the bow so that it was within easy reach. Beside me, Bryston shook himself, shapeshifting into that of his antlered form. Here, in this place, he appeared like a godling of the woods, his cloven hooves sharp and glittering.

"Harder to track." He stamped a hoof as though to make the point. "Besides, if they see me first, they may decide I'm one of them."

Talivar gave him an odd look, taking in his appearance with a curious bent before straightening. "I leave her in your care," he said formally. "Should anything ill toward befall me, you are to get Abby back to the castle."

The incubus bared his teeth. "Should anything happen to you, I'll get her out of here, but I'll be damned if I return her to your hellish little kingdom."

"Fair enough," the prince said in a chilly voice. "All I can ask for. I will have to trust that Abby will prevail upon you to do the right thing."

"Let's get this over with. And stop worrying about my virtue, okay?" My gaze flicked between both men. "We've got big enough problems." I put one hand out on Ion's arm half to steady myself and half to calm him down. The incubus could be downright testy even at the best of times, but we needed to work together.

Talivar gave us a curt nod. "Wait here and I'll scout it out. If there's an outpost here it shouldn't be too hard to find. Sulfur has a way of coating the air." The elf slipped into a nearby thicket, moving quietly in his thin-soled boots.

He'd dressed for the part, his clothes dark and tight fitting. His jaggedly cut hair was doing its best to escape from his attempt at pulling it back, and his pointed ears showed pale and stark.

A crooked half smile turned up the corners of his mouth, piercing me with a thousand things left unsaid, but there was no time now in which to say them. And then he was gone, swallowed up in a cluster of golden leaves and watery sunlight. I slumped against the bark of the tree that framed one edge of the Door. The thought of moving too far away made me nervous. No sense tempting fate, after all. On the other hand, if Talivar got stuck in a bind I wasn't going to leave him here either.

I spared a sideways glance at Ion, but he remained steadfast, his ears twitching and cupping the sound of the woods. At the moment I could only hear the leaves as they dropped from the branches to flutter to the ground with a soft hiss. My heart ached to be surrounded by such a wild beauty, and deeper still at the mess I was currently in.

There was no question I still had feelings for Brystion. Hell, the moment he touched me, I was his all over again. The fact that he obviously knew this and didn't press the issue was disconcerting. Before, I couldn't have said he wouldn't have tried something, but either his respect for Talivar ran deeper than I knew, or he'd truly decided to let me come to my own conclusion.

The question hovered on my tongue, but now was not the right time to ask it. Later, perhaps, when the world was not crashing down upon us.

Beside me, Ion suddenly froze, his hand snagging my wrist an iron grip. Before I could say a word, he shoved me against the tree, kissing me hard. I mumbled a protest against his mouth, but he was already lifting my skirts, fingers biting at my thighs, the cloth ripping under his claws.

"What the fuck—" I hissed, the words cut off as his tongue thrust deep into my mouth.

Panic flooded my brain, even as my body decided it kind of liked it. He trapped my arms above my head, his mouth nipping hot and hard down my neck. *Betrayer!* My inner voice shrieked at me, ignoring the way my hips began to sway beneath him. I blinked, realizing he was using that particular seductive power of an incubus, my skin burning with a fierce hunger in return.

And that hurt worst of all.

Blearily, I climbed out of the lust-induced fog sweltering over my brain that commanded me to submit before him. The urge to slide to my knees, take his cock into my mouth, to open myself wide to his pleasure thrummed sharp and urgent. Would we TouchStone again? The thought nearly made me laugh, but instead I let out a groan, arching toward him.

His own breath came in soft gasps, and the erection trapped between the folds of my skirt wasn't any sort of Glamour. I uttered a low cry when he mouthed my breast, chafing between his lips and the linen chemise.

"Goddess, I've missed this," he muttered. "So fucking hungry."

Lust wrapped itself over my flesh like a ribbon. His doing? Mine? "I can't do this, Ion. Not here. Not like this."

"I know." He gritted his teeth as though he fought his own inner battle. "Struggle for me and make it look real."

A harsh laugh split the quiet of the forest, jerking me out of my hazed thoughts before I could answer. I stiffened, trying to peer over Bryston's shoulder. The incubus held me back, one hand upon my neck, ignoring my protest. His ears flattened as he turned around, a chilly smile gracing his features. The gold of his eyes had damped down to an obsidian darkness.

I caught the glimpse of a shadowed face and slick scales past the ebony fall of Ion's hair.

Daemons. A shitload of them.

A hysterical shriek bubbled up in my throat and I actually tried to pull away in earnest, my ardor slamming like a pit of oil into my belly. Where was Talivar?

"Do you mind?" Bryston's voice dropped into growling purr, his tail lashing from side to side. "I'm not in the habit of sharing."

"Who said anything about sharing?" The one in front gave me an appreciative leer. "We'll watch you shag her and when you're done, we'll take her off your hands." The daemon bared his teeth. "And in return we let you go. Seems fair, doesn't it?" His voice became sly. "Unless, of course, you were to know anything about this Door here. Odd that it seems to be active when the rest of them aren't."

Bryston's hand pressed across my mouth to muffle my cry of alarm .

"Frankly, I don't give a shit why the hell you think we're here." He was stalling and the realization hit me like a slap to the face. How well had those ears heard them coming? He hadn't even thought to warn me and I could only assume that was to make his seduction of me look at real as possible. The fact that I had apparently given into him with barely a thought flooded me with shame.

The daemons snarled something rude, but Bryston turned his back on them as though he truly didn't care, warning in his eyes. The thick, meaty hand of a daemon snatched at his shoulder. "And I don't think you realize the situation you're in. This here area is off limits." His eyes wandered over me again. "And we're taking you into custody."

Anger coursed through me. "You're not even supposed to be here. Last I checked, this was Faerie . . . not Hell. Though it certainly smells like it," I sniffed, waving my hand in front of my nose, ignoring Ion's warning grunt.

I ducked when I saw the clawed hand aiming for my face, half expecting it. Not quite fast enough. The claws snarled my hair and yanked me back.

"Well, now," the daemon rumbled, staring at my breasts. "Isn't that interesting?" A sharp tug on my neck and I realized he'd found the Key, still glowing with its recent use.

Beside me, Brystion lowered his head, the glittering points of his antlers eye level with the daemon. "I suggest you let her go," he said softly.

"Or what?" The daemon's hand strolled down my shoulders with a lazy motion, even as he gestured with his head at the others to flank him. "*I* suggest you move along. If this is what I think it is, then my job suddenly got much easier." A ripping sound and I realized he'd shredded the front of my gown. I ground my teeth even as I flushed, my breasts suddenly exposed to their leers. "Think she'll service my men first, though. After all, we need her alive . . . not in one piece."

"Freeze," Brystion barked. Dimly I became aware of a high-pitched whistle. A fleshy thud and the daemon let out a low wheeze, his hands slacking upon my waist. I ducked behind the incubus as two more arrows sledged into the daemon's head.

"Talivar," I shouted, unthinking. Had he seen the incubus and me?

The other daemons paused, the largest one letting out a grim chuckle. "The Crippled Prince has killed our lieutenant," snarled the closest one. "The Fae have made the first shot."

The hum of challenge burst from behind us, a clarion call of power that made my ears ache. "Oh, shit."

We'd just declared war.

Twenty-six

In an instant I was in Bryston's arms and we were bounding toward Talivar. The tall elf let loose round after round, deadly shafts buying us a little time. Behind us, the silver pull of the CrossRoads snapped away and the Door faded. With our cover blown we couldn't possibly go through—not if we didn't want to lead the entire contingent of daemons straight into the Barras.

Not to mention a few of the fuckers had pulled out their axes and started chopping at the woven tree branches that had made up the frame.

"Bitches," Bryston swore.

I held the scrap of my dress above my naked breasts as best I could, trying to ignore the heated flush of my cheeks. Talivar wasn't paying any attention to me at all, which was probably for the best, given that the daemons were clearly lining up for some sort of attack.

He gestured at Ion. "Get her behind us. There's an empty bear den you can take shelter in. The body of the boy is not too far from it."

"Dead?" The last flare of hope I'd had dribbled away. "What are we going to do?"

The elf's mouth tightened as he eyed his quickly empty-ing quiver. "Try to find another way out."

"But that's—"

"We don't have time for this," the incubus snapped, scooping me up and heading for the woods, ignoring my feeble struggles with an air of impatience. The heat from his ebony skin was blistering against my hands. "You're distracting him and there's no sense in making us a bigger target. Besides," he added smugly, "I think the cavalry is at hand. It would seem Kitsune has tossed her hat into the ring, after all."

A high-pitched cackle sailed past me, the velvet wings of hundreds of pixies filling the air until we were nearly swim-ming through a sea of flower petals. One of them grinned at me as it sailed past, displaying a set of tiny fangs.

"What the hell can they do?" I muttered. "They're so small . . ."

Ion slid into the cover of a fallen tree and we peered through the branches, watching in awe as the pixies swarmed over the daemons, falling upon them in a flurry of tiny teeth and toothpick swords. It was strangely effective. And bloody.

The daemons retreated, unable to attack such small en-emies with any real accuracy, and most of them were getting a sharp stick in the eye for their troubles. It seemed almost comical, their arms flapping in sudden panic. And yet I was struck by how easily the pixies were able to get through their defenses. How much stronger would the Fae be as a whole if they all worked together?

Talivar watched impassively as the group was driven off. With a limping stride, he loped toward us, finding us eas-ily enough when Brystion whistled low. Crouching down, he stared at my tattered dress and then exhaled in a ragged breath. "They'll be back."

"Reinforcements," I said. "And I'm guessing the pixies won't be able to hold them for long."

He shook his head. "Not a chance. They had the element of surprise here, but now that the daemons know what they're up against, they'll take steps."

"What about Tresa's son?" A lump filled my throat.

"Aye. He's been dead for a while. There's not much left of him, but I'll see him properly buried."

"Do we have time for that?" Ion sniffed the wind, blowing out as though he tasted something bad.

"We'll put him in the cave," Talivar said. "I cannot simply leave him here; he deserves better. We have a bit of time."

"Until what?" I wondered aloud.

He didn't answer me, moving past us with his head bowed slightly. "Come here," he said, taking my hand. Our fingers entwined, tight and hard, as though he were absorbing my flesh through his. Leading us down a gentle slope, he paused at the bottom, the leaves crackling beneath our feet.

"There." He gestured to the prone form of a child curled into a fetal position, half buried beneath a hollow log.

I knelt down beside the lifeless boy. His skin was waxen and soft in places, like the rotting edges of an overripe fruit, but his face retained a terrible innocence, pale eyes reflecting a glassy confusion. I choked back a sob, sliding the ruff of red-gold hair from his forehead. The chill of his death ran like the prickle of ants' feet upon my fingertips.

"What did he die of?"

"I don't know," Talivar said, his voice thick. "But I suspect it's the same as what the Queen suffers." He pulled up the threadbare remains of a sleeve, revealing thick scratches scoring the boy's arms. On closer observation, I noticed the ragged fingernails, the rust of dried blood beneath them.

"They poisoned him," I said, tears burning hot. Had it been exposure to whatever his mother had been working with? Or perhaps Maurice had ordered it done to keep Tresa pliant, or to find a cure . . . or any number of things. It made no difference. A child was dead.

"Give me your knife." I held out my hand without looking up. He hesitated for the barest of moments before unsheathing his smaller dagger and pressing it into my palm. If he had any inkling as to what I meant to do, he said nothing as I sliced off a lock of the boy's hair.

Talivar was right. We couldn't take him with us, but some part of me wanted to take this small bit, if only to prove that he'd been alive, that he'd had a voice in the world.

Clutching the hair tightly, I handed the dagger to Talivar. He gave me a nod of approval, but there was nothing particularly happy about the motion.

"The den is over here. It's been abandoned for at least a season."

Bryston followed us in silence, his dark eyes thoughtful. Together, he and Talivar cleared a bit of space and gently laid the body into the shallow hole, collapsing it when he was fully entombed. It wasn't much of a grave, but it would have to do. At least the woods were peaceful enough, and he'd be covered shortly by a blanket of golden leaves.

Small comforts.

"What will we tell Tresa?" I said finally, breaking the silence. In the distance I could hear the sound of drums. The daemons would be on the move soon. "I doubt she'll give us the antidote now."

"If there even was one." Bryston glanced down at the hair still woven through my fingers. "We should get out of here before those fuckers come back."

The prince shook his head. "We're not going to be able to outrun them. There's an entire encampment of the bastards over the far ridge. Which is the only way out of this valley, by the way," he added dryly. "Short of scaling a few mountain peaks—and none of us is dressed for that sort of snow."

His mouth tightened and he ducked below the branches of a fallen tree. "The Key must not be allowed to fall into their hands."

His words stung, even though I knew he was right. Lover or not, TouchStone or not, at the moment I was merely a commodity and a resource. *And quite possibly the only way we had to get out of here in one piece,* my inner voice reminded me.

"Surely, there has to be another way. Another Door?"

"They won't be easy to find without the CrossRoads open," Talivar said, snapping his fingers. "But there's a set of old ruins further down the hillside . . . they've been around forever. If there was ever a place for a Door, that would be it, though I suspect it's been closed for some time." His gaze lingered at my neck. "It could be that the Key would convince it to open."

"It's worth a shot," I said.

He exhaled sharply, sliding his fingers through the sweaty fall of his hair. "All right. Let's get moving, then. I don't think we've got much time left."

The calls of the daemons rang out nearby, their great feet tromping through the golden leaves signifying they were on the hunt. Without another word, Brystion hoisted me up. "Hold on to me as tightly as you can."

I wrapped my legs about his waist and my arms around his shoulders. It seemed a bit obscene, honestly, but I was a bit past caring. A pixie fluttered by, bowing to Talivar, its voice a hissing sibilance I couldn't understand.

The prince nodded at the little thing. "He's taking his people and leaving. They've done all they can do and there's a sorcerer at the daemon camp. He doesn't want to lead his people into death."

"At least ask him if he knows anything about the ruins or the Door." I was all for exploring, but given the time constraints, prudence dictated we find the way sooner rather than later.

The prince quickly rattled off something to the tiny Fae in the same language as before. The pixie hovered there a moment, scratching his head before pointing down the hillside and gesturing anxiously.

"Time to go," Brystion said. "Lead the way."

The pixie tore off at a frantic pace, Brystion jogging easily behind it, his hooves rapping upon the ground. Talivar kept abreast, his mouth becoming a grim line when our eyes met. He seemed so much older than before, the weight of his several hundred years suddenly very obvious.

The forest had grown quiet as we moved, Brystion taking great leaping strides, carrying my extra weight as though it was nothing. The thud of his hooves became louder, and I realized we were upon ancient stone and thick marble slabs, riddled with cracks and torn by time. He skidded slightly, his grunt of apology lost in the slide of gravel and the twang of fletching beside my ear.

"Oh, shit." I twisted my head even as he rolled, ducking so that he landed on his shoulder. I tumbled gracelessly above him, his clawed fingers pressing my head down to his chest.

Another volley of arrows flew and I struggled to try to find Talivar.

"Don't move," Ion hissed. "He's fine . . . he made it behind the fallen pillar." I felt disconnected from his words, my eyes taking in the exquisitely carved arches gleaming with the burnished softness of old bone.

"What is it?" A sick certainty clenched my gut even as

I asked the question. The metallic ring of armor upon the marble answered me soon enough. The daemons had cut us off. "Do you see the Door?" I searched frantically for the pixie.

"There," the incubus whispered. "Just past the altar, in that alcove." I turned my head and saw the pixie tucked up against it, waving frantically at me.

"All right. So what do we do now?"

"Can you open it? The rest of it would be moot if you can't." He slowly turned us so that he was on top of me, snarling as he bent. A hot trickle of blood coated my fingers and I jerked my hand away.

"Jesus, Ion, you've been hit." I scrambled up despite his protest to see the arrow jutting from the perfect ebony of his skin.

"Duly noted. Don't think it's too deep." He grimaced, his teeth flashing white. "Still stings like a bitch, though."

"How are we going to get there?" I looked at our own pillar, swearing softly . This was a different set of daemons than before, and they didn't seem to be in any particular hurry to find us, though they certainly began a systematic flanking of the alcove. They knew what it was . . . and that I had the Key.

I sank to my knees, clasping the amulet. It flared to life beneath my fingers. Maybe I was beginning to form more of an affinity with it, but I'd analyze it later.

The power pulsed through me, seeking its way until I felt the underlying resonance shiver deep and low. This Door seemed . . . sleepy. It hadn't been used in a while, and I suddenly felt as though I was being weighed by some sort of otherworldly scrutiny. Which was ridiculous. Doors weren't sentient, as far as I knew.

Not that you really know dick about Doors.

"I've got it," I murmured. "I think I can get it to work. Now, how do I get there?"

"Leave that to me," Talivar said, his voice quiet. I startled. He'd slipped his way over to us.

Bryston's eyes narrowed. "Ransom, then?"

"Aye. They won't be too kind to me, I wouldn't think but they won't keep me too long either," he added bitterly. "Too much fun to throw me in my mother's face as a reason for her to bend to their wishes."

"They'll trade you," I said, finally getting it. "You for Maurice."

"Probably." His mouth kicked into a slight grin and he reached up to cup my chin. "But I suspect you're going to figure something out. You always do."

Ion stomped a warning, setting me down. "You rely on her too much," he snarled. "All of you do."

"And you would suck her half dry if given a chance, my friend. I saw the way you looked at her the other night." The prince raised a brow. "Not to mention the way you nearly just shagged her against the tree."

I flushed. "Talivar . . . I didn't mean for it to happen . . ."

"I'm sure you didn't." His mouth met mine for an instant and I could taste his sorrow upon his tongue. "And you and I aren't over yet," he whispered. "TouchStone." I shivered at the word, even as my heart ached to hear it. "Take her home, incubus. Keep her safe."

Bryston inclined his head formally.

I shook my head, panic rabbiting under my ribs. "We will *not* leave you here. I'll go and get help. There must be a way to convince—"

The prince pressed a finger to my lips. "I want you to tell Roweena to break our Contract. You'll be free of any obligation you hold to me."

"But—"

"I'm going out there now. I'll take as many of them as I can." His nostrils flared. "Don't look back, Abby. Please. Just get to that Door and go through."

I swallowed a sob. So many ways this could have gone and we got stuck with this one. Not that I was going to let it go down like this. Not yet.

Bryston shifted me in his arms and let out a chuffing breath. "Good luck," he said simply. The elf bowed his head in return and then bolted from our hiding place. The whistling twang of arrows sounded through the trees and I saw his hands moving in a blur as he let out shot after shot. The incubus hesitated a moment more.

"Go," I whispered. His legs quivered in response.

"I'm sorry." His hooves dug into the thick underbrush, swift and graceful, each thrust of his curved hind legs propelling us forward with an elegant cadence. His antlers brushed the lower tree branches, leaves catching on the glassy points like a crown of gold, stark against his dark skin.

Behind us, I heard a muffled grunt and I let out a low cry to see the prince surrounded by a cluster of daemons. His bow had disappeared and he stood in the center, sword drawn, moving in a deadly and precise motion. The silver of his blade darted and thrust until it was coated with a fine red spatter. His other hand clutched a curved dagger and with these he spun, cutting a swath of bodies as he went.

The moment hovered before us, caught in the feral gleam of his smile and the furrow of his brow, the curl of his lip and the flex and hew of his muscles. Each movement was with purpose and for the first time I could really see how the arc of years of battle had marked him, turning his flesh into its own sort of weapon.

The hitch of his stride was swallowed up by the swivel

of his hips and the twist of his wrist, the vambraces on his forearm an inky blur. He spun again and this time his eye caught mine for the barest of seconds, its blue hue blazing in a heated fury. A scant breath later and he had turned away, ducking beneath the oncoming slice of an opposing ax. Regardless of his assumptions of ransom, the daemons weren't going to just let him walk all over them.

I opened my mouth to shout a warning, but the words cut off as a clawed hand fumbled its way across my lips. Bryston shook his head at me. "Don't let his sacrifice go to waste. There's no pride in that," he added softly when I glared at him.

"Get me to the Door," I said, refusing to look away from the prince. Even if Talivar said not to, I owed it to him to watch.

Bryston edged us to the alcove and set me down. "Do it quickly, Abby . . . and don't look back." He ducked low, his antlers shielding my view even as his words mocked me. *Don't look . . . don't look . . . don't look.* I clutched at the necklace, feeling the Key spark beneath my fingertips. I willed it to open, but the magic seemed to slip through my hands as I tried to focus where I wanted to go.

"Do you have it?" Ion grunted. "He can't hold them off for much longer."

"It's not the fucking TARDIS," I snapped, blinking against the power. *Safety* I told it, my mind gibbering with the need to find us someplace we could regroup that wouldn't potentially lead the daemons straight into the palace. The CrossRoads rushed past me like a river longing to escape.

And why wouldn't it really? After all, it had been cooped up and I'd only managed to let it out in spurts. If an inanimate semblance of a road could be seen to have a personality, this one was nearly alive with its need to get out. It scrambled past me and in the distance I could hear the shouts of alarm from the daemons. A moment later and the Door blazed to life.

I glanced behind me in time to see Talivar fall to his knees, a huge daemon slamming his face into the ground. I shrieked despite myself, fighting against the suddenly iron-grasp of the incubus's fingers around my arms. "Let me go!"

He didn't, of course, and judging by the attention I'd just drawn to us, this was probably for the best.

Bryston turned toward me, his eyes golden as he kissed me hard.

"Close it behind you, sweetheart." Before I had a moment to process this, he shoved me through the Door.

"Goddamn you!" I stumbled through the other side, landing in heap in the grass of the courtyard garden . . . below my apartment.

Behind me the Door faded in a slurry of sparkles. I sat motionless for a matter of moments, blinking back angry tears when Bryston didn't emerge. Numbly, I let the Key slip from my fingers, the magic sluicing away until all that stood before me was the dead space of the old gate.

I was home.

Twenty-seven

Still clutching at the shredded top of my dress, I limped up the stairs and found the spare key I normally hid above the lintel. It was Glamoured, of course—not that it really mattered anyway.

"Buck up, Abby," I scolded myself, ignoring the twinge of panic in my chest. "Faint heart never won fair lady."

Swallowing hard, I slipped through the kitchen, wondering at the dust built up along the top of the half wall. First order of business was getting my own damn clothes. If I never saw another chemise it would be too soon. Inside, my mind raced with a hysteric sort of panic even as I attempted to disconnect from it, a false calm moving my limbs toward the bathroom.

Part of me wanted to rush right back into the thick of it, hoping beyond hope that somehow I'd be able to rescue my friends, to undo what we'd fucked up so badly. But what good would that do? I'd probably end up being captured with nothing to show for it.

I would have to go to the Queen and admit what we'd done. My fault for insisting we go to the Barras. My fault for insisting we find Tresa's son.

My fault Talivar had been forced to fire upon the daemons.

My fault.

I would get clean. I would get dressed. I would figure out
how to save everyone.

And then I would come home and sleep for a month.

I finger combed my hair quickly, ignoring the wet drips on
my clothes. My cell phone had been dead when I checked it,
so I'd left it charging while I was in the shower. I threw on
my favorite pair of jeans and a black tank top. Underwear
had never felt so good—and if it was only a mental sort of
armor, I'd take it.

I flipped open the phone, blinking as it loaded up. First
thing would be to give Charlie a call and check on Benjamin . . . and then, Katy . . . and Roweena . . . and then . . .

"Holy fuck," I breathed, looking at the date on my cell.
Three months.

Three. Goddamn. Months.

Careless of me to have traveled the CrossRoads so
lightly . . . to have stayed in Faerie. I'd known that time
could go hinky in the other realms like that, but I hadn't
quite realized it would be so . . . specific. At least Moira had
paid up all the utilities. Someone else had apparently gotten
my mail.

My hands trembled as I dialed Charlie's number. I let
out a relieved sigh when she picked up. "Charlie, it's Abby.
I'm . . . home."

"Abby?" Charlie let out a squawk of surprise. "It's nearly
midnight. Where the hell have you all been? Is Melanie with
you?"

"It's complicated," I muttered, wondering how the hell
I was going to explain it all, not to mention that I felt like a
complete piece of shit for leaving my best friend behind. My

fists clenched as I realized the daemons would take her as well. *Nobu's bargain . . .*

My fault.

I grimaced at the phone. "How's Benjamin? He doing okay?"

She paused. "Yes . . . but there have been a few changes. I think maybe you should come over here."

"Actually, do you know where Roweena is? We've got a shitstorm of massive proportions brewing and I don't think we have time to visit right now." Plus, I only wanted to have to explain this once.

"She's at the Judgment Hall. Robert is there too. It's bad, Abby. A number of the OtherFolk have started fading. They've been burying them beneath the Church."

I went cold at her words. Of course. The Door had shut when I was carried through on the deer the first time. Lack of concentration and physical distance must have done the whole thing in. I drew in a shuddering breath.

"All right. Then it's a bigger clusterfuck than I thought. I'm going to head down there as soon as I can. I've got a few things I need to do and then I'll be there. Bring Benjamin . . . and call Katy and Brandon too. They should at least be aware, I think."

She made a muffled affirmation, but I couldn't tell her mood by the inflection. It would have to be good enough.

My eyes fell on the small lock of red-gold hair I'd placed on the counter as I hung up the phone. The boy's hair.

I stroked it absently, wishing there was some way I could have saved him . . . but there was no telling how long he'd been there. No way of knowing if he'd be able to be saved even if I had found him sooner. He was so much smaller than the Queen, and if he'd been exposed to the poison longer, there hadn't been much chance of saving him at all.

Tresa probably wouldn't tell us anything now, and with

Talivar and Brystion captured or quite possibly dead and her son gone, she would have no reason to. I rubbed my thumb over the silken strands. Still.

If the hair could be analyzed in some fashion . . .

Visions of taking it to a lab, CSI-style, filled my mind but I quickly dismissed the idea. Even if I *could* find a lab open at midnight that would do such a thing, there was no possibility of getting a result anytime soon. Besides, explanations of how he'd been poisoned by some type of spider that didn't exist on the mortal plane? No, thanks.

Which left me with magical means. Kitsune said she needed access to a body, but maybe the hair would be good enough.

I was going to need currency, however. Nobody in the Faerie world did jack shit for free and if they offered to, there was undoubtedly a secret price involved. I didn't have time for a mystical geas right now, so the easy way out would be a trade of some sort. And somehow I didn't think waving Talivar's ring around was going to do me any favors with the fox-woman at this point.

Not that I had anything worth trading in my apartment. The Marketplace, however . . .

Socks. Shoes. Jacket. I threw on whatever was closest and snatched my spare backpack. In my hurry to leave, I stumbled against the coffee table in front of the TV, scattering a pile of old magazines and Dear Abby letters.

"Sorry. Got my own problems."

I didn't look back when I shut the door and replaced the key above the lintel. My hands skimmed down the rail. Despite my shower, I was sweating, but it was now July, so that was not surprising. The crickets seemed deafening in their cheerfulness. I stood in front of the brick side where the Midnight Marketplace usually opened. For all I knew, it wouldn't open at all, given that I'd neglected it for so long.

Tapping out the pattern, I thrust my hands into my pockets, sighing with relief when an arc of silver light streaked over the bricks in its usual vine pattern, though much slower than usual. Even KeyStones faded, given enough time. Shoving the Door open as soon as it appeared, I blinked as the witchlights burst to life, their pastel hues giving the shop a familiar semblance. *Hurry, hurry, hurry . . .*

My shoes squeaked against the hardwood as I dashed to the rear of the store where the forbidden and rare objects were kept. I didn't even know what half of them did, but they were freaking expensive and that was good enough for me. Crystals, spell components, mechanical devices, and enchantments. I shoved them into my backpack without hesitation. I suppose I should have felt a bit guilty for ransacking my place of employment, but I didn't have time for that sort of emotion.

Moira could bill me.

I bolted outside and tapped out the pattern on the wall, waiting only long enough to see that the Door faded again. I hedged a moment as to what to do next, the sudden weight of where I had to go paralyzing me. I glanced at my watch, the time drifting away from me, and then shook my head. It wasn't like I was going to be able to do anything about it anyway. I held the Key in my hands, willing it to activate as I approached the garden gate. One step at a time and all that.

The Key's blue glow bathed my hands in the darkness, giving everything an eerie semblance. Closing my eyes, I willed the Door to open, the familiar river of power sluicing over me once again. I let my consciousness skim over to where I wanted to go, imagining the bamboo frame located beside the Barras. The Door lit up, silver and soft. Sucking in a deep breath, I punched through the veil for the fifth time that day and stepped through.

*   *   *

The Barras was strangely hushed when I emerged. Only a
few of the denizens made their way along the muddied paths
cutting through the earth, but I didn't pay much attention to
them. No time for sightseeing this time around, regardless
of the oddness of my dress. At least I had a vague idea of
where I was going.

If the magical contraband in my bag wasn't enough to
sway Kitsune, probably nothing would be. I found the fox-
woman's tent easily enough, scratching at the canvas with an
apologetic tap. Of Tresa there was no sign, but a pile of red
thread fluttered from a post in the front. I doubted that was
anything good.

"Come in," Kitsune murmured.

"Forgive me." I ducked into the tent and knelt on the
other side of the table, the backpack sliding to my side. Un-
wrapping the hair from my pocket, I placed it in front of her.
"I've come to make a bargain."

Her golden eyes stared at me for a moment, red ears swiv-
eling forward, and then she sniffed at the hair, her mouth
wrinkling in dismay. "You've brought war to my doorstep,
Absinthe."

"We had no choice. Where is Tresa?"

"Paying the price for her treachery." Her teeth snapped
shut with an audible click. "Funny thing, destiny. Fight it
hard enough and it will choke the life out of you."

"So she's dead?"

Kitusne waved me off. "Yes. What is done is done. What
bargain would you make? I've already committed my forces
to your cause, thought it was not enough. It will not take the
daemons long to turn their eye to me. A cure for the Queen
would not be welcomed nor appreciated from either side."
She twirled a piece of red thread between her smooth fingers. "Some things cannot be undone."

I shrugged and placed my iPod on the table before her.

"It's enchanted. Last year, I accidentally managed to magic it up so that it never needs charging. It updates itself with new technology changes. It knows what I want to hear. And it has every song ever made." I hit the play button, showing her the number of the song listed as "1 of ∞."

She eyed it curiously. "How is this possible? Technology and magic rarely blend together so seamlessly."

"I don't know." I unzipped my backpack, pouring the contents onto the floor at her feet, careful to avoid the soft puff of her tail. "But I've brought you some of the things I used to do it. I don't have any money to give you, but I imagine you could sell it. Or possibly weaponize it." I hated to make the suggestion. Phineas had said firearms didn't work on the CrossRoads but my iPod did. If Kitsune could figure out a way to do the same for her people, the Unseelie Court would be on equal footing.

At the very least, they'd be a force to be reckoned with.

Judging by the sly gleam of her eyes, Kitsune grasped the implications immediately. I pulled off Talivar's ring, placing it beside the hair. "If you wish the Crippled Prince to survive, she must be healed." I was half bluffing, since I really had no way of knowing if that was true, but I did know Talivar was the only thing really standing between the Queen and the Lesser Fae. If he was gone and the daemons took over, it was a pretty good guess that the Barras wouldn't stand for long.

Something of this must have shown in my face because the fox-woman nodded her head once. "There is a way. I can brew a tea. It will blind the poisons and bring on extreme sweats." Her nostrils flared in warning. "But it may kill her."

"That's a chance I'll have to take," I said finally, mulling it over. "I have no other choice. How long will it take?"

She hesitated, her tail twitching. "Three days to steep."

"I don't have that kind of time."

"Healing potions cannot be rushed if you want them to work," she said mildly, giving me an expectant look. "This trade is acceptable. I will await your return in three days for delivery of the potion."

"I won't be here." I slid the ring closer to her. "Use this to get into Faerie. I'll tell the princess you are coming and what you bear."

She eyed me serenely, but the satisfied glint in her eye told me the rest of this was merely haggling. "A great risk for me to do so."

"One you can afford now." I nudged the pile of enchantments. "Your word?" I insisted.

Another pause and then she nodded. "The word of a fox-woman, for all that it is worth to you."

"Good enough." I got to my feet, the mostly empty backpack on one shoulder. I didn't thank her—after all, she'd been paid for her time, but I did nod politely. "Later," I said lamely, sliding out of the tent when she waved me off.

My stomach cramped with strained nervousness. I hoped to hell she came through, but this would be the best I could hope for.

I emerged from a Door made of obsidian and ice, lightning crackling down one side. Tiles of elegant ebony marble stretched out as far as my eyes could see, flanked by walls of dark thorns. Violet flowers twisted between them, crimson flecks pulsing upon each petal. Directly in front of me was a balcony overlooking a crystalline river of silver. A cloaked figure stood before it.

Nobu turned as I approached, a sardonic twist to his mouth. "I'd say I was surprised to see you, but I'm not. Though I don't recall asking for a bed warmer this evening."

I flushed. The daemon's peacock colors were gone now,

leaving him with only his own dark tresses spilling down
to his waist. He wore an emerald silk robe, belted loosely
around his hips so that the shadowed planes of his chest
showed clearly beneath.

My tongue scraped against the arid desert of my mouth.
"I thought I would come out closer to your tent in the camp.
Not . . . wherever this place is."

"Perhaps this *is* my tent. Hell keeps its own secrets, you
know." He gave me a humorless smile. "Would that you'd
taken my warning to heart, Keeper. I have no real wish to do
what I must."

"I'm sorry to have disturbed you here," I said, the words
rushing out before I lost my nerve. "I wish to make a bargain."

He nodded, slanted eyes crinkling in cold amusement.
"Yes. I rather thought you might."

The Judgment Hall was mostly quiet, though I could hear
Benjamin's babble echoing from the receiving chamber. A
smile touched my lips. At least that much hadn't changed. I
hesitated as I heard the others talking.

Coward, my inner voice hissed as I rolled the envelope I
held between sweaty fingers. I didn't deny it, merely peeked
around the corner, my body flat against the wall. I stifled a
gasp when I saw Benjamin shrieking with delight, making
an ungainly swoop toward his father. Three months had
turned the boy into a full-on toddler. With wings that far
outweighed his maturity, it seemed.

Hurtling toward Robert, he giggled madly when the
angel caught him, a smile of paternal pride upon his lips.
Nearby, Charlie gazed upon them both with affection.

Could I interrupt that?

My resolve wavered. I'd had every intention of going in
there and explaining the situation in more detail, of insist-

ing that Benjamin come back with me to be in Faerie with his mother. But a war was no place for a baby and if I didn't succeed, that's exactly what it would become.

No, I decided. This was not my call to make. Sliding the envelope across the floor, I retreated swiftly. I'd outlined everything that had happened—the Queen's illness, the daemon army, Tresa's plot, Talivar's capture, my bargain with Kitsune. The facts hung there hard and irrefutable and silent.

I did not mention Nobu.

I heard the scuff of Robert's shoes as he came closer toward the envelope with a wary grace. He picked it up and frowned at the Door.

"Abby?"

"I'm sorry," I said, meeting his eyes for one brilliant second before I plunged through the Door for the last time . . .

. . . and out of the one in the Queen's throne room. Stumbling into the midst of complete chaos, in fact. Daemons and elven courtiers flanked the walls, bristling tension and fear. I heard a gasp as I got to my feet, even as the Steward rounded on me to snatch at my shoulder.

"You!" he roared, yanking me up. "Do you have *any* idea of what you've done? Of what we're about to have to do?"

"Well, I might if you'd let me go." I pulled away, the silence crackling in my ears as he released me. My eyes darted past the blur of daemons, seeking only those I cared about.

The Queen perched upon her seat, her eyes bored as she scratched absently at her arms. Moira stood beside her with a face so pale and still she could've been a sculpture. Melanie and Phin were off to the side, I noted with relief. My gaze met Melanie's, confusion and alarm echoed within.

Of Talivar and Ion there was no sign, and my heart sank. On the other hand . . .

Maurice sat in the petitioner's chair, flanked by two daemons I didn't recognize. I arched a brow at him, my fingers
curling so that my nails cut into my palms. A-S-S-H-O-L-E.
The word spelled out in tandem with each trembling step I
took. My inner voice crowed in agreement, giving him the
virtual finger.

"Where is Talivar?" I asked aloud, aiming my question
at the daemons. The Queen looked at me briefly, a flicker
of acknowledgment passing through her eyes. I supposed I
should take it as a good sign she didn't clap me in irons the
moment I appeared for attacking her the night before.

"We have him." Nobu strode through the main doors of
the throne room, his hair sliced through with shades of pink
and blue that matched my bangs.

Nothing like being blatantly obvious, though I had to
admit the effect was damned nice.

Maurice's smirk faded. The winged daemon inclined his
head politely toward me, a sly wink gracing his features. "In
fact, we were just discussing the terms of his ransom."

"Bryston?"

"Here." Ion's dark voice rippled around me with a silent fury. I flinched as the incubus rose up from a cluster of
daemons, his antlers tied tight so that his head was forced
back, hog-tied to his hands behind him. Two more arrows
sprouted from his left leg, and his tail lashed like a snake.

I bit down hard on my lip. "I want to see Talivar too."

Nobu gestured with a careless wave and the ranks of the
daemons changed again, revealing the Crippled Prince.
He'd been stripped of his shirt and his eye patch, the scars
open to view. Dried blood rusted over his shoulders. I could
only hope it wasn't all his.

"The terms of their release?" My voice shook, but it
was anger laced with fear. I had no way to guarantee Nobu
would keep his word.

"Maurice for Talivar," Thomas said from behind me, his words quiet with resignation. "A reopening of the Cross-Roads. And . . . a presence here among our Court. In return, they'll remove their forces and overlook our provocation into war."

Maurice chuckled. "Moira for my wife, you mean."

Talivar grunted through his gag.

"The whelp speaks. This ought to be good. Been a while since I've heard a talking animal attempt a logical process." Maurice's gaze flicked toward Brystion. "I imagine it will be just the same. One merely needs to appeal to their lower natures, after all."

Ion's nostrils flared ."Not worth it," I mouthed, begging him to stay calm. If the situation exploded, I'd never be able to make this work. "I propose a different trade."

I whirled to face the Court, my eyes meeting Moira's. I had no time to tell her of her son's ability to fly or the state of the Marketplace. No time for anything.

"Tresa is dead, brought to justice by the Unseelie Court. In three days, Kitsune will arrive at the gates of Faerie with the cure for the Queen's . . . illness."

A murmur erupted among the court, the Queen blinking suddenly as if she had finally noticed what was going on. She was dressed in an elegant set of robes, the silkworms' cloth draped over her softly. At least they'd managed to do that much for her. Her nostrils flared wide. "The Unseelie Court? It no longer exists."

"This is not my fight," I said softly to Moira. "But I have done what I can." I turned to the Queen. "My lady, I beg thee to grant my boon, owed to me for saving your daughter and grandchild nearly a year ago." That I had saved them from said asshole sitting behind me was something I didn't feel like mentioning, but the truth of it hung there.

The Queen frowned, her fingers knotting in the corners

of her dress. "And what boon would you ask? I cannot grant freedom to my son over the needs of my kingdom. I have no choice but to give the daemons the mortal they claim."

I went still, my voice sounding so terribly loud inside my head. "Yes. So trade me, instead."

Behind me Talivar made a sharp noise, echoed by Ion's own growl of disbelief. I couldn't look at Melanie or Moira or Phin or my father. I'd lose my nerve if I did.

"You?" Confusion warred with a sudden shrewd awareness upon the Queen's face. I could see her working it through her mad little brain. By trading me, she'd get rid of the by-blow who reminded her of her lover's faithlessness. She'd get Talivar *and* she'd be able to keep Maurice.

Moira froze. "The Devil's Tithe," she whispered, horror upon her face. "You mean to reinstate the Tithe. Abby, you can't do that."

Nobu's eyes lit up. "But she already has, Princess. And we have agreed to it. One mortal every seven years in return for peace. Assuming the Queen allows?"

"Take me instead," Melanie shrieked, launching herself from the corner of the room to my side. "I'm already damned anyway."

"Exactly why we won't bother with you," Nobu said coldly. There was a flicker of something else shining in his eyes, but it was gone before I could really see it. "You're a sure thing."

She winced, clutching me by the shoulders, her voice a gibbering buzz in my ear. I shut her out, concentrated on my breathing. I was giving myself to the Devil to save my family. My heart vibrated with the thought.

The Queen sat up straight. "Done," she announced. "I grant thee thy boon. Thy life for my son's and the usual terms of tithing to be applied."

My father stiffened, his eyes full of anguish, but I shook

my head at him. He hadn't bothered trying to protect me for most of my life. Why would he start now?

"And Ion too," I said. "The incubus must be part of the deal."

"Now you're going and changing the terms," Nobu scolded. "In which case I've got a few of my own to apply."

Maurice reddened in fury, his eyes narrowing as they darted between me and the daemon. "You sold me out."

"You're a sure thing too," Nobu said. "And the Master can wait a *very* long time. Besides, Abby drives a rather hard bargain." He steepled his fingers, glancing at me. "I will throw in the incubus as an act of good faith, but you must drink a cup of lethe upon completion." He eyed my necklace. "As much as I'd like to fully trust your word, you've got the ability to transfer between worlds in an instant with such a device. Even with the CrossRoads open, we'd hardly be able to find you if you take it in your head to flee."

I froze. Going into my doom knowingly was one thing . . . but to drink the water of forgetfulness first? From a sacrificial standpoint I got it—much easier to make the victims pliable. But as part of a plan execution, it sucked—especially since that was pretty close to what I'd intended.

He laughed when he saw my expression. "Good try, Abby."

"The Tithe rules declare she has seven years with us," the Steward interrupted. "It's on us if we do not produce her at the specified time."

Nobu shrugged. "Abby did not specify such terms when she haggled herself over to me, therefore I am not required to follow those stipulations. I choose to collect the Tithe now."

Melanie placed a trembling hand on his arm. "Please. At least let us say good-bye."

The daemon stiffened beneath her touch, his upper lip

curling. "Seven weeks, I grant you," he snarled. "And that shall have to be enough. Is that a bargain?"

I nodded, the tinkling laugh of the mad Queen punctuating the following silence. "Release my son and the incubus and I shall open the CrossRoads as the first part is sealed."

Nobu snapped his fingers, and immediately the two men were brought forward, still bound. I took a step toward them despite myself, but the Queen slid out of her throne to crouch beside her son.

"What I did, I did to protect thee. To protect thy sister. To protect our kingdom." Lifting her face, she exhaled softly.

"This is on your head," she said to me. "Thou bastard daughter of thy unfaithful father."

Before I could respond, she blew out, a golden nimbus scattering from her lips like faded dust motes. It deafened me, as though all air had been sucked from the room into a perfect vacuum. My bones shuddered with her voice.

Talivar and Phineas had spoken of a crying sound when the CrossRoads were first closed. I hadn't heard it then, but it had surely been the Queen. How much it had cost her to do such a thing? The power fluctuated a moment more and then swept past us like a hollow wind, leaving a trail of silver sparkles and a low hum in its wake.

"Moon dust will cover you," I muttered. The hum was coming from behind me. Melanie's violin, I realized as sound became more vibrant. Controlled by her steady hand, it dipped and soared, swirling through the room like a soft sigh, tipped with deadly promise

The Wild Music had been released.

The daemons eyed her warily. Nobu grasped her arm, silencing the music. "You cannot break this Contract."

"You have *no* idea what I can do."

"You forsake all that has been spoken in doing so," he

said quietly. With a cry of frustration, she turned away, bitter tears in her eyes.

He leaned over my shoulder from behind, so that his lips brushed against my ear. His fingers played in the loose strands of my hair, grazing the back of my neck.

"You've played your part admirably," he murmured. "But the lethe is for your protection as well as mine. I took the liberty of ensuring we had some on hand."

"This isn't quite what I had in mind."

"I'm a daemon. We're not exactly known for our integrity. But you've kept my little bird safe, and that's worth far more than you know."

I fought the urge to spit at him, the realization of what I'd just done ringing through my ears. Another daemon brought a silver-lined goblet and a glass flask before me. A murky substance swirled within. Carefully, they poured until the liquid kissed the rim.

"Drink it all," Nobu said, his eyes holding mine.

"Abby, you don't have to do this." Phineas trotted toward me, his horn glowing with its own silver light.

"Yes, I do." I tried to give him a smile and failed miserably. "And you all better figure out a way to get me out of this mess." I glanced at Talivar and then Ion, my hands beginning to tremble.

Their faces burned into my retinas, until all I saw was the blue of Talivar's brilliant gaze even as Ion's golden one seared into my memory. I held myself there, balanced upon the precipice of loss and sorrow, anger and love.

"No regrets."

I drank.

Turn the page for a special preview
of the exciting third installment
in the Abby Sinclair series by
Allison Pang

A TRACE OF
MOONLIGHT

Coming soon from Pocket Books!

The fog eddied into the darkness to cocoon me in a soft haze. Something niggled at the back of my mind as I glanced down at my bare feet. They were swallowed below my calves by the mist, but the crunch of sand under my toes felt familiar. The hiss of waves slapped against the edge of a nearby shore.

Sure enough, the rolling scent of brine slipped past on a tattered breeze. Drawn toward the sound of water, I pressed forward, an uneasy chill sending clammy fingers skittering over my skin. Clamping my arms around my shoulders, I realized I was naked.

And yet a moment later, a silk dress draped over my limbs, falling to midcalf. It should have felt strange to know the merest of thoughts took shape here . . . but it didn't. My feet brushed the edges of the wet sand and I paused. I could see nothing beyond the darkness, but the warmth of the water lured me, beckoning with a soft whisper.

Flickers of memory flared up and slid away, the barest hint of scales and a cradle of blue luminescence taking form, but I shook my head and the thought scattered out of reach. Ridiculous idea, anyway. I'd never even seen a mermaid.

Another step and the foam crested past my ankles.

I hesitated.

"Abby." A name, whispered upon the breeze. The waves rushed forward, the sudden undertow sucking me into the sand as though it might drag me into its depths. I stumbled, only to be pulled back by a hand upon my wrist.

I glanced up, frowning as I made out the features of a man. Pale skin and ebony hair whipped past his face in the wind; his eyes gazed down at me, haunted and aching and terrible. I didn't recognize him, and yet his presence radiated warmly in the darkness.

Immediately the waves receded, leaving us in guarded silence. He stared at me a moment longer when I said nothing, something like grief creasing the corners of his mouth.

"If you enter the sea you will be devoured," he said finally.

"Devoured?" My own voice sounded hollow, but I watched curiously as the fog lifted at the merest gesture of his hand. And then I saw the fins cutting through the surf, moonlight shattering the darkness to reveal the sharks moving like living blades in the murk. Behind us lay tall cliffs and a worn path of sand and sea grass, a series of rocky switchbacks leading away from the beach.

I swallowed hard at my own folly. "Thank you," I murmured, my fingers finding his in the shadows to squeeze them. Abruptly he pulled away, his breath hissing as though I'd burned him.

"Who are you? Do you know where we are?"

"You're dreaming, Abby." His lips pursed mockingly. "And I am merely a shadow." At my puzzled look, he sighed. "It will be safer for you away from here. Follow me."

"Do you have a name?" The words slipped out as I dutifully trailed in his wake, bunching the dress at my hips to climb up the bluff.

"If you do not know it, I cannot tell you."

"I don't understand."

"I know," he muttered, a hint of irritation in his voice. "Believe me when I tell you this is not the way things were supposed to have been, but we have no other choice." He glanced over his shoulder at me. "And we have very little time left." As though to emphasize the point, he reached back to take my hand, helping me over a piece of driftwood. This time, his fingers entwined with mine. A wash of heat swept through me.

I sighed. "I've never had such a lucid dream before." His grip tightened but he said nothing, leading us up the cliff and down a winding path until we came to an iron gate. It was overgrown by high weeds, shut tightly with a lock.

My inner voice was strangely silent. If it knew something, it clearly wasn't saying anything. I frowned at the gate, reaching out to stroke the rusted flakes with a curious finger. The metal chilled my hands to the bone and I got a sense that it was unhappy with me.

Which was ridiculous. This was a dream, wasn't it? "Knock it off," I told it, blinking when the gate snapped open with a long-suffering creak.

"One problem solved." The man's eyes slid sideways toward me as I gazed up at the dilapidated house just inside.

A once-stately Victorian construct, the place had clearly seen better days. The shutters hung haphazardly, the paint peeling from the siding like strips of tattered paper. The rotting steps made a dubious whimper as we mounted them and headed for the outer porch.

"What a dump." The stranger flinched and released my arm. An unexplainable sorrow lanced through me. "I just meant as far as dreams go," I amended hastily, somehow wanting his approval despite myself. "I mean, I live in a friggin' tree palace, right now . . . you'd think I'd be dreaming with slightly higher standards."

"You'd think," he retorted. Abruptly he turned toward me. "Who are you?"

"You already know my name. You said it back there. Which reminds me, how *do* you know who I am?" It seemed like a fair enough question for a dream . . . but then, maybe that was my only answer.

"Name tag." He pointed to my chest. Sure enough, I glanced down to see it—just a simple little plastic rectangle, the letters spelling out ABBY SINCLAIR in lopsided relief. I frowned.

"That wasn't there before."

He gestured about us. "Dreaming, remember? Shall we go inside?"

I shrugged, intrigued by his carelessness. "I guess." I doubted there would be anything of interest in this run-down piece of crap, but I couldn't remember another dream taking hold of my mind so vividly. Might as well let it play out.

The door opened beneath my touch easily and I crossed the threshold with a slight twitch of nervousness. For all my brave thoughts, it was still a creepy old house—and that wasn't even counting the stranger who shadowed my steps with an aura of expectancy.

Inside was nothing special—hardwood floors and dusty shelves, lights flickering as though they might go out at any moment. "I wonder if there's a fuse box somewhere."

"Unlikely." He glanced at me with a ripple of amusement and I flushed.

"Yeah, yeah," I muttered. Ignoring him, I continued until I stood in what looked like a family room. The fireplace guttered with old ashes, the dying embers banked into dull sparks. A record player perched on a narrow table in the corner, a stack of records before it. I dismissed them after a moment when I read the titles. Who the hell still listened to Tom Jones anyway?

Snorting, I circled the rest of the room, noting the tattered quilt on the faded sofa and the bowl of strawberry potpourri. The man leaned in the doorway, his arms crossed as he watched me with curious eyes.

"This is all very lovely," I said finally. "But there's nothing of any interest for me here. It's so . . . empty."

He said nothing, but his gaze strayed toward the mantel of the fireplace. "Who are you?"

"I thought we'd already established that."

"I told you what your name was," he countered. "I never heard it from you."

"Abby. Abby Sinclair." I tugged on the name tag. "For all that this is apparently some sort of *Alice in Wonderland* moment." A smile drifted over my face. "I'm a princess, you know." Which in theory was sort of true. Also true was that I had absolutely no recollection of anything else before the last several weeks.

At least being a princess was better than living in a cardboard box.

"Are you, now? Surely that seems a bit lofty of an achievement." He brushed past me to the mantel, taking something from the top and tossing it to me. I caught it without a second thought, staring down at the pointe shoes bemusedly.

"Ballet slippers?" My brow furrowed. "What am I supposed to do with these? I've never danced a day in my life. Hell, even my betrothed admits I have two left feet."

He halted as though I'd slapped him. "Betrothed, is it?"

"Of course. To be handfasted, anyway." I stroked the satin of the slippers. No mere decoration, clearly. The well-worn toes were proof enough of that. "I'm not *really* a princess, though. Not yet." I glanced up at him. "But I will be. A Faery princess, in fact."

"Oh, a fine thing, I'm sure," he said sarcastically. "It

seems your fiancé neglected to mention *that* particular detail. Typical elf." He fixed me with a thin-lipped smile. "I suppose you truly have forgotten, though the Dreamer in you has not."

"Forgotten *what*? You talk in riddles."

"It doesn't matter." He sighed. "I had hoped things might be different, here. This complicates things immensely, but I will make the best of it."

I threw the slippers onto the couch. "You can try, you mean. I don't know what the hell you're talking about, but I think it's time I left or woke up or whatever." I glanced up at the ceiling as though I might will it to happen.

"Stop," he whispered, taking my hand. "Don't leave yet."

Slowly, I turned toward him, a flare of heat sliding up my arm like a welcome friend. I knew this touch. This feeling. His finger brushed my cheek, tipping my chin toward him. A dull thrum beat in my ears, the blood pulsing hot with sudden desire. A hint of gold encircled his eyes, flaring into a brilliant nimbus.

"I . . . know you," I said hoarsely, my knees going weak.

"Yes." And then his mouth was upon mine, and I knew I wanted him. Dream or not, stranger or not, the wanting of him burned the edges of my skin, flooding my limbs like liquid fire.

"What is this?" I gasped, letting him wrap his arms around me, his hand snaking down my hips to cup my ass.

"A gift. The last I can give you." He kissed me again and my eyes shut against the intensity, even as his tongue swept deep. He captured my soft groan. "Look at me, Abby."

My eyelids fluttered open and I blinked in surprise. We were no longer in a house at all . . . but a ballroom? I gaped as a cluster of masked dancers twirled by us in spirited laughter and hazy silks. Beneath my feet gleamed a checkered marble floor, the black and white tiled in a dizzying pattern. A flush of soft light shone above us from a great crystal chandelier.

"I don't understand."

"I owe you a wooing of sorts, I suspect. Consider it a parting memory." He gestured with his fingers, and the soft strains of a violin echoed from the far corner of the hall before I could ask him what he meant. I caught a dim glimpse of a cloaked player, but clearly my would-be suitor had other plans than allowing me to discover who it was, for he turned me neatly, his hand upon my waist.

A moment later and I was dressed the same as the other dancers, but in pastel blues and silver threads. "A corset?"

He shrugged. "You might as well get used to it, *Princess*. Besides, I'll like trying to get you out of it."

"Easy for you to say," I grumbled. "You're wearing pants." Which he was. Tight, low-slung leathers and a scarlet lawn shirt. "You look like some sort of ridiculous vampire."

A genuine laugh rolled from his chest. "Can't have that, can we?" He dipped me low and his shirt melted into a shimmering blue to match my dress. "Better?"

"A bit cliché, but I'll manage."

"That's my girl." He pulled me close again. The gold of his eyes gleamed brighter than before. The music took on a sultry tone, something slower and seductive. "There's only time for one dance, I'm afraid."

"Well, then, I guess we'd better make the most of it."

His lips curled into something predatory, but he clung to me harder in a desperate motion that didn't quite touch his eyes. Unaware of anything but the delicious way he swiveled his hips, I let my feet go where they would. Strangely enough, the steps flowed into each other as though I'd been doing them forever, each movement graceful and unhesitating.

Odd things, dreams.

And my partner was no slouch either.

The skillful movements soon turned the dance into something else entirely. Fingers stroked over my neck, my shoulders, tracing down my back. His hips ground into my mine, his mouth upon my jaw. And all of it subtle enough to seem as though it were part of the dance itself.

It felt as though we might have done this before.

Halfway through the piece, I realized my stays were coming undone. Struggling to keep the corset from sliding off my chest, I paused in my movements, catching a smirk upon his face.

"Charming." I snorted, wondering if he'd been undoing them by hand or by other means. Not that it mattered, really. Dreams were dreams and I was enjoying the hell out of this one. Immediately I stopped squirming and left the corset to slip off as it would.

Spinning away from him, I swayed my hips enticingly. The other dancers faded away, and even the music became nothing more than a distant echo. My suddenly bare feet touched the softest of carpets, the lights retreating to only a soft glow.

The dream had changed again.

I glanced demurely over my shoulder at him, one brow arched in challenge. My heart hammered in my chest at the thought of what I was about to do, but a certain calmness had taken over my mind. Whatever was happening here felt terribly right, even if my head couldn't quite wrap itself around the concept.

My dance partner stood several paces behind me, the rise and fall of his chest suggesting a severe lack of oxygen. "When you look at me like that, I forget why I'm here," he said hoarsely.

My breasts were about to break free from the top of the

corset—the barest of motions would send it tumbling past my waist. "And why *are* you here, exactly? Assuming this isn't pre-wedding jitters taking place by way of a dream."

"Hush." His mouth compressed at my words and I arched my back in apology, one hand casually stretching up to push my hair behind my ear. His gaze became half-lidded and hot, drawn to the taut nipple that had escaped from its confines.

"Now, how did that happen, I wonder?"

"The mind boggles," he purred. "I suppose the only thing to do is to make a matched pair." His hand found the other breast, his thumb rolling it behind the corset with the faintest of pressure. "It might get lonely."

"Can't have that . . ." I tipped my head as though to expose more of myself to him. Soft heat pooled at the base of my throat, and I realized he was kissing me there, his tongue tracing hot circles at the pulse. Something about the gesture niggled at me, its familiarity ringing true, and I said as much.

He grunted in reply, clearly too caught up in what he was doing to care, but a moment later he pulled away. "Change in plans, Abby."

My body shuddered with disappointment. "I wasn't aware there was supposed to be an agenda. This is *my* dream, right?"

He let out a humorless chuckle, shaking his head. "As much as it ever was, I suppose. Don't worry about it just yet. I'm going to ask something of you in a bit. There isn't any time to explain, but I need your word that you will do it."

My eyes narrowed. "Is it going to hurt?"

"Not exactly. Not you, anyway," he admitted. "Promise me you will do what I ask? I'm not going to get another shot at it if it doesn't work." The intensity of his expression became despairing and I could only nod in answer.

"And until then?" There was nothing glib about my

words, but my body continued to thrum with thwarted desire.

He leaned forward to kiss me, even as he gently laid me upon the bed that had mysteriously appeared behind us. "I'd think that would be obvious," he murmured. "I take what is mine."

As though this last interchange had freed him from whatever thoughts had been tormenting him, he tugged at the top of my corset, growling with approval at the newly revealed flesh. "Gods, but I've missed this." And then he was silent, suckling at the nipples until I jerked toward him, an electric pulse of pleasure shooting to my groin. I rolled my hips at him, but he was already there, one hand rucking the skirt up to my waist.

If I'd been wearing underwear, it was gone a moment later, his hand sliding between my thighs. I scissored them wide and bucked up to meet his fingers, letting out a gasp of relief when he slipped one inside. I tore at his shoulders, ripping the shirt away from him like paper. My palms stroked his naked chest and down the muscled ridge of his abdomen.

With a groan, he laid a bold claim to my mouth. I rocked in time to his movements, echoed in the way he slid against me. He chuckled at my whimper.

"Too easy," he sighed, his eyes glowing brighter still. I caught the flicker of what might have been antlers sprouting from his brow, but he turned toward me and they were gone.

"You talk too much." I brushed my lips over his jawline, grinding harder against him. Small ripples of pleasure radiated with each clever stroke. "And what's too easy?"

One dark brow arched in amusement, his fingers crooking up as his thumb pressed down. "This."

Rational thought fled as I tumbled over the edge, the orgasm hitting me fast and hard, leaving me almost sobbing with its intensity. A satisfied croon rumbled from his chest. Was he laughing? My eyes fluttered open, my body continuing to vibrate happily along.

"Delicious." His lips parted as though he was . . . drinking? His face lowered, his gaze burning at me. "Whatever happens, Abby, I have no regrets. About any of it." Confused, I frowned at him. "The mechanics are going to be too difficult to explain right now. Just do as I ask. You have the power, Dreamer. Please."

"What are you going to do?" I shifted as though to roll out from under him, but his hands tightened around me. A tremor ran through him, but it wasn't sexual.

It was fear.

Clasping me to him, he pulled me onto his lap. His erection remained beneath me, but it was as though it was merely an afterthought for him at this point. One hand stroked my cheek, the other cradled my head. "I'm going to kiss you now, Abby."

"All right," I said slowly. He hesitated for the briefest of moments, a bitter smile crossing his face, and then he lowered his mouth to mine. It was a strangely chaste kiss, hovering and light as though he couldn't quite find the right rhythm.

What the hell. I'd make it easy for him.

My fingers twined through the dark locks of his hair. He stiffened slightly, but I tugged him closer, opening myself to him as well as I could. He nipped at my lower lip, our breath mingling hotly.

"All of me I give to you," he whispered, the words slipping away into the darkness. His eyes flared painfully bright like golden waves in an infinite sea. He shuddered, his exhalation filling my lungs until they burned. "Now drink *my* dreams."

I struggled to pull back, but his hands held me firmly in place. I heard the distant chime of a bell as visions darkened my sight, wrapping me in the memories of an . . .

. . . Incubus . . .

. . . I was crouched in the darkness outside a white picket fence with thorny edges, my hands bleeding from my failed attempts to scale it. Anything to get back to the place of my birth, the warmth of the Dreaming womb and the inadvertent love of a mother who never knew me . . .

. . . I was learning to feed, gleaning off the dreams of others, taking all that I could and leaving only a hollowed longing for an unobtainable sexual perfection . . .

. . . I was singing on a stage, holding the attention of everyone. So easy to let my power roll out, lust and desire curling through the room like the flicking tongue of a snake. I could taste the scant edges of their dreams, the weight and the measure as I decided whose dreams I would visit tonight, what Contract I would make . . .

. . . I was wrapped in her arms and the darkness, her Dreaming Heart welcoming me like a beacon of light in the shadows. I would never belong there, but for a moment I could pretend . . .

"Ion." The name fell from my tongue with an easy roll. He uttered a low cry and his form wavered, his body vibrating in my arms. Golden eyes tore into me, and for a moment his humanity was stripped away to reveal blue-black skin and ebony hair tangled in a set of crystalline antlers, intertwined with twigs and red thread. He reached up to pull something from behind a cupped ear and pressed it into my hand.

A rush of energy pulsed through my limbs once.

Twice.

And then he faded, a ghostly shadow slipping away.
Remember me . . .

His voice echoed in my mind even as the white bed seemed to open up, swallowing me into darkness. The scent of rose petals and earth and decaying leaves assaulted my senses. I was falling, my fingers scrabbling at nothing as I hurtled into oblivion.

I'd been crying in my sleep. The damp trace of tears still clung to my lashes. Dimly, I rubbed at them with my hand as I sat up in my bed, trying to remember what had just happened. My body thrummed uncomfortably and I knew it had been an arousing dream of sorts, but more than that I couldn't say. I would have to ask Talivar about it in the morning.

The elven prince had a way of being able to see to the heart of my thoughts, even when I couldn't quite understand them myself. Not that he was here now. For propriety's sake we currently had separate bedrooms, although I didn't actually recall him sleeping with me before.

Not like that was anything new. I never remembered anything.

There'd been some sort of accident in my recent past, one that had apparently taken my long-term memory. No one seemed to want to elaborate on the details, though. Considering I was supposed to marry the man, it was a bitch of a thing not to remember the actual proposal.

Flopping down in frustration, I stared out the carved window at the moonless night, a rustling of branches the only sound. Usually I found it comforting, but right then it mocked me with its secrets, as though it knew more of me than it cared to tell.

I shifted onto my side in irritation, something hard digging into my back. Puzzled, I reached beneath me to find something small and round. It jingled, a lost and lonely chime that made my heart ache. I lit the bedside candle and held the object up to the flickering glow, swallowing hard when I realized I was holding a bell, tangled in red thread.

Fantasy.
Temptation.
Adventure.

**Visit PocketAfterDark.com,
an all-new website just for Urban
Fantasy and Romance Readers!**

- Exclusive access to the hottest
urban fantasy and romance titles!

- Read and share reviews on
the latest books!

- Live chats with your favorite
romance authors!

- Vote in online polls!

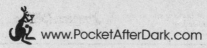

www.PocketAfterDark.com

26119

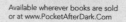

"It's a Faery concern," Brystion pointed out. "And they're using you."

"You're reckless," he whispered. "Heedless of your actions here. You think by just throwing yourself to the wolves you'll somehow master them."

"It worked before."

"You were lucky. Very, very lucky." His fingers slid from my cheek, his golden eyes filled with regret.

"So what do I do?"

"I don't know, but I owe nothing to the Faery Court, regardless of their assumptions. And this mess is of their making."

"Then it's become my mess too." I straightened up. "And if you aren't willing to help us, I have to go. I've got things to do. A world to save. You know—the usual."

Fantasy stars hail Allison Pang's masterful debut novel,

A Brush of Darkness

"First-rate . . . the world of Abby Sinclair is rich in lore, complexity, heart, and humor."
—Kelly Gay, award-winning author of *The Better Part of Darkness*

"Weird, wild, and ultimately wonderful . . . a joy from start to finish, with a completely unique mythology that's as fun to figure out as it is to read."
—Seanan McGuire, *New York Times* bestselling author of the October Daye series

"Pang's refreshingly creative world building, quirky characters, and razor sharp humor weave irresistible magic."
—Jaye Wells, author of *Green-Eyed Demon*

A Sliver of Shadow and A Brush of Darkness are also available as eBooks